MARY KAY LEATHERMAN

"For a story depicting such a seemingly ordinary life, Leatherman's novel packs a punch. The carousel of themes-abandonment, abuse, adultery, death, depression-keeps the plot lively ... A realistic, captivating portrayal of a man's life in full." *Kirkus Review*

"Mary Kay Leatherman is truly a gifted writer. *Vanity Insanity* is a deep, fabulous and fun read. I really could not put it down. Readers will recognize themselves in the various relationships and situations in this story about growing up. Mary Kay powerfully deals with life's issues. At the same time, she shows the impact that faith and spirituality have on one's growth and personal development, ultimately, bringing freedom and peace to a person. Enjoy—as much as I did!" *Father Tom Fangman, pastor of Sacred Heart Church and CEO of CUES in Omaha, Nebraska*

This book is a work of fiction. Names, character, places, and incidents either are product of the author's imagination or are used fictitiously. Any resemblance to actual events or locales or persons, living or dead, is entirely coincidental.

*Grateful acknowledgement is given to the following for permission to reprint the photos in the insert:*

Courtesy of Saint Pius Parish and School: page 249 and 250, all photos.
© Photographer Bob Dunham: page 251, top.
© Union Pacific Railroad Museum: page 251, bottom.
With permission, Warren Buffett: page 252, top.
With permission, Brookhill Country Club: page 253, top.
Courtesy of Marian High School: page 253, bottom left.
Courtesy of M's Pub: page 254, both photos.
Courtesy of Sacred Heart Church: page 255.
Courtesy of NU Media Relations: page 256, both photos.
Printed by permission of the Norman Rockwell Family Agency: page 257.
Copyright © The Norman Rockwell Family Entities.
© Curtis Licensing: page 257. For all non-book uses © SEPS. All Rights Reserved.
© Photographer Jeff Bundy, Omaha World-Herald: page 379.

Blue Wave Press

This book is a work of fiction. Names, character, places, and incidents either are product of the author's imagination or are used fictitiously. Any resemblance to actual events or locales or persons, living or dead, is entirely coincidental.


ISBN: 1489560734
ISBN 13: 9781489560735
Library of Congress Control Number: 2013910110
CreateSpace Independent Publishing Platform
North Charleston, South Carolina

*Lovingly dedicated to my husband Michael,*
*the man who was just*
*crazy enough*
*to believe in me and this story*

*A long, long time ago*
*I can still remember how that music used to make me smile.*

**Don McLean, "American Pie"**

*Vanity of vanities, vanity of vanities! All things are vanity.*

**Ecclesiastes 1:2**

*Mad Hatter: Have I gone mad?*
*Alice: You're entirely bonkers. But I'll tell you a secret.*
*All the best people are.*

**Lewis Carroll, *Alice in Wonderland***

# CONTENTS

| | | |
|---|---|---|
| PROLOGUE | Baby Bookmarks | |
| PART I | Hey, Good-Lookin' | 1969 to 1980 |
| PART II | Let's Go Crazy | 1981 to 1994 |
| PART III | The Day the Music Died | 1995 to 1997 |
| EPILOGUE | Faith of Our Fathers | |

# PROLOGUE
# Baby Bookmarks

Little bookmarks.

That's what my mom calls babies. Their debuts into this world are marking points that she refers to as reminders of specific times. If she's in the middle of a story and needs a time reference of an event, she just thinks of her baby bookmarks.

"When did the Shanahans add a sunroom to their house?"

She needs a baby bookmark.

"I think it was right after the bus accident. Remember when Al, the bus driver, drove into their house on Maple Crest Circle? Evidently, he lost his footing or something. And the Shanahans' house was right at the bottom of the cul-de-sac, so he crashed into the south side of the house. Wait, the bus crash was the year that Faith Webber was born. I remember because we were all standing out in the front yard after the accident, seeing if Al and the kids were OK before checking the damage done to the Shanahan home, and I can remember Ruth Webber waddling out to the scene. It had to be one hundred degrees. That poor thing looked so miserable. She was pregnant with Faith, and Faith was born a year before you, so that must have been September of 1960. OK, so the Shanahans remodeled in 1960."

Faith marks the events for that year.

The baby bookmarks mark all sorts of things. My neighbor Lucy Mangiamelli is the bookmark for the year of Kennedy's assassination. Elaine, Stinky Morrow's little sister, is a bookmark for the blizzard of '75. Mrs. Morrow almost didn't make it to the hospital.

I, Benjamin Howard Keller, have the dubious honor of being the bookmark that no one talks about. We all know it, though. My birth on October 7, 1961, in Omaha, Nebraska, marks the year that my father walked out on my mother, my two sisters, and me. I will forever be the neat little marker of the old man's amazing disappearing act. He left three weeks before his only son was born, as though he didn't even want to meet me, let alone raise me. I've worked that one out, though. A man who walks out on a woman and three kids without looking back—I don't want to meet him either.

Mostly, babies mark less personal or noteworthy events—like, Lovey Webber was born the year two local schools merged, or my best buddy A.C. was born the year Bob Devaney took the head-coaching position for the Nebraska Cornhuskers, not personal but important to me. At the time, the event was big news. Now it's just conversation filler. For my mom, a baby bookmark is there to help her remember what year it happened. The baby helps her find her place in time, sort of like an old song. The order of it all adds a secure feeling that temporarily lessens the pain of the death of a friend or the rejection of a husband or father. The order is functional.

Maybe that's why my mom can never remember the year that my business burned down. No baby was born that year. At least not in our little world. Nineteen ninety-seven was just a blur to her. "How long has it been since the fire? It can't be that long ago. Are you sure?"

No marker.

Most of us lost our place that year. So much more than the fire of my business burns in our memories. Great loss ravaged that fall. For me, 1997 brought about a challenge to faith, a questioning of dreams, and an incredible suffering, all for which I had never asked.

Years have a way of building up, quietly assembling upon each other. People, some random, some purposeful, have lined those years for so long, all the while demanding that we assign them as one or the other.

That's easy.

We just hold on to those who leave their mark.

# PART I

## Hey, Good-Lookin'

## 1969 to 1980

*If boyhood and youth are but vanity, must it not be our ambition to become men?*

**Vincent Van Gogh**

*You're so vain, I bet you think this song is about you.*

**Carly Simon, "You're So Vain"**

# 1

## The Creek

# 1976

We weren't supposed to be anywhere near the creek, but we were.

I looked down at Hope Webber, who was standing at the creek's edge, her head hanging low. I called to her as I ran down the hill from the Wicker house, "Hope, we've been looking everywhere for you. Everyone is worried sick."

When Hope slowly looked up at me on that awful day, I could see dirty tears trailing down her cheeks like several sad little creeks. The slightly overweight fourteen-year-old with the dark hair and blue, almond eyes cried, "Ben, I can't find Grandma. What if she got hurt? What if I never find Grandma?" She sniffed loudly and coughed. The stain of those dirty tears spilled over the front of her favorite David Cassidy T-shirt. My voice shook as I caught my breath and coaxed Hope to me, away from the nefarious creek. "Hope, we need to get out of here..."

**

The creek was a perfect place to play as a kid.

Long before the tragedy at the creek, before the adults of our world deemed it evil, my buddies and I wore a path between the Morrow and Mangiamelli houses that took us to the best area by the creek. I can't begin to count the hours we spent down along its winding bed, finding bugs, building forts, fighting off imaginary bad guys, and getting dirty.

My neighborhood was situated along a bank that hosted the Papillion Creek, quietly inching its way around our city, hiding down in low, tree-covered areas, connecting one part of the city to the other side. People pronounced the word "Papillion" in many different ways. We just called it the creek.

Seven little houses laced our curvy little cul-de-sac, each one a carbon copy of the others except for their tired colors—pink, beige, white, and goldenrod—and the backyards of each house on Maple Crest Circle sloped gradually down toward the creek, making mowing a nightmare. At the base of those backyard hills grew amazingly tall, spindly trees that reached to the sky in great clumps that we called a forest. In dry times, the creek was shallow and no wider than five feet, and in flooding periods, it was deep, wide, and dangerous. The trees that congregated all along the creek like worshipers at a church service created the best place in the world for a kid to hide and pretend to be anywhere other than Omaha, Nebraska, in the seventies.

**

As I stumbled over fallen branches, I yelled, "We found Grandma, Hope. She's fine. She was napping on the Shanahans' driveway the whole afternoon. She's never been happier. Let's head home."

Grandma, an old, overweight Basset hound, had been the Mangiamelli family pet for as long as I could remember. Lucy Mangiamelli had named the pup "Grandma" because, well, everyone loves a grandma. The neighborhood kids had taken her into their hearts and looked out for her as their own. If a neighbor spotted Grandma roaming on a nearby block, he would open his car door, let her crawl in, and drive her home. "I found Grandma a few blocks over, sniffin' in somebody's rosebushes." That's just how it was. "Grandma chewed up another shoe" or "Put Grandma outside. She stinks!" Mrs. Mangiamelli would scream from her kitchen window.

Hope ran toward me and hugged me very tightly, wiping her dirty tears on my shoulder. "Ben, thank you. Grandma is alive! Grandma is alive!"

Hope and I had grown up together in the Omaha Maple Crest neighborhood. Until my mother explained to me that Hope had Down syndrome and what that meant, I had always assumed that Hope was just a person who was born with a more forgiving nature than most.

"You're my angel, Ben." Hope patted my back again and again. "What would I do without you? Grandma is alive!"

I felt a little awkward as Hope praised me, hugging me, patting and patting. The dog had never been lost. I had done nothing to save the day, and as Hope patted, I knew that over a dozen people were looking throughout the neighborhood for her and had been for the past half hour. I had done nothing but sneak down to the forbidden creek to see if Hope might have wandered there. Hope kept patting.

A nauseating hum startled us both. Hope's head slowly turned toward the sound of a radio coming from across the creek, barely twenty feet from where we stood. A very fuzzy and almost inaudible beat buzzed as Hope hugged me. With the sun darting in my eyes, I could vaguely make out the shape of a long car hidden among trees on the other side of the creek. I finally deciphered the ominous tune as "I'm Your Boogie Man" by KC and the Sunshine Band coming from the car, the bass of the music thumping against my heart. I've hated that song ever since that day.

"Hope, we need to go back. Let's go see Grandma. She'll be excited to see you." I wanted to sound more grown-up than my fourteen years, though the truth was that I was very scared to be standing by the creek bed, and my urgency to see Grandma was more of a safety precaution than a canine homecoming—and quite honestly an attempt to break the embrace that I knew was innocent but kind of awkward for this fourteen-year-old dog hero. We needed to get back.

We weren't supposed to be anywhere near the creek, but we were.

# 2

## Feast of the Immaculate Conception

### Monday, December 8

# 1969

Several years before Hope and Grandma and the day by the creek, one frustrated nun struggled through a morning at Saint Pius X Church in the center of Omaha. The years leading up to the day by the creek and the years that followed shaped my life. Grandma and Sister Mary Matthew are linked only by my memories, but I assure you, they are linked.

Had it not been for the nun's insane organizational obsession, her intense devotion to the Virgin Mary, and her strong aversion to giggling little girls, this page might have been blank. Thank you, Sister Mary Matthew.

On December 8, 1969, the eight grades of Saint Pius X Grade School of the Catholic Archdiocese of Omaha held a procession for the Feast of the Immaculate Conception. Sister Mary Matthew's objective was to have each girl in the entire school with the name Mary, first through eighth grade, lead the procession with Father Spokinski at the all-school Mass celebrating the Feast of the Holy Day. On that day, all Marys, Mary-Combos, Maries, Marias, Mauras, and even Maureens were encouraged to open the service. First, middle, and Confirmation names were all included. In Catholic schools in the sixties, few girls did not fit this prototype.

I do not know, nor have I ever met, Sister Mary Matthew. I wasn't even there on that cold Monday in December; I attended Franklin Public School at the time. I do know, however, what happened that day in great, though disputable, detail since I've heard three different versions from three very good friends. I can clearly see the procession and the tall, rickety nun hovering over the girls and lining up the Marys all according to height, as I'm sure she assumed Mary herself would want. I'm told the Kelly girls shone that day as each was included: Mary Ann, Mary Ellen, and Mary Catherine. The shortest girls entered first, with the tallest of the Marys at the end, right in front of Father Spokinski and his two freckle-faced altar boys. In my retelling, I added the freckles and the tall, rickety nun for effect. The whole thing sounded so innocent to me, at first.

So most of what I tell is unconfirmed, but what I do know for a fact is that a first-grade girl by the name of Theresa Marie O'Brien stood quietly in front of Martha Mary Monahan, another first grader whom she had never met. The two first graders had no idea at that time that the fact that they had grown up to such a height at that particular moment, dictating their positions in that line in this holiest of processions, would change the course of their lives forever. What was to be an amazing opportunity for Theresa Marie and Martha Mary, two of the three authors of the versions of the events that day, was instead a source of frustration for the orderly Sister Mary Matthew.

In the "feast line" stood the plethora of Mary-types, quietly facing the altar as the older students, posing as song leaders, began the opening hymn "Immaculate Mary."

*Immaculate Mary, your praises we sing.*
*You reign now in splendor with Jesus our King.*
*Ave, Ave, Ave, Maria! Ave, Ave, Maria!*

The really cool part of being a Catholic song leader during the sixties or early seventies was the added bonus of playing light yet silly instruments as a pleasant backdrop for the vocal performers. Guitars, triangles, blocks, castanets, recorders, and maracas were replaced in the late seventies by a brief stint of the ever-overrated liturgical dance, featuring the "older girls" in dance slippers and graduation gowns flouncing down the aisle, leading Father Spokinski to the altar like feathery, floating flowers. The Catholic Church is not without its own passing and regrettable fads.

According to some of the versions of the story, Faith Webber was clanging her triangle, leading the "masses." I enjoyed those versions, since I like to think of Faith Webber, Hope's older sister, doing anything. I can only imagine her standing out with perhaps a special lighting around her that set her apart in the way she always appeared to me: beautiful, glowing, and ever elusive. Faith's long, smooth, dark hair lay across her shoulders as she perfectly and seriously tapped her triangle to the beat of Sister Alleluia's opening song. More on Faith later.

*Ave, Ave, Ave, Maria! Ave, Ave, Maria!*

Martha Mary Monahan and Theresa Marie O'Brien faced forward with pride as the chosen ones. The distraction that broke their perfect composure was sitting in a pew near them. Facing them with a silly grin and glasses too large for his face was the poster child for Ritalin himself: Weird, Weird Mikey Beard. He loved pretty girls and really gross things.

Fact or fiction, the recollection of that day and how it's still regarded make it what I call noteworthy; however, my apologies to Weird, Weird Mikey Beard, as I know he is somewhere out there, quite possibly reading this. I tell what I know.

I know that Mikey Beard daily pretended, or not, to pick his nose and chase the girls on the playground with his findings. I know that Mikey had once been tied with a school jump rope to his desk by a very tired, though previously patient teacher, in the days when being tied to your desk wasn't six o'clock news but a weekly ritual. I know that Mikey had once sung to

Theresa Marie O'Brien, quietly during social studies, with his menacing grin, "I'm Just a Love Machine", in a creepy serenade the teacher never heard.

I also know that Mikey Beard never went to any mental institution, since, after a healthy adjustment of his medication, he got contacts, a cool haircut somewhere along the line, and a phenomenal education in computer programming. Mikey started his own computer-programming company, one of the biggest in Omaha. I know that nobody recognized Michael T. Beard at the Saint Pius X class of 1977 ten-year reunion.

What I said to Lucy after she described the computer hunk to me following her reunion was direct and honest: "That should teach you not to make up awful nicknames for people. You, who mocked Weird, Weird Mikey Beard, could have been Mrs. Computer Hunk Beard if you hadn't been such a snob."

Her reply was simple: "Never. He will always be the kid who stuck pencil-top erasers up his nose and blew them at people. No amount of money or good looks can change that." There you have it. I guess the message to Mikey and other wild little boys everywhere is "Don't do really gross things to pretty little girls."

Weird, Weird Mikey Beard couldn't begin to put a number on the days he was cast to the passion-orange cry room of Saint Pius X or sent to the office, but he didn't get in trouble on that day in 1969. Not to say he was innocent. Martha Mary and Theresa Marie had not been singled out or targeted by Mikey. He was merely entertaining anyone who might catch his act from the pew. Rather than push his glasses-too-large-for-his face up his nose, he took them off, bent his head down, and turned around with a horrific surprise. Mikey had flipped both eyelids up, the red of the lids remaining flipped as he looked at the girls in line. If you've ever seen this immature ritual, you know how this innocent little act might throw off the strongest of stomachs. Because Martha Mary, or Marty, as she was later known, had not come across the ever-scary and kind-of-funny flip-lid trick, she shrieked at the sight.

Theresa only remembers laughing hysterically, which is no surprise. Theresa was a master laugher, the kind who made other laughers envious.

She laughed uncontrollably from the center of herself, shaking and weeping in a strangely joyous manner. As Theresa laughed, her eyes teared and nose ran; all the while, she covered her mouth in a feeble attempt to muffle the shaking convulsion. Anyone watching her in this state could do only one thing: laugh.

One person did not laugh: Sister Mary Matthew. She found no humor in the girls' irreverence for her magnificent dream. She had no choice that day but to stop the madness. Three minutes later, Theresa and Marty were sitting next to Lucy Belle Mangiamelli, the third party and teller of the final version of the story of this day, against the walls of the passion-orange cry room. Lucy is the one who named the color "passion orange."

When Lucy was born to Louis and Ava Mangiamelli, the first girl following four boys, her father chose to name her after Lucille Ball, in line with his years as an avid fan. Lucy's mom, reluctant about the name though happy with a girl, respected this wish with the name Lucille Belle Mangiamelli. Lucy was the apple of her father's eye and lived up to her name as the comic relief for the family throughout many years of economic struggles, and as a comfort to him in his later years. In 1969, little Lucy's hair was a mass of dark-brown trestles, tamed by none, feared by many. Even without red hair, she still managed to keep a fire going in any moment she lived.

With no "Mary" name, Lucy was thrown aside like yesterday's trash. Her fire was especially strong that day, and her blatant exile to the cry room had been more than she could take since she thrived in the limelight, especially during an all-school event. Lucy's misfortune also turned out to be a defining moment of her life, but she did not know it at the time. Her attempts to deal with this plight had gotten her into trouble. According to Lucy, she had simply whistled the tune "Maria" as she, in the line of boys and other non-Mary sorts, passed Principal Sister Annunciata.

Sister Annunciata, recognizing the source of the nun-provoking tune, quietly and firmly pulled the back of Lucy's "poop brown" jumper and placed her fanny against the passion-orange walls of the Saint Pius Cry Room near the entrance of the church. (Again, Lucy's color descriptions.) Having lived across the street from Lucy growing up, I knew her well enough to imagine that her pint-sized body, amazingly over-sized head of hair, and booming, scratchy voice probably caught the attention of many, accomplishing just what she felt she had been missing by not being included in the feast day's hoopla.

I never did hear how that whole Mary procession thing turned out. My strongest informants were no longer in the church past this point. The remaining details of this story took place in the back of, or outside of, a church so homely it was actually interesting.

In 1969, Saint Pius X was not a church like the masterpieces in movies, castle-like buildings etched against a mountain by a lake around which innocent children happily run in red and blue jumpers. With its straightforward design of boxes called the church, gym, and school, Saint Pius supported its young and innocent children in ugly uniforms with a big blacktop parking lot/playground next to the big box buildings, in which they received a good Catholic education, whether they liked it or not.

When I envision the architects of the great churches of the world, I imagine them taking the buildings in as clean though challenged, like many of the churches of the late fifties and sixties in the United States. Viewing Saint Pius with its "bland blond" brick and "panic green" accents, the architects might assume that the building's designers had come from the classrooms of the primary wings of that very school. They would probably not be aware of the fact that the church had originally been intended to be the gym, a decision that changed along the way, probably for financially driven reasons.

The school smelled of the cheap cleaner that I've grown to believe all Catholic schools must use. My sister used to whisper to me as she ran me into CCD classes on Wednesday nights, "Smells Catholic in here." Whether it was the smell of cheap soap or all those captive Catholic school wretches, the scent only enhanced the mood that was created in Saint Pius X in the late sixties.

Back in the cry room sat three girls who had never met before. Fate or some higher power—and I are not talking about Sister Annunciata or Sister Mary Matthew—had brought them together. All three girls believe this. In the first grade alone were 157 kids. At Pius, at the time, the last dribble of the baby boom had created one of the largest Catholic grade schools in the nation this side of the Mississippi River in little ole Omaha, Nebraska. The great numbers of kids, along with a once-lauded system of tracking children on ability, had severed any prior connection for Lucy, Theresa, and Marty.

Across the country at the time, public and private schools were experimenting with an interesting little educational hiccup called tracking. More than likely well intended, the tracking system was supposed to make it easier for the teacher to teach. In the end, the whole system, which practically encouraged children with learning disabilities or other challenges to stay put, was trashed as the "every child is gifted" era replaced it. One hiccup for another.

Lucy—my personal connection to Marty and Theresa—was in group three, though she is by no means average. To engage in a conversation with Lucy is both enlightening and intimidating. Her wit and wisdom, however, did not reveal themselves on an entrance test to determine group placement in first grade. They were filtered out with a much different assessment and a later diagnosis of dyslexia and a comprehensive written disability. In other words, Lucy's smarts could only come out of her mouth. Her written world would always be challenged.

Lucy's group three ate and "recessed" on a different schedule than other academic groups of children, which explained why she had never met or even seen tall and lean Martha Mary Monahan with long, straight, brown hair and incredible writing skills that later proved profitable. Had Lucy seen Marty prior to this day, she might never have approached the serious and often-mistaken-for-snooty first grader.

Nor would Lucy or Marty have bumped into Theresa Marie O'Brien in group two. If they had, they would have surely noticed her. To another first-grade girl, or boy for that matter, she would have been described as the "really pretty girl" admired by all. Her shiny, caramel-colored hair and bright-green eyes with dark lashes were envied by all of the groups, though she was never aware of this very obvious fact.

On that day in December back in 1969, the three girls from different groups attempted to avoid eye contact with each other for a total of three and a half minutes. The silence was broken by Lucy's laughter. Throughout Lucy's life, "opportunities" came not from scholarship money or good job offers but by making the most of moments such as this one. She proclaimed, "Let's get out of here!" All three accounts agree on this statement. Three girls who had never met one another were on a mission from God to have fun.

Lucy ran. Marty and Theresa followed, though they knew not where. Both Marty and Theresa, in separate accounts, explained that they would not ordinarily have done something like that. What with punishments and parents as they were, they would have normally avoided the consequences that could spiral from this situation. They were sure that some greater force must have been pulling them toward Lucy. Maybe the Holy Spirit, maybe the devil himself.

Lucy ran out the church door, which deposited the first graders into a corridor that surrounded the church. Another "interesting" choice of architecture. The stained-glass windows looked out into a dark corridor on the west side of the building. Sounds around the church echoed and projected, bouncing off corners and then back again. Lucy hung a left and lunged toward the window outside of the front of the church. Marty and Theresa were close behind. The girls ran to the point at which they might peek at the singers, through stained glass, of course. In a scratchy whisper, Lucy dictated, "Lift me up!" Marty and Theresa, though strangers to each other, synchronized a chair for Lucy and moved her up toward the stained-glass window.

Lucy's wiry hair got caught on the handle of the window. As Marty and Theresa fumbled and wiggled, Lucy began to howl. Her scratchy voice echoed throughout the corridor, loud and eerie. The howling, from what I hear, did not sound human. Lucy's voice echoed throughout the long corridor surrounding the church. The howling made Theresa laugh, which made her weak, thereby more fumbling, thereby producing louder and longer howls from Lucy.

Insiders I knew told me that the kids in the church had giggled and shrugged. A few thought the howl might have been a spiritually inspired sign, the howl of the Holy Ghost, a term used more often at that time than Holy Spirit. Frightening and eerie as faith itself could be, the Holy Ghost had haunted Saint Pius Church. Lucy would say, "The Holy Ghost scares the hell out of me."

Sensible Marty was able to remove Lucy's hair from the hinge, at which point the three nearly strangers ran back to the orange-passion wall before Sister Mary Matthew walked in to check on them. They made it with no time to spare.

Three first-grade girls sitting on the floor with their backs to the wall and their hearts pounding against their ugly jumpers looked up as Sister Mary Matthew's head popped into the room. Her brow furrowed as she looked each of them over. A look of mystery filled her face, just one of the many mysteries of the Catholic Church.

The girls were connected. That day the merry Mary procession gave them an intense connection that, for first graders, was bigger than ka-knockers and mood rings. In the days and years that followed that day, Lucy, Marty, and Theresa would meet whenever they could, after school, on the weekends. Their worlds blended even more as their classes mixed in the middle grades to create a world of ugly uniforms, super balls, troll dolls, K-tel records, and overnights at which Lucy would jump on her bed, holding a brush and doing her best impression of Jeannie C. Reiley singing "Harper Valley PTA."

Their world was the only world.

At that time, the dawning of the Age of Aquarius, Lucy, Theresa, and Marty were oblivious to the fact that Grateful Dead played in Omaha that year on February 2. The girls didn't know that the hit song "Build Me Up, Buttercup," with its bubble-gum rhythm, sitting in the number-three spot on the Billboard Hot 100 in February that year for eleven weeks, was actually about a dysfunctional relationship. They had no clue that a guy in Omaha named Warren Buffett, who bought his first share of stock at age eleven, had returned an average of almost 30 percent in 1969, in a market where 7 to 11 percent was the norm. The girls had never even heard of a man named Gordon Matthew Sumner, son of a hairdresser and milk man, raised in New Castle, England. Gordon turned eighteen that year.

And I know for a fact that Lucy couldn't have cared less that the Nebraska Cornhuskers won their final seven games that year, including a victory against Georgia in the Sun Bowl thanks to golden-toed Paul Rogers, who booted four field goals. This was all in the first quarter, setting off a thirty-two-game unbeaten string that didn't end until the first game of the 1972 season, Coach Bob Devaney's last as head coach. He had planned to retire as coach after the 1971 season but was persuaded to stay one more year to try to win an unprecedented third consecutive national title. This, I cared about.

I'm not sure of most of the facts of this Feast of Mary story in 1969. What I do know is that when Lucy, Theresa, and Marty were brought together that day, they stayed together for a very long time, and their union affected my life.

# 3

## Lucy Mangiamelli: Haircut, Trim Bangs, First Communion

### Saturday, May 15

# 1971

Two years after the procession of the merry Marys, I met Lucy Mangiamelli.

My mom swears that Lucy spent an afternoon with us when she was five or six while her parents moved into their home on Maple Crest Circle. Neither Lucy nor I remember this first meeting, but supposedly we played Chutes and Ladders and lunched out in the sandbox. Maybe we weren't impressionable enough or interested enough in each other to remember that four-hour treasure of a day, but my mom seemed to think that we connected over peanut butter and jelly.

Lucy and I see it differently. We both remember our first meeting on the day Lucy was getting ready for First Holy Communion. Lucy remembers the clothes. I remember the music.

Marcia Keller, my mother and my boss, ran a salon in our basement for thirteen years. A driven single parent, she worked very hard to keep her work separate from our home, and because she didn't want business to march past the breakfast dishes or possibly a sleeping child or two, she asked that patrons to Marcia's Beauty Box enter the shop through the basement door. To make the route more inviting, Mom made a sign using black and what she called "a perky pink" paint and placed it just off to the north of the house, where a flower-lined path began that led around the house to the back basement door. In the spring and summer, my two older sisters weeded and maintained the pink and perky roses that lined the same path I shoveled on snowy winter days.

Marcia's Beauty Box was everything a hair salon should be in the 1950s. Unfortunately, it was 1971. My mother put big, bold pictures of women with outdated hairstyles on the walls of her twelve-by-sixteen room with two chairs and one sink. If you had to pick a color, you could choose from two in this room: pink or black. On the wall near the door leading out to the back path was a little framed print that had been given to my mother by one of her clients through the years. The faded cartoon showed a hair stylist leaning next to her client in the styling chair, both with outdated hairstyles; the character in the chair had permanent rods all over her hair. The caption read *Ours Is a Permanent Relationship*. On the wall behind the sink was another plaque with the words *I'm a Beautician, Not a Magician*. Even though the days of stinky permanents were long over, several of her clients still asked for the tight and close curls. This time in my life can be brought back in a blink with the pungent smell of chemicals.

Most of my mom's clients were neighbors and friends and friends of the neighbors and friends. A few of them even called her a "beauty operator." These women, permanent and set in the ways of their hair, had been loyal to Mom even prior to the great disappearing act of my dad. My mom's reputation was solid, since she was known for maintaining and grooming the same style repetitively for the women who wanted the exact same look, week after week. "Let the client feel comfortable with what you're about to do to his or her most prominent and identifiable physical feature. The nerve endings to the mops of trestles are most sensitive." As my mom put it: "People are very particular about their hairstyles." My slant on this: people are just weird about their hair.

In Omaha, during the early seventies, great numbers of these "permanent and set" women showed up as regulars at our basement door, and they were welcomed warmly by a single mother whose income depended upon them. She took good care of them as she organized a file of the history of each client's hair. A green recipe-card box holding index cards sat near her combs. My mom marked the date, the hairstyle, and any special event of her clients, she said, to keep organized. I think she kept those cards to make her clients feel special. Each index card was a life. The fancy times and the hard times, the Christmas parties and the changes, the graduations and the funerals, all on a neat little index card. She would pull the index card of hair history and say, "Looks like last time we only took off an inch. What are you thinking today?" or "Your hair was permed for your party last week. Maybe we do a hot oil treatment this time. What do you think?" My mom would write notes on her index cards for the next appointment. They liked her order. They liked her style. They must have been OK with the pink-and-black decor.

The day Lucy arrived at our basement door that spring afternoon in 1971, hours before making her First Communion, I noticed her. She was livid, and as usual her hair was noticeable and wild. The tension between Lucy and her mother entered the room before they did. Her mother had felt that Lucy's hair was out of control and un-Communion-like, so Ava Mangiamelli wanted it "taken care of" now. Lucy disagreed. Her reply to her mom was something along the lines of "OK! Fine! I'll be ugly for my First Holy Communion if that will make you happy!"

I overheard the two bickering while I swept the hair of my mom's earlier customer from around the chair in which Lucy would soon be "taken care of." I had been helping my mom out in her shop for as long as I could remember. I was nine at the time, so my jobs included sweeping hair, straightening magazines, and cleaning scissors, combs, and brushes. I was the "best little helper," my mom would tell her clients.

This comment made me blush and cringe at the same time, since my grandfather had told me on more than one occasion that I was the man of the house and that my mother needed me to be strong. No pressure there. That's something I would never tell a child under ten.

Sensing the tension, Mom asked Ava Mangiamelli if she would like a cup of coffee up in our kitchen and a chance to look through books of children's haircuts, allowing the hot-headed Italian females some time to cool down. What this did was leave me alone with the younger of two fiery women. The silence was broken as soon as Lucy realized I was in the room.

"My very best friends, Theresa and Marty, and I are making our First Communion today," Lucy announced as if she had prepared a speech.

"Oh," I replied. I wasn't really that impressed. I had made my First Communion the year before.

The song "Knock Three Times" by Tony Orlando and Dawn was playing on the black radio that my mom kept on the windowsill. The outdated, black radio was always a bit of an embarrassment to me. The louder you turned the volume, the louder an irritating static boomed with the bass in the background to any song. I couldn't complain, though. Even though the décor of Marcia's Beauty Box was antiquated, the music was always up-to-date. Mom was pretty good about playing WOW, the station my sisters and I listened to.

"My dog's name is Grandma," Lucy proclaimed.

"Oh." I acted disinterested, but I smirked at the implications of that name for a dog.

"I saw *The Aristocats*. It was dumb." No comment. "My brother Subby got in trouble for seeing *The Exorcist.*"

This time I was impressed. "How did your parents find out?"

"He slept with the lights on all night and then finally confessed out of fear."

"Of the devil or your parents?"

"My parents. Where do you go to school?"

"Franklin Public."

"Oh. I go to Saint Pius."

"Oh."

"You don't talk much."

"My grandpa met Bob Devaney once."

Lucy's face showed that she had no idea that Bob Devaney was the coach of only the greatest football team ever: the Nebraska Cornhuskers.

"Did I tell you about my dog already?"

When Lucy and I later talked about that first meeting we remember, she had to mention my brown corduroy pants with my brown K-Mart zipper shirt. Hey, brown goes with brown. She gloats as she recalls her elephant bell jeans with a purple smiley-face shirt. Big wow. Me, I remember the music.

My entire life, I've looked to the music of the day as an anchor, tying me to my memories. Songs, good and bad, have entangled my calendar, and the strong association of a song can carry me back to that moment, either good or bad, in a second. The opening measure to the song "Dream Weaver" by Gary Wright connects me immediately to the first kiss of my adolescent career with Julie George, who turned out to be disappointingly ditzy. I guess that would be both good and bad.

Somewhere between a possessed, prepubescent girl—I'm not talking about Linda Blair from *The Exorcist*—and a phenomenal season for the Huskers, Ava and Mom came back, well coffeed and slightly calmed. Ava still felt that something must be done to the mop on Lucy's head. Lucy still felt differently. Ava won.

Ava and Lucy were two peas in a pod, even though they did not approve of sharing the same pod. Ava was a tiny woman who usually got her way. Lucy was a carbon copy, though she would vehemently deny it. Lucy came from a true Italian family. Her father was Italian. Her mother was Italian. Enough already. She was the baby girl following four brothers, all of whom were admired by my sisters and others for their dark lashes, big, brown eyes, and great stature. Louis Mangiamelli was a tall, handsome man, and his boys followed suit. Lucy—short, feisty, and blunt —resembled her mother though she was the only namesake of her father. Louis, Lucy. It works.

"OK, we'll keep the back messy but do something with the sloppy bangs." If Ava felt that she was meeting Lucy halfway with the issue of her hair, she hadn't considered the serious outcome of such a request. Lucy, also oblivious to what might come of such a combination, actually smiled as though she had won. She had always wanted long, flowing hair like her friends and Marcia Brady.

My mom and I were both aware that cutting the bangs of a person with frizzy and wiry hair is not good. And furthermore, leaving the rest of her hair wild was not a great combination with pinhead bangs. But Mom stuck to her philosophy: let the client make the call. Fifteen minutes later, Lucy's bangs were trimmed.

As Lucy and her mother got ready to leave, her bangs began to dry and slowly creep up her forehead like little worms on the sidewalk after a big rain. By the time the duo was at the door, Lucy's bangs were one-quarter of an inch at best. Lucy's hair looked really bad. Even though I had only spent thirteen minutes talking with her, something told me that Lucy would not like her hair. And as has most often been the case with my instincts about Lucy, I was right. She hated it.

As Lucy and Ava walked out of Marcia's Beauty Box, another strong woman entered the room. My life has been filled with a great number of strong women. Octavia was an old friend of my grandma Grace, who had lived in Fremont, Nebraska. My mother, who grew up in Fremont, had started doing hair in Fremont before she moved to Omaha in her early twenties. Once my mom moved to Omaha, Grandma Grace and Octavia were loyal to Marcia, making the half-hour drive once a week to Omaha to have their hair done. They would then do lunch and head home to Fremont, looking good, feeling good.

When Grandma Grace died, Octavia continued the routine, claiming that no one else could do her hair right. For the sake of vanity, the drive was worth it. She stayed with what she knew was good.

On that spring day in 1971, I stood as a witness to the brief exchange, while sweeping the shrapnel left under the chair. Octavia looked down at Lucy. Lucy looked up at Octavia. Two strong winds. Two radical jet streams in a Nebraska spring. As James Taylor's voice crooned from the little black radio about some tough times in his life in the song "Fire and Rain," maybe I imagined it, but I would swear the two cocked their heads to the side, raised one eyebrow each, and looked away. Almost mirror images.

While Lucy's world was focused on her First-Communion hairstyle and POW bracelets, Octavia was dealing with the recent death of her husband of forty-two years. At sixty-six, she was learning to drive herself to new places and praying for the souls of all she knew at daily Mass at Saint Patrick's in Fremont. Warren Buffett was keeping an eye on the American economy as it was experiencing current account deficits, which led to the Dollar Crisis in 1971. Later that year, the Nebraska Cornhuskers would win the game of the century on Thanksgiving Day, a game that went up and down with more thrills than a roller coaster. Johnny "the Jet" Rodgers played in that game. On the other side of a big ocean, young Gordon Sumner was training to become an English teacher at Northern Counties Teacher Training College in England.

And a strong little girl and a strong older woman made great efforts to look good in my mother's basement.

# 4

## Evelyn Perelman: Jerry Curl, Relaxer

### Friday night, October 20

# 1972

What I remember more than anything else was how she smelled.

Mrs. Perelman, the mother of my best friend, A.C., would enter a room and fill my head with a beautiful scent that triggered the pleasure center in my brain. Of course, it made me feel very uncomfortable as an eleven-year-old in the presence of his best friend's mother, feeling so strange. I always squirmed and found a reason to leave whenever I saw her. Later I realized on a date in college that the fragrance she always wore was White Shoulders. I couldn't date that girl again because of the strong smell association. Dating my best friend's mother? Just weird.

Evelyn Perelman was an anomaly. And not just to me. Something of a mystery always hung around her. She was tall and beautiful. She was a black woman in the white side of town. She was quiet, intelligent, and serious. Few people knew her well, yet she was very warm and approachable if you were ever able to engage in a conversation with her. My mom was one of those lucky ones, or perhaps one of the few who did not look critically upon a black Catholic woman married to a white Jewish man, living on the west side of Omaha in the late sixties and early seventies.

That cool Friday night in October of 1972, Evelyn and A.C. Perelman showed up at the front door of our little, white house. Few if any clients that I remember ever entered the front door except for Grandpa Mac. Evelyn Perelman had a standing appointment with my mother one Friday night a month. Because of her heavy schedule as a microbiologist at the Med Center, Evelyn was unable to have her hair done during the workweek. I suppose she could have come on Mom's busy Saturday shift, but I always assumed that she preferred not to be around the other women. My mom, an oddity herself as the only single parent that I was aware of, and Evelyn Perelman found an ally in each other, I guessed. More than likely the two enjoyed their girls' night, and I know A.C. and I never complained about it. A.C. Perelman could hang out as long as our mothers talked; we always hoped they would get into a long, serious, and deep discussion.

This week, when the doorbell rang, I raced to the front door as always. As I turned the knob, A.C. exploded into our tiny living room doing his best imitation of our most recent hero, the one and only Flip Wilson. "Hey, what you see is what you get!" The eleven-year-old, imitating Flip Wilson's Geraldine persona, wiggled his body as he walked in the room and flashed his lashes up and down at me. "Heya, Killer. This pink dress I'm wearing? The devil made me do it!"

I snorted and hit him. Mrs. Perelman darted a disapproving glance at A.C. as she greeted my mother. A.C. was notorious for his silly imitations and stupid antics, but I think the black accent and extreme cultural stereotype, more than the feminine whiles, perturbed Evelyn. A.C. and I were unaware of the racial tension in our city and most other cities even though the adults were hyperaware of the awkward relations between black and white people at that time. It had only recently occurred to me that A.C. was both black and white—chocolate milk—and I envied his unique birthright.

Before *The Flip Wilson Comedy Hour* started, I quickly pulled A.C. into the kitchen to show him my mold garden that I was growing for my science project.

"Man, Ben, you're going to get some major extra credit for that!"

My mom popped her head in the door and interrupted our serious discussion. "This may be your last night to go out and play since winter is around the corner." My mother scooted us out the door as she spoke. "You can look at that another time and watch Flip Wilson on the snowy Fridays when A.C. and his mom come by. Now go. Grab your windbreaker, Ben. And don't go near the creek."

My mom's words hung in the air around us like anxious moths at a light. Not like we hadn't heard the warning every day for the past two weeks. The words forced us back to the reality that a twelve-year-old paperboy had disappeared weeks earlier. His bike had been found down by Papillion Creek. Next to the boy's bike was the bag of newspapers, not one of which had made it to its destination. Many phone calls to the *Omaha World-Herald* from paperless homes led to a phone call to the parents of Johnny Madlin, which ignited the nightmare they must be living as we stood in my safe little living room.

Just before the bad thing at the creek, before the unspeakable and reprehensible crime, my buddies and I spent any non-school-or-chore moment down at the bed of the creek. A.C., Will Mangiamelli, and I led the younger boys down by the creek bed as we orchestrated our "projects," as A.C. called them; A.C. was our idea man. We shed our shirts and our childish games as A.C. directed us to build tree forts and underground forts and commiserate until our moms called us. As soon as breakfast was forced down our throats, we grabbed food, tools, and pitchers of ice water so that we were equipped for the day of building and scheming. Whatever we could sneak from our homes—boxes, stools, a transistor radio, utensils, and old *Playboy* magazines that Stinky Morrow smuggled from his father's stash in the back of his parents' closet—became treasures that the group praised. Though we didn't know it at the time, pending testosterone was quietly beginning to pump through our veins; we only knew that we felt eager and alive. Daily we prepared to fight the enemy. We were brave in defending our territory, all the while hoping that Lucy Mangiamelli and her friends were watching us from the backyards, admiring our naked upper bodies that were anxiously anticipating manhood.

No one wore a watch at the creek, so our mothers whistled and rang bells to call us home on perfect summer nights to wash our faces and hands and eat dinner as quickly as we could so we could race back down to the creek with coffee cans under our arms to catch fireflies before we were summoned again for the night.

The creek was a perfect place to play as a kid.

It was also, evidently, the best place to abduct children on the way to their afternoon jobs of delivering papers. Johnny Madlin's red banana-seat bike had been found by the creek several miles south of our neighborhood, and consequently, the children of Maple Crest subdivision were thereafter warned daily and emphatically: don't go near the creek. The very nature of the warning had most kids worried that the creek itself was guilty of snatching the boy and harboring him, waiting for more children to come. But I knew differently. I loved the creek. The creek was no criminal.

Speculation would continue for years about the case. Most agreed that the boy had been abducted. Some thought his body had been swept away in the creek and just never found. Still, a few believed that Johnny might have run away. Though views were inconsistent, the reality around the speculation was clear: we were no longer allowed to play by the creek.

A.C. and I opened the door into the dark, cool Friday night. I forgot Johnny Madlin for the moment as I embraced the night air. I loved the fall. The fall meant two things to me at that time in my life: sweatshirts and football. The sweatshirt was important since I had spent the summer and most of September feeling self-conscious about my skinny arms. Chicken arms, A.C. called them. I would remind him that chickens didn't have arms and that the expression was supposed to be about legs. My sister Tracy would laugh and say, "Are you worried about the girls looking at your arms? Don't worry. They aren't looking at you at all." I was still relieved to be wearing long sleeves again.

Beyond the sleeves, fall signaled the best sport ever known to mankind: football. Football meant Friday nights lost in high-school games and Saturday afternoons lost in college games. I couldn't get enough. I thrived on the intensity every week as the analysis of the past victories and losses still lingered in the crisp fall air and the anticipation of the next set of rivalries made my eyes widen with excitement. Living in a home as the only male surrounded by fits of estrogen and an overabundance of nail polish, I held the conversations about the games in my head as though I were one of the sports announcers commentating on a game.

A.C. and I were heading out to throw the football to each other when we heard a group of voices coming from the other side of the cul-de-sac. The streetlight in front of the Webbers' created a silhouette of a large group of kids gathered beneath it. As we walked toward the gathering place, I zipped up my green windbreaker. Winter was knocking.

I knew once winter hit, I would not see most of the kids under the streetlight, who were from different grades and schools, till the first nice spring day in late March or early April. That's how winter worked for us. Nice weather and vacation from school meant going outside. Division was gone when we were in our yards. I liked that. The kids of the Maple Crest cul-de-sac were a gang of convenience.

Fifty-two kids living within a two-block area usually gathered in the cul-de-sac down by the Webber home. I'm not kidding. One time Mrs. Webber counted us. She said we had a full deck of cards. That is, if you counted the handful of babies, who never came out to the cul-de-sac, and a few older kids who were too cool to hang with us. But nonetheless, we had fifty-two kids in the Maple Crest area that summer.

At any given time, a group would be gathered, usually with bikes. We were always planning. One summer we built an underground fort behind the Mangiamellis' backyard fence. From five feet away, you couldn't see anything but dirt and weeds. That was the plan. Once upon it, you could see the square opening in the large piece of plywood covered with dirt and weeds that served as our roof. A ladder would take you down to the secret room where we usually planned other things. Another year we had a trash carnival, probably one of our stupidest endeavors, though you wouldn't hear me say that around Lucy, who planned the whole thing in the great, altruistic hope of cleaning up our neighborhood and having fun.

I could see the breath spraying from the mouths of the kids under the streetlight, clouds of conversation filling the fall air. They were definitely planning. A few basketballs bounced as they talked. Several kids were on their bikes.

"We can't play Capture the Flag. The best places to hide the flag are down by the creek." The same voice quickly moved to another subject. "How about Kick the Can or German Flashlight?" The voice belonged to the tallest silhouette, whose face became clearer the closer we got to the group. Will had the dark Mangiamelli features that impressed any girl around him. His height, looks, and strong voice gave him the commanding presence that made people want to follow him.

Another voice chimed in. "Hey, A.C. What are you d-d-doing here?" The question came from Stinky Morrow, a kid who was a few years younger than us, but his inferiority never kept him from hanging around the older boys all the time. Stinky was sometimes annoying, but we always felt something was missing if he wasn't hanging around. Stinky stuttered.

"We miss you, A.C." No one laughed as the slightly overweight eight-year-old girl came up and gave A.C. a big, long hug. Hope Webber was the second daughter of Ruth and Ed Webber.

"Hey, Hope, I miss you, too," A.C. said as she continued to hug him.

"Let him go, Hope!" This time the voice, which had a nasal and obnoxious edge to it, was that of Hope's little sister Lovey. Ruth and Ed Webber had a clear plan in naming their children. The very religious couple felt that Faith, Hope, and Love were beautiful names for the three daughters of whom they were so proud. The three little Webber girls had very dark hair with blue eyes and freckles on very fair skin. A knockout final look, if you ask me. A few years later, Robert was born. The Webber plan became a little less clear at that point, but the Webbers remained proud of their clan. Lovey, the third daughter, through her very vibrant and rather flamboyant personality, was able to transform the religious intentions of her name into something of a parody. At the very end of the hippie era, "Lovey" took on a different flavor. Lovey would constantly remind us of how she felt about herself, usually twirling her hair as she canted, "Faith, Hope, and Love... and the greatest of these is Love!"

That night under the streetlight, with one hand on her hip, Lovey tilted her head and said, "You can't go around hugging every cute boy you see."

"Lovey!" Hope retorted. "Be nice."

"Hope, you can hug me any time you feel like it." A.C. Perelman was a complex kid. This not-really-black and not-really-white kid lived in a world that asked he be clearly labeled. The waters muddied as you threw religion and socioeconomic factors into the pot. A.C. would always say, "At least I don't have a split personality."

Arthur Charles Perelman was born in the same year I was born, when his parents still lived next door to our house. He and his little sister, Elizabeth, had been among the neighborhood gang until a year ago when his parents decided to move to a bigger house. An older couple, Mr. and Mrs. Anderson, moved into the Perelmans' old house and kept to themselves. Evelyn and Howard Perelman agreed to stay in touch as they moved closer to the downtown area and transferred their children into Brownell Talbot, a private school in the Dundee area. Both Howard and Evelyn were extremely bright and had met at Harvard getting their doctorates, Evelyn in medicine and Howard in business. Financially, they had outgrown our humble neighborhood, though they struggled to leave it, not quite knowing the best environment in which their two uniquely defined children could thrive.

"Hey, Will. My cousin T-T-Theresa is spending the night at your house tonight. Lucy, Marty, and Theresa are having a slumber party or something." Theresa's aunt Sheila was my neighbor and Stinky Morrow's mother, who seemed to be in a perennial state of pregnancy, with a few kids around her and one on her hip. Theresa's family lived about six blocks from our little cul-de-sac in the Dogwood subdivision. The houses there were a little newer than the houses in our subdivision. They were still small, but the carbon-copied floor plans in Dogwood touted the dawning of the split-level house that grew to be a favorite in Omaha's twenty-year era of Boring Construction. Split-level, raised ranch, whatever you wanted to call it, the guests of those homes had immediate options upon entering the doorway. *Do I go up; do I go down? Maybe I should leave.*

Theresa lived in Dogwood, but she hung out in Maple Crest, and we were all too proud of that decision. Stinky's comment to Will was really an attempt to get his attention or impress him. He must have sensed, as we all did, that Will had a crush on Theresa O'Brien.

"She really is spending the night, Will."

"I think I know that, Stinky. Can we get this game thing figured out? I'm freezing."

The circle of kids was again interrupted as three figures walked from the Mangiamelli home. Lovey shouted, "Hey, Lucy, hurry up, we're gonna play Capture the Flag. We need a few more kids."

Lucy, Marty, and Theresa hurried toward the group with hands in pockets. Will scowled as he muttered, "We are not playing Capture the Flag." Will looked up and caught a glimpse of his little sister. "Wow, Lu, looks like you three fell into a humongous pile of makeup. Yikes. Must have been some accident."

Lucy ignored her brother, though he did have a point. She ran to A.C. and squealed in her scratchy voice, "Hey! This is perfect. This is the greatest! A.C.'s here. We almost didn't come out, but we just did each other's hair and thought, 'Hey, let's go see who might be hanging out on a Friday night.' Good thing we did." Lucy's hair was covered with all sorts of colorful barrettes and ribbons. It looked more like a carnival than a hairstyle, though she seemed very proud of the new and almost trampy look as she tilted her head and said, "We're staying up late tonight to watch *Creature Feature.* Dr. San Guinary's going to make an announcement before *Teenage Caveman.*"

"I heard about this. He's announcing haunted-house kits you can order." Stinky stepped into the center of circle as he spoke.

"Yep," Lucy continued, "and we're thinking of having one before Halloween. You all can help if you want. We send the money we make from the haunted house to Dr. San Guinary. He's collecting money for muscular dystrophy."

"Who's she?" Stinky asked seriously.

Marty stood with her usual solemn expression behind Lucy. Her straight, brown hair had been braided and finished with ribbons as well. As for her makeup, I thought she looked as though she had been hit a few too many times in the face. Theresa O'Brien was another story. She looked beautiful. The makeup had done what makeup should do. It accented her already striking features. Not even childish adornment could hide the amazing beauty of Theresa.

"Where's Faith, Lovey?" Lucy looked over at Lovey Webber.

"She went to Cheap Skate with the older kids." Lovey rolled her eyes and moved her head and shoulders in an exotic swish. I'd be lying if I said I wasn't disappointed that Faith was off skating that night. I could learn to roller skate if it meant that I could look at Faith, the older, more mature girl that I found myself staring at too much. A.C. would catch me gawking and whisper, "Out of your league…"

"Who needs her anyway? I know what we can—" Lovey stopped in midsentence. Her eyes froze on something as she looked past the group toward the entrance to our cul-de-sac. Her lower lip dropped. Her upper lip rose to scream; nothing came out. The group turned in the direction that Lovey was looking. The glare in our eyes from the streetlight above us all made it very hard to see the large shadow moving toward the group. I wanted to be brave and calm, but my gut did a somersault as my eyes tried to detect the large, lumpy body moving toward us. Why none of us ran will never be clear to me, but I was planning, as I'm sure Will and A.C. were, how we were going to attack this man—heck, maybe even kill him if we had to, to protect the ladies and youth of the neighborhood. I'm certain that everyone in the group, grateful for the safety-in-numbers factor and the close proximity to our parents in the houses behind us, was wondering if Johnny Madlin had run into this same creature down by the creek.

Once the man had moved to the point in the street where the light showered down, we all visibly sighed in relief upon the realization that the coulda-been-a-monster-coulda-been-a-killer who now stopped and looked at the group was only Mr. Payne. Corky Payne looked tired and confused as he looked at each face under the light. His eyes stopped on me and stayed there.

Corky Payne, unkempt and unsure, carried a grief in his heart that came from his son Tommy's tragic accident six years earlier. Tommy Payne and I were born on the same day back in 1961. On October 7 of that year, my mother and Patti Payne delivered healthy baby boys within forty-five minutes of each other. For Patti and Corky, this event was amazing since this was their first child delivered after years and years of trying to achieve a pregnancy. They were elated, and this may have been a good or bad thing for my mother since the two women shared rooms following the births of their babies. My mom was a newly single parent giving birth to me.

Grandpa Mac shared with me that, though my own father was gone by then, obviously he and my sisters were there for mother and would visit her on the days she stayed at Immanuel Hospital. He mentioned that Corky Payne was up there every moment he could and kept the two ladies in stitches as he entertained them in his father-high state at the time. "He was good to your mother. Made her see that some fathers do stick around. Maybe caused her a bit of pain, though."

A few years later, Tommy Payne and I had little play dates, my mother called them. Though we didn't look that much alike—Tommy had red hair and one of the biggest heads I have ever seen on a kid—the mothers loved to call us the twins. Tommy and I used to ride our Big Wheels all over the neighborhood. The Paynes lived behind us a few doors down, so the mothers would walk to the corner to meet and tag off with us following behind on our Big Wheels. Tommy had this loud, scratchy voice that sounded like Charlie Brown when he belted out gravel commands in his driveway. "You're Batman and I'm Superman! OK?" He always got to be Superman.

The summer before we turned five, Mr. Payne was backing out of his driveway. He had just seen Tommy in the backyard and didn't know that Tommy had climbed the fence and grabbed his Big Wheel from the side of the house. Corky had no idea what he'd hit as he backed out to head to the hardware store. The Paynes drove Tommy to the hospital as fast as they could, and though the doctors did everything they could, Tommy didn't make it through the night.

Six months later, Patti Payne left Corky, and from that day on, Corky pretty much wandered. Some said he was a drinker, but Grandpa Mac said that Corky was doing the best he could. Corky stayed in his little house and did fix-it jobs here and there for people, but he mostly wandered.

That chilly Friday when Corky came upon our group under the streetlight, not one kid snickered at the strange man who had singled me out.

"You the Keller boy?" he asked me.

"Yes, sir."

Corky looked deep into my eyes. "How old are you now, kid?"

"Eleven, sir."

"Eleven?"

I nodded my head.

Corky dropped his eyes and then his head, and then wandered back out of the cul-de-sac. Bummer baby bookmark. That's all I have to say about that.

Lovey broke the silence.

"Well, are we going to play something or what? How about Sardines? We can keep warm, don't you think?" Lovey elbowed A.C. and tilted her head. She was only seven or eight at the time, but I swear to you that the girl exuded sexuality in her every movement.

I can't recall if we played Sardines or German Flashlight or just talked and bounced basketballs. Aside from the moment with Mr. Payne, I remember feeling really cold but not wanting to go inside since that would mark the end of another season with the neighborhood kids.

# 5

## Octavia Hruska: Weekly Set, Going to Dinner

### Friday, November 16

# 1973

The dread would always start slowly up my spine as I waited to be picked up for CCD.

During my elementary-school years, I spent two hours each week "learning to be Catholic." The letters lined up together—CCD—scared me, though I didn't even know what CCD stood for until I was an adult. I thought it was Catholic Children's Detention, a place for unworthy children to be tested and to learn about purgatory as the divine spanking, common "misconceptions" about the Immaculate Conception, and other Catholic stuff like that. Although my mom struggled with the Catholic Church and its treatment of divorced Catholics at that time, my grandfather quietly encouraged my religious journey. When I asked Grandpa Mac his thoughts on the whole lurid CCD conspiracy, he laughed and said,

"Ben, I myself think that faith is more caught than taught, but that's how it works here. You gotta go, kiddo."

My sister Cheryl and A.C.'s mom took turns taking us to the Saint Pius classrooms on Wednesday evenings where A.C. decided that the devil himself would have cried uncle to get out of the militant sentence. One of the only memories I have is when an elderly priest with thinning gray hair visited our class and scribbled all over our board words regarding transubstantiation that I could not understand. When he was concluding his lesson, he asked our class in a quiet, holy voice, "Now, do any of you have any questions?"

A.C. responded without even raising his hand. "Who cuts your hair?"

Mrs. Perelman was running late the day I remember first talking to Octavia Hruska. Octavia had been a name my mother and Grandpa Mac talked about, but I had never really engaged in conversation with the Fremont icon. The day I had walked down to my mother's salon, my plan was simple. I would do my best to look disappointed as I informed Mom that I didn't think that Mrs. Perelman was going to make it and that I should probably just watch *Gilligan's Island* or *Get Smart* instead of going to CCD—if that was OK with her.

"Come on in, Benny. You know Mrs. Hruska, don't you?" my mother prodded me. CCD or an old lady conversation. I was being tested.

"Oh, yes," I lied. "How are you, Mrs. Hruska?"

"Why, I'm just fine, Ben. Your mother tells me that you are doing real well in school."

"Thanks. Mom, I don't think Mrs. Perelman is going to make it tonight."

"I'm sure she's on her way, Ben. Did you know that Mrs. Hruska lives in Fremont, a few blocks from where I grew up?"

"Wow." *Get Smart* was probably already starting. Maxwell Smart would be walking through all those doors about now.

"Octavia is meeting an old friend for dinner."

"Old is the key word," Octavia chided. "I haven't seen her since high school. She read my husband's obituary and sent me a lovely card. I called and asked her to dinner."

"And you're going to look fabulous." My mother sounded sincere as she spoke.

"Oh, I don't know about that. I used to look a bit different in high school...Meredith asked how she would recognize me. Did I still have red hair and freckles? I said, oh no, I'd be the one with old hair and liver spots."

Octavia Hruska made the drive from Fremont, a town just outside of Omaha, into town as one of her many routines that helped keep her looking refined and well-groomed. These routines would have been very foreign to the little girl she had been growing up on a farm outside of Fremont, Nebraska. She had been one of twelve kids, daughter of a struggling farmer with a drinking problem that may have impacted his financial failure.

My mom told me that Octavia's mother had named her eighth child Octavia, possibly having run out of names for her babies. Maybe the unique name of Octavia Edith True helped keep her positive through the poverty and family shame of her childhood. Isolated from the town's folk and stigmatized by birthright, Octavia had few friends other than her siblings. Her most loyal ally had been her beauty.

During a trip to the county fair when she was fourteen, Octavia attracted the attention of David Lee Hruska, the son of the wealthiest farmer in eastern Nebraska. The farming skills of his father, Wayne Hruska, barely matched his ability to buy and sell land. Because most of Fremont was owned by Wayne and his wife, Darlene, many people called Washington County "Wayne County." The eldest son of Wayne made no effort to hide his interest in the True girl, who had blossomed since he had seen her at the last Washington County Fair. Octavia had been showing her prized sheep when David Hruska made claim to her heart.

As a young man, David Hruska had enough gumption, confidence, or whatever you call it to rise above the town talk and marry Octavia True, the poor girl from the wrong side of the Fremont tracks, on her eighteenth birthday. She held her head high as she made the jump over the tracks that not one person in Washington County could have predicted, and Mrs. David Lee Hruska never looked back. Octavia ignored the fact that she had ever been made fun of by most of the women who came to her garden parties. On bridge night, no one could have guessed that she had never graduated from eighth grade. The only thing she carried with her from her childhood to her new life was her Catholic religion. She could always buy new clothes.

From the stories I've heard, I think I would have liked David Hruska. He died before I met Octavia.

That day in my mother's shop, an older yet still beautiful version of Mrs. David Hruska still held her head high as she glanced in the mirror. "Marcia, do you think we need to do something with this side?" From the little black radio in the window, Carly Simon sang to her mystery ego case about his vanity. Her background singer Mick Jagger, notorious for his own escalades of vanity, chimed in with "You're So Vain."

I heard a door slam upstairs. A.C. interrupted Jagger and Simon when he called down to the basement from the top of the stairs in our kitchen, "Hey, Ben, c'mon. You better hurry up if you plan on going to heaven!"

"I'll be right up." No *Get Smart.* No more old-lady conversation. The slow dread began to race up my spine. *CCD, here I come.* "Good-bye, Mrs. Hruska. It was good to see you."

"Have a lovely time, Ben," she advised as she patted her hair in the mirror.

I headed up the stairs, knowing that once I saw A.C., the dread would disappear. I should probably give A.C. most of the credit for me learning anything about the Catholic Church since he always made the journey fun. If he didn't make me laugh, he made me pay attention.

During the year that we were preparing to make our First Confession in our CCD class, I held the greatest fear during the weeks leading up to that first time I would walk into the confessional closet and sit in the dark, alone with my sins and my fear. A.C. held no fear, as he devised a master plan based on the information he had received from some savvy fifth grader, who had told him that Old-Fart Father Dailey was stone deaf. The fifth grader had told A.C. that Father could not hear our sins and would usually bestow upon the confessor some pretty minor penance. The fifth grader had tested the rumor by reporting to Father Dailey during one of his confessions that he had committed adultery once, committed suicide twice, and had fought with his sister a few times. Father told him to be sorry for his sins and to say one Hail Mary and two Our Fathers.

A.C.'s plan was for the two of us to race to the line to the confessional of Father Dailey, avoiding the possibility of being directed toward one of the younger, nondeaf, and more-penance-heavy priests. I was happy about the plan and proud to have such a schemer for a friend. Once Sister Alleluia announced that we could go to the confessionals to make our First Confessions, the entire class raced to form a line outside of the confessional for Father Dailey. Apparently, the fifth grader had told several people his little secret.

After the other priests sat for several minutes in their confessionals, awaiting their first confessors, they each poked their heads out and looked to the line for Father Dailey. Young Father Gusweiler—we later added Uptight to his name—walked over to me, tapped me on the shoulder, and pointed to his confessional. "Now!" My sins were indeed heard that day by a grumpy priest who gave me more than a deserved amount of penance.

A.C. and I ran to his car to go to Pius for another episode of "CCD in the Seventies," a great premise for a reality show long before its time in which second-rate Catholics were sentenced by tired parents/CCD teachers to memorize prayers and rules. For what? Why, the prize was the experience. Every Wednesday we got to sit at another kid's desk, who would then blame us public-school kids for messing with his stuff.

And maybe we did.

6

## Mrs. Webber: Something "Fun," Sports Banquet for Hope

### Wednesday, July 10

# 1974

Even though the nation cried "ouch" during the national fuel crisis of 1974 due to the OPEC oil embargo, the crisis did little to affect my life that summer. The lines for gas were ridiculous, but they didn't hold me back from wheeling around on my royal-blue, ten-speed bike every day.

That summer I rode several times a week to Brookhill Country Club, the neighborhood hangout. I hung with the kids on my block and A.C.—when he could get a ride to my house. We rode down to Ben Franklin Five and Dime for junk food. And as usual, I helped my mom out in our basement.

Around that time, I began to sense my mother's limitations in running a business. She knew people and she knew hair, but she had never been good with money. I always knew that we "struggled" in the financial area; I can remember more than once witnessing my grandfather hand something to my mother in an envelope and quietly say, "You're taking it. And that's that."

Several times a month, even during those summer months, Grandpa Mac would pick me up and take me to Saint Pius to serve Mass. The schedule I picked up each month from the sacristy announced days and times that I would serve. Daily Mass was offered four times and Sunday Mass five in our parish. My name popped up on the schedule about six times a month. I always picked up an extra schedule for Grandpa Mac.

That evening I sat on the porch in long dress pants and church shoes even though it was ninety-seven degrees out. Always, I made a point to be on the porch ready to go so as to avoid those awkward exchanges between Grandpa Mac and Mom. Long ago, whether one of my sisters told me or I had acquired special powers of tension osmosis, I became aware of the situation, as it were, regarding the Catholic religion in my home. The imaginary conversation between Mac and Mom would have gone something like this:

*Mom: "I'm angry at the Catholic Church."*

*Mac: "I can see that."*

*Mom: "I am afraid that the Church doesn't like me because I am divorced."*

*Mac: "You had no choice."*

*Mom: "I don't think I should have to go through the so-called annulment process to prove my innocence. Why should I be the one who has to work so hard? He left me."*

*Mac: "What about the kids?"*

*Mom: "I don't know."*

*Mac: "Let me show them the Church. They need the Church."*

*Mom: "Just don't talk to me about it."*

*Mac: "I love you."*

So that's how it worked. We all ignored the big Catholic elephant in the room. We all pretended that I wasn't really going to serve Mass. I was just putting on the ugliest and most uncomfortable clothes that we all knew I hated and heading to sit on the porch. We just didn't need to talk about it. That's what it was like growing up in a not-quite-Catholic home.

My shirt began to stick to my back from the sweat trickling down my neck. Such suffering was offered to my grandfather, as I would do anything for Grandpa Mac. I knew, for whatever reason, that it was important to him that I serve Mass. My trivial suffering was soon interrupted by a loud and off-key song walking toward my house.

"Grounds in my coffee, grounds in my coffee, and you're so vain, I betcha think this song is about you, Ben!" Hope laughed loudly as she and her mother walked toward my porch. "That's how Lovey sings that song. Everybody knows that it's 'Clouds in your coffee.' Duh!"

"Let's not say 'duh.' Can we think of a different word to say, Hope?" Mrs. Webber was holding Hope's hand.

"Not really."

Hope's reply was genuine. It was not in any sort of tone, typical of girls her age. I agreed with her, though. "Duh" was pretty much the only word to use there. Hope's comment was regarding what in time came to be known as "Loveyisms." Loveyisms were the strange spin that Lovey put on lyrics. Hope's little sister, Lovey Webber, was notorious for belting out her own erroneous versions of the most popular songs at the time. What damage Lovey could do to a song could sometimes never be repaired.

Hope smiled at me. "Hey, Ben. Guess where I'm going?"

"Uh, crazy? Can I come along?"

Hope's head went back, and her authentic laugh made me smile. "Ben, this is serious," Hope said. "I am going to a rewards assembly."

Mrs. Webber chimed in. "Ben, Hope is being honored today at a sports banquet. She's receiving an award for success in track at the Special Olympics. Hope holds the state record for the mile run last year. Your mom is going to do something fun with her hair." Mrs. Webber was always kind and quiet. The only time I saw her mad was when little Robert went streaking toward the pool yelling, "Ethel, don't look!"

"Congratulations on your award, Hope. You should feel really good about that."

As Hope and Mrs. Webber headed toward the path to the back door to the salon, Mrs. Webber asked me the question that every adult had asked me that summer. "Hey, Ben, have you decided where you'll go to high school in the fall?"

I dreaded the usual dialogue. I knew that we couldn't afford for me to go to the Catholic all-boys Jesuit school, Creighton Prep. Mac had offered to help with that, but my mom knew she couldn't pay him back. She'd said no to offers for my sisters to go to Marian High School. With our financial situation, my family would stay on the public-school track.

"You know, I'm not sure yet..."

Grandpa Mac honked from the curb and waved at Mrs. Webber. "Gotta go. Congrats, Hope." I ran to the big silver boat of a Buick that Grandpa called Babe.

"Heya, Benny," Grandpa Mac yelled. Note: Grandpa Mac is the only person who got away with calling me Benny besides my mom.

"Heya, Grandpa, heya, Babe," I addressed his silver femme-auto that only slightly embarrassed me as we drove by the kids on the block. "It sure is hot."

The talk would remain on the surface during the ride to the church. Weather, ball games, and gas prices. Pretty much it. I think our great effort to sound nonchalant was an attempt to make this little ritual seem natural. And for sure, we never talked about my mom during those ten-minute drives. Mac always allowed me to turn the radio in his car to WOW. That evening, the Righteous Brothers were singing about heaven in the song "Rock and Roll Heaven."

As we pulled onto the blacktop parking lot at Saint Pius, I took a deep breath. Going to a church that I didn't feel much a part of. Standing up in front of large crowds of people watching me try to remember every little cup I must give Father. Lighting candles twice as tall as me. Kneeling for what seemed like an eternity. Wearing a dress that I guess was supposed to make me look like a "minipriest" or maybe an angel. This was not easy.

But Grandpa Mac would be sitting out in the pews. He would drop me off near the sacristy and then park out front. Mac would enter the church through the front doors and would sit on the left side, halfway up the aisle, always. He was never too far, not too close or obvious. He would make eye contact with me only once, as I walked down the aisle in the procession with Father Whelan. Grandpa Mac would wink.

Grandpa Mac dropped me off, and I headed toward the back door to the sacristy. Just outside the door against the building leaned Father

Whelan, smoking a cigarette. I can still hear A.C., as he puffed on a candy cigarette from Ben Franklin Five and Dime Store: "Winston tastes good… like a cigarette should."

Most of the priests that I knew at that time smoked. Heck, most of the adults that I knew smoked at that time in my life: Grandpa Mac, most of the dads, and some of the moms on our block. I had my suspicions about a few teachers. A.C. and I used to think that Father Whelan was one of the coolest smokers ever, though. He seemed deep in thought as he inhaled and squinted. Maybe he was contemplating his sermon for this five thirty p.m. Mass. Maybe he was praying for someone he had visited in the hospital. Maybe he was thinking about some of the more awful or interesting confessions he had listened to recently.

"Good evening, Ben." Father exhaled as he spoke. Father Whalen was the only priest who knew my name. Father Whelan was cool. A.C. and I had names for each priest in our parish. Big Father Laverty, Young Father Gusweiler, Old-Fart Father Dailey, Fun Father Spokinski, and Cool Father Whelan.

"Hey, Father!" I always liked serving for Father Whelan. He didn't make me feel nervous if I forgot to bow or get the wine right away. I ran into the sacristy hoping that he would think that I was eager to serve.

Calling these men "father" was always strange to me. They weren't my father. My own father wasn't even my father. The name, I figured, even then, was to show that a priest held great responsibility to the people of the church. He was supposed to nurture the people and be their strength and safety during challenging times. People looked to the priest in this way. I could see that in the older women in the church as they told Father Gusweiler he gave a great sermon, or in the faces of children as they ran to Father Spokinski on the playground.

One Thanksgiving as the choir pounded out an impressive performance of "Faith of Our Fathers," I listened to the words:

*Faith of our fathers, living still,*
*In spite of dungeon, fire and sword;*
*O how our hearts beat high with joy*
*Whenever we hear that glorious Word!*

I pinched my eyes together to see what face would pop up in my mind as the father, living still. The father who made my heart fill with joy. I saw Grandpa Mac. Not the priests of Saint Pius.

*Faith of our fathers, holy faith!*
*We will be true to thee till death.*

A.C. and I had analyzed the whole priesthood thing. Having people look up to you and call you Father would be kind of cool. Giving our lives to God would certainly gain us some points and impress the adults in our worlds. If I knew that I could be as cool as Father Whelan as a priest, I might consider the priesthood, especially if that whole girl thing never worked out.

A.C. had already committed his life to God in the second grade following his First-Communion ceremony. He had announced in front of the cake and coffee at the family party that he was going to be a priest. He would live his life and offer all he did up to God. He also wanted to be a zookeeper and an NFL football player. If anyone could juggle the three, Father A.C. would be the man.

As soon as I signed in to serve that summer evening, I bumped into a kid whose last name must have been right next to mine in the altar server roster since I more often than not got stuck serving with him. Ken or Keith Kemper or something like that. I just remember I didn't care much for him.

"Dibs on the book. Oh and I'll do the bell, too!" Ken-or-Keith skipped off to light the candles on the altar—another fun thing I wouldn't get to do. The "book" happened to be the easier of the two jobs assigned to the servers. These jobs had been taught to me earlier that year during a forty-five-minute training session where Young-Uptight Father Gusweiler magically made me an altar boy. A flock of half minipriest hopefuls and half this-was-not-my-idea youths sat listening to Father while their mothers sat in the back of the church.

Hey, I have an idea! Let's get the boys in their most awkward, self-conscious state of puberty and put them on the altar for all to gawk at during Mass. Oh, and don't let the girls up there. Did they really want to give the key to the tabernacle to a sixth-grade boy? Did they have any idea how hard it was for a twelve-year-old boy to keep a straight face when he saw his friend from the pews crossing his eyes? Did they not know how tempting it was to shine the shiny-crumb-catcher thing right against the light so that it would reflect on the ceiling? Did they know how hard it was to get up at 5:45 in the morning on days that boys served at the 6:30 a.m. Mass and stay awake for that next hour? I think they knew. Oh, they knew. No one had spared them, either.

Those who schemed up this whole altar-boy thing must have felt that young men might gain some character taking part in the liturgy. They must have hoped that the overwhelming, nauseating stench of the incense would knock some sense into the young boys. Maybe the holy-water thingy that the priest shook at the congregation would look like something fun to do. Maybe some of those young participants would consider the priesthood. I'm sure they had an agenda. I just know that the roller coaster of emotions every time my name showed up on the altar-server roster was absolute. From the moment I put on the ugly church clothes to the moment I was dropped off after the Mass, I would endure that anxious feeling that I might screw something up.

Occasionally, while enduring my "anxiety and suffering" offering to God, I would have moments of awe. As I held a gold plate under the communicants' chins as they stuck out their tongues for the Holy Eucharist, some people looked hungrier than others to me. Hungry for something. Hungry for what? Of course, the younger communicants focused more on the style of receiving the Eucharist. After watching and anticipating their time to partake in the Communion, they wanted to do it right. It was the older people of the community who always struck me. They looked so hungry.

During the mornings that I served, I had to wonder, what had gotten these older people out of bed to come to Mass? I know that if Grandpa Mac had not prodded me along, I certainly would still be in a nice, warm bed. What made these people get up so early to come? They could have slept in. If you are over one hundred years old or so, you shouldn't have to go to 6:30 a.m. Mass. Right? Yet they all looked so hungry. They actually wanted to be there. It was during this time that I felt completely unworthy. Unworthy to be standing on the altar. Unworthy to be partaking in this amazing ritual. Unworthy to receive such grace I did not understand.

After Mass that evening in the summer of 1974, once Ken-or-Keith and I had cleaned up, snuffing out candles and putting everything in order for the next Mass, I hung up my robe and headed out to the blacktop parking lot. Grandpa Mac and Babe were waiting for me. The ride home was pretty much the same as the ride to church except that every once in a while Grandpa Mac would stop by Goodrich Dairy and get two chocolate malts for us. That night on our way home, we saw a small black man walking down Blondo Street with an armful of brooms and a white cane. Mac waved at the man. The old man, in a suit and tie, wearing a capped hat, held about five brooms over his shoulder. He moved the cane back and forth as he walked down the sidewalk.

"That's Reverend Livingston, Ben," Grandpa Mac said quietly. "He's a blind man who sells brooms for a living and preaches God's word. Makes the brooms, too. The man's a saint, a quiet little saint weaving around the city."

"He's blind? How does he know if people are paying him the right amount of money?"

"He just trusts them, I guess. I bought a broom from him when I was working downtown. He was walking around the UP building at lunch time, but I've seen him all over Omaha."

Grandpa Mac turned Babe past the Wicker Witch house and onto my cul-de-sac. He parked in the driveway. "Thanks for serving, Benny."

"You bet. Hey, Grandpa?"

Grandpa Mac looked at me as I opened the door to get out of his car.

"You waved to a blind man." I started laughing. "Did you know that?"

Grandpa Mac smiled. "Wondered if you'd caught that."

I ran up to my porch and went into the house. The summer of 1974 was stinkin' hot. Gas prices were wacky. An old, blind man sold brooms on the streets of Omaha. And over in England, after a stint as a ditch digger and an English teacher, my future hero, was playing music wherever he could get a job. Gordon Sumner, music man of England, was starting to make a name for himself.

And Ben Keller, not-quite-Catholic kid of Omaha, was serving the evening Mass at Saint Pius X in Omaha, Nebraska.

# 7

## Mrs. Mangiamelli: Wash and Set, Delayed Graduation to Attend

### Thursday, June 5

# 1975

The winds across the state of Nebraska misbehaved during the year 1975. They mastered the perfect blizzard in January and later performed a mind-dazzling "ten" of a tornado in early May. Those same angry winds blew Ava Mangiamelli into my mother's basement in early June for a wash and set.

The official icebreaker for any hairstylist is the weather. In Nebraska, this was most definitely a volatile topic. How 'bout that blizzard? Hey, how 'bout that tornado? "If you don't like the weather in Omaha, just stick around an hour or two. It'll change."

So much to talk about in 1975.

In January, when mothers were hurrying to get their children back to school following two weeks of Christmas break, the blizzard of '75 hit.

Major winds and almost twenty inches of snow took fourteen lives in Omaha. The National Guard rescued four hundred stranded motorists. Employees of businesses around the city were stranded for days in their offices. Mr. Webber spent three days at a light company that was near a gas station and a liquor store. Mr. Webber and three other employees found a TV in the storage area and played cards until the snow plows unburied their cars. I still have a picture of A.C. and me standing on a drift that was as high as the roof on his house. No joke. We had the longest Christmas vacation that year since school was canceled an additional week. The city was paralyzed. The kids were ecstatic.

As if we hadn't already missed enough school, in May we had another unexpected break from the classroom since, barely an hour after school kids made it home for the day, some of the classrooms were no longer there. At about 4:15 p.m. on May 6, several major tornados, with winds gusting up to 260 miles per hour, decided to blow down the center of town, turn left on Seventy-Second Street, and swing by the Ak-Sar-Ben Racetrack and Archbishop Bergan Mercy Hospital before driving out of town and lifting at 4:38 p.m. The afternoon tour chopped a path across ten miles of streets and residences. Nearly a year after Elvis Presley sold out performances in his "Tornado over Omaha" concert tour of June 1974, the real-life tornado of '75 caught our city's attention.

The miracle of it all is that this F4 natural disaster took only three lives. Omahans were proud to say that their sound-warning system was the real hero; one of the three fatalities had been a hard-of-hearing elderly lady who had not heard the sirens.

Omaha drew a breath as the paralyzed community picked up toasters and wallets in their yards belonging to people who lived miles away. An entire block wiped out near Saint Pius had only one wall standing, with a cross hanging soundly. Lucy's friend Beth Taber, who lived two blocks from Pius, spent the next three months in a town house while her home was rebuilt. When the sirens sounded on that day in May, Beth and her three sisters and mother had gone to the southeast corner of their basement and hid under a mattress during those twenty-three minutes. The tornado lifted the house from above them and replaced it with a car. Within seconds, glass whirled around the basement. Beth and her sisters watched from under the mattress as the corner of the house lifted off the foundation. Beth remembers bobbing up off the floor, holding onto her sister.

When the tornado passed, the girls found their neighbor's car suspended just above their heads and their mother on the floor bleeding from a deep cut, apparently inflicted by the car's bumper. Mrs. Taber was knocked out by the blow but revived by the gasoline that was pouring out of the car onto her face. When Mrs. Taber came to, she and her girls noticed that the house was gone. The Tabers didn't realize at the time that one of the twister's three victims lay dead in their backyard.

Saint Pius X, Lewis and Clark Junior High, Creighton Prep High School, and many other schools were out of commission for weeks that spring. No one complained as every normal tradition for the end of a school year was turned upside down. Creighton Prep's graduation was delayed until early June that year. Louis and Ava Mangiamelli's son Sebastian, or Subby, would graduate in the auditorium at Boys Town. Ava came to Mom to have her hair done for the event.

About fifteen minutes before Ava blew in to have her hair done for her son's graduation, I was eating breakfast in our tiny kitchen. Couldn't get enough of Super Sugar Crisp. I was studying the back of the cereal box when Tracy, my second-oldest and most annoying sister, plunked down in the seat next to me. The minute she got her driver's license, Tracy chose to use her driving powers for evil rather than good. When my mom asked her to take me places, she thought it was funny—once we were alone in her clunky Volkswagen—to taunt me by saying, always in a deadpan tone, that Mom had really asked her to drive me to Boys Town and drop me off since she no longer had room for me at home. The seventh time she performed this little antic—the time that she actually drove to Boys Town and parked in front of the *He Ain't Heavy, He's My Brother* statue out front—it was no longer funny.

Tracy would also pull the ole "I'm flyin'—Buckey's buyin'" routine. I would be playing the role of Buckey. This translated to A.C. and me that Tracy would drive us to her favorite fast-food spot, but we had to buy her lunch. When you're housebound with only a ten-speed for transportation, you tend to get a little desperate.

Tracy slammed her transistor radio on the table from which Rufus and Chaka Khan were singing "Tell Me Something Good" and attempted to take a knot out of the cords of her earplugs. She may have been older than I was, but she was just a brat to me. I chomped on my cereal and ignored her.

"Oh, my gosh, I *love* this song…OK, Ben, you need to do me a favor. Tell Grandpa Mac that I went to Confession. I don't want to go to Pius since the priests we see all the time would know my sins, and that's just creepy. OK, so I'm going to Saint Walter's. I want Grandpa Mac to know 'cause if he thought I hadn't gone, he would take me when he takes you. I'm running over there right now. Ben, are you listening to me?"

Tracy was sixteen going on nine. My apologies to nine-year-olds everywhere.

"I heard you, but how do I know if you're telling the truth? Maybe you're lying. Maybe you *need* to go to Confession with me since you would need to confess that you lie about going to Confession. Aren't you the one who sent me into church one time to grab a bulletin to show Mom that we had gone to Mass? I believe you called it a receipt. And why do you think that the priests at Pius even care about your stupid sins?"

"Just tell Grandpa!" Tracy got up and headed out of the house, leaving the earplugs on the table, throwing the radio, still playing, in her fluorescent, oversized bag.

"You have to live with yourself!" I yelled. I went back to studying the back of the Sugar Crisp cereal box. In addition to the fun yet useless toy I would find in the bottom of the box, I could also cut out a forty-five record of Bobby Sherman's hit "Easy Come and Easy Go" right from the back of the box. My mind was buzzing with all sorts of ideas, like how I was going to cut the record out when the box was still over half full. Should I cut the record out or dig for the plastic sugar bear first? Could you really play a cardboard record on a record player? I heard the basement door slam, shaking the table holding my cereal. My spoon was suspended in midair. I heard the muffle of a conversation.

Ava.

My mom.

Ava.

My mom.

Ava sobbing, "What am I going to do, Marcia?" I sensed they weren't talking about the weather, though in a strange way, the meteorological events that year had certainly started to wear down the adult community that I knew. Maybe Ava was barometrically frustrated.

"She's the thorn in my side, I tell you. She will drive me to my grave!"

I heard my mother muffle a laugh. "Oh, Ava! Lucy will be fine."

Aside from this moment, my memories of Mrs. Mangiamelli were all of a well-oiled mother-machine of many children who, despite her stature, maintained a high position of power over her children in a very organized household. When I speak of the tiny houses on our street, I can't stress enough the word "tiny." Ava, in her motherly wisdom and driven adaptability, raised four very large sons and one very bossy daughter under a very tiny roof. With a floor plan quite similar to my little white house, the Mangiamelli home was a lesson in resourcefulness.

While my mother maintained a business in her basement, Ava directed her husband, Louis, to build the frames of two sets of bunk beds against the cement walls of their own underground Boys Town. No one ever complained about the accommodations except during the colder days in the basement in the winter. With four twin mattresses and carpet remnants, the room served as a dormer of sorts that I found resplendent. Posters of the Huskers, The Who, Adrienne Barbeau, and Raquel Welch covered the cinder-block walls, warming the look of Mangiamelli cellar. The summer before, the boys had bought a gigantic *Jaws* poster that was cooler than snot. The four boys slept there year-round. Lucy shared a room on the main level with Grandma, the sewing machine, and a desk from which Mr. Mangiamelli did his bills.

Ava's order and resourcefulness went beyond the home when she told Louis that all of her boys would go to Creighton Prep High School for a fine Jesuit education. Paying tuition for four boys when the public school was right down the street would surely be a challenge, so Ava went up to Prep and gladly filled a position in the cafeteria kitchen. Children of employees were given free tuition. Problem solved. With all of the order and control she maintained in her life and in her home and with her children, Ava was not one who was comfortable when something went awry. Case in point—that day in my mother's shop.

"This. This is awful! Do you think that my baby girl is turning into a floozy?" Ava shouted.

I muffled a laugh. Lucy, a floozy? *Luuucy, you got some 'splaining to do!*

I slowly put the spoonful of cereal into my mouth. I knew that any noise I made in our tiny little kitchen would send a loud, creaking sound to my mother's shop. If I wanted to run away, I would make it known that I had heard the exchange. If I ran, I might miss out on what sounded oh so much more interesting than the Sugar Crisp cereal box.

"Even though we're out of school, I got a call from the principal at Pius this morning. Evidently the day before the tornado, Lucy and seven other kids were called into the office. Lucy was the only one who admitted to… you know. They had to put the punishment for their crime on hold because of the chaos with the tornado. Sister Annunciata said the janitor had found the kids in the tornado shelter between the two locker rooms…doing stuff!"

"Stuff?" my mom asked.

"Stuff!" Ava shouted. "Boys and girls doing stuff." I heard her crying as my mom soothed her. The milk and soggy cereal mellowed in my mouth. I swallowed quietly.

"C'mon, Ava. Sit down."

The tornado shelter or crime scene was yet another interesting architectural decision in the Saint Pius facility. The guy in charge of the blueprints must not have been wearing his thinking cap the day he drew the plans for the Pius tornado shelter. Stairs leading down from the girls' locker room took children to a long, dark, safe hallway. Stairs leading down from the boys' locker room took children to the safety of the same hallway. Great for tornado protection. Not so great for adolescent hormone protection following seventh and eighth-grade basketball games.

Even I, simple public-school boy, knew about the Hall. Some called it Horror Hall, as the lights were not on when kids went there to do stuff. Some called it the Whore Hall. Whatever. The Hall was known. Ava seemed concerned about the scarlet "H" or "W" Lucy would wear the rest of her life with the news of this heinous crime.

She may have been guilty of being in the wrong place at the wrong time, but I knew for a fact that Lucy was innocent of the Whore Hall charges. She was always where the action was; however, Lucy was not one bit guilty of the "stuff" that flustered her mother. I knew this. Now I was in an even more-awkward position since the valuable piece of information that I had in my little kitchen was pure and simple: Lucy was innocent.

I wanted to run downstairs with this information and shout it out loud. I wished I'd left with Tracy for Saint Walter's. I suddenly had to go to the bathroom.

"I know she has her moments..." Ava sobbed and then blew her nose. "She's not a bad girl...What if she doesn't get confirmed?"

"She's a very good girl," Mom consoled Ava during more quiet sobbing.

What if she didn't get confirmed? Did Ava really think that someone other than Lucy had control over her soul? Did she think that someone other than Lucy could confirm her faith? I felt a bit stormy. Linda Ronstadt's song "You're No Good" echoed in the basement as Ava sobbed.

I should know about Confirmation. I had gone through the whole process the year before the tornado with A.C. We were the CCD kids who were tucked in the pews between the Saint Pius school kids on the Sunday of Confirmation. I remember the looks from kids, the same looks we got during First Communion and First Confession. *Who the heck are you? Are you the one that messes with my desk on Wednesday nights?*

Confirmation in the Catholic Church is usually the fourth sacrament that a precious, young Catholic might experience, following Baptism, First Communion, and Confession. Though the ages of those to be confirmed may vary across the nations, most young boys and girls confirm their faith in the Catholic Church around the time that their hormones start clicking away. *Hey, your body is growing up; now you need to be an adult, spiritually as well.*

In the traditional Roman Catholic rite of Confirmation, the sacrament indelibly seals us to the Holy Ghost, hence its name. During Confirmation, a young Catholic publicly "confirms" his or her Catholic intentions in this crazy world. Parents have spoken for these kids at Baptism and up to this point. Now these young men and women come forward and say, "I am Catholic because I say so!"

The added bonuses that go along with the whole Catholic Confirmation process include naming a sponsor, who stands by the child during this big decision, and taking on a new name, one added to the birth-given name. That name should be one that a person takes on because of its significance. It looked really good to the teachers and other adults if you picked a name of a saint.

My sponsor was Grandpa Mac. This was an easy decision. He had stood by me all those years while I served Mass and confessed my sins. He would stand by me as I confirmed my faith.

Then there was the name picking. A young person could really make a statement about himself by picking a certain name. Marty, for example, picked the name Ann since she had intentions of going into the medical world. Saint Ann was a nurse. Theresa was unique, as she chose the male name Gerard, taken from Saint Gerard, the patron saint of mothers. I don't need to tell you that Lucy had been planning her Confirmation name for years. Quite possibly, she'd made her mind up years earlier when she had been excluded from the great Mary procession of 1969. You guessed it: Lucille Bell Mary Mangiamelli.

The year before, A.C. and I had picked out Confirmation names with careful consideration. Of course, A.C. had to be unique with his decision. While the rest of the to-be-confirmed chose names like Elizabeth, James, and Thomas, A.C., after studying many books on the saints, chose the name Aloysius. Saint Aloysius Gonzaga was the patron saint of compassion and Catholic youth. Maybe A.C. couldn't pronounce it. He certainly could pull it off.

I chose the name Joseph. Benjamin Howard Joseph Keller, a no-brainer decision. Joseph, father of Jesus, was the great Background Guy. He married a young pregnant woman, knowing that he had not fathered her child. He protected her and her child through many a turbulent day. That good-father factor certainly weighed heavily on my decision. Jesus was not even his biological son, yet he loved Jesus like a father should.

From my chair in the kitchen, I listened to more sobbing. Would Mom ever do Ava's hair? I sat at the kitchen table with the truth and my soggy cereal. I knew that Lucy was not a floozy. I knew that the only thing Lucy was guilty of was being honest and being in the wrong place at the wrong time. She had not done any of the stuff that seemed to be bothering Mrs. Mangiamelli. I knew this because Lucy had told me.

A month earlier, before the tornado, Lucy had her first baby-sitting job. Because she was twelve, she had taken the Red Cross class on baby-sitting. In perfect Lucy style, she handed out flyers to everyone within a three-block radius that shouted "Pick Me!" My next-door neighbors, Ted and Nancy Shanahan, were past the years of needing babysitters since their "baby" was thirty-two years old, but their daughter, Tammy, and her husband and four-year-old twins would be visiting. Mr. and Mrs. Shanahan, who happened to be one of the only non-Catholic families in our neighborhood, had asked Lucy to baby-sit their grandchildren while they went to a wedding reception. A perfect baby-sitting job for a first-timer.

When I answered the phone that Friday night in April, I didn't recognize her voice. Lucy was terrified.

"Ben!" Lucy cried. "I'm scared to death. You've got to help me."

A million things went through my head as I felt panic growing in my gut. *What! Where? How much blood?* Before I could say a word, Lucy continued, "You've got to come over here. I just watched *Wait until Dark*. My mom's gonna kill me..."

"You've got to give me a little more information, Lucy. What are you talking about? Where is 'here'?"

Lucy explained that, after putting down the kids, she had watched a movie about a blind woman and some bad guys hiding in her house to steal a doll stuffed with drugs that had been planted on her—something her parents would never have allowed her to watch. The Red Cross had prepared Lucy for feeding kids, giving baths, reading bedtime stories in goofy voices, and putting them to bed. She even knew what to do in case of an accident. What the Red Cross failed to do was teach Lucy not to watch scary movies after the little ones were down for the night.

"I can't call my house because my brothers would just tease me and my mom and dad would think that I couldn't handle baby-sitting. Every sound I hear…it's like I think someone is watching me. Can you come to the back door? I don't want anyone to know that you're coming over…Oh, my gosh, what was that?"

Lucy couldn't hear my smile over the phone. I told her I'd meet her at the back door in sixty seconds. Once I got to the door, I saw the silhouette of Lucy in the doorway. Behind her every light in the house appeared to be on. She could still hear if the twins woke up, but she didn't want me to come in just in the event that the Shanahans got home. I felt so sneaky. I guess there were some kids in Omaha our age who were doing some sneaking around. Maybe they were having fun.

For the next hour, until we heard the Shanahans drive up, I kept Lucy company on the back porch. Did she really think that I could protect her from a trio of thugs while they searched for a heroin-stuffed doll? I guess she just felt a little safer for the moment.

The radio from the countertop in Mrs. Shanahan's kitchen was on a low volume, and I could hear Casey Kasem announce the top forty songs of the week with little stories of dedication tucked in between the hits. "This next song is a dedication from Nancy Anderson of Evanston, Indiana. Nancy met a boy years ago at a Bible camp in Illinois and has since lost touch. That boy was never forgotten. Nancy said that the two weeks she spent with Christopher were the best two weeks of her life. Tonight Nancy sends this next song out to that very special young man from Bible camp. Christopher, we hope you're listening."

Casey Kasem played the nauseating and extremely dumb song that had been played to overkill in 1975: Captain and Tennille's "Love Will Keep Us Together."

Lucy talked nonstop that night, I think to avoid sounds of drug dealers. "OK, so for all the stories about the Horror Hall, not an awful lot went on down there. We mostly just talked. Even though the boys are fun and interesting, I don't like the dark, and I definitely do not like holding Joe Weller's hand or the thought of kissing him."

"But isn't that the point?" I knew what I had heard in the roaming rumors about the Hall. "Whatever...Joe told Will who told Marty that if I didn't kiss him soon, he'd break up with me. I'm OK with that. Mostly the Hall is something to do. Besides, I have my eye on one of Anthony's friends from Prep. He makes me laugh, and he's so cute."

"And he's in high school and you're in sixth grade."

"Tom Ducey." She said his name like she was savoring a spoonful of ice cream.

"Never heard of him."

"He's from Saint Peter and Paul." Like that mattered. "He's this big, handsome South Omaha boy with awesome eyes."

"Wow," I said and smirked.

Lucy rolled her eyes. "Sometimes the Horror Hall feels like what death would feel like. Dark and scary. No, death could be worse than the Horror Hall. I wouldn't know anybody in heaven. How fun could that be?"

"And no one would ask to hold your hand. It's not like it's a party... You're dead. Maybe you'd make new friends."

"Ben, I feel kind of stupid about getting so scared tonight...I know you won't tell anyone."

How did she know that?

Lucy stood alone in her admission to her presence in the Horror Hall. I doubt if Sister Annunciata could even threaten to take Confirmation away from Lucy for telling the truth. The principal held much-more-interesting punishments for those Horror Hall criminals. All by herself, Lucy did the time for her crime of admitting being in the wrong place at the wrong time. She served her sentence for three days, helping out the janitors who were cleaning up the mess in the classrooms that was left by the tornado.

Lucille Belle Mary Mangiamelli did "confirm" her Catholic faith later that year in what she called the ugliest tangerine dress, which Ava had insisted she wear. "I mean, really, who wears the color tangerine?" Lucy may have worn the dress, but she refused to wear her glasses that she had just gotten that year.

So, once again, from the top.

Sister Annunciata called seven kids to the office. All but one said that they had never been to the tornado shelter below the locker rooms. Later that day, a tornado visited Saint Pius X in the late afternoon. A month later, Sister Annunciata called Ava. Later that morning my sister went to Confession. I think. After that, my mother tried to do Ava's hair but instead calmed the fear in her that her daughter might go to hell, or worse, not make her Confirmation. Right after that the phone rang. I dropped my spoon.

"Can somebody get that?" my mother yelled from the bottom of the stairs. I ran to the phone. No one was there. This time, someone saved me.

# 8

# Grandpa Mac: A Trim, His Best Friend's Funeral

## Saturday, July 31

# 1976

A little off the sides was all he ever wanted.

Mom and Grandpa Mac would always argue.

"You took off too much."

"It's not too much."

"Just look at the floor, would ya? Look at all of my hair."

Mom would wink at me as they argued. This Saturday seemed different as they verbally sparred, splitting hairs. While he threw in the usual grumbles and jabs, he seemed distracted; I noticed that Grandpa Mac didn't have the usual sparkle in his blue eyes.

"Going fishing today, Grandpa?" I asked, hoping to reignite that sparkle.

"Not today, Benny. Not today. Got to bury my buddy Bill."

"Bill the fighter pilot?'

"One and the same." I thought I caught a slight sparkle.

"Wasn't he the best man in your wedding with Grandma Margaret?" I knew this as a fact, but I also knew that Grandpa Mac loved to tell the stories of his life.

"Yep."

No story today. His role as a pallbearer was imminent. Grandpa had been burying a good number of his buddies and their wives that year, and the weight of the dead was wearing him down a bit. He looked tired and alone. I thought it was funny he would worry about his hair looking nice. Heck, his friend was dead and didn't care about hair anymore. It was more for respect, I guess. As my mother brushed the stray hairs from his collar, he got up and grabbed his hat.

Grandpa Mac had accomplished much in his life. Warren Alvin MacClintock had served his country during World War II. He married the love of his life at twenty, raised three daughters with her, and buried her too early—way too early, as he would say. He then married her best friend and spent another twenty years in marriage, only to bury another wife. He was sixty-five. He worked as a civil engineer for the Union Pacific Railroad for forty years, although he would just say "the railroad." What other railroad is there? He taught me to salute a Union Pacific train whenever we stopped for one.

Grandpa Mac, with his blue eyes and well-developed laugh lines, would fill a room with what I found to be his most salient character trait, his strong, positive spirit in everything he did. If I introduced him to you at this very moment, I would bet my life savings that he would reach out to you with one of his calloused, honest hands to shake your hand while simultaneously patting it with his other calloused, honest hand. He would tilt his head and look straight into your heart with his blue eyes and say, "Hi, friend." My life savings.

Mac ushered every Sunday 7:30 a.m. Mass of his adult life at Assumption Church down south of us. He was born to usher. No one was left standing at the back of his service. Two? He would quickly find a place for two and smile as he escorted you to your place to worship. He lived out west as long as I knew him but continued to support the Czech parish in which he grew up in South Omaha. The Czech church was where Scottish Mac had learned all of the pre–Vatican II ropes, only to totter and sway through the sixties; eventually, he politely acknowledged the "changes" of the Church with his usual positive, though sometimes hesitant, spirit.

He shared with me, more than once, the story of poor Father Begley informing the many staunch Czech Catholics of Assumption—can you get more staunch than a Czech Catholic?—that the Mass would now include a new little ritual called the Sign of Peace. This "interruption" would take place following the Lord's Prayer. During that time, the congregation members would turn to each other and shake hands or hug or kiss as an endearing, beautiful sign of peace to each other. This would probably have been better received in a touchy-feely Southern Baptist Community, but back in South Omaha in 1968, in a community that was quite content with showing peace without saying or demonstrating it, it was unsettling and, well, silly. Implications should carry more significance, right? You already know that I wish you peace; why should I have to be all goofy?

Father Begley had anticipated this Catholic indigestion as a result of some spicy little get-togethers held in Rome earlier that decade. He reassured the community that in time, this little added gesture would feel like a normal part of the Mass. Try telling that to Dorothy Skromak. She was offended by the overanxious Norma Antonelli—a few Italians had snuck into Assumption—who appeared to show too much peace to Dorothy's husband, Joe. Her sign of peace came in the form of a shove and an elbow as poor Father Begley and Grandpa Mac, the usher, attempted to calm the waters. Peace came slowly to the Church in the sixties.

Mac shot me a tiny twinkle as he opened the door. "Have a good one, Benny."

"You bet I will." I lowered my voice a bit.

My mother mumbled as she grabbed her purse and patted the back of her hair, "I'll lock up the outside door if you lock the one into the laundry room. Don't forget to turn off the radio. If Mrs. Bittner calls, please tell her that I'll reschedule. She was the only one I couldn't get a hold of."

I was in complete shock. My mother was closing Marcia's Beauty Box on a Saturday. The quiet of the room had not hit me, as I'd been searching for Grandpa Mac's sparkle. I'd missed the empty waiting area. Saturdays were her "meat" and the rest of the days were "potatoes." My mother had never closed her salon on a Saturday before; in the world of hairdressers, Marcia Keller had just committed salon sacrilege.

"Mac needs me. Lock up," Mom reminded me.

"You bet I will." This time my voice squeaked.

I was an almost-fifteen-year-old sitting on a wobbly fence of torment. On the one hand, I knew I should feel sorrow for my grandfather. I should feel concern for my mother's tight financial record for the next week. I should feel confusion about my mother walking into a Catholic church, when she had not stepped inside one since she cried over a torn and crumbled pile of annulment papers years ago. On the other hand, I felt the greatest joy in my selfish stomach as I leaped to leave the room, almost forgetting to silence Elton John singing "Someone Saved My Life Tonight" from the black radio. I had never been free this early on a Saturday since I could remember. After cleaning up after my mom's last client, I would usually not get done until late afternoon.

What made my guilt even stronger was that the day was absolutely perfect. A perfect Saturday with endless possibilities. I thought I might just get on my ten-speed and cruise around the block to take in the concept. The guilt was starting to dissipate as I considered the day. Should I go to the pool? Maybe Will would want to ride down to Ben Franklin Five and Dime for a ton of junk food.

On my way out of the door, I grabbed a cold bottle of TaB. If Mom had been there, she would have looked at me disapprovingly and then looked away. No look today. I opened the bottle with a bottle opener and checked under the lid to see if I had won anything. I guess my luck went only so far. With a skip in my step, I headed out to the cul-de-sac after downing half of the TaB. Cool and refreshing, with a very nasty after-bite. I grabbed my transistor radio and turned it on. The song "Afternoon Delight" was playing. If Mom had been here, she would have made me change the station, frowning at the risqué lyrics. I turned the song up.

I saw a clump of the neighbor guys with towels on their handlebars, heading to the pool: Will, Stinky, his little brother Andy, A.C., and Will's older brother, Anthony, who never hung out with the younger kids. Will was pulling his bike out of Satch as I rode up to the group. "Satch," short for Sasquatch, was the name we had given the gigantic evergreen tree in the front of the tiny little home of Louis and Ava Mangiamelli.

Satch was the kind of evergreen on which the lowest branches were poised just so that they covered about four feet of space beneath them, enough that a group of kids could use the underbrush as a fort. Don't think we didn't spend plenty of rainy afternoons under the gentle giant of a tree, planning and scheming about nothing and everything. I remember one noted afternoon under Satch, playing spin the bottle with most of the kids from the cul-de-sac. Lovey Webber had brought an empty Pepsi bottle from the Webber trash and dictated the diversion under the tree. She started by spinning the bottle until the mouth end pointed toward Stinky Morrow.

"Dare! I take the d-d-dare!"

"OK then." Lovey batted her eyes. "I dare you to touch the Wicker Witch's back door."

Upon Lovey's request or demand, Stinky raced about thirty feet to the Wicker Witch's back door, touched it, and ran back, panting, narrowly escaping death. Stinky's spin pointed toward me, and I squirmed at my options.

Truth meant I would risk the question that I couldn't answer. *Why don't you have a dad?* I doubted that Stinky would ask it, but I found a dare more enticing than the truth, so I went with that. Maybe Stinky would make me drink Pepsi on top of a mouth full of Pop Rocks to see if my head exploded. Better than the truth.

Stinky looked right at me and said, "B-b-ben, kiss Faith Webber."

Kiss Faith? Out-of-my league Faith? If pleasure and panic can coexist, they did in my stomach that afternoon. Everyone laughed at the look on my face until Faith said that she had to go baby-sit and mumbled something about a "silly game." Relief and disappointment took over my stomach while Faith left, the branches of Satch moving around her.

For most days, though, the Mangiamelli kids used the base of Satch as a storage unit for their bicycles, footballs, and squirt guns. Will pulled his bike to the curb and looked at the top of my head and teased, "Clip, clip, buzz, buzz. Liked it better the way it was!" Mom had cut my hair the day before.

Will was shirtless, tan, and proud of his physique. Not a flaw except for a big scar—even that looked good—that served as a reminder of an operation that had removed his appendix when he was seven.

"Grab your towel, Ben. Hey, aren't you supposed to be working?" A.C. came back to the neighborhood more often than not.

"I got the day off!" I boasted and finished off my TaB. "I'm just taking my bike." No swimming for me today. No need to show off my big arms and muscular physique at the neighborhood pool.

"No towel? Just going to watch, Ben? Not a bad idea..." Anthony Mangiamelli rarely talked to me, so I was both impressed and embarrassed by his comment. Of course, I would watch. It was perfectly legal to go stare at all the cute girls in their swimming suits.

Up until three years ago, during the summer months on Maple Crest Circle, a little blue kiddy pool sat at the edge of most driveways to cool the children down on humid, hot days. The Mangiamelli family also had the ultimate Slip-N-Slide in their backyard, which was actually three Slip-N-Slides hooked together that would practically throw a kid down to the creek if he got to sliding too fast. We took turns spraying the slide with the cold water from the hose. Mrs. Mangiamelli was really great about letting us run the hose for a long time. That was how we tried to get comfortable in the heat until we were older, and our parents decided the fee to the local pool was worth giving the older kids something to do. Brookhill Country Club was three blocks from our cul-de-sac and the highlight of our summers. A.C. would use a British accent when he talked about the club. "You can buy frozen Three Musketeers and greasy hamburgers from the Snack Shack if you want. I'm a member of the *club*."

"Hey, Ben, I just picked up a new Wacky Pack. The st-st-stickers in this pack are awesome. Check it out." Stinky Morrow pointed toward his bike.

Stinky's entire bike was covered with stickers from Wacky Packs. His green bike had a banana seat and long handlebars, and we were all pretty sure that it was his sister's old bike. He called his bike the Rock and saturated it with any of the latest trends to give it personality. The name came from the Pet Rock he had gotten at Christmas; Stinky was so amazed by the fact that some guy had come up with the idea to sell rocks in a kit and become "like a bazillionaire or something like that!" Stinky's little brother, Andy, was riding a clunker bike that day, painted red, white, and blue in what looked like paint that had not been intended for bikes. Andy's bike was his own personal contribution to the celebration of the country's bicentennial celebration that year.

Stinky went on, "Check it out, Ben. I have Kentucky Fried Finger, Choke Wagon, S-s-spit and Spill, Windhex, Lip-Off Cup-o-Slop, B-b-blunder Bread…My favorite is Dr. Pooper…"

Andy chimed in, impressed with his older brother's finds: "Shit, you gotta be kiddin' me. My favorite is Liquid Bomber. Get it?" Andy was seven with a mouth like a drunken sailor. Reacting to or laughing at his potty mouth encouraged him to pull out his filth repertoire, so we learned to ignore his expletives. "Liquid Plumber—Liquid Bomber? Get it?"

"We got it. When you ladies are done chatting, we can head to the pool," Will growled.

"OK, Evil Knievel," Andy retorted. "I forgot you're too cool to understand Wacky Packs."

At that, six bikes started moving in the direction of Brookhill Country Club. Even though the pool was only three blocks away, we chose to travel in a group on wheels to avoid the Saragossas' chow, which looked cute and fuzzy but had bitten Lovey Webber the summer before. There was also the cool factor that weighed in taking our bikes. We weren't old enough to drive, and only the dorky kids walked; we did everything on our bikes. The last reason for the bikes was mostly unspoken though probably the most important motivation not to walk to the pool: the Wicker Witch—our very own neighborhood witch. No neighborhood should be without one.

Technically, we didn't know for sure that Ms. Wicker was a witch, but we did have what we considered several experiences and observations that certainly added up for us. First off, she just looked wicked. Her hair was always muddled and frizzy, at least during the few glimpses we had of her peeking out her windows. She never interacted with anyone on the block, and the few times we did see her, she was watching us from her kitchen window, her head half hidden by the curtain. She never, ever left her little green house. Eleanor Wicker stayed home all the time with nothing but time to cast spells from her window. Every once in a while, we saw a deliveryman bringing groceries—milk, bread, and probably some eye of newt.

Now the experiences. They may seem a little farfetched, but if you had lived them, you would have agreed that we might have a witch on our hands. We were pretty sure that the Wicker Witch had put a curse on the Shanahans' cat—not that this was a bad thing. Precious Christmas Morning, the most spoiled pet on the planet, was a snooty, fuzzy, gray-and-white thing. She was a gift from Mr. Shanahan to Mrs. Shanahan one—you guessed it—Christmas morning after all of Mrs. Shanahan's children had grown and moved out. She named the feline and spoiled it like a bratty grandchild. "Precious Christmas Morning! Precious Christmas Morning! Mommy needs you to come have your lunchy-poo now. Precious Christmas Morning!"

One not-so-precious morning, said cat walked onto the lawn of said witch and never returned for his lunchy-poo. Stephano Mangiamelli said that a guy he knew from the next block over had seen the precious fur ball walking onto the lawn of the Wicker Witch. We never saw that cat again. Enough said.

Lucy said her dog, Grandma, had a protective, witch-proof aura since Grandma had been known to meander over to the Witch House and take a nap on the sunny side of the wicked, green house. Eleanor must have liked Grandma. We weren't about to test our own auras. Because our destinies on those grounds were uncertain, none of us risked the fate of poor Precious Christmas Morning.

Every Halloween, our neighborhood looked like Bourbon Street during Mardi Gras. Fun, silly, and scary costume-clad children marched down the sidewalks, parents stood out on the lawn with big bowls of Mike and Ikes and Baby Ruths, and houses lining Maple Crest blazed with light—all except the tiny, green Wicker house, the last house out of our little block, waiting. It sat dark and eerie, welcoming no one on a night when most witches are probably pretty busy.

So, while most of the evidence was questionable, we still justified any evil activity on the circle as the work of the Wicker Witch. When we were not directly in front of her house, we felt pretty safe. Proximity meant fear, and so speed was the answer as we flew by the green house.

I shared a secret with A.C. about the witch.

"I swear, I feel like the Wicker Witch is watching me. Like she singles me out. It kind of creeps me out."

"Ben, she's watching all of us. You're just paranoid. Paranoia will destroy-a."

Whenever my mom overheard us swapping witch stories, she would scold us and tell us that we should mind our own business. "Leave that poor woman alone." Once she pulled me aside to further reprimand me, seeing this as an opportunity to teach her only son a little compassion. "No one knows what a person's life is really like." She explained that Eleanor Wicker had been married once. Though my mother was not sure of the details, she knew that Eleanor had never had any children and was somehow able to maintain her residency without working. She explained to me that life is just a little more overwhelming to some than others. I figured the world must have been extremely overwhelming to Ms. Wicker.

This did not stop me from wondering, and it certainly didn't stop me from racing by the last house out of the cul-de-sac on Maple Crest. On that perfect summer day back in 1976, our clump of bikes directed our thoughts to the pool as we whizzed past the green house. Thoughts of the Wicker Witch vanished as girls and freedom filled our minds.

About a block before we got to the pool, we could hear the pool sound system blaring WOW radio station playing the top-forty songs, over and over again. The song "Shannon" blasted out of the pool speakers. I remember because A.C. starting singing it really loudly as we got closer. His high-pitched nasal bellow made the rest of us laugh.

It's no wonder that this stinker song was a shoe-in for the A.C. and Ben's Top Ten Dumb Songs of All Time. Theories abound about its dumb yet well-known lyrics. One theory suggests that one member of the Beach Boys, the writer of the song, had a dog named Shannon that drowned, and so he wrote a song about it. This would explain the part of the song that whines about the dog finding an island with a tree, just like the one in the family backyard. How dumb is that? First, the dog is dumb because it loves to swim away and so it drowns. Then the guy singing the song is dumb because he's crying about how his dumb mom and dad are missing the dumb dog. If your dog was that dumb, why would you write a song about her, even if her name was Shannon? Dumb. Dumb. Dumb. No-brainer for the list.

Our list was called the A.C. and Ben Top Ten Dumb Songs of All Time, but we had more than ten songs on it. Over time we lost count, but we could make strong arguments for each and every song on the list. Most people wouldn't argue, though. Our list included "Muskrat Love" (duh, dumb), "All by Myself" (the guy is assuming someone is listening to his dumb song), "Having My Baby" (what a lovely way of saying how dumb the song is), "I Am, I Said" (Neil Diamond sings to a chair that doesn't reply), anything by Neil Sedaka, and most songs by Barry Manilow. Just to name a few.

A.C. was best at making sound arguments to justify placement on our list. Lucy and A.C. once went at it over the presence of the song "The Candy Man" on our famous (or infamous) list. A.C. looked Lucy squarely in the eye and asked her, "Do we really need to argue about sprinkling a sunrise with dew?"

Lucy could not answer.

A.C. responded, "I rest my case."

The dumb dog song was just ending as we got to the fence and was replaced by Elvin Bishop's "Fooled Around and Fell in Love." Not on the Top Ten Dumb Songs of All Time. Perfect background music for checking out girls.

We rode up to the fence on the side of the pool where the diving boards were. Our unspoken plan was to stand by our bikes acting not very interested, as though we were just stopping by on our way to another and more interesting place. Soon one girl might come up to the fence, followed by a friend or two, and in time we would be hanging with a group of girls—granted, with a fence between us. That was the plan.

While waiting for the group to assemble, we would stand there looking cool and talking about not-so-cool things, like the fart machine and the Farrah Fawcett poster Will had bought at Spencer's Gifts in the mall. Is that a paradox or what? Will was boy enough to think that foul bodily noises were hilarious and man enough to think that a woman's body was beautiful. I thought it was kind of stupid to buy the poster of the Charlie's angel wearing that amazing, orange swimsuit, but that didn't stop me from looking at the revealing pose that hung above his bed in his basement.

That day by the pool, we also discussed important issues like the mental state of the master on the TV show *I Dream of Jeannie*. Like, why was Larry Hagman so uptight when he had this gorgeous woman who lives in a bottle, calls him master, and says that she will do anything he wants? Was Larry dense or what? Our debates were disrupted by the loud, irritating singing of Lovey Webber. Lovey, who was now thirteen and developing nicely, sang loudly as she sauntered toward our clump. She wiggled over to the fence and giggled. She looked directly at me.

"Somebody got a haircut!"

"I got them all cut..."

Exaggerated laughter exploded. Maybe some other, more interesting girls would hear us and want to know what was so funny.

"Oh, Ben." Lovey rolled her eyes and tilted her head. "Hey, we're all asking our moms if they will take us to Peony Park tomorrow night for Sprite Nite. You want to meet there?"

Peony Park was the Omaha amusement park located in the center of the city at that time. Grandpa Mac told me that he used to go listen to the big bands at Peony Park Ballroom when he was a young man. In 1976, the older Mangiamelli boys worked the rides at the amusement park, and my sister Cheryl was at the big pool every day. My friends and I were more excited about a dance called Sprite Nite, where a DJ played the same top-forty songs we had listened to all day at the pool.

Will answered for the group. "It depends on who 'we' includes." Careful now, not too cool.

"Oh, Lucy, Theresa, Marty..."

"Theresa's here?"

"Lucy has her as a guest. Didn't you know?" As Lovey spoke, our eyes darted around the pool area for a glimpse of Theresa. The radio in the background, the smell of chlorine and suntan lotion, the sun on my back...My senses all seemed heightened.

A scratchy voice yelled from the door to the Snack Shack. "Hey! Did you tell them about Sprite Nite, Lovey?" Lucy may have appeared to most as a bossy little thing, but on closer observation, those around her appreciated her bossiness as a gift. She organized fun. She directed them to enjoy life. She was the Julie McCoy of Maple Crest Love Boat.

Tiny little Lucy walked toward us with what appeared like two bodyguards towering behind her. Theresa and especially Marty had grown tall and slender as they entered their early teen years, while Lucy stayed petite. One small disappointment of the day was that Theresa was wearing shorts and a T-shirt. No swimming suit for us. They had already finished swimming and were heading home. The girls all looked at Will. To me, Will was just a grump who bossed us all around. To the girls, he was very attractive. I wasn't stupid. I'd figured that one out all by myself.

Lucy looked at Will. "If Mom says we can go, we can have Subby or Stephano drive us there. On the way we were going to stop by that billboard where the DJ from WOW is living in a huge banana. He's broadcasting from up there and not leaving for a whole week."

"WOW has gone bananas!" A.C. used a deep voice and held his pretend phone to his ears. During that week, the radio station was calling listeners. If you answered the phone like A.C. instead of saying hello, the station was offering prizes. The big prize was a trip to Kansas City.

"How does he go to the bathroom?" Stinky wondered out loud.

"Just let us know if you guys want to go."

More girls walked up to the fence, sensing that Lucy had found a new adventure. Our plan was working.

Lucy shared her most recent discovery with the large audience. "OK, I have to tell you all what I just found out from this high-school girl who works in the Snack Shack." As she spoke, her mouth sparkled. Lucy was wired for sound with the entire orthodontia works. She even wore the whole headgear thing at night, which only further encouraged my theory on the barbaric things that our own parents impose on us for the sake of vanity.

Lucy looked serious as she started her performance. "If you listen to the beginning of the song 'Rollercoaster' by the Ohio Players, you will hear a really high scream."

"Son of a bitch. I've heard it!" Little Andy Morrow's eyes were big and round and glued to the Lucy.

"Anyway, that's the scream of a woman who was killed during the actual recording of the song. Her murder was recorded!" Lucy paused for effect. "It's like her murder is repeated every time we hear that song."

I was stunned by the big eyes and opened mouths in the group that had gathered. *Really?*

"It's true." Lucy shook her head slowly and pursed her lips with the burden of this sad awareness. Theresa and Marty shook their heads in unison and agreement, looking like the Supremes behind their lead singer. I worked hard to hide my smirk. In the shuffle of expressions in the group, Theresa looked at Will and smiled.

A deeper voice from behind me added, "And if you listen really, really closely to the end of that song, you'll hear the drummer fart." The voice came from a kid who had been sitting on his bike a couple feet behind the group, listening to Lucy. She looked at the boy perturbed but said nothing.

Eddie Krackenier laughed louder at his joke than anyone else. Eddie, a very fit fifteen-year-old, was from a nearby neighborhood that fed into the Saint Walter's parish and school. In Omaha, parishes were like little puddles all over the city, with the little tiny Catholic fish that in time would jump into the bigger ponds of Catholic high schools, connecting all those little puddles.

"This pool sucks!" Eddie said to no one and everyone as he moved his bike up to the fence and looked around the deck of the pool. The crowd that had gathered was silent.

"Then why are you here?" Anthony Mangiamelli, a good year older and a foot taller than Eddie, had been silent until now. He wasn't afraid of the bully from Saint Walter's.

"Well, you see, I was just on my way to the housing development under construction out north of here, a place where me and my older buddies like to go when the workers aren't around. Anyway, on my way, I see what appears to be a group around a fire or tragic accident or something. Turns out to be some stupid story about a roller coaster and a murder. Ahhhhh!" Eddie screamed in a high pitch so loud that I thought the lifeguards would come by.

Eddie was a bad seed. That's what Mrs. Webber had told the kids after her tree had been TP-ed one time. Eddie called himself Chief and asked that others do the same in his presence. Kids in Maple Crest heard that Eddie had seen R-rated movies before he was ten. He also had a big birthmark on the back of his neck that was allegedly in the shape of a star. From where I stood, it looked more like a drunk amoeba that hoped to be a starfish someday. He didn't have a dad, and his mother was never home, either working or whatever. The freedom he had meant that he had more connections with his older buddies finding all sorts of interesting things to do. Evidently at construction sites.

"You're all welcome to come with the Chief to the construction site. Hell of lot more fun than this place." He spoke to the group with an evil grin.

We were no idiots to the reputation of Eddie Krackenier. Eddie lore trickled from his puddle to ours, and we all felt as if the devil himself had just invited us all to hell. I wouldn't allow some self-proclaimed chief to ruin my perfect day. I wanted Eddie Krackenier to go back to his puddle.

"I'll go." Will's voice sounded strange. Now the group of wide eyes looked at him. What was he thinking? We all looked to the Mangiamellis' oldest brother, Anthony. Was he going to stop Will or what?

Eddie's grin grew into a creepy shape. "OK, Mangiamelli, the Chief says you may follow."

I really do believe Will would have gone with Eddie that hot Saturday. Something in the way he looked at Eddie said that he was serious. The interview with the devil was interrupted by Faith Webber, who forced her way through the group up to the fence, panting and catching her breath. She had run the three blocks to Brookhill pool. Breathless and anxious, Faith still looked incredible.

"Lovey, is Hope with you?" Faith leaned against the fence and tried to catch her breath.

"You should see how red your face is, Faith." Lovey laughed and looked at me.

"Lovey, is Hope with you?" Faith repeated with panic in her throat.

"No, she didn't want to swim. I asked her. I really did…"

"We can't find her anywhere. If she's not with you, she's been gone for a while. Hope never goes off by herself. The last thing I remember was that she was going over to the Mangiamelli house to visit Grandma. We know where Grandma is, but we can't find…"

Faith had already turned around and was running back to the house. The group started moving with her. Lovey made her way back to the pool front desk and around the fence, and ran barefoot toward Faith in her swimsuit. The rest of us on bikes moved quickly. The others ran behind: Lucy, Will, Theresa, Stinky, Anthony. Everyone but Eddie.

"Hey, who's this Hope? And just how often do you lose your grandma?" he yelled to us, laughing at himself.

The Chief stood alone.

We all took off without a plan, moving quickly in our alarm. The Johnny Madlin thing was a few years behind us but never forgotten. Hope was too sensible to just take off without telling anyone. My own mind was racing as I rode. Where could she be? The three blocks back to our circle took forever, even on my bike. All I could think about was Hope.

As everyone rounded the corner near the green house, I slowed down. My heart pounding and a full bottle of TaB swishing around in my gut, I threw my bike down on the lawn of Wicker Witch and, without a second thought, ran quickly through the yard by the side of her house, taking a route I had never taken to the creek. I doubt if anyone on Maple Crest had ever taken this route. We didn't even consider it growing up. During the days when we were allowed to play down there, we'd always walked between the Morrow and Mangiamelli houses.

From the back edge of the Wicker yard, I jumped into the weeded area that quickly turned into a steep hill and took me down to the area where we built forts and played Capture the Flag. Hope might have gone there to look for Grandma. Everything was overgrown. I fell twice but recovered quickly as I made my way down to the area where we had spent most of our creek-playing days. Nothing looked familiar to me.

About halfway down, I stepped on something that, with a quick glance, looked like the leg of a GI Joe. I kept moving. I couldn't remember the last time I had been on this steep, bumpy hill, creeping and twisting down to the wooded creek. The ground beneath me began to level off, and I found my bearings, adjusting my internal compass.

I was now looking at the area I knew so well from a completely new viewpoint. I could see, through the overgrown trees, the dark area protecting the creek. The trees told the time. I recognized a few trees that had unique marks or trunks. They were so much bigger and wider, providing more shade than I ever remembered. My heart pounded as I stood on the forbidden ground, squinting as my eyes adjusted from the bright, sunny day to the darker woods.

That's when I saw her, head hanging low, right at the creek's edge. I didn't yell. I just stopped. She looked up.

"Hope, we've been looking everywhere for you. Everyone is worried sick."

"Ben, I can't find Grandma. What if she got hurt? What if I never find Grandma?" She sniffed loudly and coughed.

"We found Grandma, Hope. She's fine. She was napping on the Shanahans' driveway the whole afternoon. She's never been happier. Let's head home." She ran toward me and hugged me very tightly, wiping her dirty tears on my shoulder.

"Ben, thank you. Grandma is alive! Grandma is alive! You're my angel, Ben," Hope patted my back again and again. "What would I do without you? Grandma is alive!"

During the silence of her patting, we both became aware of the static of a radio. A very fuzzy and almost inaudible beat buzzed as Hope hugged me. KC and the Sunshine Band sang "I'm Your Boogie Man" from the other side of the creek.

"Hope, we need to go back. Let's go see Grandma. She'll probably be excited to see you."

Neither of us moved as we squinted our eyes, looking across the creek to the side on which I had never been. The music was coming from the radio of a car that was tucked between two very large trees. I knew there was another side to the creek, but I had never stopped to think about the area beyond it. Just north of the area were several farms that the city was looking to acquire in order to start building more little parish puddles, and there must have been a dirt road for access. The fear in the center of my chest turned to confusion when I realized the car was the old Morrow station wagon, a funky and easily identifiable metallic color of blue. What was their car doing down here? How had it gotten here? My confusion turned to shock as Hope and I witnessed two heads popping up. Mr. Morrow and—not Mrs. Morrow.

That's when the staring started. Hope and I stared at Mr. Morrow and the other person, whom I quickly discerned as Casey Worthington, a sometimes friend of my older sister. I knew that Stinky had mentioned that Casey baby-sat him and his four other siblings every once in a while. He thought she was a babe. I was thinking Mr. Morrow must have thought the same thing. He and Casey stared at us as the reality of the situation became sickly apparent.

KC and the Sunshine Band stopped singing about the boogie man, and the voice of the DJ living in the big banana on the billboard came in with less static than the song.

"Debbie Andrews has answered her phone correctly and wins two tickets to Cheapskate Roller Rink. We'll also put her name in the final drawing for that trip to Kansas City. What do you think of that, Debbie?" Static. Blurry voice. Static.

Thoughts racing through my head jumped from Stinky to his mother to Stinky's cousin, Theresa O'Brien, to the little Morrows. All of these people were somewhere at this moment unaware of the clandestine meeting. Hope and I knew, though. I hadn't asked to be a part of this. My stomach reacted, and I fought hard not to throw up a carbonated mass in front of this very private gathering.

Within a microsecond, my mind took me back to a birthday party for Stinky in the Morrow kitchen. Years earlier he had invited most of the kids from the neighborhood, and we were all standing around him singing "Happy Birthday" as Stinky smiled at the candles on his cake. He may have been five or six. I can't remember. What I do remember was Mr. Morrow standing behind Stinky smiling, with both hands on Stinky's shoulders. The perfect father. I remember feeling so jealous that I wanted to run out of the kitchen before I cried. I sang louder and saved myself from tears. That was what I would never have.

Anger zapped me back to the moment. Mr. Morrow had been pretty savvy to come to the one place that no one had been in years, but the fact that his secret meeting place was so close to his family left an even worse taste in my mouth.

Dumb songs, stupid jokes by the pool, and a self-absorbed bully seemed less irritating and harmful and, unfortunately, a million miles away. I wanted to be there instead of here.

Everything moved in extreme slow motion after that. Mr. Morrow looked very worried as he slowly moved to start his car, never making eye contact again. Casey smiled at us—kind of a powerful agreement with a wink that spoke volumes to Hope and me that day. *Oh, you know not to tell.*

She looked very powerful as the car slowly backed up. She had each of us in a bad spot. Mr. Morrow definitely stood to lose the most with any public awareness of this covert get-together.

Hope looked bothered, but I wasn't sure if she was aware of the implications of what we were witnessing. I know that if Hope and I told what we saw, placing us both at the creek, a place that our parents had repeatedly warned us not to go, we stood to lose privileges.

Everyone might lose something.

Finally, I stood to lose, no matter what. Telling any soul what I'd just witnessed could lead to the breakup of my friend's family. I already knew what it was like not to have a father around. Stinky didn't need that. Not telling, which was what I planned to do, meant that I would have to carry this secret alone, always knowing, always wondering.

Another face flashed in my head out of nowhere. It was the face of Johnny Madlin, or rather the face from the photo that was plastered everywhere following his disappearance five years ago. I wondered about him. By the creek. Losing his life.

A bunch of losers. I lost a piece of my soul down by the creek that day.

**

"That was weird. Who was that lady with Mr. Morrow?" Hope whispered as the car went out of sight.

Now for the next moral dilemma. Did I tell Hope that we needed to keep this a secret? I didn't want Hope to feel any guilt about today. She'd done nothing wrong, just gone looking for a dog and found a neighborhood affair. She shouldn't feel bad about this afternoon.

"Hey, Hope. Your mom would really worry if she knew you had come down here. Let's not talk about it. OK?" I wondered if the "it" had covered enough.

"Yeah." Her word was numb.

"You were just looking for Grandma and then went for a walk. OK?"

"Yeah."

"We don't really need to tell anybody..."

I may have worked hard to eliminate guilt for Hope, but I could never take away the sickening guilt that started seeping into my heart about my decision not to talk about what we had seen. Was that wrong? Was I responsible to report what I'd seen? Was it any category of sin not to tell the truth if you thought the truth was worse than silence? I hadn't asked to be here.

Guilt was something that I usually left to Lucy. She knew all the sin levels and stuff for Catholic guilt—it was what defined her as a good little Catholic girl. Lucy would say, "You're not alive if you're not feeling guilty." If that were the case, I had never felt more alive. But why was I feeling such guilt? I hadn't had the affair. I felt bile in my mouth mixed with TaB.

We would walk the back way up the hill from the creek and enter the neighborhood as if we were coming from outside Maple Crest Circle. Everyone would be happy to see Hope. I would be a hero.

So I walked up the hill with Hope.

The perfect day was just a mirage slowly dissipating into one of the worst days of my life. I worked hard to catch my breath as Hope took my hand. I looked up at the Wicker Witch's green house and saw a curtain move in the back window. My stomach hurt as I trudged up that creepy, twisted hill with Hope, carrying a much greater, more uncomfortable guilt than that which had started my day.

9

# Lucy Mangiamelli: Something Like Olivia Newton-John, Graduation Dance

## Tuesday, May 24

# 1977

I'm not sure when giggling girls turn from obnoxious to interesting, but I know that it wasn't in 1977 for me. Though I was intrigued by their bodies, I was confused and annoyed by their minds.

As I stood at the top of the stairs to my mother's shop, I heard obnoxious girl laughter coming from below. I knew that Lucy was coming to get her hair done for her junior-high graduation from Saint Pius, and it sounded as though she'd brought her backup singers. To avoid any awkward exchange with those who were of the opposite sex, I yelled down the creaky stairs to the basement to let my mother know that A.C. and his dad were driving over to pick me up to go see *Star Wars*—for the seventh time that year.

A year after the incident with Hope at the creek, most of the neighbor kids no longer played outside, as we focused on more mature interactions than getting dirty and planning forts. We were all getting older. Before you think that I'm some kind of *Star Wars* freak, I need to explain that A.C.'s dad was the one driving every time. He drove and paid. We went. I'm not saying he's a freak. I'm just saying.

Better than the movie was the theater that we went to each time: the Indian Hills Theatre, the coolest theater ever known to mankind. All movies there were shown in a Cinerama wide-screen format. A 105-foot screen, inclined, purple plush seating, a smoking section, a balcony, and the biggest variety of candy offered to my imagination to date. For A.C. and me, Indian Hills was the best movie-going experience of our lives; however, at almost sixteen, we were pushing the age factor and realized that we needed to start acting like teenagers. Sneaking into R-rated movies and going to concerts were next on the age agenda, and we begrudgingly yet excitedly decided that we would let go of our youth and grow up that year—after we saw *Star Wars*, just one more time.

"I'm heading out, Mom!" I yelled, sounding hurried.

"Hey, Ben. Come down for a minute, would ya?" Mom yelled up.

I took a breath and descended the creaky stairs. Walking into my mother's salon, I could hear the voices talking hairstyles and colors of dance dresses, and with that, their beauty quickly dissipated before my eyes.

The good friends that they were, Marty and Theresa wanted to make sure that Lucy looked beautiful for her first dance that followed the Mass and graduation in Saint Pius church. Following a graduation Mass, Cool Father Whalen would bless their junior-high souls and push them out of the puddle. The boys in their suits and the girls in their long dresses would march right out of the big box church, across the black top/ playground, and over to the big box gym where cookies, punch, a DJ, and the moms and dads who signed up to chaperone would be waiting. The parents would gawk at their kids the remainder of the night, occasionally offering a steep karate chop between two bodies that had snuggled too closely. Of course, they would remind the couple, "Let's just keep enough room for the Holy Spirit between you two while you dance..."

Eighth-grade graduation was a rite of passage. In the Catholic universe, eighth-grade graduation was the almost equivalent to a Jewish bar/bat mitzvah. *These boys and girls are growing up to be such fine pubescent Catholic individuals that they should start to take responsibility for themselves. Heck, why don't we have a big dance and send them off to the next phase of life: Catholic high school? A big send-off from the puddle to the pond.*

Suits? Long dresses and a dance? Really? This was not college or high school. *For heaven's sake*, it was just eighth grade. Maybe the Catholic schools could have learned a thing or two from the Omaha public schools in the seventies. I survived without the party.

Theresa and Marty stood on each side of Lucy during the great transfiguration. Marty stood taller and thinner than ever with her Dorothy Hamill haircut, which looked like a goofy eraser top to a really long pencil. Theresa smiled with the hair of the day, flowing and feathering with an effect that would make Farrah Fawcett look dumpy. They stood behind her and giggled a hello.

"Hey," I said.

"Ben, we're getting Lucy ready for her big dance tonight. What do you think?" my mom prompted me. What did I think of what? Hair? Long Dresses? Stupid graduation dances?

"You bet," I guessed.

The trio laughed with Lucy leading, of course. "What do you think of my hair, Ben? I'm going for an Olivia Newton-John look."

This was going to be harder than I'd thought. Lucy and her frizzy dark hair looked about as much like Olivia Newton-John as I did John Travolta.

"Looks good, Lu—" I started walking toward the stairs.

"Wait, here's the really exciting part! We're going to pick up our dresses from Theresa's aunt. Mrs. Morrow made all three of them from the same pattern."

"I'm subtle peach," Marty said.

"And I'm sky blue," Theresa added.

"And I am mint green," Lucy said, concluding the wimpy rainbow parade. My mother smiled weakly, and then I heard my own voice speak the very words I was thinking.

"And you did that on purpose?"

The giggling stopped. The three looked at me, confused and annoyed. The room was quiet with disappointment in me. Fine by me. I was about as interested in their fluffy conversation about bland-colored dresses as I was in the final episode of *The Brady Bunch* when they went to Hawaii and found a Tiki doll.

"What a lovely plan, girls. You'll all look lovely," my mom said as she shook her head and gave me a dirty look. I guess I was dismissed.

I was then sharply ignored as the discussion moved on to the dance, ABBA, Lucy's love of her life, Tom Ducey, and the movie *You Light Up My Life*. I hadn't realized it could be that easy to get out of a silly conversation. Of course, Lucy would later scold me and then forgive me. Lucy always forgave me. "Blinded by the Light" played on the little black radio on the windowsill.

I ran up the stairs and walked out to my front yard, praying for more intellectual stimulation than the Pale Rainbow Coalition. A.C. was the kind of guy who was always pontificating, and I was the friend who not only didn't mind but truly enjoyed his mountain of insight. Out of the blue, A.C. would proclaim, "The devil wears a Girl Scout uniform…Why else would Girls Scout cookies be delivered during Lent?" This was some profound thinking for kids our age.

Once A.C. got to my house, we would talk sports and music and about that whole plan to grow up this year. Sometime this summer we were hoping to sneak into the movie advertised all summer that would be coming out in a few months: *Saturday Night Fever*. I looked up toward the Wicker Witch house and waited to see Mr. Perelman's Cadillac appear. It was actually pretty impressive that A.C. and I had stayed connected through the years. We hadn't lived near each other for what seemed forever. A.C. went to the private high school Brownell Talbot while I attended Burke High School. Still we managed to keep the ties tight—thanks to his dad driving us to movies and his mother getting her hair done.

The white Cadillac seemed to emerge from the green Wicker house as the car turned the corner onto the circle. When A.C. got out of the car, he looked like he could throw up on the lawn. I wondered if he was sick.

"You look white!" I commented before I could filter the words.

Through his pale face, A.C. smiled. "Well, I am, partly." The smile disappeared. "You won't believe what we just saw."

At this point Mr. Perelman got out of the car. A.C.'s dad always reminded me of a gentle giant. I think A.C. told me that his dad was six-four or something like that. He always seemed taller to me. Though he hadn't practiced his Jewish religion in years, John Perelman looked like an oversized rabbi with his beard and olive skin. I guess that made it even more peculiar that this colossal, quiet professor liked *Star Wars* so much.

"We don't have to talk about it, A.C.," he said softly.

"I can with Ben, Dad. He can handle it. We aren't even sure what happened. We were driving near Ak-Sar-Ben Racetrack when we saw all these police cars. Maybe twenty. Don't ya think, Dad?"

"About ten."

"Well, they were all surrounding this tiny little house. Tiny."

A.C.'s body moved as he told the story. He was thin like me with gigantic feet that made him look like a clumsy puppy. He seemed puny at fifteen, but A.C. would grow into those feet some day and into his own father's shoes. He admired his quiet parents, though he was anything but. Rather than attempt to disappear so that his blended racial and religious inheritance did not draw attention, A.C. chose to embrace the anomaly of his state of affairs and demand attention through humor, strong opinions, and animation of the moment. His sister Elizabeth took the quiet path. I barely knew her.

"The house was right off the golf course, you know, about seven blocks or so from my house. Twenty cop cars. Can you believe it?"

"Ten police cars, A.C. We still don't know the details." His father grew more uncomfortable as A.C.'s story progressed.

"OK, ten. Anyway, Dad and I turn on the radio and find out that a woman was murdered last night. They think it's some guy who worked at

Ak-Sar-Ben. He walked horses or something. He murdered her and then just left her. Her parents were worried when they hadn't heard from their daughter..."

Their daughter was twenty-six-year-old Jane McManus. Harold Lamont Otey, who was also known as Walkin' Willie, a nickname he'd acquired from handling horses at the Ak-Sar-Ben track in between races, was in custody and arrested for her murder. Per usual, stories through the years varied. Some say he was high on PCP, saw her through the window, and just decided to attack her. Another account claims that he walked by her house after he left work and decided to steal a few things. He took a stereo, but when he reentered to remove other items, McManus awoke. They say that Otey raped McManus, then stabbed and finally strangled her with a belt.

A.C. had been that close to such a gruesome scene. I was standing near him at that moment. By the theory of transitive property, I felt somehow too close to something pretty evil. Other than the disappearance of Johnny Madlin, I was unaware of such shocking events in Omaha. A.C.'s dad quietly rushed us to the car, explaining that Luke Skywalker couldn't be waiting all day for us.

When Mr. Perelman, A.C., and I got to the Indian Hills Theater that evening for our farewell-to-immaturity viewing of *Star Wars*, all three of us were not as focused on Princess Leia Organa as we had been the first six times. I noticed that A.C. was quiet when he and I usually whispered our favorite lines from the movie.

We sat in the comfortable, purple plush seats in the darkness of the theater, feeling unsettled with the residue of A.C.'s story sloshing around in our heads. Our fair city was a safe city. Now something was awry. And just where should we direct our fear and anger now? Willie Otey looked like a good bet.

As we left the theater and walked to Mr. Perelman's car, we spotted Corky Payne walking up and down the rows of cars. At first I didn't recognize our strange neighbor from Maple Crest. His hair was long and dirty now, and he had grown a much-disheveled beard that matched his wrinkled shirt and pants. I closed my eyes and prayed that we would get into the car before he neared us or recognized me. Corky spotted Mr. Perelman first and then noticed A.C. and me behind him. Mr. Perelman politely waved and acknowledged the sad man we all knew.

"Hey, Corky, haven't seen you in a while."

Corky tilted his head and squinted. "John?"

"That's right. John Perelman. How are you, Corky?"

Corky didn't answer but looked over at us and then directly at me. "Keller?"

I nodded my head. Guilty.

"How old are you, son?"

"Fifteen."

Corky shook his head and mumbled something that sounded like "See ya, John" to Mr. Perelman, and then continued on his aimless journey through the Indian Hills Theatre parking lot.

The Willie Otey thing and our unplanned meeting with Corky Payne had left an unpleasant feeling in our guts. Other things were happening around the world in 1977. Well, you know about the big hoo-ha dance at Saint Pius. In 1977 the Huskers were still looking good. Coach Tom Osborne was now coaching the Huskers as Lyell Bremser, the best Nebraska announcer ever, announced the home games. "Man, woman, and child, they're jam-packed to the rafters for this one today…" That year, Warren Buffett lived in three-bedroom home in midtown Omaha. The extremely wealthy and humble man said that he was the man who had everything he needed in that house, with no wall or fence surrounding it.

In 1977 my hero, Gordon Sumner of England, and his friend Henry Padovani started playing in a new band formed by Steward Copeland—they called themselves the Police. They had a kind of punk-but-not-really-punk and a pretty-much-reggae-influenced sound to their music that changed my view toward music completely. Before they cut their first album, the band—hoping to make some extra cash—was asked to do a commercial for Wrigley's Spearmint chewing gum on the condition that they dye their hair, and it was most likely during that time that Mr. Sumner gained his nickname. "Sting" wore a black-and-yellow striped jersey, that a fellow band member Gordon Solomon had commented had resembled a bee. The nickname stuck.

Oh, and in 1977, the sadder and the wiser A.C. and I said good-bye to our childhoods and to the innocent and safe feelings that went with it.

It only made sense that Grandma died that year.

# PART II
## Let's Go Crazy

# 1981 to 1994

*The definition of insanity is doing the same thing over and over and expecting different results.*

**Ben Franklin**

*Did you write the Book of Love, and do you have faith in God, above?*
*If the Bible tells you so*

**Don McLean, "American Pie**

# 10

## Marty: Wash, Trim for Prom

### Friday, May 1

# 1981

Marty rhymes with smarty.

*Appropriate.*

Marty rhymes with party.

*Ironic.*

Marty rhymes with farty.

*Funny.*

People should really consider the lyrical ramifications of a name when they're placing one on a baby.

When Marty Monahan showed up at my house for a wash and trim for her high-school prom, she looked serious as usual. Every comedy act demands a straight guy. Every trio needs the one with the brains. And that is what Marty offered Lucy and Theresa.

"Have you talked to Lucy yet?" Marty fired away as she stood in the doorway, her short hair from the seventies now grown out to a long, straight un-style.

"I'm fine. Thanks for asking. Nope, I haven't talked to Lucy, but she'll be in tomorrow for an appointment with my mom. It just happens to be your lucky day since I will be taking care of you today." I had been filling in for my mother the past year for "easy dos," as she called them. A wash and trim she knew I could handle, so she scheduled those appointments when she was working her second job at Boys Town. With the extra expense of my older sister in nursing school at College of Saint Mary's, my mother now worked odd hours in the administrative offices at Boys Town. I had become the filler guy, moonlighting as a business student at University of Nebraska in Omaha in 1981.

"Sorry, Ben. I was just worried if Lucy had asked you what we...what she was going to ask you. You're doing my hair?"

"As long as you're OK with that. My mom's working her other job today. She said you're getting ready for your prom."

"Right, I'll be too busy tomorrow decorating for the dance. We're worried that we won't have enough fish cut out by then for our 'Enchantment Under the Sea' theme."

"Well, there's no time to lose then. You need a perm and color, right?"

Marty's brain was on overload as she juggled my stab at humor with the other trillion things splattering around her brain, along with this latest concern about Lucy asking me something.

"Kidding, Marty. Kidding. We can start with the shampoo over here. So what does Lucy need from me?" I actually hadn't seen Lucy in a while. The past several years had scattered the neighborhood gang across the city. We might see each other driving to school or jobs, but no one had the time to hang out anymore. Our world was getting bigger, and our busy schedules and new interests limited the chance of us meeting at the streetlight on our bikes.

Lucy, Theresa, and Marty had gone on to Marian High School, a school run by the Our Lady of Sorrows Servants of Mary, the same order of nuns that ran Saint Pius. Oh, the order of it all. The girls stayed tight in their friendship while making their mark in the secondary flight of Catholic education. Marty was the president of the National Honor Society while Theresa and Lucy made their marks socially. Faith and Lovey Webber had also gone to Marian while Hope attended Madonna Specialty School. The Mangiamelli boys all went on to make their marks athletically at Creighton Preparatory High School, also known as Prep, Ava working in the cafeteria.

I'd always known A.C. was smart, but he made a major academic splash of a mark at Brownell Talbot, landing an almost-perfect ACT score that awarded him several different scholarship offers his senior year. His brilliant mind did not stop him, however, from going to the grocery store before dates to pull cologne samples out of magazines and rub them on his neck and wrists before throwing the magazines back on the shelf. And during those same years, I didn't make any sort of mark at Burke High School, unless you counted all of the hours spent helping my mom run her business.

A.C., Will and I—who had spent every day of every summer of our childhoods together—had each graduated from different high schools and gone on to different colleges. I was at UNO, A.C. was at Creighton University, and Will went to University of Nebraska in Lincoln. Like I said, we pretty much scattered.

Over the past several years, the cul-de-sac began to look different from the one on which I'd grown up. The yards and street seemed more and more bare as kids of the block grew up; so, too, the driveways were missing something—Grandma.

I won't leave you hanging with the whole Grandma story. It was strange for the person who took the time to look around our neighborhood to note her absence. While we were growing up, we could calculate the time of day by her napping schedule as she moved from driveway to porch to driveway, I suppose following the sun or her karma. Our youth. She was just part of it all. She died around the time we were all heading off to high school.

In July of 1977, the Mangiamelli family had gone on one of the only vacations I ever remember them taking. They were going to meet some really old and important relative who had traveled over from Italy for only one visit and would only go as far as Cincinnati, Ohio, to meet all of the American Mangiamellis. The Mangiamelli family packed into their station wagon and drove the trek to Ohio to visit Great Uncle Mosticolli—or something like that.

Grandma was definitely getting older, and her naps were getting longer; and so Ava Mangiamelli employed the older Morrow brothers, Stinky and Andy, to take care of Grandma while they were gone. The two Morrow brothers took this great honor as a grave responsibility, feeding her and attempting to take her for walks. At night they walked her over to the back porch of the Mangiamelli home where she slept in an old, stinky doghouse till morning. Everything was going along nicely until, a few days after the Mangiamelli family left, Andy went to get her for the evening routine and noticed that she was napping in the Webber driveway, a place she usually started her day. Grandma hadn't moved all day. Andy ran to get Stinky before doing anything. They poked at Grandma and yelled at her. Andy cussed at her, but Grandma did not move. The two together figured that Grandma was taking her Great Final Nap.

In their panic, they made a plan. They would wait to bury Grandma until the Mangiamelli crew came home. The whole neighborhood could give her a beautiful send-off in the backyard, looking over the creek. The two agreed that she would not "keep" till the next week, so they put Grandma in a giant trash bag and loaded her on their wagon, taking her back to the deep freeze in their garage.

The Morrow freezer was awesome, always loaded with popsicles for anyone who stopped by. The freezer was the kind that looked like a chest and opened upward. Stinky and Andy put Grandma in a huge yard bag, hauled the overweight basset into the freezer, and said a special blessing over her and orange push-up pops and ice-cream sandwiches. The not-so-good part of the story is that Mrs. Morrow went into hysterics when she went to get the roast to thaw for dinner a few days later and found the solid and beloved dog among her frozen foods. She screamed, "Grandma's in the freezer!"

The Mangiamelli family was touched though a bit freaked out by the stiff homecoming they received when Stinky and Andy brought Grandma over. We all held a sort of impromptu funeral in the Mangiamelli backyard. I brought flowers for Lucy, who, of course, cried her eyes out. Will and Anthony snickered a bit as Grandma's thawing paw poked through the plastic bag while they were laying her to rest in the grave they dug for her, and we all said our good-byes to Grandma.

The first bookmark for death.

Grandma's death marked the end of an era. Sometimes I break my days on Maple Crest Circle into two parts: the Grandma Era and Post-Grandma—PG. I didn't see my Maple Crest friends Post-Grandma that much. Like I said, Grandma died, and then we scattered. So my response to Marty in 1981 was that I hadn't seen Lucy much lately.

"Well, just so you know, she's looking for you."

"I'll keep that in mind." This mafia-like threat did not scare me. "Now, how much would you like trimmed from your ends today? And just who are you taking to this underwater dance?" I had learned well from my mother that the attention must always be centered on the client, his or her hair, and his or her events and concerns. When a person is in *the chair*, it's all about that person. Never, ever talk about sex, politics, or religion. Just talk about the person sitting in the chair.

Marty spent the next forty minutes filling me in on the details of her life. Colleges she was looking at for next year. How excited she was for Lucy and Theresa because they had both been selected as prom candidates for the Marian prom. And, even though she was not a prom-princess candidate like Lucy and Theresa, she was fiercely proud of her two best friends, guaranteeing me that one of them would be crowned by the night's end.

"I'm going to the dance with Max Van Husen. He's very smart."

Max was a senior at Prep who had challenged her in one of her debate matches. She had beaten him, but maybe something in his argument had turned her on. Finally, Marty answered the dress question. Nothing rainbow this time. She would wear to her senior prom the same elegant dress she had worn when she was a debutante at the Ak-Sar-Ben Ball two months earlier.

Just like in *Cinderella*, each year, this century-old coronation event gives the rest of Nebraska a peek at some of the state's richest and most influential families dressed in gowns and whatever it is men wear to a ball. Until Marty Monahan enlightened me as to the history and donations to this city that the Ak-Sar-Ben Knights had presented to the city of Omaha, I didn't really get it.

Growing up in Omaha, a kid saw the phrase Ak-Sar-Ben several times in the course of a day. Of course, we had the horse racetrack that put the name on the map in 1919. But, if you drove down the street, you would also see Ak-Sar-Ben Heating and Cooling, Ak-Sar-Ben TV and Radio Repair, and Ak-Sar-Ben Sewer Cleaning, and Draining. Kind of got a pattern here. Any kid could tell you that Ak-Sar-Ben was Nebraska spelled backward, although Lovey Webber didn't have the great epiphany until fifth grade when she figured it out in the middle of math class one day when she wasn't paying attention.

For the Ak-Sar-Ben Ball, my mom had done Marty's hair in a not-so-Marty swooped-up style for the la-de-da affair. Growing up, I'd never known that Marty came from big money. She never pushed it in anyone's face. Money was not of great value to her, unlike her intelligence and serious approach to life. Money never mattered in her friendships with Lucy and Theresa, who had grown up in our humble, little neighborhood.

Marty left Marcia's Beauty Box that day to run around and do whatever you do to get ready for a fantasy underwater adventure. I sat and wondered about the impending, ominous request from Lucy Mangiamelli.

11

# Lucy: Something Different for Prom

## Saturday, May 2

# 1981

Events were cake to Lucy. Getting ready for events was the ever-so-sweet frosting.

That's why I was confused when I saw the sad and serious expression she wore as she sat in my mother's chair, awaiting a transformation from ordinary high school girl into Pow-Zowie Prom Princess.

"Did somebody die?" I asked. My mother shot me a stern glance.

Lucy's eyes teared up as she whispered, "They found him. He told them. "

I had come down for the big question Lucy allegedly had for me, and she threw a bunch of blurry pronouns at me.

"A man confessed from his prison cell. They went where he told them he was buried. He was there all that time. And his parents didn't know it…" Lucy's eyes were watering.

Kool and the Gang begged us to "Celebrate Good Times" from the little black radio. Bad timing, bad song. Put it on the list. I looked at my mother, who whispered, "Johnny Madlin."

The name of Johnny Madlin sent a chill up my spine. I shivered.

I hadn't heard the name in years, but I still thought about him every time I saw a paperboy. Every time I looked down at the creek. Every time I heard a song that brought me back to that year. We'd never met the young paperboy, but we all felt like we knew him. Time passed, but Johnny Madlin would still pop up in our heads. We had never found any closure about the boy at the creek.

While we were all moving forward in our lives over the past decade, Johnny Madlin's murderer had gone on to kill many other young boys until he was finally caught on the East Coast the spring of 1981. He boasted of his many victims and mentioned a kid in Omaha, Nebraska. He could even tell authorities where the body was if they wanted to know. He had hidden the body deep in the woods of Hummel Park of North Omaha. With the details, the police were able to uncover Johnny's body, which had remained the age he was the day he disappeared.

We all grew up. Johnny Madlin remained dead and eleven.

Lucy's voice was stronger as she whispered, "I'm starting a novena today for his parents. I know that Johnny is in heaven, but his poor parents have to grieve all over again. Not that they haven't every day for the past ten years. But their hope that...Those poor people." Just when you thought that Lucy was as fluffy as her hair and all about accessories and the next event, she went ahead and prayed the rosary for sixty-three days for somebody she didn't even know.

Lucy may have been bossy and popular, but none of those traits was as strong as her devotion to Mary. Lucy and her mother, Ava, disagreed on many topics, but they both agreed that Mary, mother of God, deserved daily attention. The rosary suffered a momentary lull in the seventies; I'm not sure why. Before then and since then, the world mission of saying the rosary daily has been intense, but in the seventies, not so much. Leave it to Lucy to keep the fire burning. She said a daily mystery and spoke of it just as every young girl at the time spoke of eating breakfast. You just did it!

My mother shifted from the novena to Lucy's hair as the time crunch hung above them. "OK, how would the princess like her hair for the big event?"

"I can't even think about my hair right now. What do you think, Mrs. Keller?"

My mom looked at me, and I looked at my mom. Had we just heard Lucy ask what someone else thought? *Jump in, Mother dear. You may never have this chance again.* Not that I wanted anyone to take advantage of Lucy during her grief of the moment, but the possibilities were endless.

"Well," my mother started slowly, "we could always allow the natural curl to come through." She waited for a response. "I think you would be surprised how beautiful it would look."

Lucy had fought her hair for as long as I could remember. She had ironed her hair with a real iron. She had pulled her hair up on her head and wound it around a giant juice can. She had attempted any and every hair-straightening technique known at the time. She never gave up the hope of getting that Marcia Brady gleam. Unfortunately, the result of all her efforts was a bumpy, frizzy look that was nothing close to Marcia Brady. It was no secret to any of us that Lucy absolutely hated her curly, thick, Italian head of hair.

"Sure, fine."

Swiftly, my mother started the process of sculpting the heavy and thick head of hair in the chair before her, fearing that Lucy might change her mind. The shampoo she used was called Mane 'n Tail—horse shampoo for those who don't remember it. She put a power protein pack on for several minutes following the shampoo and began the drying and styling of Lucy's new look. Lucy's mind was busy with the grief of Johnny Madlin and the concern for his family. Maybe she began that novena for them in my mother's chair.

The brunette curls framed Lucy's face, and I would have to say that I had never really noticed how pretty her eyes were before the new *look* my mother gave Lucy. Lucy lifted her long hair, twirled around, and smiled in the mirror.

"I look great!" She shook her locks and gathered her belongings, paid my mother, and started walking out the door. Her eyes were puffy from crying, but she was attempting to push the sad mood away as she thought of the night ahead of her.

"Have fun tonight, Lucy," my mother said.

"Uh, Lucy, the word on the street is that you've been lookin' for me..." I did my best mobster impression.

Lucy looked dazed. Her confusion slowly turned to alarm. I had just slapped her back to the present. She shrieked, "Oh, my gosh! I almost forgot. We need you, Ben. We really need you!"

"I'm right here."

"Would you take Theresa to the prom?"

I laughed out loud. I had a few questions for Lucy, such as the following: What guy wouldn't want to take Theresa O'Brien anywhere? Wasn't prom that night? And didn't Theresa have a big boyfriend named Gooey or something like that who had gone off to college to major in being arrogant and conceited? So many questions. So little time.

"I'm serious, Ben. Chewey plays in a big baseball game this weekend at the University of Iowa. We just found out his coach won't let him come back. Theresa's a prom princess. She *has* to have a date. Chewey told Tom, who told me that she could only go with a safe guy. We thought of you immediately. You'd have a blast, Ben. Oh, please, please, please."

This time I had been slapped.

A safe guy.

A gentle kiss on the lips with a major whack to the back of the head. A kind compliment with a stabbing undercurrent of an insult. A warm wish with a wicked laugh.

A safe guy.

Ouch.

"That's me. Safe guy...You know I don't own any ugly tuxedo or..."

"We have that all planned. Chewey is as tall as you are. He's a bit bigger in the shoulders. You'll be fine. Tom is picking it up when he picks up his tux. He said he'll drop it off by three..."

"You've had this all planned out, and you almost forgot to tell me? What if I'm busy? What if I'm already going to prom with someone else?" I smiled.

Lucy laughed. "Thanks, Ben. You're the best."

At least I was the safest.

# 12

## Theresa: Finishing Touches for Prom

### Saturday, May 2

# 1981

A.C. laughed his butt off and then told me to behave. I wasn't so sure that a phone call to him with my news was worth it.

Just as Lucy had dictated, Tom Ducey, the love of Lucy's life and a sophomore at Creighton University, dropped off Chewey's tux three hours later, along with a corsage, and then left to go get ready to pick up Lucy. My mother gave me the "it's the right thing to do" speech while I adjusted the peach bow tie and cummerbund on one ugly, brown, suede tuxedo.

And finally, as Lucy had predicted, I did not completely fill out the Chewey-ordered tux, and as I looked in the mirror, I could only laugh. I was going to prom. Let's have a little refresher here. In May of 1981, I was a freshman in college. I'd never been to a dance, even when I was in high school. I was spending the evening with one of the most beautiful girls I had ever known. I was wearing a really bad tuxedo that was loose where bigger biceps should be. Feel refreshed?

Once I got over my pity party of being named Omaha's Safest Guy, I focused on the up side of it all. For one, I didn't have to go through the whole pre-prom fret of "whom should I ask" and "what if she says no." I didn't have to talk on the phone endlessly deciding where to eat, with whom to double, and that whole color-of-the-tux thing. I didn't spend days or weeks on end playing the "evening" over and over in my head. Oh, and my date was beautiful—have I mentioned that yet? A.C. said that I had the best deal in town.

A.C.'s laughter upon my news was pretty ironic. Throughout all of my not-going-to-dances years in high school, I endured that pain vicariously through A.C., who would call me with all of the details ad nauseum. Dance after dance, girl after girl, disappointment after disappointment, A.C. came upon what he called his Prom Theory. It took him only eleven dances—winter wonderlands, proms, homecomings, and probably even one or two enchantment under the seas—to realize that the whole "prom" process was a setup.

The many generations before us had built up the whole scheme with a must-not-miss enticement that sent most teens racing to be part of it all. They made sure that the night was held up on a high pedestal as a magical jewel so that no reality could ever come near. Once the event had come and gone, preconceptions and dreams shattered like cheap costume jewelry on a garage floor, and teenagers would spend the day after the big dance with thoughts of disillusionment. Cleaning up the broken pieces of the bogus gem, teens quietly feared that sharing this thought with other teens might not be the best idea. Most of those young and naïve individuals, A.C. concluded, would go to yet the next dance that came along in fervent hope that the jewel on the pedestal might eventually be real and obtainable. I had never bought into the scam, and therefore, I had no preconceived notions of the evening. I guess it helped that I had only three hours to anticipate the night of my first dance.

My mom pulled out her camera from the kitchen drawer and said, "I forgot to tell you. Theresa's coming here first for me to put some finishing touches on her hair after she picks up her dress from Mrs. Morrow. She should be here any minute."

*OK, are there any other women in my life who want to drop something on me at the last minute?*

The plan, and I use the word loosely, was to have pictures taken at Lucy's house, drive to dinner down at Mr. C's, an Italian restaurant in North Omaha that kept its Christmas lights up and on all year round, and then head to Marian High School to dance the night away, check out the decorations, and watch the queen crowned. The plan seemed plausible. The remainder of the night, I kept an eye on the clock. I was no fool. When midnight rolled around, the magical evening would end for this simple and safe guy. Instead of a pumpkin, a baseball is what I feared turning into—a big baseball that Mr. Chewey might smash with a bat if my safe factor waned with the hours.

From our kitchen I heard the door to my mother's shop downstairs open. Mom looked at me. I looked at her. She grabbed the camera, I grabbed the flower thingy, and we both headed downstairs. From the stairs I could see Theresa laughing, her skin tan against a beautiful cream-colored dress. She looked gorgeous.

"I tripped over my dress on the path around your house." Theresa covered her mouth with one hand, laughing hard as she adjusted her long dress and shoes with the other. "These big Candy shoes are a hoot. I'm not sure I'll make it to dinner…"

"Great dress." I was grateful for the filter that retracted any thoughts like "Great body" or "You're so hot" or "I dream about you more than I should."

"This ole thing?" Theresa said in a sweet, Southern accent. "I only picked it out since I really don't care how I look."

"Sounds like…wait for it… *It's a Wonderful Life*."

Theresa and I were two great movie-lines people, and we tested each other whenever we could. I hadn't seen her for about a year, and I had almost forgotten our little exchange that we had whenever we ran into each other. We called our little verbal volleyball the Sounds Like game.

We put our own slant on lines and challenged each other. I can't remember who started the whole thing, but I do know that there are few people out there who can keep up with me when it comes to movie and music trivia. Sure, most can recant the well-known lines, but the more obscure lines and lesser-known great movies were recounted by only the great trivia buffs. That would be Theresa O'Brien and Ben Keller, prom dates for the evening, thank you very much. I left my anxiety on the stairs and joined Theresa with renewed excitement for the night.

"Good call! Now, whose line? Which scene?" Theresa continued the challenge.

I took the challenge: "On the street. The chick that Jimmy Stewart is flirting with...her name..."

"Violet!" Theresa finished my sentence. "I'll give you the point anyway!"

My mother put the "final touches" on Theresa's already-perfect hair while I sat hoping to entertain her. She really did look great.

"Hey, how was the concert? I heard that you and A.C. went to see the Police in Mexico City. Was it awesome?"

"Never got there. Between our schedules and bank accounts, it didn't happen. We're saving for the next time the Police are in Chicago."

I'd accepted A.C. into my Sting Fan Club a few years ago after he, driving around with me one summer, had heard every song by the Police. He was hooked after hearing "Roxanne" only once and soon became as obsessed with their music as I was. The first time we saw them in concert was in Kansas City in March of 1979 when we were both seventeen, almost eighteen. We camped out all night to get the tickets and then drove to Kansas City to see them in concert on March 15. Beware the Ides of March. The concert was incredible, and we started planning for the next tour. I would have given anything to get tickets to the world tour in Mexico City.

I carried Theresa's shoes, purse, and bouquet as she hiked her dress up knee-high and tossed the bottom of the gown over her wrist. In her bare feet, Theresa walked ahead of me around the path from my mother's basement door to the front yard. Mom followed close behind with her camera.

We were halfway across the street when the crowd that had gathered in front of the giant Mangiamelli evergreen began to clap. For me.

Lucy shouted, "Cheers to Ben. The lifesaver!" Everyone laughed and clapped.

I squinted and took a glance across the Mangiamelli lawn as a huge wind blew over the group. Ava and Louis Mangiamelli stood laughing and waving. Most of the Mangiamelli brothers were sitting on the front porch. Lucy leaned into the large body of Tom Ducey while Marty kept at least eighteen inches from her debate guy. Beyond that, several other bodies flooded the tiny front yard. Several of the younger Morrow kids, most of whom I couldn't name, ran around or rode bikes back and forth, commenting on how funny the prom people looked. Hope and Mrs. Webber heard the commotion and had grabbed their cameras as well. The prom princesses and the decorator of halls held their dresses and hair in the next wave of wind.

"Quick, get a picture. We need to go before our hair is ruined," Marty scolded anyone who would listen.

Ava gave me a big hug, and Louis Mangiamelli gave me a firm handshake, mumbling, "You're a good kid..." I glanced up from the handshake to see a sullen Will Mangiamelli on the Mangiamelli porch, his eyes red and squinted, leaning against the railing with his hands in his pockets. He was staring at Theresa. He was either high or upset that he was not included in the gala events of the night. Only one response there, buddy. *Safe guy*. Guess you didn't qualify. Still I yelled out to him, "Hey, Will."

"Hey," Will mumbled.

Will and I had gone our different ways for many reasons. Different high schools and some not-so-legal extracurricular activities on his part played a big role in that. Will had dabbled in a few activities other than sports, as Lucy informed me. His junior year, Will rekindled a connection with the Chief. Eddie Krackenier, who went to another public school I can't remember, had led Will down a wobbly path of drug experimentation and risky living that Will juggled for a year or two with his high-school sports career. The many balls in the air caught up with him his senior year.

A month into his last year at Prep, Will and a carload of buddies drove over to Marian High School. Prep had a free day while Marian was in session. The driver of the car, allegedly Eddie, dropped about five or six guys off at one of the school entrances and drove to wait for them at the other end. The boys were naked except for skivvies, ski masks, and Converse Chuck Taylor sneakers. Each guy was armed with two loaded squirt guns and a gut full of inopportune self-confidence. They hooted and hollered and squirted down the main hallway, exiting to the getaway car, buoyed by false immortal assurance, minus support in other areas.

The prank sounded harmless until you hear the second part of the story. When Sister Mary Edna, librarian and Latin expert, came out into the hallway to scold the source of noise and mayhem, she slipped and hurt her hip. No longer funny.

Principal Sister Rebecca announced somberly over the sound system to the Marian student body that this sort of activity was unacceptable and that anyone with information regarding the identity of the members of the reckless act should come immediately to the office. Lucy had glanced out into the hallway and recognized legs and shoes that had been to her house in recent years. She hung her head and prayed.

Before Lucy could feel any guilt surrounding this Catholic crime, rumors slithered through the school faster than the patterns of light on an oil slick. Ellen Richter, class officer and a perennially self-righteous classmate of Lucy, had named one naked squirt-gun runner, and one only: William Mangiamelli.

Will's huge scar on his perfect physique had become a traitor along with Ellen. Long ago—I vaguely remember—Ellen had a crush on Will, though he had no interest in her. He may not have paid attention to her, but Ellen had paid attention to his upper body during the summer days at Brookhill Country Club. She recognized the scar and immediately turned Will in to Sister Rebecca. Lucy immediately placed Ellen Richter into a box clearly marked *self-righteous.*

The Jesuit leaders at Creighton Prep anguished in making an appropriate punishment for Will his senior year. The following two weeks, Will was not allowed to participate in any school-affiliated activities. This would have been frustrating to most, as the homecoming dance was the next week, but for Will Mangiamelli and the Creighton Prep varsity football team, this was a huge problem since the state playoffs fell within that punishment time. Will and his team, who lost in the playoffs—though we will never know if his absence played a role in the loss—had to live with the consequence of his little run through Marian.

That windy day in 1981, Will stood back and took in the chaos. Ava waddled from Lucy to Theresa to Marty like a little hen, pecking and fixing their hair and dresses. Ava moved Tom Ducey, the debate guy, and me in place and told everyone to step back. Several cameras flashed as we all formed a great pose that said, "Hey, look at us! We are young and dressed up and…it's all about us!"

I saw a car pull out of the Webber driveway and drive past the group. Faith slowed down and smiled. I waved to her, and she waved back. Then she drove out of the cul-de-sac as A.C.'s green Camaro turned onto it with him honking over and over again. He parked, jumped out of the car without shutting the door, and ran up to the group. Stephano Mangiamelli grabbed the top of A.C.'s head, which was now sporting an Afro. A.C., who had grown into his big feet, towered over Stephano and looked at me, holding up his camera. "Hope I didn't miss it!"

Either Mrs. Webber or Ava announced that she wanted a picture of the old neighborhood gang. Tom grabbed A.C.'s camera, and Debate Guy went and stood under the safety of Satch the Evergreen. A.C. joined the growing group as Hope and the Morrow kids squished in. We all huddled together and smiled, eyes squinting in the sun and wind.

Tom Ducey turned into a comedian as he directed us into our neighborhood shot. To say Tom was South Omaha means more than just a direction in our city. Calling someone a South Omaha Boy, or SOB, implied you were dealing with a very proud and loyal guy. Tom was loyal to the end. To his mother—oh, they loved their mothers. To his father, who had worked his whole life at the Falstaff Brewery. To his buddies. To his girlfriend. The order of the loyalty was questionable, but having a guy from

South Omaha in the area meant he was taking over and we were going to have fun.

As the group moved in for the pose, something to the left of me caught my eye. I turned to movement from the green Wicker house. The dark image of a head looked out from the back porch. Our neighborhood witch had joined us, too. Ava took only one picture as a huge wind forced everyone to his or her cars.

From that point on, the evening moved at warp speed. We did make it to dinner and to the dance. Theresa laughed that she didn't recognize most of her classmates since they had all washed their hair and put on makeup. With no boys in the school, daily hygiene rules for the Marian girls include a ponytail and teeth brushing before heading off to class. I discovered that night that the Marian girls could care less if their dates danced; they danced all night whether their dates got up or sat. Marian girls knew every word to "Paradise by the Dashboard Lights." Oh, and, there is such a thing as too many cutout fish.

Finally, the DJ played "Free Bird," something I could enjoy. Last year's queen came to crown the new prom queen, who also happened to be my date. Marian girls swarmed Theresa like bees on a warm glass of lemonade. I bent down and whispered to Theresa, who looked shocked and uncomfortable at the attention, "Gee, your hair smells terrific."

"This prom thing is goofy, right?" Theresa asked, her voice quivering. I knew she was uncomfortable with all of the attention. I also knew that when Theresa O'Brien and I had walked into the gym, all eyes moved in our direction. This happened everywhere we walked, every place we stood. All eyes. Something I realized Theresa must have to endure every day. Something I was sure she was unaware of as she went about her life. All eyes.

**

As we drove home that night, the Police sang to us on my car radio: "Every Little Thing She Does Is Magic." The lyrics are about a guy admiring a girl he can never have. Lucy and Tom fought in the back seat the whole way home about a girl named Charlotte—or Charlotte the Harlot, as Lucy called her—a girl Tom knew growing up in South "O."

"You were flirting with her." I could see Lucy pouting in the back seat.

"I wasn't flirting with her. I said hi. She went to Saint Peter and Paul…"

"Do you still like her?"

"I took you to the dance…"

I dropped Theresa, Lucy, and Tom off at Lucy's house since Theresa was spending the night there. Lucy slammed the door as she ran to her house. Tom mumbled as he walked to his car. Theresa looked back at me as she left the car. "They're just crazy about each other."

I drove a few houses down to my home with a smile. When I got in, I locked the door and threw my keys on the kitchen table. I was taking off my shoes when I heard soft tapping on the door. I looked out the window and saw Theresa with no shoes shivering on the front stoop in the chilly, early May night, holding the tuxedo jacket I had put around her shoulders as we left the Marian gym. "You're gonna need this when you turn your tux in, Ben. I'll let Chewey know. Thanks…"

I didn't say a word as she stood on her bare tiptoes and kissed me on the lips. "Thanks, Ben. I had a blast."

I watched Theresa turn and run to the Mangiamelli house. I watched her until she was safe inside. A light went out at the Wicker house.

Somewhere in Iowa, a cocky baseball player was feeling an erroneous sense of security.

# 13

## Octavia: Wash and Set for Funeral Meeting

### Friday, July 24

# 1982

"I'm sitting under the spout from which the glory of the Holy Spirit flows out." Octavia Edith True Hruska always made an impressive entrance into a room. That day in the summer of 1982 was no different than any other.

"And just where can I find this spout?" I asked the stately, sometimes-mistaken-as-stuffy, impeccably dressed woman whom I had been "washing and setting" for the last couple months.

"Honey, if you have to ask, you've got bigger problems than you think," Octavia teased as she sat in the pink styling chair of Marcia's Beauty Box. I learned right away that Octavia needed what my mother had called warming-up time in the chair. She didn't like to be rushed; her Friday-morning appointment was an event to be savored like a nice dinner with a good bottle of wine and not just another thing to check off the weekly list.

"Well, it's time to make me beautiful for my meeting this afternoon. Do you know where I can get that taken care of?" She was dead serious as she tested me. Could I play the game? Would I feel intimidated by her presence, or would I jump in and make the team?

"I could make a few calls and find out. You're welcome to hang out here until I get word. We've got to find someone to do something with your hair." I pretended to organize my combs.

A half smile slowly curved up from the left side of Octavia's mouth, though it appeared on the right side as I looked at her in the mirror. The mirror played an interesting role in my job. For a good part of the time spent with each of my clients, I did not look directly into their eyes. I looked at the mirror image of them. I looked directly into the eyes of the mirror Octavia and grinned back.

This mirror-interaction felt natural to the people who sat in this chair, though they had spent most of the waking hours of their lives interacting with others by looking directly into their eyes. The indirect interaction might appear impersonal, but it was anything but. One human being was allowing another human to manipulate an extremely personal part of his or her identity—appearance. If anything, the entire experience could be seen as something of an intimate exchange.

Music blared from the little black radio on the windowsill. The Rolling Stones were calling "Start Me Up" to Octavia.

"Who in the hell is that?" Octavia's eyebrows burrowed together, and yes, she did say "hell," in a very ladylike tone.

"That would be Mick."

"Mick sounds like he should have chosen a different career. That's awful."

I was relieved that Octavia was focused on the voice and not the words Mick Jagger was singing. "So where is this big meeting that you want to look good for?"

"Oh, honey, I'm meeting with those altar-society girls, who are all a little too sappy, if you ask me." The thought of Octavia working in a group with other women made me laugh. "We're planning the funeral for

Edmund Rump, and they all start to tear up every time we say the name of the person who has passed. It's silly, really. We have so much to plan. We don't have time for all their slobbering and sniffing. Anyway, the funeral is Monday, and the man was so blasted old that most of his loved ones have died themselves, no disrespect meant. We need to recruit some more women to make sure that we have a good number to send him off."

"Oh, the fun you can have with funerals." I picked up a comb and scissors from the tray in front of the mirror.

"Depends on the flavor of the funeral."

"Flavor?"

"You've got your happy funeral, like Mr. Rump's. He lived a good, long life, and now it's time to die. Then you have some really unpleasant funerals. You know, the untimely ones. Just a nasty taste all around." Octavia made a face and then changed the subject. "Getting kind of crowded in this basement, don't you think?"

My mom had told me that beneath her grumblings, Octavia had a very sincere and concerned nature. Worrying about an old man having a good group to send him off was just the surface of her altruistic approach to life. My mom told me that Octavia made large donations, anonymously most times, to different causes each year. Octavia had even told Mom, though she didn't tell many people, that she volunteered once a week in the nursery at the little hospital in Fremont to help feed the newborn babies, with the ulterior motive of secretly baptizing their little souls. She would bless their heads, marking them with the sign of the cross with the holy water that she had smuggled in her purse. She hoped to cover them all before her shift was over. The antiquated thought some Catholics still believed was that a baby who died before it was baptized might not make it to heaven. She told my mom that she figured that was probably a bunch of bologna, but she wasn't taking any chances.

Octavia had jumped on board with Warren Buffett in 1981 as he created the Berkshire Charitable Contribution plan, allowing each shareholder to donate some of the company's profits to his or her personal charities. She'd met Mr. Buffett at a fundraiser bridge tournament. Octavia, who had brought her fortune from Fremont into Omaha, offered support to many causes with Buffett in the eighties. Although Buffett's personal fortune was approximately $140 million at that time, he was living solely on a salary of $50,000 per year. He was not one to wear his wealth openly. Warren and Octavia had a lot in common in that respect.

I always felt that Warren Buffett must have appreciated Octavia's straightforward approach. What you see is what you get. No verbal clutter. No pretense. Octavia called out, named, and scolded the elephant in any room. After that first appointment, she'd looked me directly in the eyes, through the mirror, that is, and said, "You do my hair better than Marcia. This stays between the two of us. Can we work it out so that I'm scheduled on your shift?" No verbal clutter. Got it.

What threw most people off when dealing with Octavia Hruska were her occasional sidewinders that went completely against the personality she displayed most of the time. I remember that the first time I did her hair, she was a bit late. Her apology was clear and sincere: "I'm sorry for being a little late today. I met with my rosary group today, and I looked throughout the whole damn house for my rosary beads before I realized that they were in my purse the whole time." Did she just say damn?

"I usually have a rosary in every room. On the table next to my bed. On the kitchen counter. In the car. How I couldn't find a rosary is beyond me."

"You do know you have a problem, Octavia."

"Excuse me?" She tilted her head and raised her eyebrows.

"And the first step is admitting it."

She tilted her head again.

"You're addicted to the rosary, woman."

Octavia's laughter filled the tiny room in my mother's basement shop.

My mother was putting in more hours as an office "temporary" person at Boys Town. At first, she claimed she was looking to make some extra money, but she seemed to enjoy getting away from the salon. I was juggling more of her clients as she seemed to miss more and more of the appointments that had once meant so much to her. At first, the recipe-card holder that protected all of the index cards with client information and history helped me out as I got to know the ladies, occasional men, and hit-and-miss children who were loyal to Marcia's Beauty Box. In time, I created my own cards, which I put in a shoebox that I kept under the bin that held the brushes and combs.

My routine went something like this. After a client left, I marked the date and the procedure done to his or her hair, just like my mother had. What I added were my own comments based on interests, events, and favorite subjects. This was helpful as I pulled the card out before the next appointment so that I would have some opening line to break any tension that the client had about getting his or her hair done and any apprehension I might have about talking to people I didn't know very well.

With Octavia, I worked a bit differently. I still wrote the notes on her cards, but she usually started the ball rolling. If anything, she calmed me and tapped my curiosity as to just what big topic she would tackle that day. What would I walk away with from my hour with the Octavia wash and set? I never knew.

"Well, if we can't find someone to do your hair, I'd be happy to take a stab at it." I held up the scissors and comb.

"That would be lovely."

As I worked on her silver, fine, and thinning hair, her expressions would direct me as to whether I was doing OK. "I just don't get it, Ben. How did you get to be so good at this when you never went to beauty school?"

"A gift from God, I guess." She grinned in the mirror. "And just so you can add it to your gigantic mountain of knowledge, they no longer call it beauty school, Octavia." About a month into doing her hair, Octavia told me not to call her Mrs. Hruska. First of all, I pronounced it strangely, and secondly, she had never liked being called "Mrs." by other adults. I guess she considered me to be one.

"All right then, what do they call it now since beauty school doesn't quite cover it? And is it legal for you to be doing my hair? Are you committing a crime with this shampoo?"

"Cosmetology school. It sounds more impressive, don't you think? No, I'm not a criminal, though some of my first haircuts should have been against the law. I lucked out on that one, Octavia. By way of a little loophole or whatever you might want to call it. After a few years of illegally doing hair, I took the test to get a license, I aced it, and boom, I'm legal.

Someone starting in the field today would have to go to school. I fall under a grandfather clause or something like that...I still have to keep up hours in education, but on most levels anyhow, I am legit!"

"Well then, you need to post that license somewhere before someone reports you, honey. I think that might be a good idea."

"I'll do that...but I'm just filling in for my mom anyway. This is helping pay for college. Just a temporary thing."

In one of my first appointments with Octavia, she felt compelled to tell me a story I'll never forget.

"My husband David was gone to war during World War II. My boys and I didn't see him for four straight years. Letters only."

"I think I remember my mom told me that. That's crazy."

"Well, the worst part is that he missed four big years of the boys growing up. When he got home, he kept calling Teddy 'Truman' and Truman 'Teddy.' They had changed so much. David was so consumed with guilt and sadness."

"I bet." A father missing his kids. I couldn't imagine.

"He spent all of his time with the boys. After they were in bed for the night, he expressed his disappointment in some the money decisions I'd made when he was gone."

I didn't say anything.

"Only time I have ever been that angry with the man."

Again, I chose not to comment.

"So you know what I did?"

"Join the circus?"

Octavia laughed to tears. "Oh, Ben, almost. Almost. I went to the train station...I was so angry."

"You ran away?"

"Well, I didn't know where to. I stood in line to buy a ticket out of Fremont."

"I was just kidding."

"Well, I didn't buy a ticket. You want to know why?"

"Sure."

"I was afraid of what the neighbors would think." Octavia laughed again. "I went home and unpacked my bags, and life went on."

"The circus is overrated…"

"Ben, sometimes we make the right choices for the wrong reason. But that's OK. You can write that one down."

Conversations with Octavia would go from politics to religion—both topics you shouldn't talk about with clients in the chairs. One topic we never talked about was the death of her youngest son. I knew the story, though. Grandpa Mac had pulled me aside, when he knew I'd begun doing her hair, and warned me not to talk about him or ask questions. Octavia had grieved like no other mother when Teddy was killed by a drunk driver in the middle of the day. The whole town of Fremont felt for the family. Grandpa Mac said that it was standing room only at the funeral of the son of one of Fremont's best-known leaders and his beautiful wife. Nasty flavor, I'm sure.

The two sons of David and Octavia Hruska, Truman David and Theodore Nathanial—called Teddy by his parents—were their pride and joy. And, as Grandpa Mac had put it, they were darn good boys, too. When thirteen-year-old Teddy walked downtown to meet his grandfather for lunch, he had no idea that Realtor Edward Allen would be finishing up a power lunch of martinis and cigars at Clark's Bar and Grill. Allen, who didn't even see Teddy on the drive back to work, killed the boy on Main Street, in the middle of the day.

Mac said that some people like to talk about the dead to keep them alive in a sense. This was much too painful for Octavia. No parent should have to endure the pain of the loss of a child. No parent. I followed Mac's advice. During our hour once a week, I made no mention of her loss. Of course, I wouldn't. Mac's story did help me in understanding Octavia and her great, edgy approach as a sort of protection from any other pain.

In time, Octavia and I developed a little routine of sorts, which I must admit even I looked forward to. I could always count on her to say the same thing every time I finished her hair.

"Well, what do you think, Octavia?"

"Well, honey, at least it's clean."

As I took off the apron around her neck, I noticed a square piece of material on a string or ribbon sticking out from her collar.

"Hey, Octavia, your price tag is showing."

Octavia looked down and broke into a beautiful chuckle. "Oh, dear, Ben. My price tag!" She laughed a beautiful reaction. "Do you not know what this is? Weren't you raised Catholic, honey?"

"I have no idea what that is."

"Oh, now what are they teaching kids today in those Catholic schools? Evidently not about the scapular." She pulled the whole scapular out from under her shirt to show me the "sacramental" piece. It was really rather simple looking. Two small square pieces of material, laminated. The two were joined by a slender band of material that looked something like a thin shoestring.

"It's a scapular, honey. 'Those who die wearing this scapular shall not suffer eternal fire.' You need a strong trust in Mary to handle this little cloth pendant, Ben. I just hook it over my brassiere and keep it with me at all times."

"Well, there you have it. I guess without a bra, I might be out of luck."

"Don't worry. I took care of you already. I put one under your chair long ago. It's there to collect your prayers and protect you."

Rather than risk looking like I didn't believe her, I waited until Octavia was gone to check. I wasn't sure if I felt impressed or creeped out by that little act of kindness. I was protected from eternal fire, at least.

Following her appointment, I escorted Octavia out of the basement and up around the little pink-flower-framed path to her big, light-blue Cadillac. With her hand hooked in the crook of my arm, Octavia and I talked about how the path needed weeding. We predicted the coming weather; I opened her car door and waited until she found her keys in her gigantic purse.

That day, I threw one more jab at her as she started her car. "Hey, Octavia, you've got to do something about that hair of yours." And then I shut the door.

I smiled as I thought of her behind the wheel of that huge Cadillac, chuckling all of the way out of our neighborhood.

# 14

## Marty: Trim, Back from College

### Thursday, July 28

# 1983

She looked like she had just spent a few months off the coast of Anorexia.

Marty was different somehow. Not that different looked that much better on Marty. She was thinner, that was for sure. She was wearing her hair with an angular cut just beneath her jaw line. She was still serious.

"So how's DC?" I asked Marty as she walked down the stairs to the shop. "Is it OK to call it DC?"

"It's as different from Omaha as you can get. I can't wait to get back. It's going to be a long summer."

"Don't you miss *anything* about Omaha?" I placed the apron around her after she sat down.

"Oh, Lucy and Theresa, maybe...and you."

Earth, Wind and Fire sang "Let's Groove" from the windowsill.

Graduating from Marian High School, Marty had received what Lucy called humongous bucks in scholarship money to attend George

Washington University. She couldn't have been more excited to get the hell out of Dodge and blow the Nebraska dust off her boots as she rode out of town. This was always a sore spot for Lucy, who rolled her eyes as she talked about Marty's attitude toward her hometown. She felt a personal attack as Marty chose to spread her wings. "Omaha's not that bad. We have lots of fun things to do. Marty thinks the world has more to offer her than we do."

Marty would retort that Omaha wasn't "bad." It was just that moving away and seeing a more exciting city made Marty aware of just how slow Omaha was to "grow up" as a city.

Marty's argument, as stuffy as it may seem, was probably true. A.C., who became an expert on Omaha one summer after reading anything he could find on the history of Omaha, told me that Omaha was supposed to be big. I mean really big. The truth was that long ago when those pioneers of American development looked to the future of this country, they saw Omaha's role in this country's economic success as being as great as that of New York and Los Angeles. After the Nebraska Territory was opened for settlement, the city was officially founded in 1854. Omaha was named for the Omaha Indians living nearby, whose tribal name means "upriver people" or "those who go upstream against the current." Omaha was destined for great things.

A.C. said that Omaha was the center of America, conveniently perched on the Missouri River. Businesspeople and government officials chose Omaha for the World Fair in 1898. This three-day festival in North Omaha brought 2.5 million people to Omaha and helped establish it as a center of commerce and culture. So what was Marty barking about? Why did A.C.'s roommate at Creighton University say, after we took him out on the town, "This city sucks!" With all of its potential for greatness, had Omaha not lived up to its name? Instead of Omaha, Chicago bumped in to take that spot. I have to say, I started to take it a bit personally myself; after all, I had grown up here and turned out fine.

Hadn't I?

In 1983, a look around the downtown area was certainly not impressive. But we were working on it. Finally. Throughout the sixties, seventies, and eighties, Omaha had turned away a number of big companies, financial suitors wooing our city as a site for their big-company fannies. Omaha, fearing that the corporate presence would take away from the family-oriented nature of Omaha, said no one too many times. All of that protection brought our commercially challenged city to a point where Omaha became sort of a joke to the city planners. They looked at each other in the early 1980s and said, "Last one out turn the lights off." Omaha didn't feel so "upstream" anymore.

Marty may have had a point. That didn't make it any easier to swallow.

Despite their disagreements on Omaha, Lucy, Theresa, and Marty were good letter writers and protectors of their friendship, doing lunch and taking road trips to Kansas City or Okoboji whenever Marty was in town.

As I shampooed her hair, Marty talked about her pre-med classes and a guy she had met before she stepped outside of herself for a minute to ask about me. "I almost forgot to congratulate you on your big decision to open a salon. Theresa told me about you moving. You're leaving your mom's beauty shop?"

"Newsflash, Marty. We no longer call them beauty shops. Didn't your hair sugar daddy in DC teach you anything? Yep, Mom's shutting down the business. She approached me a few months ago with the news that she was done with Marcia's Beauty Box and the whole industry. She was getting burned out, I guess."

"Where are you looking?" Marty asked.

"Taking my time and just looking all over Omaha," I replied.

My mom's feelings regarding Marcia's Beauty Box couldn't have surprised me more. I had always thought that this was who she was, what she liked. She styled hair. The timing of her news was also rather strange since I had been working on my business degree at UNO in hopes of helping her with her dragging business. I'd done some research on the industry following a lecture from one of my more interesting professors, who talked about the emphasis on product sales for many small businesses. The large, balding man with a big smile and goofy ties lectured about sales promotion in many fields as playing a much bigger part in many industries, one of which was the beauty industry. I took lots of notes as he preached, "The products on the shelf are becoming more of the bread, especially for smaller businesses. The service to the consumer is just butter."

Not only the small salons but also the bigger and better-known franchises were filling their front windows with displayed shampoos, conditioners, and hairsprays of those ever-so-elite lines that refused to allow their products on the shelves of Hinky Dinky and Safeway grocery stores. *You want to look beautiful? Sit in our chair, and hey, pick up a bottle or two on your way out of the salon.*

Watching my mom's poor business practices and unsuccessful bookkeeping, combined with this latest information on product sales, I now understand why she struggled to make ends meet keeping a "shop" in her basement. Even with my encouragement to her and suggestion of promoting products to increase revenue, my mom quickly replied, "Ben, I've already decided. I just need to do something else for a while."

For a while? What about her clients? What about the ladies who drove miles and miles to have her make the difference for them? What about her license? What about her shop? Did she mean that she would come back when she wasn't so tired? What about me?

Over the next year, I took over all of the remaining clients in my mother's basement while she worked full-time at Boys Town, working as an administrative assistant. She giggled as she said she was really just a secretary, but she enjoyed the new title that went along with her new little adventure. As she learned to administratively assist, I made a plan.

I decided to go for it. I would start my own business. I already had the clients for it, and with the other research I had done, I knew that, along with product-sales promotion and the addition of a few other employees, I could double what my mother had been earning in the past several years. My goal was to start combing the city to find a place to start my business.

Marty moved on to another subject: my love life. I guess Omaha gossip had traveled all the way to Washington, DC. "So, how's Mitzy?"

"I'm sure she's fine. We're just friends now, so I don't have any fun news for you..."

If a lie detector machine had been hooked up in the room, flashing lights and blaring horns would have betrayed me. I'm not a big fan of knowing the personal drama of clients that sit in my chair, but I detest sharing any drama in my life—and Mitzy was definitely the drama in my life for about two months.

I met Mitzy at Lucy's Christmas party over Christmas break that year. In hindsight, I'm sure that Lucy had an agenda in asking me over with all of her new sorority friends, but at the time, I'd just stopped by to see a friend I hadn't seen in a while. Mitzy Culligan came up to me the minute I stepped into the Mangiamelli living room. She introduced herself and didn't leave my side.

For two months.

At first, I was pretty into her. I must have needed something like Mitzy at the time. Standing four feet eleven inches on a good day, Mitzy was a tiny little firecracker with short hair and a beautiful gymnast body that never sat still. Her birth name was Mathilde, a bummer name for anyone growing up in the sixties and seventies, so her nickname, Itsy Bitsy Mitzy, given to her by her father, stuck. I still believe the name is more appropriate for a killer Pekinese dog.

During our first week of dating, we were together every day. This made sense, since we were both on break from school. When I had to work, Mitzy hung out at the salon, getting to know each client as if she might be related to him or her some day. By the time UNO started its new semester, I hoped I might have some Mitzy-free time. Not to be.

If Mitzy and I were not together, she needed to know exactly where I was. A.C. called her the pit bull since anyone who came within a few feet of me was quickly scared away. By the end of our first month of dating, we had celebrated the first anniversary of anything we had ever done. The first date. The first time we drove downtown. The first time we went to a movie. By the end of our second month of dating, Mitzy had named all of our future children.

When I told Mitzy I just wanted to be friends, she screamed some pretty awful things at me, which sounded hilarious coming from her tiny body. After her tantrum, I thought I would lighten the mood and even make her laugh when I said, "So I guess this means that we can't smooch anymore?" I thought it was funny. She threw her purse at me.

The breakup did not go well. Mitzy called several times a day to tell me how stupid I was to walk away from the best thing that had ever happened to me. A few times, during the stalking weeks following the breakup, I did wonder if I was like the man who used to be married to my mother. Maybe it was in my genes to walk away. To prove that I could handle relationships, a month after the breakup, I took a girl I had met in my business ethics class to dinner at Piccolo Pete's. Our waiter had just served us each a big plate of spaghetti when, from the corner of my eyes, a tiny, spastic figure marched into the restaurant and up to our table, picked up my plate, and poured the spaghetti on my lap.

A.C. advised me, based on his prelaw knowledge, to take out a restraining order or to enlist in some witness-protection program if I didn't want to be killed by the mad Pekinese. By the time Marty came to my chair that May, I was still a little jumpy whenever a door opened. Marty gave me a look in the mirror, suspecting that she wasn't going to get any information from me.

"I'll ask Lucy for the details…"

Spandau Ballet was singing a very dumb song from the windowsill. "I Know This Much is True" just might be within the top-three spots of the Top Ten Dumb Songs of All Time list.

"Oh, I love this song!" Marty squealed, and squealing does not look right coming from Marty.

"You've got to be kidding me. This is the worst song ever. The guy finds it hard to write the next line of his song, and he tells you this and then whines about wanting the truth to be known or something like that. It makes no sense."

Marty sang with the radio.

"See, right there. Just what that does the mean?"

"Maybe it's too deep for you to grasp." Marty started writing me a check.

"Yeah, that's it. I guess I need a ticket to the world. I thought the big-city life would give you some taste in music."

I swear I saw a smile on her face as Marty pretended to storm up the stairs.

# 15

## Theresa: Trim and Style for New Year's Eve Party

### Saturday, December 31

# 1983

Nineteen eighty-three was a big year for Warren, Sting, and the Huskers.

Mr. Warren Buffett enjoyed watching Berkshire end its year with $1.3 million in its corporate stock portfolio. This, along with Buffett's personal new worth at $620 million, probably convinced *Forbes* magazine to put him on their list of the wealthiest Americans for the first time. Feeling some of that money burn a hole in his pocket, Buffett purchased Nebraska Furniture Mart for a cool $60 million, a decision that turned out to be one of his best investments yet. The man knew money.

In 1983 Sting, formerly known as Gordon Sumner, proved that he was not only a great performer for The Police but he was also a brilliant songwriter on the band's new album in 1983: *Synchronicity*. "Every Breath You Take" won a Grammy for song of the year, beating out Michael Jackson's "Billie Jean."

For the Huskers, who were having a big, undefeated year, "big" also came in the form of a big play in that 1983 season: the Fumblerooski. Lineman Dean Steinkuhler was the big player who picked up quarterback Turner Gill's intentional fumble in the 1984 Orange Bowl and ran it seventeen yards for a touchdown. Big.

Oh, and in 1983, something else was big: hair. I still have to live with myself because of some of the hair that I allowed to walk around Omaha during the early eighties. Most girls looking back at photos of themselves from those years, shake their heads and wonder, "What was I thinking?" Bangs teased a mile high stiffened by a ton of hairspray were what the clients asked for. The look gave new meaning to the concept of the Big Bang theory. Big hair and lots of it meant that people could see the hair coming down the road long before they saw a face. Men were asking for a little hair mistake called the mullet: business in the front, party in the back. Wrong on about ten levels. I didn't always agree with the trends, but people asked for it. So they got what they asked for.

I couldn't wait to get out of the tiny basement on Maple Crest Circle and move the salon into a bigger property away from this corner of Omaha. And while the process to get to this point had taken a lot longer than I'd planned, I was still ready to make the move.

After months of looking at strip malls and equipment, I had found a vacated bay in the Old Market in downtown Omaha. The Old Market was several blocks from the river, lined with restaurants, art galleries, and unique stores. The uneven brick roads and old buildings had so much character that people felt like they were walking back in time when they spent an evening in the area. When Grandpa Mac used to take my sisters and me for ice cream in the Old Market, I remember being fascinated by the horse drawn carriage rides and the street performers. The renovated area was starting to grow, and though the price of the space was more than I'd hoped for, my gut told me this was the place if I was going to try my luck in a fickle business. With a loan from Grandpa Mac, I was able to procure the space and equipment. I was on the verge of my own new adventure. I just wasn't sure how I felt about it.

The salon was a mess since I'd spent all week packing and organizing for the move. I'd moved several boxes of hairspray near the door and was down to packing the last few boxes of blow-dryers and curling irons that would be used by the new employees I'd be hiring soon. My hope was that order in the new place would make me feel better about everything. Maybe calling all the shots would make doing what I did feel right. I planned on interviewing people for the open spots next week and slowly growing a business as I finished my last few classes at UNO.

As I placed the last bottles of hair dye and permanent solutions into one of the smaller boxes, I looked up to see Theresa, the only person I knew who could pull off the big-hair look, standing in the doorway of Marcia's Beauty Box, taking in the clutter of the small room. She was wearing formal clothes since she was coming from work.

"'Looking good, Theresa!" I said, sincerely sizing Theresa up and down.

She took the bait and handled the movie-line challenge: "'Feeling good, Ben!' Sounds like… *Trading Places.* Eddie Murphy and Dan Ackroyd." Damn, she was good. "I can't believe this is my last visit to your basement, Ben." She looked around and picked up the black radio that was sitting on top of a larger box. "This is going down to the new place, right? We need a link to this place, where it all began. Right?"

"Right."

"Can I plug it in? Just one last time?"

"Sure." I grabbed an apron for Theresa and walked toward the pink chair.

"The pink chair is moving, too, right?" Theresa turned on the radio to the sound of "Maniac" from the film *Flashdance.* She sat down and smiled at me through the mirror. I smiled back.

"Yep."

From the radio, Michael Sembello sang about how everyone thinks the steel town girl is crazy. Theresa looked around the room at the empty shelves and walls. "Wow, this is really going to happen."

"Pretty sure."

"Oh, I wanted to tell you to go see the movie *Risky Business*, crazy good," she said as I started combing through her long hair. "Stinky is working at Six West Theaters, and Michael and I got in free on a Friday night. You have got to see that movie, Ben."

The Iowa baseball player, Chewey, had become chunky and overbearing, and Theresa had moved on right after her high-school graduation. I had heard that a new guy was in the picture. Must be Michael. Theresa and I spent the next few minutes catching up. She was still living at home, putting herself through the speech-pathology program at UNO. I had run into her occasionally on UNO's campus as I finished my last few business classes.

"Oh, I heard another Loveyism the other day. This DJ was talking about some girl who sang that one song by Elton John about a tiny dancer, but said Tony Danza instead of tiny dancer. Sounds like Lovey, right?"

Lovey was almost magical but surely comical in her incessant twisting of lyrics and stories. Growing up, most of the neighborhood kids found her annoying. I found her entertaining and kind of cute. *Lovey, Lovey, pants on fire.* Hope used to say that Lovey lied. She did lie a little, but Lovey was harmless.

"She just conveniently makes up parts of her story to make it more interesting. Lovey's just misunderstood." Theresa defended our childhood friend and finally took a seat in my chair, safe and sound.

Through the years, Lovey bopped around from hairdresser to hairdresser. I hadn't cut her hair in a while.

"Do you think I need another perm?" Theresa asked as she ran her hands through her hair.

"What do you think?" Always throw it back at 'em.

"Probably not right before a New Year's party. I don't think so. Let's wait until next time."

"Sounds good. Hey, how's Lucy? She seemed pretty grumpy last time she was in."

"Oh my gosh, she's such a head case whenever Tom has finals. She starts getting all neurotic about things. I see her more during his finals than ever since she doesn't know what to do without Tom Ducey." Lucy was in her third year at UNO studying to be a teacher or something. Tom was in his second year of law school at Creighton. A.C. was in his final year of undergrad there. He was also planning on heading down the legal path.

Theresa continued, "Those two are crazy. They are either all lovey-dovey or fighting. Did you know she still worries about Charlotte? That's usually one of their bigger fights. Now and then."

"Charlotte the Harlot?"

"Yep. She will never get over that girl. It was his grade-school girlfriend, for heaven's sake."

"Who flirted with him through high school," I added.

"And now we are in college. When's Lucy going to realize that Tom is so crazy for her? Oh, I forgot to tell you, Lucy and I drove by the new place downtown. Ben, it's going to be awesome. You must have come into some money to get a place in the Old Market."

"Yeah, I'm loaded. Actually, I got the last deal before prices went up on prime real estate in the downtown area. I was pretty relieved when the ink dried on all of the paperwork. I bet I signed 'Benjamin H. Keller' one hundred times at the closing." I motioned for Theresa to walk over to the sink so I could wash her hair.

"H? Your middle initial is H? Harold? Henry? Hamlet?"

"Howard…don't ask."

Theresa laughed. "Howard is a great name. A solid name. Why Howard?"

"I'm named after the man who used to be married to my mother."

Theresa was quiet. I knew she was sorry that she had stumbled into awkward territory. Most people backed away from that piece of my life like a kid finding a bug under his bed. Ignore it; maybe it will crawl away.

"Have you ever heard from him, Ben?"

I shook my head as I tested the water's temperature and then gently moved Theresa's head to the water.

"Do you ever think about him? Ever?"

"Nope."

"You don't have to do this," Theresa said.

I stopped and looked into Theresa's eyes.

"Are you OK, Ben?"

"What do you mean?"

"With this move? With doing this whole hair thing?"

I massaged Theresa's head as I shampooed her hair. After I rinsed it clean, I put in a conditioner.

"I could think of a million jobs I would rather be doing than doing hair. I kind of fell into this whole mess when Mom pretty much abandoned it."

"You're good at the 'mess.' You're good with hair and the business part, but is this what you really want to be?"

"I thought about what I wanted to be when I was young, but I haven't thought about it in a while...I never wanted to be a fireman or an astronaut."

"Football player?"

"Oh, sure. But with my lanky body? I know everything about the game, but I'd get killed out there."

"Sports announcer?"

"Big fantasy. Big."

"You don't have to do this. You know that, right?"

"If I can make a go of it, I think I could make some pretty good money."

"And if not?"

"Haven't thought about it." A final rinse. I helped Theresa up to go back to the pink chair.

"Your dad was crazy to do what he did, Ben..."

I took a towel and dried her hair. I grabbed a pair of scissors and started checking out the ends of Theresa's hair. I looked up at her in the mirror with a goofy look on my face. "Speaking of crazy. Who is this new Darrin guy? I mean Dagwood?"

"His name is Michael."

"Right, Michael. That's what I meant."

"Michael is awesome."

"I'm sure he is," I replied with one raised eyebrow.

"Really, he's great. I met him at the Ocean Wave."

The Ocean Wave was a bar just on the other side of the mighty, muddy Missouri. It was both humorous and horrifying to realize that all of the college-age kids—and a few high-school ones, too—who were unable to legally drink alcohol till the ripe age of twenty-one in Omaha could just cross over a bridge to drink in Iowa, where their eighteen-year-old souls were deemed ready and legal to drink. It only took another three years before the adults discovered this bizarre discrepancy. Hey, our children are going to bars. This had been going on since 1973 when Iowa changed its legal drinking age from twenty-one to eighteen. Evidently, some eloquent eighteen-year-old had convinced governmental officials that eighteen was a great age to go to bars. Voila! Eighteen it was. In 1978, one or two officials wised up and thought, "I don't know, maybe we should go with nineteen." Finally, in 1986, with pressure from a few neighboring states, they joined the twenty-one club. Until then, the upper youth of Omaha went on secret road trips every weekend to the other side of the river.

I replied to Theresa, "Go on."

"He's from a little town in northwest Iowa. He works at First National Bank. He's a great guy!"

"A great guy from Iowa? Sounds like the kiss of death."

"Ben!" I started cutting off a short amount from the ends of Theresa's hair. "He's not at all like Chewey…I mean, Chewey was good guy, but… You'd like Michael."

"Then we'd better get to work on your hair. You want to look good. And we're gonna need some big hair to do that. Big."

The door at the top of the stairs opened. A voice yelled down, "Hey, who's down there?" The voice sounded like Lovey Webber, loud and sensual.

Theresa recognized the voice, "Lovey, it's me! Come down."

"Theresa's here!" Hope sang out. "I didn't know Theresa would be here, Ben."

Lovey and Hope rushed down the stairs. Hope Webber had begun cleaning my mother's shop and helping out with little odds and ends after I started getting busy with clients. As I inherited almost all of Mom's clients, I had less and less time to do the little jobs that I had done growing up. I liked having Hope around. She came in twice a week now, leaving with towels to clean at an independent-living group home for adults with Down syndrome. Usually Mrs. Webber picked her up and dropped her off at the salon; Hope would then walk over to the Webbers' house and have dinner, and Mrs. Webber would take her home.

Lovey chimed in, "Theresa, I haven't seen you in, like, forever! Ben, don't hate me…I've been cheating again…" Lovey hugged me, pressing her body against mine. Over the hug, I glanced at Theresa. We exchanged a can't-believe-we-were-just-talking-about-her glance.

"Can't believe you strayed again, you little hair whore."

"Mom was so busy, so I told her that I would get Hope here. Why is this place such a mess?"

"Lovey, that's not nice. We're moving; I told you that." Hope was part of the whole moving deal. Package deal. The boxes, pink chair, and Hope would carry me to my new place.

Hope turned to Theresa and touched her hair. "Theresa, you are so beautiful."

"Thanks, Hope. Hey, what is Faith doing these days?" Theresa asked both Hope and Lovey.

"Yeah, where is Faith?" I added before I realized that I'd said the words out loud.

Everyone looked at me.

"Faith is everywhere," Lovey said, annoyed. "It's like she needs to travel the whole world, but she can't get back to visit us. Whatever." In a nutshell, Lovey talked to everyone, bouncing around like the pinball in an overused pinball machine. Hope was always by my side. But Faith. Faith was elusive.

Hope filled in a few holes for us. "Faith is graduating from TCU this year."

"And then she gets a teaching job overseas with her friend Thomas, or something like that." Lovey, growing tired of talking about someone other than herself, continued, "Hey, guess who I'm dating now?" Before we could even take a stab, she exploded, "Jim Kinney! Remember him. We all thought his dad had died or his parents were divorced or something 'cause he was never around..."

Lovey looked more at Theresa but sensed all of our confusion. "Jim Kinney. The guy who could do triple flips off the high board at Brookhill."

"Oh, Jimmy." Theresa and I both remembered Jimmy Kinney. Why hadn't she just said so in the first place? Hope began sweeping up the areas of the floor where I had moved furniture out.

"Well, his dad was in prison that whole time we were growing up. Not sure why. Don't even want to know, but I'm going as Jim's date to the welcome-home party. Can you believe I am going to a back-from-the-slammer party? Hey, Ben, did you go to see your guys when they were in town?"

Keeping up with Lovey was like riding bumper cars. You might think that you were going one direction when suddenly something bumped you into a different direction.

"My guys?"

"The Police. I thought I heard that you and A.C. were going to a concert or something."

"As a matter of fact, yes." A.C., his girlfriend at the time, and I had seen The Police at Rosenblatt Stadium in August the previous year. "My guys" had won a Grammy the year before for the song "Don't Stand So Close to Me." The song is about a girl who has a crush on her teacher while the teacher is not very comfortable with the situation. Sting has never confirmed if the song was based on a personal experience from his years of teaching.

Lovey bumped us all again after she looked at her watch. "Oh, I've gotta run. Hope, you know you need to go over to Mom's after you finish."

"I think I know that, Lovey." A perturbed Hope started pulling towels from the hamper. "I know."

Lovey bopped out of the messy basement. I'd be seeing her in a few months, probably.

Hope looked at me after Lovey left. "Thomas is not Faith's boyfriend. He's just a friend." She started putting the clean towels she had washed at home into an empty box, then turned back to me. "Hey, what are we going to name our new place?"

"Yeah, what is the name of the new place?" Theresa asked.

That question I couldn't answer yet.

Hadn't even thought about it.

# 16

## A.C. in the "New Place": Entire Head Shaved

### Saturday, February 4

# 1984

"Her name is Angel, and she's beautiful."

A.C. was in love again.

I was wiping the shaving cream from the different areas of A.C.'s head as I tolerated another love story. Because A.C. had helped me move boxes and equipment from my mom's basement salon to the new space in the Old Market one cold Saturday morning in late February of 1984, I had given him a free shave. The "fro" was out; the shiny skull was in. I guess the deal also included me hearing about his love life.

I looked in the mirror at my best friend admiring his new look and shook my head. No matter what he did with his hair, no matter what different and sometimes bizarre clothes he threw together, A.C. always looked good. And he always had a girlfriend. The short, skinny kid I had grown up with had hit a major growth spurt our sophomore year in high school and now stood six feet three, fit and trim, and appealing to girls of all races. A.C.'s green-gold eyes framed with dark lashes and not-black, not-white skin came together in a look that blended the best of both races together. I wouldn't call him cocky, but I am pretty certain that A.C. knew he was attractive. He looked at himself in the mirror and smiled. He rubbed his head and looked around at my new place in the Old Market.

"Now that's what I'm talking about. I bet Angel will love touching my head…"

Because A.C. and I had helped move every Mangiamelli boy out of the house on Maple Crest, A.C. decided to call all four of them to ask for help when we moved everything from my mom's basement to the new salon downtown. They all said yes and showed up that morning, all except one brother: Will. Stephano mumbled something about a hangover, and we got right to work so that the entire move on a fourteen-foot by seventeen-foot U-Haul truck took only two and a half hours on one of the coldest days in Omaha that year. Anthony made a few predictable comments about me going into a field that he thought was a bit "girly," but he changed his tune after he saw the new place in the Old Market with high ceilings, one brick wall, and big windows, floor to ceiling, looking out on an outdoor mall a few blocks from the Missouri River. He thought the place looked like something in downtown Chicago. I bought the guys lunch and a couple pitchers of beer at the Blue Jay Bar near Creighton, and they all took off for their Saturday afternoons.

Except for A.C. He stayed to help me interview the last few applicants for the two chairs I needed to fill when I opened the following week. The three candidates I had interviewed the week before were eager to learn but inexperienced. As much as I would have loved to help them out, I needed help that would bring loyal clients with them from the last job. Before the applicants came, A.C. helped me unpack while he finished the Angel story.

"She's like an angel dropped down from heaven."

"Whatever happened to Butter Face?" I asked about the girl from Texas in his theology class he had been dating a month earlier.

"Butter Face?"

"The girl you said you loved everything about her…but her face?" I laughed. "I thought you said that *she* was the one."

"I know I always say that this one's the one."

I raised my eyebrow.

"But this one is the one. I mean it, Ben. Angel gets it. She gets me. She gets everything about me. About why I'm going into law. About why I've decided to convert to Judaism…"

"You what?"

"Well, I haven't yet, but I'm researching it. I need to explore my roots. She gets that."

"Weren't you just a Methodist, yesterday?" A.C., the guy who had announced he was going to be a priest at his First-Communion party over fourteen years ago, had recently gone on a world tour of the churches of Omaha. He wasn't angry with the Catholic Church, he told me; he was just curious. The hunger that drove him to experience as many different religions as he could was that same hunger that drove A.C. in anything. His ravenous appetite to "know" was exhilarating and draining as he read everything he could get his hands on—even while going through law school. A.C .had read anything and everything by C.S. Lewis, whose words he looked to for inspiration and guidance just as I looked to Sting from the Police for my direction in life.

The pursuit of the Jewish religion threw me off a bit but didn't surprise me. A.C.'s father came from a strong Jewish background. When he fell in love with A.C.'s mother, his family, overwhelmed by racial and religious flags waving in their strict culture and society in general at the time, decided to part ways. Grandma Perelman did send A.C. and his sister Elizabeth a birthday card with money each year. Evelyn's family was really not much more supportive, and so Evelyn and John were alone on their island of diversity. Familial influence was infinitesimal. I was the closest thing to a cousin for A.C. growing up. Early on, A.C. embraced the Catholic religion. Around the time of high-school graduation A.C. began questioning the Catholic Church—not attacking, just questioning.

"Now don't make fun. Growing up Catholic was an education of sorts...but I know that I need to check out a few things while I'm on this earth. Besides, there were some awfully attractive women in the Methodist church. You wouldn't know. You haven't even been to check out the women in your own church."

"OK, so is your little Angel someone you met at Creighton, Arthur? In a law class or something?"

"Not exactly. She works in the cafeteria. She is a bit younger, but that doesn't matter. She gets it more than the older women I've dated. And don't call me Arthur."

Here's where A.C.'s hunger or passion annoyed me as a lifetime observer of what, occasionally, could be considered impulsive or even reckless. "A.C., is she in college? How old is she?"

"She's eighteen, almost. Her birthday's tomorrow. And she's saving money to go to college."

"Angel may get you, but I don't get you. You're converting to Judaism, you're robbing the cradle...Is there any other bomb you want to drop on me today?"

"We're getting married."

Even the shampoo was silent.

I took a deep breath after this sucker punch. No music was playing since I hadn't set up the new sound system yet. I looked at A.C., but I felt I was looking at a stranger. The fluorescent lights of the new place shone on the side of A.C.'s bald head.

"I really love her, Ben. I want you to be my best man."

I looked down at the box I was holding and placed it on the ground. I walked over to the pink chair from my mom's old shop. The "beauty chair," which had been outdated in the sixties and seventies, now held a retro look that I was incorporating in the new place. I'd bought two other chairs for the new, yet-to-be-hired employees, but I would use the pink-and-black chair for my own. I stooped down to look under the chair and noticed that the scapular from Octavia was missing. In the move from Maple Crest, the little Catholic charm must have fallen off along the way.

I walked over to another box that I knew held the black radio Mom had let me take, kind of as a housewarming gift. For me the archaic radio held comfort and memories. For the new place, it would provide a conversation piece; I plugged it in and looked for a good station.

"Angel and I are going down to the courthouse next week. I'd love for you to meet her. Come down. Stand up for me, Ben. Her sister will stand up for her. We'll take you both out to a little wedding lunch after..."

The excitement of my moving day had fallen like a weak balloon following a long party. I felt tired as I considered all of the flags waving in my face right now. No church wedding. No Mr. and Mrs. Perelman. I had never met this girl, and I was to stand up for a marriage I didn't really support. I found a clear station playing Prince's "Let's Go Crazy." I turned the song up.

A.C. stared at me, his green eyes waiting curiously.

"Sure. What time, Arthur?"

A.C. exploded. "My man!" He jumped over several boxes and shook my hand. "My best man! I'll get the details to you...You're gonna love her. I just know it. Love her!" He looked around the room, and as if to ensure my answer, he started moving boxes and emptying them without knowing where things went. "Now, we've got some interviewing to do."

"Yep."

"Looks like we have about fifteen minutes before candidate number one shows up. What do you need me to do? Do you want me to start putting these things over there?"

A.C. wanted me to talk. To say something, say anything. His energy was really starting to annoy me.

"Well," I slowly said to A.C. without looking at him, "you could help me come up with a name for the place." He did owe me.

A.C. knew that my creative talent went only as far as the hair on the head in my chair. For the past several months, I had been considering name upon name for the biggest risk I had taken in my life. Grandpa Mac had loaned me more money than I felt comfortable borrowing, and I hoped to pay him back sooner than later. I would, of course, have to put up a temporary sign, a quick sign made by Kinko's. It would take weeks for the permanent sign to come in. The pressure to come up with a name was really hitting me hard, especially as I stood in the new place with all of the equipment that I had just bought. Sinks, hair dryers, furniture. If this place didn't fly, I would be in debt for a long time. My goal of moving out of Mom's house was either around the corner or a year out—dependent on the success of this venture. The name of the salon would need to bring in more clientele to cover my overhead. For a moment, I shifted all of the pressure toward A.C.—and without remorse, because of what he had just dumped on me.

I stared at him, waiting with raised eyebrows.

"You definitely need something catchy but not goofy…no more Marcia's Beauty Box." A.C. had never made fun of me working in the hair industry. He respected the work I did. "Curl Up 'N Dye is already taken." He smiled.

I frowned.

"Sheer Pleasure…no, too erotic…Hairanoya? What do you think of that?"

I crossed my arms.

"Give me some time on this one. How much time do I have?" He sounded sincere.

"Three days." At least I had deflated some of his annoying energy. A.C. looked as though he were really working on something.

The sound of the bell above the door announced the entrance of a candidate. The previous renter of the bay, who had managed a candy store that tanked, had put a bell above the door. Where Jolly Ranchers failed, I hoped that conditioner would succeed. I'd kept the bell but hoped the energy would shift as I moved in with my business.

Toby Windsor, candidate number two, stood in the doorway and looked uncomfortable as he noticed A.C. and me. "You must be Toby." I motioned for him to come in. My first candidate must have been running late. Jenae Tolliver should have been here ten minutes earlier, and Toby was about fifteen minutes early for his appointment. A business owner and manager only a few minutes, I was already learning to be flexible.

Toby was a slightly overweight young man who was average in all other physical ways. Average height. Average style of dress with his khakis and white, button-down shirt. Average brown hair with average eyes framed by his average big glasses, which were average, at least in the eighties. The average façade lasted for thirty seconds until he took a deep breath and reached up to touch the top two corners of the door, each twice in a row before he walked to stand right in front of me with a folder in his hand. He said nothing. Behavior, not so average.

"Take a seat." I grabbed a chair from behind two boxes in the mess that was causing distress to Toby, whose eyes scanned the room, his cheeks red and his eyes rounder.

"We just moved in today, Toby. The place will be cleaned up by opening." It wasn't that I cared what he thought; I just hoped that my comment would calm him down. Toby looked at the chair, and walked a full circle around it, and then sat down. I grabbed a stool for A.C. and sat down on two boxes, avoiding eye contact with A.C., who would probably be making a face about the interesting candidate and trying to throw off my attempts at being professional.

"I'm Ben." I held out my hand to shake Toby's; he looked at it as though it were obscene. He nodded his head his head twice and looked down at the folder in his lap. I put my hand down.

"From the resume you sent me, I can see you've established quite a long list of clients."

"Yes." His first word was spoken in an average voice.

"I actually called a few clients and your present boss. They all speak highly of you."

"Yes, they do." As Toby spoke, his cheeks filled with redness, as if someone had just slapped him very hard on each cheek.

"I guess, then, it would make sense if you let me know if you have any questions for me. Any comments? Anything?"

Toby cleared his throat and offered the folder to me as he stood up. "This is a list of requests and special contingencies I have." He cleared his throat following the word "special." "I will know that you cannot concur with them if I do not hear from you."

"Great. I'll just give the folder to my assistant," I said, again without looking at A.C., handing him the folder. I didn't offer my hand to say good-bye.

Toby got up to leave as the bell above the door rang again, this time announcing the late candidate number one, Jenae Tolliver. A beautiful woman with what A.C. would call a naughty body rushed in past Toby, who avoided eye contact with the knockout. I yelled to Toby, "Thanks, Toby. Have a nice day." A.C. snickered behind me.

Jenae smiled at Toby, who disregarded her as he walked around her, touched the two top corners of the doorframe again, twice each, this time in the opposite order, and left the salon.

"Wow. This place is awesome! I love the retro look." Jenae took in every little detail as she walked toward A.C. and me. One side of her hair was a bright magenta, lying smoothly to that side, with a good portion of it covering one eye. The remaining side was an almost-black color. The ridiculous hairstyle could not hide her beauty. Jenae wore a black, fitted, short skirt and a tight, white, revealing blouse. Her large earrings and high-heeled shoes were the exact color of the magenta side of her hair. Three of her fingernails were without the magenta nail polished that coated the remaining seven nails as though she'd run out of time as she was getting ready for her interview.

"I'm telling you. This place is soooo different from any other place I've worked in. I love it! Oh, look at the pink chair."

"I'm Ben. You must be Jenae."

"Ben!" Jenae squealed as she shook my hand with one hand and grabbed my other arm with her other hand. "You are too cute…and who is this guy?"

"This is A.C., my assistant." Not really.

"A.C.? What does that stand for? Absolutely charming?"

A.C. smiled a toothy smile that made him look goofy. "You got that right."

I gestured to Jenae to sit down, and she pounced down on the chair, crossing her legs in an angle, a well-rehearsed pose.

"I got your letter, but I didn't get your resume or references." I began the interview.

Jenae's huge, dynamic, blue eyes were complimented by dramatic eye shadow. When you erased all of the magenta and most of her makeup, Jenae was stunning. Really stunning.

"Oh, I brought them with me." She pulled several papers out of her oversized purse. "You can call any of these people any time. Actually, call this guy late at night. It drives him crazy. So funny." I looked over Jenae's list of clients and then handed the papers to A.C.

"I'll get in touch with some of these people soon, but until then, do you have any questions?"

"Questions? Uh, no, no questions." Jenae seemed to sit up straighter with a serious expression. "I think I should let you know that doing hair is my life. It defines me. I have been doing other people's hair for as long as I can remember. I love helping people feel good about themselves. Don't you?"

"Well, that's a big part of the job, I guess…" My laugh sounded awkward. A.C. cleared his throat.

"Sorry I was late. I hate being late." Jenae looked over at A.C. and winked. "Why don't you two call me if you have any questions? I think we would work well together. Just a feeling. I do get really strong feelings sometimes…Oh, great radio. It's so fun!"

Both A.C. and I rose to walk Jenae to the door. She glanced out at the parking lot and put her hand to her forehead. "No, no! Oh, gawd, am I really getting a parking ticket? Gotta go. Call me!" she screamed as she ran out the door.

Neither A.C. nor I said a word as we watched Jenae run to her car. We both turned back to sit down when I heard an eruption of laughter from A.C. He was laughing so hard, he was crying.

"Those were two major wackos! The girl was hot, though. Wait, you've got to hear this." A.C. pulled out the folder that Toby had given me. "That Toby guy's requests include the exact layout of his station, where he wants his combs and hair dryer…when he wants to take his breaks…And that Jenae, what a trip. She was a looker, though. So do you have to start over, or do have any more candidates tomorrow? You do open in three days."

"I think I'm done."

"Done?"

"Yep. I only have two extra chairs and stations."

"You're kiddin' me. You are not hiring those two head cases."

I said nothing and started emptying boxes.

"Benny, I won't let you do it. You'll bomb. You need to think clearly about the money you've put into—"

"A.C., did you see the number of clients on Toby's list? Did you see how long most have been coming to him? Following him each time he moved to a different salon? I called some of those people. One lady said she wouldn't have anyone else do her hair. He has the clientele that will follow him to the Old Market. I have a business that can benefit from that. And don't call me Benny."

"He is messed up!"

"He'll be to work early."

"Yeah, touching doors and ceilings and…"

"I'm hiring both of them."

A.C. wrinkled his face and shook his head. "The girl? You haven't even seen her resume. She was late…"

"I liked her energy."

A.C. looked into my eyes with a serious expression. "Either you want to date her or you feel sorry for her…" He was shaking his head, trying to think which made more sense for me. "So glad I could help. You really listen to my advice."

"I didn't really want your advice. I just wanted you here to help me feel better about the process, and pretend to be my assistant."

"Crazy House."

"Excuse me."

"Looney Bin. Dysfunction Junction. You *did* ask me for help with a name for this place. You choose to enter a whacky industry and you hire a bunch of…Vanity Insanity…Vanity Insanity. I like it!" A.C. stood up. "Seriously, what do you think? Vanity Insanity!"

I started to laugh. "I actually kind of like it."

"Vanity Insanity." A.C. stood up and smiled, repeating the name over and over. He was starting to annoy me again.

A week later, on February 14, 1984, A.C. and Angel got married.

The temporary sign went up the next day. A month and a half later, the permanent sign, which cost more than I'd paid for my first year of college, was hung above the bay in the Old Market.

Vanity Insanity.

17

## Lucy: Highlight for Graduation Party

Wednesday, May 8

# 1985

Lucy squealed as she ran into the shop. "Looook! Look! Don't you just love it?"

She didn't have to open the door to Vanity Insanity since I'd propped it open all afternoon on what was one the nicest days in May I can remember. Lucy, very tan and more bubbly than usual, ran in wearing yellow Bermuda shorts and a matching shirt. Flat pumps, purse, and jewelry matched as well. I'm pretty sure if you researched the origin of the name Lucy, you would discover that it translates to mean "tiny collector of many matching clothes."

"What? What should I love?" I pretended not to notice the ring she was waving in my face. "What am I looking for here?"

"Not funny. My engagement ring. Do you love it or what?"

"Wow." I held her hand, looking as hard as I could. What did I know about rings? "It's one of the nicest I've seen…Now who is the lucky guy?"

"Don't you know the rules of what you're supposed to say to someone who has just gotten engaged?"

"Rules?"

"OK, I'll help you. You first ask when the big day is."

"OK, when's the big day, Lucy?"

"Well, we're getting married on Tom's fall break in October." Another squeal. "I have so much planning to do."

"Am I supposed to ask about the planning next?"

"No. You're supposed to ask what my colors are."

"Colors?"

"The color theme I'm using for the wedding. Like bridesmaids' dresses, napkins, decorations…colors!"

"Color theme?"

"I'm going with a jewel-toned fuchsia. And I'm accenting it with a cream color called moon shadow."

"Wouldn't it just be easier to have a wimpy-rainbow wedding?"

"OK, now you're bugging me. No more questions." Lucy marched over to my chair and plopped down, arms folded, a smirk hidden under her frustration.

"Sorry, Lucy. It's just I'm in graduation mode, thinking that your next big event was your graduation, and you threw me off with the whole wedding thing." I stood behind her with my hands on her shoulders and looked straight in the eyes of the mirror Lucy. "Seriously, congratulations, Lucy. Great news for you and Tom."

Lucy frowned.

"Was it something I said?"

She shook her head. Her eyes started to water as Madonna sang about living in her material world from the radio.

"Congratulations?" I guessed.

"No…. graduation…you said graduation. I'm not graduating, Ben."

"Sure you are, I have the invitation to your graduation and party at your parents' house on my counter at home. It says that unless it rains, the party will be in the backyard of your house on Maple Crest Circle."

"Nope. I just got my grades…I flunked meteorology. I bombed the final." Lucy put her head in her hands, sobbing. I put my hands on her shoulders.

"Hey, who really cares about the weather anyway? We can't control it. We just have to live with it. Yet some guy gets paid to be wrong most of the time about what the weather will be tomorrow. Heck, that guy probably didn't do very well on his final either…"

"I haven't told my parents, Ben." Lucy sparked up. "But I have an idea. I was thinking that the party they planned for my graduation can be Tom's and my engagement party. What do you think?"

"Have you talked to Tom about it? Marty? Theresa?"

"No. Nobody knows but you…about the class or the engagement. What do you think?"

"Does Tom know you're engaged?" I smiled and started combing out Lucy's hair.

"Of course he does. He proposed to me last night, outside on Creighton's campus. Under the stars in Jesuit Gardens…He doesn't know about the class."

The "class" was just one of many that Lucy had tolerated over the past four years. She'd started out at Kearney State College but missed Tom too much, so she came back after just one semester and enrolled at UNO in Omaha. With Tom at Creighton University, Lucy was just a five-minute ride away. I'd run into her several times on campus, and I can say this much: the girl never studied. Lucy loved everything about college except the classes. They were an inconvenience that she endured so that she could do what she did best, socialize. I had always suspected that her grades were not stellar. Louis Mangiamelli wanted each of his kids to have a college education, but as far as Lucy was concerned, what she would do with that degree was as much a mystery to Lucy as it was to me.

Our secret discussion, packed with all sorts of things she had told no one else, was interrupted as Jenae got off the phone. "Hey, what did I miss, girlfriend? I had to make some stupid appointment for Toby. Where is he anyway?"

"He ran to pick up supplies." The running tension between Toby and Jenae was amusing more than intrusive in the daily interactions of Vanity Insanity. Jenae irritated Toby. Toby irritated Jenae. And for that reason alone, I positioned their stations right next to each other.

"Jenae, I'm getting married!" Lucy shouted and thrust her hand out to Jenae, shrieking louder than before. So much for the big secret.

"Married!" Jenae joined the shriek fest. "Lucy Lu, you will be the most beautiful bride." Jena's black ankle boots in May were a statement alone. She'd toned the look down with a deliberately ripped pin sweatshirt over her leather miniskirt. Her now-brown hair was pulled in a tight ponytail to the side and two chopsticks—at least that's what they looked like—were poking out of her head as though they had been forced into the back of her neck, through her brain, and up and out of her head, perfectly poised like two antennae.

"OK, now when is the big day?" Jenae asked with big, blue, sincere eyes.

"Well, my fiancé," Lucy started, "I can't believe I can finally say F-I-A-N-C-E…" She dragged it out. "My fiancé is in law school, but neither of us wants to wait, so we're getting married on Creighton's campus at Saint John's over his break in October."

"And the colors?"

Jenae knew the questions? Jenae didn't strike me as the type who would know the questions. Lucy couldn't answer since Jenae's next appointment was standing in the doorway. Jenae gave a congratulatory hug to Lucy and ran up to the small, older woman, smiling at her.

"All right now, Miss Colleen, let's go make you look fabulous." She held the older lady's hand all of the way to her chair.

Once you could get past the latest Jenae getup, you were overwhelmed by her warmth and exuberant energy. I know this is why her clients were loyal to her, that and the fact that she was great with hair. Ironically, about 75 percent of her clients were woman over the age of fifty. They were not threatened by her effervescence, taste in clothing, or beauty. In fact, they might just have been hoping that some of her edgy looks would rub off on them as she shampooed them. The final look Jenae gave them as they walked out the door was usually conservative, but she would style it with some gel and extra hairspray so they walked out with an extra, little, zippy something-something.

Lucy cleared her throat. "So, what do you think?"

I had to be careful here. "Well, that depends. Are you asking me about your hair or the lies that you're living?"

"Ben, I haven't lied to anyone—yet. I'm going make up the class this summer while I'm working at UNO. Did I tell you that I got a new job in the dean's office? Anyway, I'll be on campus, so it'll be no big deal to retake the class. I'll graduate in August. No big graduation. I don't even want a party."

Lucy may have had her share of inappropriate guilt in life, but she felt none as she looked to her college education as something "to get over with." The degree was not a means to an end. The piece of paper would not catapult her to her dream career. Most of her girlfriends were entering careers they would embrace until marriage and baby came along, only to find that *guilt* was an unavoidable state of mind for the remainder of their lives. Guilt if they remained in their jobs to succeed and reap the financial benefits that would afford a lifestyle they might not have known as children. Guilt if they stayed home and "wasted" the years in college. Parents had cheered them on, "You go, girl! Run for president!" until that first baby came along, and "Of course you are going to quit." A young woman in the eighties was facing new problems. The smart ones handled it well. That would include Lucy.

The money her parents had paid for her college education was not wasted, in Lucy's opinion. She had met a ton of interesting people and learned a lot of interesting things—except meteorology. Lucy had a real career goal in mind: marry Tom Ducey and have a lot of babies. She had not gone to college to get her MRS degree. She was not "pre-wed." She had no hidden agenda. She would tell you that herself. She'd always known that she wanted to get married and stay home with her kids. You got a problem with that?

"I'll take Mom and Dad to dinner or something to celebrate when I do finally graduate. I'll be working full-time until Tom gets a job; I'll work to put my husband—I just said husband—through law school. I can't believe I'm getting married."

"I think that the graduation ceremony and party were as much for Ava and Louis as for you, Lucy. They'll be disappointed." I could tell this was not what she wanted to hear.

"I didn't plan on flunking meteorology, Ben"

"I know. When are you going to tell your folks? Graduation is in three days."

"Soon…Do you think they'll be happy for me? I mean about the engagement?"

"I think they'll be very happy." I would hear the full reaction when Ava came in to have her hair done the following Tuesday. "You might want to bring Tom with you to buffer the school news. Once they see how excited you are…and hear about those wonderful color themes or whatever you called them, they'll be fine."

"Ya think?"

"Are you kidding me? They will get off the couch and hug the future Mrs. Ducey." Then like a light bulb going off and falling directly on my head, the thought hit me. "Lucy Ducey?"

"Yeah, yeah. I figured that one out when I started having a crush on Tom. I think I was in seventh grade. Haven't you ever thought about that? I probably wrote it a million times on my notebooks in study halls."

"Lucy Ducey." No, I had never gone there before.

"I love the sound of it, so don't make fun or you won't be an usher at my wedding. Now, what funky thing should we do with my hair for my engagement party?"

"Something big and poofy, I'm thinking. Or spiky! I'm an usher?" I walked Lucy over to the sink.

The good news about Lucy's hair in 1985 is that she was finally "in." Other women were paying sizable amounts of money to get the curl and volume that Lucille Belle had been born with. If anything, I was still calming her locks a bit to give her a Julia Roberts style, but she shone in the middle of that decade.

I warmed the water as Lucy sat down by the sinks and babbled on and on about her plans for the big day. I listened and nodded as I shampooed her hair. No longer did we talk about the "newness" of my salon, and that was more than all right with me. I had grown tired of talking about the place, so I couldn't have been happier when clients stopped asking if I was "getting settled" or if I was "going to make it downtown" or if I was "happy with it all." We were back to the clients' hair and their event or disaster of the day, and I liked it.

That day in May, I was finally settled. Vanity Insanity had been up and running for a full year and two months or so. I had a lot of ideas for changes with the bay, but I chose to put any extra money into new equipment and additional employees. What remained—until an unknown future date when I could put money into fixing up the place—was a hodgepodge design. One wall of the bay was brick. The previous renters of the bay had painted the remaining two walls just before their business tanked in what I guess was a last-ditch effort to save it. The owners of Candy Fantasy or Candy Addict or something like that had painted one wall a bright yellow and one wall an obnoxious pink before the last bell had rung for their sweet endeavor. I was stuck with yellow and pink, colors I would have never chosen. Fine for now.

The sinks and counters of the hair stations were black, the cheapest choice I could afford. By the entrance were church pews, anchoring the big door, with their backs toward the windows that climbed from floor to the ceiling. A.C. and I had picked up the pews from Saint Pius X after the parish remodeled the church. Anyone who could load the old pews and take them away could have them for free. A.C. helped me load them on a borrowed truck from Subby Mangiamelli one weekend.

That same weekend A.C. and I had picked up an old desk from the Union Pacific Railroad building downtown. Mac informed me of a similar you-move-it, you-own-it deal, as the UP was getting rid of several floors of old furniture. A.C. and I moved the gigantic, sold, cherrywood desk from the tenth floor of the UP building. The guard on the main floor had felt sorry for us and helped us move the desk as far as the sidewalk before he needed to go back to his guard duty. Once we'd gotten it back to the Old Market, we'd set the desk by the pews near the door.

The desk was definitely my favorite piece, an anchor of integrity that seemed to be floating like a circus balloon in a bubblegum disaster of a room. I kept the appointment book open on the desk at all times next to an old, black rotary phone I'd found at a Goodwill thrift store. The desk served as a receptionist desk, even though I didn't have a receptionist, though Hope liked to think that she was the receptionist on the days that she came in to drop off towels and clean sinks and the back room. She drove Toby crazy when she got to the phone before he did, since she took twice as long to make an appointment. She was slow and cautious on the phone, and some callers could not understand her very well, but I was happy to have her around throughout the week.

Customers could not see the back room, which was really just a big closet that we'd rigged as a break room where Jenae, Toby, and I put our coats and made a coffee station. What the clients did see was a scattered and homey room. Scruffy and comfortable. One of Toby's clients called it "eclectic," kind of a stretch if you asked me. "Unplanned" would have been better, more appropriate. For me, the guy who liked a plan and a sense of order, this room was a great challenge. Out of my comfort zone. A learning opportunity. I was learning to let go a little. I'd become more and more OK with the unplanned look.

Along with saving for more equipment and employees, I was also socking a little bit of money away each month for moving out of the house on Maple Crest Circle, which was getting smaller and smaller, even though

Mom and I were the only ones living there. Cheryl had gotten married right out of high school to a really nice guy that she'd dated her junior and senior year. Tracy, who was always dating older men, was living with two other friends in an apartment. Mom wasn't home much, as she put in full days at Boys Town. She had also met a new "little friend," whom I had met only once or twice, but he seemed to fill any remaining hours. I saw my mom in those years mostly when she came in to have her hair done. Someday I would move out.

As I was styling Lucy's hair, I filled her in on the most recent hires. "You might want to come back and get your nails done, Lucy Ducey. I have two new girls here Monday, Wednesday, Friday. One works every other Saturday."

"You have nail people now? You can afford that?" Lucy knew about my early struggles to get the place together financially. I was only about a year and a half from paying off my loan to Mac.

"Yep. Caroline is really quiet but hardworking, and Kelly's a young Vietnamese woman who's working for her citizenship. Her real name is Hmong Huy Nygen, but she's taken on an American name to feel more American. We all call her Kelly. She's changing her name legally when she passes her citizenship test."

"Ben, I didn't mean to flunk the final…"

"What final?" I took Lucy's apron off and handed her a mirror to look at the back of her hair. "Just tell your parents."

"Oh! Scoop! I almost forgot." Lucy's little scoop updates were entertaining to me since I rarely remembered the people she was scooping to me. Still, she enjoyed keeping me in the loop, or she just enjoyed talking scoop.

"Ellen Richter. Remember her?"

I tilted my head with my eyebrows raised, feigning a serious attempt to recall Ellen What's-It.

"Ellen Richter. She outed Will when he streaked through Marian. She was Miss High and Mighty Better Than Thou. You know. Ellen."

"Oh, Ellen."

"Pregnant. Not married."

"Wow."

"Yeah, wow. She was so pure and judgmental. Right and wrong. And guess what?"

"Pregnancy." I knew the answer this time.

"That's right. Miss Self-Righteous Richter may not have been so pure after all…and, oh! Charlotte. Do you remember Charlotte?"

"Charlotte the Harlot?"

"Yeah…how do you know Charlotte?"

"I don't. I've just heard her name. I thought she was a mythical creature."

"She's real all right. She gives me major gas. She loves to flirt with Tom whenever we run into her. Blond, skinny thing. Anyway, Charlotte went to California for the summer, and she came back with…" Lucy looked at me, dangling her context cue at me like a piece of meat in front of a dog. "Come on. She came back with…"

"Are we playing Password or something?"

"She came back with…"

"The flu? A new dress?"

Lucy gave me her best disappointed look. I tried again. "She came back with Sylvester Stallone?"

"Boobs! She came back with boobs! She got a boob job, Ben."

"That was my next guess. Really." California had more to offer than I'd thought.

I think Lucy felt better as she left my salon that afternoon. I know that she looked good. Before she got to the door leading out to the Old Market, I yelled out to her, "Hey, you just got engaged last night and you already have your 'colors' figured out?"

"I had my colors picked out years ago." Lucy never looked back as she answered.

The truth? Lucy had been planning her wedding since fourth grade, years before Tom Ducey had come to her house to hang out with her brother.

Lucy Ducey.

She was a planner.

# 18

## Lucy's Wedding Saturday

### Saturday, October 12

# 1985

"Nebraska must be the most unexciting of all states. Compared with it, Iowa is paradise."

Bill Bryson claimed this in his book *The Lost Continent*, a book that documents his travels and humorous commentary on places as he sets out to rediscover America in his search for the perfect small town. A.C. had loaned it to me a few years ago.

I think that Mr. Bryson was trying to be funny by playing the "let's make fun of those states that people don't know much about" card. Hilarious. Like people from Nebraska have never heard those jokes. But then Bryson went a little too far when he decided to play the "let's make fun of one state by comparing it to another state that people don't know much about and essentially make fun of two states at once" card. He would have no way of knowing that he'd hit a huge Nebraska nerve, in this native, at least.

The Iowa card in and of itself is a big no-no. People in Nebraska don't like their state being compared to Iowa. We sense a big difference in our states. Sure, a bit of healthy ethnocentricity may account for our strong point of view. Maybe the adults of our youth, grumbling about our neighboring state, had poured some of their state perspective into our minds. Maybe we were all brainwashed to think that the bad drivers in our city were all the people from Iowa who had gotten lost and ended up on this side of the Missouri River. Just look at the license plates. Oh, and while you're at it, figure out that IOWA stands for Idiots out Wandering Around or I Owe the World an Apology. You probably thought it was an Indian word or something.

In time, my friends met or married some really nice people from Iowa, and we realized that Iowa wasn't so bad. Honestly, most of the people from there seem just like us. Sorry, Iowa. We just don't like being told that you're paradise compared to us, that's all. Come to find out, Bill Bryson, who actually made fun of every state in our united fifty in his book, is from Des Moines, Iowa. Go figure.

I'm inclined to believe that Mr. Bryson has never been to Nebraska on a beautiful fall day. Anyway, if Mr. Bryson would like to come back on, say, a beautiful October day in Omaha, I extend the invitation to him wherever he might be right now. He would then probably want to edit that little line in his book. There is nothing, and I repeat, nothing, boring about Nebraska on a fall Saturday.

Huskers, the fall colors, and perfect weather. Oh, and the occasional beer that coats the whole effect as something very much like paradise. Growing up, I looked forward to autumn Saturdays in Nebraska like the kid counting down days to Christmas. With each day of the week, I knew that Saturday was that much closer. Even though Saturday was also the day that brought in the bulk of my business, I still knew that it would be a day to be savored. Without argument, anymore, at least, the people I call employees, and the clients for that matter, knew that the pregame, the game, and programs following the Husker game would be playing on the sound system all Saturday. When the game was televised, I brought a small black-and-white TV from home and set it on the UP desk.

So when Lucy mentioned her little wedding secret back in May, don't think I wasn't already worried about the Husker schedule. Then I remembered that she was marrying Tom Ducey, season ticket holder for decades in his family, who would be the voice of reason in finding the "right" game day on which to wed. Most guys would ask, "Who gets married on a Saturday in the fall in Nebraska?" But rather than be slapped by a woman who couldn't wait to marry the love of her life, Tom found an away game in Stillwater, Oklahoma—Oklahoma State, not Oklahoma—on which to marry. All men, and many women, opened their invitations for Lucy and Tom's wedding, checked the Cornhusker schedule, and sighed, "I guess that will work." That didn't mean that there wouldn't be a few discreet earplugs on an usher or two.

For Lucy's Wedding Saturday, as I called it, I planned ahead. I announced to Jenae, Toby, Caroline, Kelly, and to any Saturday regular clients that October 12 would be a little out of the ordinary. The pregame would still be on all morning, but we would be doing hair and nails of the wedding party and special guests only. And we would be closing early so that everyone could go get ready for the wedding; Lucy had invited the entire Vanity Insanity staff.

Jenae said that she could keep the salon open later for a few other clients and come late to the wedding. In the past, both Toby and Jenae had argued that they were competent and able to open and close for me on occasions that I wasn't able to do so. I offered no argument ever but stood firm in my rule. Only I would open and close Vanity Insanity. Jenae had called me a control freak and a few other things I had never heard before, but I was all right with it all. You could call me Mr. Flexible on most of the issues and policies surrounding my business, but I stood firm: that if this ship stayed afloat or went down, I would be the only captain to answer for it. I had, at a very young age, ventured out on a very risky ocean. I had opened a business in an incredibly fickle and often unkind industry, and I wanted to control that. Call me all the crude names you want.

Lucy's Wedding Saturday began with Lucy, who came in very early, alone and calm. My wedding gift to her was styling her hair and having

Kelly give her a manicure and pedicure. Kelly and I were the first to open the salon. Lucy was waiting for us at the door. I gave her a big cup of coffee and stuffed a danish into her mouth and then went to work. I made sure that I had enough time to make Lucy beautiful and send her out the door before anyone else arrived.

The rest of the morning was very hectic as we serviced Ava Mangiamelli, Tom's mother, Lynn Ducey, all of the bridesmaids, Mrs. Webber, and Hope and Lovey, who were participating in reading and carrying up gifts during Mass. Every person had to ask at least twice, "How was Lucy?" "Is Lucy doing OK?" She wasn't in a terrible accident. She was getting married. I was happy to repeat that she was fine. Toby and Jenae were on their best behavior that day, avoiding squabbles with each other or scenes that might take away from the focus of the day.

Marty came in midmorning with a scowl bigger than Nebraska and Iowa combined. She had flown in from Washington, DC, earlier that week with news that had already made it to Vanity Insanity—Marty had broken up with DC Guy. I guess I should remember his name, but I never met him. I just know that Marty had been expecting an engagement ring from him on her birthday in July. DC had given her a pen set or something. Nothing says "I love you" like a pen set. He had called things off two weeks before Lucy's wedding, and Marty was not handling the news well. By all accounts the breakup was most likely Marty's first failure. Throughout the years, she had gotten everything she tried for—jobs, awards—that erroneously equated to her that if you worked hard, the outcome would always be good. This breakup had been a huge blow to her theory.

If she had asked for my advice, I would have told Marty to quit expecting so much from life. Nothing every matched the great expectations of Martha Mary Monahan. I would have also given her advice on her latest hairstyle. She was wearing her hair in the latest—regrettable—eighties hair fashion: the asymmetrical cut. I think the New York stylist who first came up with the look was hiding under a table somewhere, laughing uncontrollably. Kind of like "The Emperor's New Clothes" of hairstyles. *Let's tell the women who have really short hair on one side of their head and long, poofy hair on the other side that they look great. Isn't it obvious to most of us that your hair is crooked?* I didn't know how to tell her that when she looked back to 1985, DC Guy would not be the only regret. If she had asked my advice, I could have helped on both accounts. But unlike other clients that sat in my chair, Marty never asked for my advice.

Marty would need to keep her chin up that night alongside my buddy, A.C. While Marty had been getting the boot from a guy in Washington, DC, A.C. was putting the final papers on his divorce to Angel in a back drawer somewhere. The marriage to his psycho child bride with a serious drinking problem and enormous intimacy issues did not turn out to be such a heavenly experience in the end. I could have told him that as we'd stood in the courthouse on the cold day eighteen months earlier. The first time I'd met Angel at the courthouse, A.C. was beaming with the beauty of life and love, and Angel was looking at some girl's hat, annoyed that "this thing" was taking so long. A.C. saw her as the person who made him whole and absolute. He really believed this and threw himself completely into the commitment. Nothing I could have said to him at that time in his life would have changed his mind. Frustration floated over that whole day for me as I could see, so clearly, something to which A.C. was oblivious. How could my brilliant and logical friend, who read *War and Peace* and *Atlas Shrugged*—and anything else by Ayn Rand, just for grins—not see that Angel was so unworthy of what he had to offer. I could have tried to stop it, but that would have only damaged our friendship. Now, standing near the debris of A.C.'s disappointment, my role, once again, was to be quiet and supportive. "I told you so" would mean nothing now.

I didn't do A.C.'s hair that day, but he did stop by Vanity Insanity, smiling and talking to all of the ladies, choosing a much-different approach to his heartbreak than Marty, but suffering nonetheless. His latest profound statement: "the devil wears a bra", was always followed by a huge grin.

All morning I had my hands on hair and my eyes on the clock, and by noon, I wondered where Theresa was. She knew that I would be closing early, and I hoped that she would make it in time to have her hair done before pictures. Maybe she was good with her hair on her own.

Fifteen minutes before I was set to lock up, Toby and I were the only two remaining in Vanity Insanity. Toby was sticking around to clean up, but

I knew he was listening to the kickoff on the radio. I was entertained by the fact that I had turned the staff to the light. The Husker Light, that is. Toby, who had never understood the game of football, had finally caught on, due to no choice of his own, and was listening to games and asking me questions that really stupid girls would be embarrassed to ask. He liked football now.

The bell above the door rang as Theresa ran in, looking at the clock and asking, "Am I too late?" Her hair was pulled back in a ponytail, stray pieces coming out here and there. Her eyes were red and puffy.

"Never." I knew we had about a half hour. "Let's get you started over here."

Toby attempted an awkward greeting. His cheeks red, still he was getting better at connecting with clients. He began organizing his station.

"Hey, Toby! Ben, if I'm too late, I totally understand."

"Take a deep breath. We're fine on time. So Marty tells me the dresses are ugly."

"She said that? Was Lucy around?"

"I think her exact words were that the bridesmaids were going to look like several overly frosted cupcakes. Do you care to comment?"

"I can't believe Marty said that. Is she doing OK?"

"Marty's just fine. And no, she didn't really say that. I was trying to make you laugh."

"Ben, Marty is going through a really tough time."

"How about you? You look like your day has been crazy. You all right?"

Theresa's hand held tightly to the arms of the chairs as if she were bracing herself for a crash landing. Toby left without saying good-bye. He did remember to touch the top corners of the doorway, though. The bell above the door rang.

"I do? I mean—I am having a bad day. I really need to regroup before tonight." Theresa's voice cracked.

I walked her over to the sink to shampoo her hair as she continued, "Do you remember my friend Kathryn Bertelli from my speech pathology classes? The one who looked kind of like Jaclyn Smith from *Charlie's Angels*?"

"The one you were always going to set me up with and never did?"

"Sorry about that. That's Kathryn. Well, anyway, she and I have been through four years of classes together. Study buddies and all that. She alone is the reason I made it through statistics…Anyway, she called me from Immanuel Hospital this morning. Actually, she's been calling all week. She calls me up…She asks me to bring wine and cheese to her party…She has all of the guests coming. I have been bringing up wine and cheese all week."

"Must be some party. Does she work at Immanuel?"

Theresa's eyes began to water. "No, she doesn't work there…She's in the psych ward. When I get to her room she tells me to shut the door… that no one there can know about the party."

"How can you have a party if no one knows?"

"Ben, Kathryn is under evaluation for schizophrenia. She tells me every time I go to visit her that the people who work in the hospital are all spies. Never to trust them. The others. They won't support it. They don't understand it. They will never understand it…"

"Wow."

"The last year in school, she got a little strange when we studied. We would meet in her basement where she felt safe…I never thought about it at the time. I mean, Kathryn! She's brilliant. She's beautiful, and right now, she lives in fear of the posse that's listening to her wine-and-cheese-party plans through the vents of her room. It's so sad."

"You keep bringing wine and cheese to her?"

"Yeah, the staff knows. They monitor and know that she's safe. All of the wine is under her bed. The cheese is collected when she's sleeping. Why? Why would God allow such a brilliant…? I shouldn't say that. I just don't get it. She had goals. She had dreams. Now she'll live a completely different life. It won't be a bad life. It just won't be the life she set out to live. It almost makes me feel guilty for having such a great life."

"You should never feel guilty about that, Theresa." I didn't know what else to say. I was wondering the same thing.

As I was drying Theresa's hair, she looked at her watch. "Oh my gosh! I can't be late for pictures!"

"Almost done. I can fix anything you need when we get to the church."

As I was curling the last section of her hair, Theresa looked at me in the mirror and smiled. Her first smile. "No, I shouldn't."

"Shouldn't what?"

"I really shouldn't tell you."

"Tell me what?"

"If I tell you, I'll have to kill you." Theresa laughed and looked at the clock on my wall.

"Then by all means…"

"Ben, I'm getting married, but you can't tell a soul."

"You gotta be kidding me."

"Seriously, Ben. No one knows."

I shook her hand and then gave her a hug. "Congrats! Uh, when's the big day?"

"Oh, heck, I don't know. Michael asked me a few weeks ago, but we both agreed that I would wait to wear the ring and tell people till after Lucy's wedding. This is her time." Theresa looked in the mirror and shook her hair. "Thanks, Ben. It looks great!"

"I'll see you at Creighton."

"Oh, and don't tell Marty. I don't know when I'll tell Marty. Just don't tell a soul."

"I'm pretty good at that."

Theresa grabbed her purse and headed toward the door when she stopped. "I almost forgot. Happy birthday, Ben!" She shuffled through her purse for something. Her eyes were no longer red.

"Technically, it's not my birthday. I celebrated a few days ago."

"I know. Lucy told me. Did you know that you were born on the Feast of the Most Holy Rosary of the Blessed Virgin Mary?"

"I'd have to say that I did not know that."

"I'm pretty sure that you already have several, but I got this for you at the Immanuel Hospital gift shop. It was either white or black. I got black since it seemed more manly."

"I am pretty manly."

Theresa laughed as she handed me the gift-shop bag with the rosary in it.

"I think I had a glow-in-the- dark rosary that some nun handed out in CCD, but I'm sure I lost it along the way. Thanks." I took the rosary out of the bag.

"Happy birthday. See you at the church, Ben."

I handed Theresa a stale, crusty danish as she left Vanity Insanity. I yelled to her as she walked to her car, "I'll keep your secret if you don't tell anyone about my birthday. Fair?" Theresa gave me a thumbs-up as she ducked into her white Subaru Justy with the danish in her mouth and then took off.

I knew I was running late, but I took my time as I ran through my closing ritual. If Toby could have his rituals, so could I. I made sure that curling irons and hot irons of any type were unplugged. I unplugged everything in the break room: hot pot, coffee pot, and microwave. I kept the small fridge plugged in and grabbed all of the towels that had been used that day to take home in a big white laundry bag. Toby had already taken the trash out to the alley. I unlocked the only locked drawer of the UP desk and pulled out a bag holding checks and cash for the day. I knew that I needed to get to the church for pictures before the wedding, so I planned to take the bag home and get to the bank on Monday. As I placed the last few checks in the black bag, I noticed a small piece of paper on the corner of the desk. The note was scribbled in Jenae's handwriting.

*Ben, Octavia called. Wondered if she could use Lucy's wedding flowers for a funeral Monday. Some poor guy died.*
*—Jenae*

I smiled as I put the note and my new rosary in my pocket. Isn't every guy who dies a poor guy? Even though Octavia didn't know Lucy, she knew that I had a friend and client named Lucy who was getting married. When people in Octavia's parish could not afford a proper funeral, she saw to it that they were given the most decent of send-offs. Of course, Lucy would say yes to my request. Of course, neither woman would see this logical act as amusing and almost morbid. I took one last look around the room, grabbed the laundry and bank bags, and turned off the light. I locked the door to Vanity Insanity and ran to my car in the parking lot.

I was about a half hour late to pictures, but no one noticed. I was just an usher. I found a group of bridesmaids gathered at the altar with Lucy anchoring them as the haggard photographer attempted to organize another shot. Lucy looked radiant and happier than she had ever looked. Meteorology was light-years in the past. She waved to me. This little West Omaha girl was marrying her good old South Omaha boy, and she looked pretty excited about the whole thing. During one of the many haircuts I had given Tom Ducey, he'd told me that South Omaha girls he knew thought that Lucy and her friends were fluffy, whatever that meant. West O girls laughed too much. Their hair was too big. Tom took no issue with the fluffy factor. He was going to marry Lucy no matter what.

Ava Mangiamelli, Lucy's mom, appeared from nowhere and directed me to the side of Saint John's Church nestled on the campus of Creighton University. As she pushed me out the door, Ava fussed, "Tom must not see Lucy until the wedding. Now go on, Mr. Keller."

I walked out on the grassy area to the side of the church and found a gaggle of black tuxedos, waddling around like confused penguins. Tom knew almost every guy in South Omaha, every student in the Creighton Law School, every boy who grew up on Maple Crest Circle, including all of his soon-to-be brothers-in-law. How do you decide whom to have in your wedding? Evidently, you ask them all. A different photographer was directing the penguins to stand in a long line. He signaled to me to head to the back of the line. The photographer grinned and yelled to the group, "Now you all need to show an expression of complete horror on your faces as you look at Tom!" I didn't think the picture was funny, but I joined in. Lucy would get a kick out of this one.

I'm not a big wedding guy, but I figured that Lucy had made sure that she included every little wedding gimmick she had dreamed of her whole life. Once Lucy headed down the aisle, the other ushers and I remained in the back of the church for the rest of the wedding. Just as with the merry Mary procession, I heard the wedding was perfect. My informants told me so. The plan with the ushers was to take turns listening to the Husker game on the smaller radio I'd brought with earplugs. The usher on Husker duty would report any big plays to the other ushers.

Music, ring bearers, of course colors, and whatever else there is at a wedding—everything was perfect and normal as a wedding should be, with the exception that Lucy had two maids of honor: Theresa and Marty. She argued that there was no way in the world that she could choose one over the other. Tom went with one best man, so Tom's childhood best friend, Buddy, escorted Marty and Theresa down the aisle with one very cheesy expression on his face.

What I remember most about Lucy and Tom's wedding in 1985 was not the wedding but the reception. Following the ceremony at Saint John's on Creighton University's campus, the wedding party and guests caravaned twenty minutes south on Ollie the Trolley to Sokol Hall, in the heart of South Omaha. South Omaha has been called the Ellis Island of Omaha, a pool into which poured many different cultures and communities that built small churches on every corner—across from a family-owned bar. The Italian, Hispanic, Czech, and Polish cultures found their niches and stayed there for many generations. Remember the staunch Czechs at Assumption Catholic Church? Grandpa Mac remembers them, having grown up with them. Sokol Hall was situated in South Omaha's Bohemian neighborhood, just south of downtown.

The reception decision was probably the best that Lucy and Tom had made among the million wedding decisions: an old dance hall, which included a stage and dance floor. Instead of a DJ for the dance, which most weddings I went to had that year, Tom and Lucy picked a band. Not a rock band. A big-band band. No top-ten crap from the eighties would be played. The Fred Waring–type band played music, sprinkled heavily with polkas. No, I repeat no, *no* dumb songs were allowed in Sokol Hall that night. Songs like "We Built This City," "Take on Me," and "We Are the World" had to find another hall that night.

Following dinner and toasts, the wedding party gathered on the floor for the opening dance between Tom and Lucy. A loud, hornlike alarm sounded, and everyone moved in slow-motion unison toward the door. The fire alarm had not been on any of Lucy's lists of things to do. I followed Subby and Anthony out to the parking lot; each Mangiamelli brother held a beer as we waited for the drill to end.

"Probably Charlotte the Harlot pulled the alarm," Subby mumbled under his breath.

"She wasn't even invited," Anthony said as the two fire trucks and several police cars drove up near the hall on a fall night that was cooling down as we stood together.

"My money is still on 'er, though," Subby said as he lit a cigarette.

Lucy would not allow anything to ruin her perfect evening, so she dragged her new husband onto the fire truck with a photographer close behind, who took several shots of the freshly married couple, until the fire marshal gave us all the approval to return to Sokol Hall following a false alarm. As I was heading back to the hall, I felt a tug on the back of my tuxedo.

I turned around to see Faith Webber, looking more beautiful than ever. Her long, dark hair was pulled back and up. Her black evening dress paired with a string of pearls made the blue of her eyes glow in the fading daylight. I had not seen her at the wedding.

"Ben, you look great in a tux."

I don't remember Faith ever saying my name.

"And you are the classiest-looking world traveler I have ever seen, Faith. Where are you now? Germany? Japan? Been trying to keep up." My beer confidence was throwing out phrases I would never have used.

"Really? You've been tracking me?"

"Well, not in a stalker way at all…Really, Hope gives me updates."

"I'm in Australia now. Loving it, but I had to make it back for Lucy's wedding."

The fire marshal was yelling at the people who would not return to the building. Faith grabbed my arm.

"Ben, do you realize that you owe me something?"

The woman I'd had a lifelong crush on was telling me I owed her something. Wow. Whatever I owed her, I was heading to the bank for a loan if I needed one. I tried to think about what I owed Faith Webber while most of the crowd moved back into the building. A favor? A haircut? Money? Maybe I really owed her money.

"I do?" I pulled out my wallet, attempting to look entertaining. "How much do I owe you?"

Faith put her hand on my shoulder, stood on her toes, and kissed me. I was rattled by the sneak attack, but it took me exactly a fifth of a second to kiss her back. We kissed for a long time—a really long time—even after the fire trucks pulled away.

Faith laughed as she came down from her tiptoes and pulled away to look at me. "Do you know why you owed me that kiss?"

"It doesn't really matter. I believe you."

"Spin the bottle? Under the branches of Satch on Maple Crest? Is it coming back to you?"

I shook my head and smiled. I hadn't thought about the gigantic tree in years. I'm sure it was still protecting animals and lost toys from our childhood. I remembered the day under the tree when I'd been mesmerized by Faith. I couldn't remember at the time who'd dared me to kiss her.

"I saved you, Ben. The look on your face told me that you weren't ready to handle the dare that day."

"I handled it pretty well tonight," I defended myself.

Faith and I walked back into the reception, her hand holding mine. Not a date, but we hung out the rest of the evening. By the end of the night, everyone looked overheated and happy, dancing every dance, eating and drinking plenty. At one point, I remember seeing Tom Ducey talking to one of the band members and moments later taking a microphone out in front of the band. In 1985, Tom's beer belly had made a debut, and though he still had plenty of hair, his hairline was starting to creep, slightly but noticeably, back onto his head. On the stage that night, he held the microphone and a cigarette in one hand and a plastic cup filled with beer in the other. Tom Ducey, sweat dripping from both sides of his face, shirt untucked, jacket and bow tie long gone, smiled the most awesome grin as the band stopped playing.

"Hey!" he said as he looked through the crowd, looking for his little vanilla-frosted cupcake. He spotted Lucy talking to a group of guests at a table. He nodded to the band, and they began music to a song that I've never heard until that night but have never forgotten since that day.

In a voice that swooned like the great ones, Tom Ducey belted out a spectacular rendition of Bobby Darin's song "More." The crowd took note of the singer on stage and started laughing when Lucy glanced up to see Tom point at her with his beer in hand.

This guy must have really loved this girl. He'd married her on a football Saturday during his final year of law school because that was what she wanted. He'd followed all of her plans and then, knowing exactly who Lucy was, topped her perfectly planned day with something that every woman in the hall that night secretly wished would happen to her. Little Miss Perfect Planner had had her hands on every decision that day except this one, and the surprise bought her hands to her cheeks and tears to her eyes. Tom had surpassed her plans and dreams of the perfect wedding.

The older guests liked the performance as they smiled at singing groom, and the crowd starting swaying at that moment. In between lyrics, Tom shouted out, "This is all about you, Lucy Ducey!" I looked around the faces in the room and found Marty, smiling with all her might. A.C. wasn't far behind her, clapping with the group, a serene look on his face. For anyone enduring a broken heart, a wedding would have to be a huge bummer. I think the temptation would be to oscillate between wanting to cry out loud for your lost love and laugh out loud in mockery of what you doubted could ever be real. A.C. and Marty did their best, hanging on the edge of faith—faith in love, faith in believing that goodness prevails when you feel so rotten.

Theresa caught my eye as she leaned against Michael, the two watching Tom sing. She put her finger to her lips in the international sign for "remember the secret." I could see that the night had temporarily allowed Theresa to forget about her friend Kathryn, who would probably never have an evening like Lucy was having.

I swear Tom held that last note for over a minute as the crowd cheered. He then quickly chugged his beer, watching Lucy come toward him from across the room. As Lucy Ducey hugged her husband, I felt Faith's hand on my arm. I looked at Faith as she watched Lucy and Tom and wondered if tomorrow I would find this unusual connection had been only a dream.

Later that night, as I put my hands into my pocket for a bartender tip, I felt the rosary beads and Jenae's note about Octavia's request. I had taken everything out of my work pants and put it into my tux pockets before heading to the church. I needed to connect with Lucy about her flowers before she took off that October night in 1985.

**

In Omaha in 1985, my clients were talking about Enron, a result of Houston Natural Gas merging with InterNorth, which had brought many job opportunities for Omaha. In the same breath, Warren Buffett predicted that recent gains in the market would not be sustainable; he knew his stuff, as a stock-market crash was less than two years away. The Huskers finished the game that evening with a 34–24 win against Oklahoma State. We ended up being ranked 11th after the bowl games. Sting released *The Dream of the Blue Turtles*, his first solo album only a year after the Police had unofficially broken up.

While the Huskers, Sting, and Buffett were busy, Lucy Mangiamelli of Omaha, Nebraska, became Lucy Ducey. Her bridesmaids' dresses did not look like overly frosted cupcakes. Faith Webber promised to send me postcards through her world tour. A young and beautiful woman planned an imaginary wine-and-cheese party in a psych unit, and Ben Keller received his first rosary gift, bringing his rosary collection to a total of one.

The next Monday, some poor guy would have the send-off of all send-offs at Saint Patrick's church with Lucy's wedding roses all around.

Oh, and in 1985, author Bill Bryson received an invitation to Omaha on a beautiful fall day.

Anytime, buddy, anytime.

# 19

## Mac: Just a Trim

## Saturday, November 21

# 1987

When Grandpa Mac stepped into my place in the Old Market that Saturday in 1987, he looked the entire room over with a smile, nodding his head the whole time. Mom had continued cutting his hair at home the past few years, where he claimed that he felt a little more comfortable. He would always ask me how the new place was, but he took his time making his way downtown for a haircut. I had just recently paid off my loan to him—surprising myself and everyone who knew how quickly I was able to do so—which must have prompted him to make a trip to the no-longer-new place and take a look at the business enterprise that I had made work.

The staff hustled around him setting up for the day as Mac walked in and placed his hand on the old Union Pacific desk. George Michael's voice sang about "Faith" over the sound system. Mac ran his hand slowly along the side of the wood and said, "Ben, you did it. You really did it."

More nodding as he walked to the pink chair that he recognized from Mom's shop. Of course, Mac would be positive. That's how he always was. I looked into his eyes as he looked at the high brick wall, hoping to grasp the heart of his response.

"You're a real fine worker, Ben. Marcia told me the place looked great, but oh…you did a fine job." Mac sat in the chair as I placed the apron around him and tried to make mirror direct eye contact with him.

What Mac thought of Vanity Insanity meant a lot to me. My whole life, I had gone to him for advice on problems and plans. His wisdom and patience had been my anchor. I remember as a kid going with my mother and sisters to his retirement luncheon down at the Union Pacific. I sat right next to him, and he introduced me to everyone as Ben. Just Ben. Not as grandson. I pretended that I was his son, that he was my father. I savored that whole afternoon.

I needed to know what Mac really thought of the place.

"But what?" I asked, not in defense but with curiosity.

"But what? I didn't say 'but.'" Mac looked at me in the mirror with his cool, blue eyes edged with deep, well-earned smile lines.

"No, but I know you, Mac. But what?"

Mac paused and then grinned and shook his head. "The name, Ben. I just don't get it. What does Vanity Insanity mean? What's wrong with Ben's? That's what a guy called a barbershop when I was growing up. I always knew what Frankie's meant? I just…"

I started laughing before he could finish. Mac wasn't judging me for being a man owning a salon. He wasn't wondering why I'd opened up a business that focused on people's looks every day. He just didn't get the name. Vanity Insanity.

"Crazy, isn't it? I guess because it's not a barbershop. I have to give A.C. the credit or blame here. He came up with the name. I couldn't think of anything catchy…and I guess that's what works in this business. Something catchy. It's A.C.'s fault." I smiled at Mac in the mirror as I picked up a comb and sheers.

"A.C.'s fault. I could see that…" Mac grinned.

"Kind of a gimmick. A name just has to stand out when you're competing with a town filled with a bunch of other places where you could run in and get a haircut. If you think about it, people spend an awful lot of the waking day thinking about their hair...It's kind of crazy...Get it now?"

"Sounds like you have it figured out. It works for me if it works for you. I still like Ben's better." He winked. "So how are A.C. and the kids from the old neighborhood? You ever see any of them?"

I walked to the back room to turn on the Husker pregame program on the radio. "Mostly A.C., Lucy, Hope, and a few others who come in for appointments. You ready for the game, Mac? I don't know why, but I think we're gonna thump Oklahoma today."

Oklahoma was not a rival to the Huskers in the eighties. Oklahoma was *the* rival. If a Husker Saturday felt like Christmas to me, then a victory against Oklahoma felt like the Christmas that you got the exact red bike you had asked for. We loved beating Oklahoma.

Lucy had a cousin—Sissy or Cici or something like that—who sometimes visited from Cincinnati. That Ohio girl would always say that she liked visiting us all here in Oklahoma. Four kids on Maple Crest would correct her at once.

"Nebraska! Not Oklahoma!"

"Omaha sounds like Oklahoma. What's the difference? Your states all blend together to me."

"Big difference! Those are fightin' words, lady," Stinky Morrow scolded her. "*They* are the Oklahoma Sooners. *We* are the Nebraska Huskers. You better write that down."

"Nebraska Oscars? What's an oscar?"

OK, Nebraskans don't like to be compared to the state of Iowa, but we really hate to be confused with Oklahoma. No one ever really liked Cincinnati Cici.

In the world of sports, the Huskers were all we had, and thank God for that. We had no professional teams, so when our football team put Nebraska on the map in the seventies, we just assumed that the rest of the world was as impressed with us as we were with our state. All of those people from the big-time states could at least comment on something besides corn when Nebraska came up in a conversation—at least, we hoped.

And as our fight song boasted "There is no place like Nebraska," an entire state of fans could give you at least a hundred reasons why. We would tell you that we've had consecutive sellouts since 1962. We could tell you how many years we had without a losing season. We would mention the number of Academic All Conference players that came out of NU. Just ask us.

We don't like to air our dirty laundry, but if people must know, we haven't always been the most unified state. At one time, our state was extremely divided. Since most of the industry and population of Nebraska is in Omaha, the western part of the state held a great deal of resentment toward Omaha for the power in government and agendas throughout the early years of our statehood. Stories float around the state of how a group of officials in the late eighteen hundreds sneaked into Omaha and stole the capital, or the papers that went with the title, right out from under Omaha's sleeping nose. Lincoln, known as Lancaster in its younger years, denied it but agrees that they fought for the title in the early years of the state since Omaha had the river and Union Pacific Railroad, and a few "you can't have it alls" were thrown our way. At least Mrs. Foster, my fourth-grade history teacher, had told us this story during the Nebraska history unit. She said that the Republican Omaha said, "OK, have the capital, but you Democrats have to change your name to Lincoln." The newly named Lincoln was so excited that the growing community ignored the fact that their now-capital town was named after the famous Republican president.

So when the Husker football team started to do well, the state came together, at least on game-day Saturdays with our common bond, and we really liked to talk about the Huskers. On a home-game Saturday, Memorial Stadium in Lincoln, Nebraska, is the third-largest city in the state.

"I'm not sure about the game today," Mac replied. "We've got our work cut out for us. Nice touch, though. Playing the games for your clients." Mac looked around and stopped. "What about William? Do you ever see the one Mangiamelli boy you spent your summers with? That old Will. He never met a mirror he didn't like."

"Not so much. Will kind of went his own way. He was supposed to go with A.C. and me to Chicago last summer. We all had tickets to see a band we follow. We planned the trip for weeks, and the day we left for Chicago, he never showed up." Too bad for Will. He missed the last concert that The Police had before they split up in 1986.

"Sounds like he has some problems in his life right now." Mac's way of saying that he had heard about Will's struggles with alcohol and drugs. He changed the subject.

"Turn up the volume, Ben, could you?"

As I turned up the volume, Jenae burst into the salon like the spray from a shook-up Pepsi bottle. Definitely on an "up" day, she squealed at the sound of the announcer's voice. "Oh, game day! I just love game day!"

Jenae's tight, black minidress with short, black boots and high, skinny heels needed no spotlights. All eyes in the salon zeroed in on her fishnet stockings. Jenae had pulled her hair—now dyed black—back as tightly as she could. A big, red N was painted on her left cheek. Her red, bold lips brought the whole look into one Robert Palmer video. Jenae stopped and looked at Mac.

"I'm wearing my 'Blackshirt' outfit. The guys on defense are so cute." She winked at Mac.

"Jenae, this is my grandfather. Mac, this is Jenae."

Mac's eyes were large and round as he held out his hand.

"Oh, my gawd! Ben has a grandfather! Well, Mac, you have a really cool grandson. We just love Ben!" Jenae skirted around to stand in front of Mac.

Mac cocked his head to one side as Jenae shook his hand. "Ben is pretty cool. We think so, too, Janelle."

"Jenae," she corrected him. "But that's OK, I answer to anything."

"Jenae," Mac corrected himself. "You look lovely for the Husker game."

Jenae shrank back at the compliment. "You really think so? I thought that the stockings might be a little too edgy. I thought twice and then said, 'You know, the stockings really finish off the look.' Don't you think?"

"I think you look very pretty." Mac smiled. "Are you going somewhere special all dressed up?"

"No, I'm just here to do hair."

Mac hadn't considered that Jenae was an employee. I could see that he was working really hard to take it all in when the bell above the door announced Toby, Caroline, and Kelly, who all hurried in to set up for our big Saturday. Toby touched both top corners of the doorway and shut the door, rubbing the doorknob three times—a new little something he had added recently—and he worked hard to avoid the staff chatter so he could focus on setting up his station.

"Hey, guys, come meet Ben's grandpa. He's adorable!" Jenae called.

Mac sat in my chair as the staff surrounded him like he was a puppy to be pet and admired.

"I didn't know Ben had a grandpa," Kelly commented as I motioned them all back to their stations. Throughout the haircut, Jenae flirted with Mac and babbled to him as she worked on her own client's hair, and Mac pretended to pay attention while he listened to the pregame commentary. I wheeled a cart with an old television from the break room out to the front area once the game started.

Mac stayed to watch the first half of the game after I finished his hair and started working on my next client. He pulled up the chair from the UP desk. I caught him a few times looking around and taking in the whole room. His eyes stopped on Toby occasionally with a "what the hell is going on there" expression on his face.

At half time Mac gave me a firm handshake and said his good-byes to the staff.

Jenae ran up and hugged him before he left.

"I'm having a Broken Berlin Wall Party later tonight. We might go see *Dirty Dancing* again. I've seen it three times. Have you seen it? You should come. We'd have fun."

"I'm sure we would, Jenae, but I'm going to have to decline. Old people don't stay out that late." The bell rang as Mac walked out of Vanity Insanity.

My gut feeling was way off regarding the game. Seven to seventeen, final score. Our only loss of the season if you didn't count the bowl game.

The disappointment felt worse than the stomach flu on Christmas morning. Lucy's cousin in Cincinnati probably watched the news that night and thought her cousins' team had won.

Mac returned every few weeks to Vanity Insanity for his haircuts. He would adjust. He might not have understood the name of my new place before he walked in that Saturday, but he got it by the time he walked out.

# 20

## Octavia: Wash and Set for Holiday Shopping

### Friday, December 18

# 1989

At first I was elated, and then I was deflated.

Going through the mail that cold morning in 1989, I found a letter from Faith, a Christmas card I presumed, since most of the other correspondence from her came in the form of postcards from her worldly travels. Faith moved around so much that I couldn't even send her a card or Omaha Steaks for Christmas since she would likely be moved by the time they were delivered. I opened the UP drawer to get my letter opener for the card, and I was surprised by my own excitement in hearing from her. Was she going to be more personal this time? Would she let me know that she missed me, couldn't live without me, and would be coming to Omaha for Christmas? Maybe she'd been thinking about that long kiss as much as I had. I opened the red envelope to find a UNICEF Christmas card cover, which I quickly opened.

*To see the sacred in the season, we must slow down. We wish you a Merry Christmas from the UNICEF team.*

In Faith's handwriting beneath the form-letter Christmas card were the words *Thinking of you! Faith.*

Thinking of you? "Thinking of you" was something I wrote at the bottom of a sympathy card. Just what did Faith think of me? I had no way of saying to her, "Thinking of you…more than I should." I was disappointed in my overexcitement about Faith. I had always been good about managing expectations, and I knew I'd better start making adjustments to my feelings about her. I needed to compartmentalize that kiss and move on to the new year. I decided to look over my schedule for the day and was happy to see that both Octavia and Lucy were appointments that I could look forward to.

The bell above the door interrupted my pity party as Jenae used her hip to push it open. She was carrying an oversized stuffed snowman and a bag with Christmas silver tinsel spilling out. Exactly two minutes after the Thanksgiving turkey bones were thrown in the trash, Jenae became obsessed with the next big holiday on the calendar. She set down her snowman and took off her coat. "Don't you just love him? I think his name should be Jimmy. I don't know. He just looks like a Jimmy." She had on green tights with red boots and a little pixie dress that looked as though it had been painted on her. Not that that was a bad thing. Toby mumbled something about a Keebler elf. Jenae told Toby exactly where he could shove his little cracker comment.

Jenae refused to allow Toby's annoying remark to dampen her holiday spirit as she adjusted her headband, which supported two pieces of mistletoe shooting out from her head like alien antennae moving back and forth. Jenae "fixed" the decorations of Vanity Insanity all day between shampoos and highlights.

A few weeks earlier, Jenae had started working on setting up Christmas and stayed well past closing without any intimation of slowing down or quitting.

"I need to get to the store before I head home," I told Jenae as I began unplugging all of the equipment. "We need to wrap this up, Toots."

"I'm just starting. I'm picking up the tree tomorrow morning."

"Tree?"

"You can't have Christmas without a tree. Oh, and the glow-in-the-dark nativity scene is going to have to sit on the UP desk next to the wall. That's the only place that makes sense…"

"If all of your decorations are here, what are you doing in your apartment?"

"Painting."

"Painting?"

"I stayed up all last night painting. I got through most of the place. I have one more room to do tonight."

"Your apartment complex allows you to paint?"

"Oh, I don't know. I guess I should have looked into that…Anyway, it looks awesome."

Of course, the thought of drugs did cross my mind as I wondered about the source of energy that Jenae had tapped into during her hyper holiday, but she was a walking antidrug announcement. She had mentioned to me that she had suffered through trying to help her brother break a serious cocaine addiction, unsuccessfully.

I was the picture of patience as Jenae's plan took over the salon for a month, but I drew the line when she started taking over the music selection and insisted that we play her Bing Crosby Christmas tape over and over again, which threw Toby into such a funk that he cleaned out all of the cabinets and closet and reorganized the display case in the front window. Even quiet and kind Kelly had enough as she pulled me aside and, in her best broken English, voiced her frustration.

"I know all de words to this tape. I don't want to know all de words to this tape. 'Mele Kalikimaka' no more."

As leader of the crew, I had a responsibility to maintain the sanity of the season. I informed Jenae that from now on, I was the only person in charge of the music; that way the staff would not squabble. This was not the first staff argument over music. The summer before Jenae had tried to convince everyone that customers would receive a growth opportunity if they were exposed to Guns and Roses' "Welcome to the Jungle." Cultural growth and a hairstyle for the patrons. Caroline politely told Jenae that one of her manicure customers had been offended by Def Leppard's "Pour Some Sugar on Me" and that we should consider playing music without sexual implications. Toby thought we should just skip the music thing all together and focus on our work.

So we tried the stipulation route when it came to the music selection of the day. No naughty words allowed. We even tried a schedule of the Music Monitor of the day. That Christmas of 1989 was the tipping point for trying to please the whole staff. If Jenae thought I was a control freak about opening and closing the salon, then she probably felt that I was a power freak when I took over the music completely that Christmas season.

I played some Christmas music during the days until December 25, but I gave old Bing a break. I introduced the staff to Mannheim Steamroller, a local group that took Christmas music to an entirely different level, and we pulled out some Nat King Cole. I wove in a few non-Christmas tapes I'd brought from home. Sting's *Nothing Like the Sun* became a staff favorite.

As I set the bills aside on the UP desk, I looked up to see Octavia enter Vanity Insanity. "Well, you do look ready for Christmas," she said as she took in the room that looked like a page in a Dr. Seuss book. Jenae, who had taken it upon herself to be the holiday decorator, had brought all of her outdated decorations and encouraged the staff to join her in the trashy Christmas tradition. Caroline brought in an ugly wreath, and Toby brought a bright-green garland that he had been planning on throwing out anyway. Kelly brought in a string of blue lights, and I brought in a giant, plastic Santa impersonating Elvis that I had found at a thrift store. If we were going tacky, we would take it to the extreme.

"Actually, Jenae is responsible. I just own the place."

Octavia's son had dropped her off for her regular Friday-morning appointment that snowy morning in 1989 as he had for the last several weeks. I never asked but figured that Truman felt the time had come for Octavia to stop driving. There are just some things you don't talk about. When I did my calculations, Octavia was in her mid to upper eighties. I never asked that question either.

"This is the life, I tell you." Octavia walked into Vanity Insanity like a queen. "It doesn't get any better than this. I have my own chauffeur. Truman knows how much I hate looking for parking downtown."

"You're living the life, woman." I helped Octavia take her coat off of her shivering, small frame. She hooked her hand into the crook of my arm as I escorted her to my chair. Octavia's booming personality, so big and strong, and blazing opinions, so sharp and current, caused me to overlook just how delicate she was physically.

Octavia had moved into Omaha in 1987, and while she held tightly to her hometown Fremont ties, she embraced the city life with fire and enthusiasm. She bought a big house two blocks from Saint Cecilia's Cathedral, one of the ten biggest churches in the country at the time of its completion in 1959. She made it a point to get involved with her new parish and the altar society as soon as her little pumps hit the doorway of Saint Cecilia's floor. The Cathedral community probably didn't know what hit them when Octavia Hruska filled out forms to join the forces.

Once Octavia had found her bearings in the local restaurants, boutiques, and museums, she began investing more time and money in the missions of the city. Following her first visit to my new place, she spent the entire afternoon drinking in the Old Market area. M's Pub, with its mirrored back wall and a large green marbled bar that anchors the center of the room with stools surrounding it, became a favorite of Octavia. In time, the owners of M's found a favorite in Octavia as they reserved a special table for her on the days that she visited.

My mom told me that a friend of hers knew the lawyer who had handled an investment Octavia had made in one block of the Old Market. That little rumor was also making its way through the Market grapevine, and vendors wanted to know who this Hruska lady was.

The Old Market had seen big changes just to the east of the area in 1988. The city planners who had once talked about Omaha as a dying city in 1981 had decided to give one last effort to revive the fading metropolis. ConAgra was the company that gave mouth-to-mouth resuscitation to the downtown area and succeeded in "saving the city." The jobs and continued growth of the headquarters on the 113-acre ConAgra campus jump-started the economy and encouraged other big businesses to take a look at Omaha as a place to set up.

Not everyone was happy with expansion in what was the once-bustling historic area called Jobbers Canyon, however. The historic site was nationally recognized, and conservatives were appalled that anyone would consider demolishing the area that ConAgra took over. Omaha did not want to let go of the area and had been about to break up with the company when Octavia jumped on the bandwagon. She and her money joined the force that planned to keep downtown Omaha economically alive. In the newspaper picture of the task force to bring in ConAgra, she was the little lady standing in a group of men. Octavia had told me, "What Omaha needs to realize is that change is always uncomfortable. In order to grow, we are going to have to suffer a little." And in the next breath, she threw up her hands and sighed, "Get over it!"

The city planners, who had for years listened to the voices that resisted change, decided to go ahead with what they knew would benefit Omaha. Much like the parent who knows that the nasty-tasting medicine will only help the child, the city planners had demolished the area earlier that year. In the end, ConAgra built a billion-dollar campus that included the city's Heartland of America Park, transforming the Omaha skyline.

In the years that followed, Octavia's Friday mornings were a picture of predictability. A neighbor took her to 6:30 a.m. Mass at Saint Cecilia's Cathedral, as she did every morning, and then Truman worked his schedule at TC Property Investments so that he could pick her up and get her downtown to Vanity Insanity for her hair appointment with me. Truman would then conduct business downtown until Octavia's hair appointment and lunch appointment with a friend were over. She was probably right. Octavia was living the good life.

"Once I get my shopping done, I'll feel better," Octavia told me.

"Now don't be telling me what you got me, Octavia. I don't want to know."

Octavia chuckled and went on. "The big thing on the list this year is a Cry-Like-a-Baby Doll. Have you even heard of such a thing? My granddaughter Sara has a star next to the doll on her list. I can't find one anywhere. Seems like companies have to make a damn game of it for the consumer to find the toy. And then the doll costs an arm and a leg."

"Why don't you just get her any doll? Do you think she'll know the difference?"

"Are you kidding me? She pulled out a picture from the Sears catalog and pasted it on a piece of paper for me. The doll cries and then says what she's not happy about..."

Truman's eight-year-old Sara sounded as precocious and demanding as her grandmother.

"Sara reminds me of Truman when he was about that age," Octavia continued. "The only thing he wanted for Christmas was a Tudor Electric Football Game. Made of metal or something. That was all he wanted. Nothing else. We searched everywhere for that thing and finally had to order it. Shipped to our house Christmas Eve morning. I almost kissed the deliveryman.

"Anyway, Truman loved the game and played it all of the time. Then, halfway through the YMCA flag football season the following year, he came home crying and crying. He was mad that I hadn't signed him up to play. Of course, I didn't sign him up. He never asked. He told me that he thought I would know that he wanted to play. I told him I needed to hear him ask. Sometimes we need to ask for what we want...We signed him up the next season..." Octavia drifted off in thought.

Kelly hesitated to interrupt. "Ben, you have a phone call."

"I'll be right back, Octavia. We'll let your hair dry a little more."

When I got to the phone, Kelly said, "Ben, it's Lucy. She doesn't sound too good."

I dried my hands and grabbed the phone. "Hey, Lu, gonna be late?"

"Ben, I've never been so sick...throwing up all morning. I'm not even going to our Christmas party."

"You OK?"

"I'm pregnant."

Lucy had wanted to be a mother for as long as I could remember. The years of baby-sitting and watching over neighbor kids had prepared her for this day.

"Go lie down, Lu. We can reschedule when you feel better."

When I turned to Octavia, the chair was empty. She was heading to the coat rack and getting ready to leave.

"Hey wait a second, Octavia. I refuse to let you out in the cold until your hair is dry and done. Go sit back down."

"Are you bossing me around?" Octavia forced a confused smile.

"Yes, I am."

"All right then. You're the only one I let boss me around. I do have to watch my time here. I'm meeting a friend for lunch at M's Pub. They treat me like a queen over there. My friend Sylvia was an orphan on the orphan trains that went through Nebraska from New York. It's really a fascinating story."

"Hello, Octavia. I introduced you to Sylvia. Remember, I told her story, and you were so interested you wanted to meet her. I do her hair every Thursday. Remember?"

"Well, I'll be."

Nat King Cole sang of Jack Frost nipping at the door as I finished Octavia's hair. When she was patting the back of it, I grabbed a bag from the side of my hair station and handed it to her.

"I know it's not wrapped or anything, but this is my gift for you."

Octavia opened the bag and pulled out a big gray T-shirt that I was sure she would never wear. She held it up and looked in the mirror and grinned. The shirt read I MAY BE WRONG, BUT I DOUBT IT.

Jenae interrupted us both with furrowed eyebrows and her purse in hand. "Ben, can you start my next client? I have a pounding headache. I'm running over to get some aspirin at Cubby's."

"Sure. Are you going to be able to finish your shift?" Maybe Jenae's crazy Christmas was getting to her.

"I'll be fine. This headband is pinching my head and..." Jenae was out of the door before she finished her sentence.

I looked at Octavia in the mirror, shook my head, and raised one eyebrow.

Octavia put the shirt in the bag, tucked it under her arm, looked me in the mirror, and said, "Ah, vanity, too, must suffer."

# 21

## Lucy: Trim and Style

## Ash Wednesday, February 13

# 1991

The bell lay on the ground between the two pews on a cold and windy February morning in 1991.

I had known it was loose for several weeks, but I'd kept hoping that I could buy some more time before I needed to get up on a ladder and fix it. I usually parked in the alley lot and opened the salon an hour earlier than the staff showed up. I liked to have a cup of coffee and see one or two clients before the chaos exploded. Lucy was that client that Wednesday. Once I opened the shades to the front of the salon, I stepped on the silver bell lying in the doorway. It must have fallen during the night. I picked it up and put it in my pocket.

I jumped up on the pew and looked up at the upper rim of the door, hoping to devise a plan to fix the bell. The logical part of me knew that I should just throw it away, but I was surprised at the urgency in me to get the bell back up where it had been for the past seven years. I was thinking that I would have Subby Mangiamelli take a look at it when he came in for a haircut when my eyes diverted to a clunky green Honda Civic parked in front of the shop. I recognized Jenae's car and wondered why she was at work so early and why she hadn't parked in the alley. I saw a body slumped over the steering wheel. I jumped down from the pew and unlocked the front door as quickly as I could.

The extreme cold slapped me as I ran out to the driver's side of her car. The DJ on my drive to work had announced that the temperature was not quite ten degrees. I tapped on the window.

"Jenae! Hey, Jenae!"

I pounded the window with my fist, looking for movement. Jenae slowly lifted her head from the steering wheel and looked up at me, confused. Her hair was wild and nappy, covering a good part of her eyes. The dark uneven smudges around her eyes jumped out against her gray complexion. Her big, blue eyes now appeared dark gray and distant. I kept pounding and calling her name.

"Open the door, Jenae. Unlock the door."

Slowly, as if moving underwater, Jenae unlocked the door. I opened the door and moved my hand to her shoulder to maneuver her out from the front seat.

"Hey, Toots, what are you doing up so early?"

Jenae said nothing as she gazed in my direction. No coat or jacket. Jenae was wearing some summer flip-flops, loose gray sweatpants, and an oversized T-shirt with a picture of Michael Bolton on the front. We moved toward the door of Vanity Insanity. I kept one arm around her, struggling to open the door as my foot pushed it open. I laid Jenae down on one of the pews, grabbed my coat, and covered her.

"Hey, girl. You've got to be kidding me with this Michael Bolton thing you've got going on. What were you thinking?" My voice echoed against the empty room with high ceilings. "I'm gonna go grab you a hot coffee. Be right back."

Jenae did not move.

I came back hoping that she would be Jenae again and start flitting around with endless chatter, but I found her curled body facing the back of the pew.

"I've got coffee! Hey, Toots, why don't you sit up for second…?"

Jenae didn't move. I placed my coat behind her and pulled up her body.

"Jenae. What's going on here? Are you OK? Jenae."

"He's in the storm," she whispered.

"Somebody's in a storm. Who's in the storm, Jenae?" I held the back of her head and moved the cup of coffee toward her. She took a sip.

"My brother."

I knew very little about Jenae's family. What little I knew was not good. I did know she had a brother. The bubbly and loquacious woman who inhabited this body on most days would offer all kind of information about her life, her opinions, and her ideas—more often than not much more information that we needed to know. What she never talked about was her family or her childhood except for her younger brother, Scott, whom she would occasionally ask us to pray for. I knew that he struggled with drugs, and that bothered her. I knew that much.

"Scott? Is Scott in a storm, Jenae?"

Tears welled from her eyes as she rocked back and forth. "No. Not Scottie. Poor Scottie."

"Jenae, help me out here. What's going on? Did somebody hurt you? Tell me…"

"No!" Jenae shouted. "Kevin is in Desert Storm. Not Scottie!"

"OK, you have another brother. He's in Iraq. Is that the storm?"

She shook her head.

"Can we find out how he's doing? What do you need here?"

"No—I don't want to know how he is. No."

Jenae tucked her knees under her chin, rocking and tapping one foot. I knew she wouldn't make it through her shift, and I also knew I didn't want her to be alone. I would need to contact her clients to either reschedule or shuffle to Toby or myself. I needed to figure out what I could do with Jenae so that I knew she'd be safe.

"And poor Caroline." Jenae shook her head and sobbed.

"Our Caroline?"

"Yes, our Caroline. She's going to die if we don't do something. She throws up, you know." Jenae looked like a little girl with pouting lips.

Of course I knew. We all knew that every day following lunch, the already-too-thin Caroline would go to the bathroom and flush the toilet, run water, and throw up her lunch. We all knew this. What did this have to do with Iraq?

"Kelly can't get enough money together to bring her sister over from Viet Nam…and poor Toby…"

Poor Toby? This was worse than I thought. Jenae had never said one nice word to or about Toby. I looked into her fuzzy eyes and leaned in to smell her breath.

"Toby tries so hard, and that witch is so mean to him. So he fires her. And then she comes right back and is so mean to him…"

Jenae was referring to Delores Welks. She had been coming to Toby for years, even before he worked for me. She was demanding and demeaning, and she shattered Toby's world by complaining and criticizing how he did her hair, so he had "fired" her—at last count, four times. And each time, she came back announcing that no one else could do her hair as well as Toby and would he please, please take her back.

"What's going on here, Jenae?"

"*Jenae*, ha!" Jenae started laughing. "*Jenae*! Did you know that my real name is Jane? Janie, not Jenae. Just Jane! Jane Schmeling. I changed my name legally, but deep down I will always be Jane Stinkin' Schmeling."

"Look at me." I grabbed Jenae's shoulders and moved closer to her face. "You are Jenae Tolliver to me. You are bright and beautiful, Jenae." I gently pulled her head closer to my shoulder; her tears wiped against my neck.

Under all of her makeup and sass, Jenae was a delicate child. I remember how she'd reacted to a client leaving her a few weeks earlier. Jenae thrived on making her clients happy so much that she'd cried in the back room when she found out that client was seeing another stylist. I told her that "it" happened to the best of us. People were fickle. But she cried back to me that all she wanted was an exit interview or something. *Let me know where I failed.*

"What's wrong, Jenae?"

"Everything…" She sobbed into my shirt. She lifted up her head. "Everything is so, so sad. Everything is bad…and I don't want to take them anymore…I really don't."

"Take who?" I thought that we had covered everybody.

"My stupid meds. They make me feel icky. I want to be someone who doesn't need pills. I don't want them."

"Well, I'm thinking we need to find this medication if it helps you to be the Jenae that I know and love." I had suspected from Jenae's high and low days that she struggled, but I had not known to what degree.

Jenae began sobbing again.

"Jenae Tolliver, where are your pills?" My voice bounced off the pink and yellow walls.

She cried a muffled answer into her hands: "At home."

"We're gonna get this figured out, Toots." I grabbed Jenae's face and moved closer to her. I looked into her eyes. "We need to get you back."

"I'm so tired, Ben. I'm just so tired…"

My mind was racing as to where this day was headed. I needed to call Kelly, who had the day off, so she could cover Caroline's shift. Since Kelly didn't drive, I would then have Caroline drive Jenae home and watch over her while I rescheduled appointments so I could get over to Jenae's apartment to find her medication. Clients called us and canceled and rescheduled appointments all of the time, but when a stylist canceled, the response was not always as forgiving on the other end of the phone. The days that followed would be hectic since most people would want immediate consideration.

Jenae's head was against my shoulder again. She was falling asleep.

"Lucy will be here soon," I told her. "Do you want to just lie down here, Toots?"

Jenae sat up and grabbed my arms. "Lucy? Ben, don't let her see me like this. Ben, please." Jenae looked like a little girl begging me for help. She looked beautiful in her pain.

"Jenae, I'm here. You're gonna to be OK."

I pulled her up and started walking her to the back room. Once I settled her on the floor with my coat covering her, I called Kelly. When I told her about Jenae's rough morning, Kelly, who had seen a hint of this side of Jenae earlier that week, said that she would call Caroline and ask if she could pick her up on her way. As I hung up, I heard the sound of a babbling baby. Without the bell above the door, I felt unsettled.

"Happy Ash Wednesday! Anybody here?"

"Hey, Lu!" I held out my hands to Maria, her baby girl who would never be excluded from a merry Mary procession. I learned after Lucy had asked me to be her first child's godfather that high expectations came along with the role. Rather than have brothers fighting over the honor, she picked me. I helped her out, I guess.

"Say hi to Uncle Ben, Maria."

"You girls look like you need to wash your faces." I heard a sound from the back room and looked at the clock. Kelly lived a block away from the salon and would be here soon.

"Don't be messin' with our ashes, and where are yours, by the way?"

"Sit down, ladies. I'll be right back." I checked on Jenae. She was still lying on the floor. I knew that Lucy would help me if I needed help, but I wanted to respect Jenae's wishes for Lucy not to see her like this.

I walked out to Lucy and Maria and smiled at them both in the mirror. "So did Father Whalen say Mass?"

"Nope, we have a new guy. Father What-a-Waste. Our new assistant pastor is the most gorgeous man ever."

"Good for him." I gave Maria some combs to play with as I washed Lucy's hair.

"Hey, did you forget to tell me that A.C. was Jewish?" Lucy asked me. "Anthony heard it through the grapevine."

"That's a long story. I'm sure he'll be Buddhist by your next appointment."

Lucy spent the next half hour updating me on her latest scoop as I kept one ear listening to any sounds coming from the back room. Maria sat on Lucy's lap and smiled at me as I dried Lucy's hair.

"Don't let me forget to show you what I have in my trunk before we leave, Ben."

"Don't tell me…Father What-a -Waste?"

"It's a dresser-drawer thingy that Stephano just finished for Michael."

"I think you'd probably have more fun with Father What-a-Waste."

"You know, the little mirror table where a lady puts on her makeup and does her hair? Like a makeup desk. What is that called? Anyway, Michael found it at a garage sale last fall and had Stephano strip it down and restain it. Michael's going to give it to Theresa for a Valentine's Day gift tomorrow. I'm dropping it off at his office after I leave here. I want to show it to you."

I hesitated. I didn't want to leave Jenae.

"A vanity!" Lucy exclaimed. "That's what they call it. A vanity. It has this beautiful mirror, and Stephano discovered after he stripped it that the wood was mahogany. The guy from the garage sale had painted it white! Can you believe that? Anyway, it has this little stool with a cushion. You have to see it." Lucy was putting on Maria's coat and gathering the little books and toys that she had been playing with.

Kelly and Caroline walked in the back door from the alley. The cold air blew in with them. I directed them with my eyes to the back room. Caroline disappeared into the room.

"Hey, Kelly!" Lucy called.

"Hi, Lucy. Your baby getting so big."

"I'm helping Lucy to her car. I'll be right back," I told Kelly as she ran back to help Caroline.

I carried Maria to the car and covered her against the cold as Lucy threw her bag into the back seat and adjusted the car seat. I handed Maria to her, and she buckled her in and shut the door. Then she ran back and opened the trunk. The mahogany vanity was actually pretty sharp. I had never seen anything like it.

"Isn't it beautiful?"

I smiled. "Just like Theresa."

"She's going to love it!" Lucy shut the trunk and ran to start the car. "Don't forget to get your ashes today, Ben."

I smiled at Lucy and put my hands in my pockets to warm them, feeling the broken bell.

# 22

## Octavia: No Show, Reschedule

### Friday, October 25

# 1991

"Oh my gosh, he is so hot!" Jenae knelt on the pew looking out at a man walking toward Vanity Insanity. It was late October, but Jenae was wearing a fluorescent-green tank top, a short, short jean skirt, lime-green high, high heels, and a matching green scrunchie, pulling all of her hair to the top of head, shooting her hair up like stalks on the top of a pineapple.

"Who?" Caroline asked, looking around Jenae toward the tall, twenty-something man with a thin, black leather tie over a peach dress shirt.

"That gentleman walking toward Vanity Insanity!" Jenae said.

"That's no gentleman," I said. "That's the smarmy sales guy coming to push Summit products. He's been calling me all week."

"Whatever he's selling, order ten of them."

We had our Jenae back.

I had kept my eye on Jenae the past six months, as had the rest of the staff. On dark days, Kelly would nudge me and then look at Jenae and shake her head if Jenae's demeanor hinted that she might need to be guided back to home base. Jenae had plenty more good days than bad.

Jenae may have been stabilizing, but Caroline's affinity for throwing up escalated as her weight dropped. Kelly, who had gained her American citizenship, was getting closer to having enough money to bring her sister over to Omaha from Viet Nam, and Toby had fixed the bell over the door. He was more familiar with the upper casings than anyone.

"Phone, Ben." Toby handed me the phone as I took a breath to prepare myself for Peach Sales Guy. "It's Truman."

"Hey, Truman." Octavia had been a no-show for her usual Friday morning appointment. In all of the years that I had been doing her hair—religiously—on Friday mornings, she had never once missed an appointment.

"We can't find Octavia, Ben. Lately she's been taking these random walks. For the life of me, I can't believe she forgot her hair appointment. I know when we find her, she'll want to get in…Do you have any time today?"

I looked over the schedule and saw that the day was stacked, but after tossing a new client at Jenae for a cut and dry only, and another at Toby, I told Truman that I could fit Octavia in at one o'clock that afternoon. I would need to cut short my meetings with Peach Guy and a woman who was coming by at twelve thirty to promote her product. That was fine by me.

"Thank you, Ben." Truman sounded tired.

Until Octavia's appointment, I had to entertain two competing salespersons for the spot in my window. Two different companies, two different, brightly colored product packages, the same cajoling and aggravating approach. The bell rang as Peach Guy smiled his way through the door.

"Hey, Ben! Trent Schaefer. We talked this week." Yes, we had. "Love the place. I just wanted to show you a few of our new products. Actually, what I want to show you I haven't shown to anyone yet. It's a secret. "

"I love secrets. Don't you?" Jenae stood next to Peach Guy and smiled. I gave Jenae my best get-lost look and started looking through the products that were laid out on the UP desk.

A half hour later, Peach Guy walked out, and an overly bubbly little redhead with smooth hair walked in. Siena, whose speech was sprinkled with sharp *s*'s, represented a new company called Head JAM. "Thissss Frizz Paste is not coming out until ssspring, but I will give you a few ssssamples for you and your ssstaff to enjoy."

"Super."

Both "salespersons" were obnoxious, and from the extent to which they took their schmoozing, I reveled in the fact that every company wanted to promote its products in a salon in downtown Omaha. Within the past year, availability of bays in the Old Market two-block area had become scarce and costly, and I knew if I grew tired of this gig, I would make a sizable profit on selling the business alone. For now, the large bags of free products that Peach Guy and Little Red left were perks that came with the territory.

The bell above the door rang again as Octavia walked in at one o'clock sharp. "I haven't lost my mind, but sometimes I do misplace it."

"Well, look who's here." I greeted Octavia as I held out my elbow for her to hook her hand in.

"Don't even start with me, Ben. It's been a damn day, that's what it's been."

"And already, she's cussing."

"I never once used foul language when I was raising my boys." Octavia pointed her little finger at me as she set her purse on my station. "Never. I'm entitled now 'cause I'm old. I've earned the right to say exactly what I think."

"Well, lucky me." Hope, who had been in the back room folding towels, came out to see Octavia when she heard her voice. I mumbled, "Keep it clean for this one, eh?"

"Miss Octavia! You look beautiful today."

Octavia beamed as she sat down in my chair. Years ago, Octavia had told Hope that she could call her Octavia, but Hope, obedient to the rule her mother had given her that she should address adults as Miss, Mrs. or Mr., and in spite of the fact that Hope herself was over thirty, had politely replied, "No, thank you, Miss Octavia."

Octavia held up her hands to hold Hope's as she spoke to her. "Now, honey, have you read through the prayer book I gave you last time I was here?"

"I'm still working on it, Miss Octavia."

"Good, good. I thought you'd like it."

Hope leaned over to hug the little old lady in my chair. "Thank you, Miss Octavia, but I've got to get back to work." Octavia smiled at Hope as she collected all of the spare towels from each station.

"Hey, how come you're so nice to her? You're never that nice to me, Miss Octavia."

Octavia belted out a laugh. "Oh, because you're a poor wretch, Ben, that's why." She paused. "Oh, Ben, I am just so out of kilter since I missed Mass this morning."

"And your appointment with me."

"Mass is what gets me going."

"Why do you go to Mass every day, lady?"

"I'm cramming, honey."

This time I laughed.

"Now, I have a question for you, Ben. How come you don't go to church at all?" She paused and raised her eyebrows. "I know these things, you know."

"You could tell?"

"I'm serious, Benjamin Keller. You can't get to heaven on good looks and my prayers alone."

"I was kind of counting on it."

Octavia tilted her head. I walked her over to the basin to wash her hair.

"I think I'm comfortable with where I am right now…I guess."

"Comfortable? Well, there's your problem."

I put an apron around Octavia, stopped, and looked at her in the mirror.

"Ben, you need the gospel. The gospel comforts those suffering and conflicted, and it roughs up those who are too comfortable."

"Good to know. I didn't really plan to stop going to church. I think I kind of slowly fell away from it all. Once I moved out of Mom's house,

I just fell out of the rhythm…and Mac stopped picking me up. Not his responsibility…I don't know."

"Do you pray, Ben?" Octavia raised her eyebrows and looked at me in the mirror. I wished we could talk about politics or even sex.

I started shampooing her hair. "I pray that the next color I do on someone's hair works out…"

Octavia said nothing.

"Boy, you're getting kind of nosey here," I said. "I don't know. I think I pray. You know, I think around the time that I graduated from high school, I ran up to Mass on the feast of the Trinity. Father Old-Fart Dailey was talking about connecting with each part of the trinity. The Father, Son, and Holy Ghost. I remember so clearly him saying that to truly know God, we need to understand or know the love of a caring father."

I helped Octavia up as I put a towel around her head. "I guess I pretty much struck out in that category. 'I'm very angry with my father. It cost me thousands of dollars to pay a therapist to say…'"

"It cost you what to what?"

"It's a line from a movie. *Pretty Woman*. Richard Gere's character is telling the prostitute played by Julia Roberts that he's…"

"Angry with his father. Got it." Octavia stared at me in the mirror.

"I'm not angry or bitter. I just look at it all differently. I believe in goodness. That's kind of praying. Does that count?"

Octavia scowled.

"Hey, I shared some kind of private stuff here. Are you gonna be mean again? You're the one who missed Mass." I hoped that would get a laugh.

"I think that's a damn cop-out."

"And we're back. Here comes the potty mouth."

"Ben, did you ever read Coleridge's *Kubla Kahn*?"

"Sorry, I was a business major."

"That Coleridge may have been a great poet from the Romantic era, but he was also a pretty serious drug addict. Half stoned writing most of his stuff."

"So you've heard." I didn't know that Octavia knew what "stoned" meant.

"Anyway, he has this drug dream and wakes up inspired to write one of his most beautiful poems." Octavia recited some of the poem:

*In Xanadu did Kubla Khan*
*A stately pleasure-dome decree:*
*Where Alph, the sacred river, ran*
*Through caverns measureless to man*
*Down to a sunless sea.*

"I thought Olivia Newton-John created the whole Xanadu thing."

"The point, my dear wretch, is that when a messenger from town knocked on his door, it interrupted his hallucination or rhythm, he never finished the poem."

"OK."

"And wouldn't it be nice if we could blame all of our unfinished projects and disappointments in our life on a poor, little messenger?"

"Father Old Fart?"

"Father Old Fart and your father."

Ouch.

"I think that sure is an easy way out," Octavia continued. "If I based my faith on the father that I knew, then God takes a whack on me a few times a day and more than a few drinks from the whisky in the back of the barn. If it could be that simple."

"Sorry."

"I think that your Father Old Fart probably needed to expand more. You've got other people in your life that have shown you fatherly love. Right?"

"Right."

"Get over it."

"Are you done scolding me?"

"I think so. I might need to go to five thirty Mass. That should help me feel better."

"And hopefully be nicer."

Octavia hooked her hand in the crook of my arm as I walked her to the door. We saw Truman pulling up. Octavia gave me a hug, something that she had never done before. I don't know if she made it to Mass that evening, but I knew that my day was a bit off-kilter, thanks to Octavia. I thought about Sting and his new album, which I had been playing a lot lately. Sting had dedicated *The Soul Cages* to his recently deceased father.

I thought of Mac.

# 23

## Tom Ducey: Same Old, Same Old

### Tuesday, July 21

# 1992

"Merry Christmas, y'all!"

Tom Ducey stood at the door, opening and closing it several times so that the bell rang along with his ho-ho-hos on that humid day in July. Toby's cheeks were red as he stared at Tom, who was holding in his hand the customary baker's dozen donuts he had just picked up from Petit's Pastry.

"Merry Christmas, Vanity Insanity!" His voice was thick with nicotine gravel, lined with many years of cigarette breaks.

Jenae ran up to Tom and gave him a big kiss on his cheek as he handed her the box of donuts.

"Now that's what I'm talkin' about. That is exactly what I am talking about." His voice boomed throughout the salon.

Tom Ducey came into Vanity Insanity every two weeks on Tuesday mornings at ten o'clock, always with a box of donuts. I would trim his conservative style, shave his neck, attempt to disguise his receding hairline, and attack the gray hairs sprouting on his sideburns. "I swear, the little buggers grow faster than my other hair," he'd say. "They're just like old age making fun of you. Wheeeeeeee, here we are. Try to get rid of us...We just grow back faster."

Jenae looked out at Tom's new "Husker Red" Jeep Cherokee out front with his standard vanity license plate: LEGL SOB. "Boy, somebody must be doing well. Check out the wheels of our 'legal South Omaha boy.'"

Kelly and Caroline came up to the window to see the new car. Caroline nervously eyed the donut box as Kelly looked at the car. "Nice car, Tom!"

"Why thank you, Kelly. Just traded in the old one. Kind of like it myself."

Tom had been doing well, as Jenae put it. He and Lucy had just built a new house out west, where construction was popping up everywhere. I have to take a little credit for his good fortune since I was the one who'd "set him up" with my good friend Octavia. Truman had shared with me during one of his haircuts that Octavia was looking for a lawyer to do some work for TL Enterprise. I knew that Tom was happy with his job, but I'd asked him if he would consider a little extra work.

"What? Are you kidding me? Work for *the* Octavia Hruska?"

The chemistry was perfect. After Tom had advised and written up a few agreements for Octavia during the whole Jobber's Canyon deal, Octavia had told her son Truman to hire Mr. Ducey full time in their growing company, TL Property Acquisitions and Consulting. Octavia was on the board and had the largest vote in decisions since her money was what directed the company. Truman ran the firm with a solid hand but always followed the orders of the little old lady who knew what she was talking about. As TL prospered, so did Tom Ducey.

"Well, your little friend Octavia is at it again. I tell you, that brassy broad knows what she wants, and she knows how to get it," Tom said as he sat down in the chair in my station. "She just bought herself a radio station."

"Radio station? What is Octavia going to do with a radio station?"

"Whatever the hell she wants…or nothing at all. She did her homework, and so she says to Truman, buy it. And Truman jumps and buys it. And I jump and write up the papers." Tom laughed till he coughed a long, rough cough.

"Is this one of those things where I'm not supposed to know about the radio station when I see Octavia?" At least once a day, somebody sitting in my chair dropped a confidential bomb on me. It went with the territory, but I never got used to it.

"Hell no! Just read your morning paper. Front page of the *Midlands* section. I figured she would've told you, though. You rate pretty high in her book, man. Just what did you do to get in such good graces with Octavia Hruska?"

"You mean when she's not chewing me out? I just do her hair and do as I'm told. Works for me."

"Right there with you, buddy. And on a more serious note, on the same page as the radio-station article was an article about the priest from Saint Walter's."

We'd all been hearing a lot about the priest from Saint Walter's: Father Frank Camen, pastor during the late seventies. The man had been accused of sexually abusing three boys in the parish during the time that he was there. All three plaintiffs, now grown men, claim that the archdiocese knew of the abuse at the time when Father Camen was reassigned to a parish in a town west of Omaha. The allegations and the rumblings throughout the community mirrored similar cries across the country, as many adults were now coming forward with the appalling stories.

"One of the plaintiff's names jumped out at me," Tom continued. "E. Krackenier."

"Eddie?"

"The paper just said 'E,' but I'm guessing. Same era. Wasn't he from Saint Walter's?"

"Yep."

"The Chief. Wow."

Tom and I were quiet for several minutes, attempting to take in the lurid implications that came along with these kinds of stories. The thought of innocent children being taken advantage of was hard enough to fathom. The piece that made this more horrific was the fact that these children had been abused by a person whom they should have been able to trust. A person who should have protected them. These children, who were no longer children, became adults who were haunted daily by that exploitation for years until some impetus stirred them to find peace in naming the act.

"Didn't Eddie use to work with Will at the racetrack?" Tom asked "I remember seeing them when we went to bet on the horses."

"Yeah, and A.C., too, one summer."

"A.C. How is that guy doing? Things with his job working out?"

Making barely enough money to make ends meet, A.C. took the cases of people who did not have enough money to afford proper legal representation. A year earlier, A.C. and I had moved into an apartment in the Old Market that we were subletting from the owner of Trini's, who had decided to go spend some undetermined amount of time in Europe. The price was right, so we lived, day to day, knowing that any day, the owner would come back and we would be looking for a new place.

"He's doing great. A.C. is A.C. Ya know." Universal Guy Talk for *can't really talk about it.* "Now how's my goddaughter handling her new little sister? Sounds like Lucy has her hands full."

"Let me tell you that little Maria loves to poke her little fingers in baby Diane's eyes when no one is looking. What do you make of that, Godfather? Didn't you teach her anything?"

"Not that little trick. I told her not to do that."

"OK, so Lucy gets her feathers all in a tizzy like we have this devil child or something. My wife—I'm telling you, her hormones are all whacked out. She gets off the phone with our new neighbor, and she says to me, 'Googy Bear'—'cause that's what she calls me sometimes."

"Really?"

"No. But anyway, Lucy says, 'Tom, I didn't know that the Hendersons weren't Catholic. They always seemed so nice.' And I'm like, give me a break."

"That's just some misunderstood Catholic confidence talking there."

"Ya think? Hey, you and I are Cradle Catholics, just like Lucy, and we don't go around with that confidence—borderline arrogance—like the whole world revolves around us. Just what would my lovely wife do if she was dropped in the middle of the South, say in the heart of the Bible Belt? She just wouldn't get it."

"So you've got your Cradle Catholics and your Cafeteria Catholics."

"Yeah, pickin' and choosin' what works for them."

"And don't forget the Convert Catholics." I untied the apron around Tom's neck.

"I like to call them the damn-convert Catholics since they make the rest of us look so stupid. After they get through the training camp, they know all of the stuff we were supposed to learn a long time ago but weren't really paying enough attention to. OK, so let's call Lucy a Kookie Catholic, OK?"

"I'll let you call her whatever you want to. What about the Quiet Catholics?"

"You mean like your grandpa? Never talking about it but living it?"

"Yep."

"And that A.C. He's a Query Catholic. Questioning everything and thinking about it all of the time." Tom stood up and shook some hair off of his pants.

"Query Catholics. I like it."

"Man, we could go on all day. Crazy Catholics, borderline fundamentalists I call 'em. They think they're all that and a bag of chips."

"They're all pretty much crazy."

"Pretty much, and then there's you."

"OK, and what am I?"

Tom thought about this one. "Um, Comatose Catholic. Asleep at the wheel."

"Thanks…"

"Not that there's anything wrong with that. It's like that Catholic stuff is in you somewhere." Tom slapped me on the back as he pulled out his wallet. "Oh, all the many different flavors of Catholics. We're like a Catholic ice-cream store. One scoop or two? I'll just take a Kamikaze Catholic sundae. With extra dispensations sprinkled on top." Tom laughed so loud at himself that everyone in the salon stopped and looked at him. He didn't notice as he put his credit card in his wallet after paying me at the UP desk.

"Oh, one more Lucy story for the road. Vintage Lucy. Vintage. Lucy has this picture that's been on our fridge for years. Taken right after Maria was born. The picture is awful. I have a beer in my hand and a wicked sunburn. I don't even know where it was taken. Maria's crying her head off. Not centered. Barely focused. You can see the shadow of the finger of the person taking the picture. Bad picture. So Lucy puts this picture on the fridge as soon as we move into the new place, see. I'm like, Lu, we have another child. Why don't you put this one away and put up some new pictures. Right?"

"Right."

"I ask her why she keeps that one up. And she says to me, ''Cause my hair looked really great that day.'" Tom's laughter boomed on all four walls of the place, and he coughed all the way out the door and to his car.

Tom was still laughing as he lit up a cigarette before getting into his new Jeep.

# 24

## Lucy: Pregnancy Hair

### Thursday, November 5

# 1992

Toby—wearing a tucked in Husker T-shirt that read *Fear the Corn!*—was spraying his chair with the special disinfectant he'd brought from home. After each spray he would wipe the seat of the chair in a strong, circular, rhythmical motion. His cheeks were splashed with the agitated red that flared out of nowhere when he was upset about something.

"Hey, Toby," I ventured. Toby either ignored me or was too focused on his chair to notice me.

From my almost-nine years of experience with Toby, I knew better than to ask directly if something was wrong. Sarcasm was another approach that staff members would never use with Toby when he was in "a mood." Just ask Jenae. What I knew was that Toby would get to his breaking point and then let it all go. He was definitely upset about something. The phone rang. I watched Toby's wiping ceremony as I answered it.

"Vanity Insanity."

"Hey, Ben. Stephano here. I have the blueprints for the new bay. I can drop them off when I get my hair cut on Thursday."

Stephano Mangiamelli, owner of Mangiamelli Brothers Construction, had put together a plan for the bay next to Vanity Insanity. I was still waiting to hear from Tom Ducey if the owners of Tres Chique were ready to move on with my acquisition of their unit. We were crammed tight in the bay alone, and I knew that I needed to hire one more stylist in addition to the one I'd hired last week. Virginia had a great track record and a funny personality. I liked her, so I hired her on the spot.

"Sounds good to me. I'll be able to let you know what Tom knows by then. See you then."

I hung up and glanced over at Toby again. He was now staring at me, glaring.

I avoided the obvious. "Did you read last night's article about the Huskers? I don't think that Kansas will be ready for us Saturday."

Toby walked around the chair and then sat in it.

"I'm thinking it'll be a blowout." A.C. and I were heading to the game on Saturday. We had an extra ticket, which we were thinking of giving to Will, who always canceled the last minute. The words were out of my mouth before I realized. "A.C. and I have an extra ticket if you want to join us. It's a night game." A.C. would kill me.

"Somebody stole one of my combs."

This was about a comb?

"I count them between every client, and one is missing. It's either Jenae or that new girl." Toby said "new girl" like he was tasting poison. I couldn't speak for the new girl, but I knew that Jenae would never steal. She's been known to sneak over to Toby's station when he left for lunch and move things out of order just to rattle his world a little. A cheap thrill, she called it. But steal? Never.

Toby had come a long way from the khaki-pants-white-shirt, not so normal guy who'd interviewed for a job at Vanity Insanity. With clients and staff, he was much more relaxed than when he'd started. Now, he mostly wore jeans and T-shirts, but the shirts were always tucked into his jeans. After Jenae had made fun of the big eighties goggle glasses, Toby invested in an expensive pair of much smaller 1990s glasses. He lightened up some and maintained his strong clientele base, but he still hung tightly to his order and rituals. Personally, I'd never found fault with his little obsessions; a guy had a right to do what worked for him as long as it didn't get in the way of the big picture.

"Toby, I have a few extra combs."

"Virginia, the new girl? And now another stylist!"

This was not about a comb.

"And all of these renovations. Really? And…"

"And what?"

"I left Baldwin Salon because things got out of control. The place got so big and so busy that I couldn't hear myself think. Things are fine the way they are. That's just what I think." Toby looked at the combs on his station.

"We won't get that big, Toby. It's just that we're crammed in here, and we could use a little more help."

Toby looked down, and then, as if speaking to the floor: "What time are we leaving?"

"Leaving?"

"For the game on Saturday."

I looked over to my station and saw Lucy already sitting in my pink chair. She must have sensed the tension and sneaked past us during the Mystery of the Missing Comb. "Oh, right, around three o'clock if that works," I replied.

Toby shook his head and walked to the back room.

"Hey, Lu." I pulled her card out of my shoebox.

"Everything good?" Lucy looked over at Toby.

"Think so." I pulled out an apron and put it over Lucy.

"Well, aren't you going to tell me how pregnant I look? Everyone else has. 'Oh, look at the short, little pregnant woman. Are you having twins? You could be eleven months pregnant. You're all baby…'"

"You're pregnant?" I teased. "You know what causes that, don't you?"

Lucy did look pregnant. This would be girl number three. Tom had wailed in delight when they were told at the ultrasound. Maria and Diane, the two big sisters, were pretty proud. The good news about the baby coming helped to divert Tom and Lucy's attention from the recent news that Maria was showing signs of mild autism. Theresa had worked with Maria and directed Lucy and Tom to a specialist.

"Just do something with this mop. Cut it all off. Shave it! Just do it." Lucy's hair was experiencing the old pregnancy transformation. For some women, the hormones affected the color or texture of their hair. For Lucy, her hair was growing faster with the hormones speeding through her system at the moment. "Hormone hell," she sniveled.

I read my notes from Lucy's last appointment and walked her to the sink to wash her hair. "Looks like we just trimmed it last time before your big home party."

"Home *interior* party."

"What you said...What is that?"

"You wouldn't believe me if I told you. That night was a huge disaster. Theresa came over to help me get ready, you know, with the food and stuff. About a half hour before guests would be coming, she heard some commotion at the front door and saw a woman had fallen on the porch. It was the lady who was giving the party. She had dropped a box holding some of her products."

"Products?"

"Lamps, candles, pictures, foo-foo stuff for decorating your house. It's called Home Décor and More or something like that."

"OK."

"Anyway, it had been raining, so the front porch was kind of slick. Theresa helps her up and then notices her son, maybe ten years old, behind her carrying another big box. So we get this lady and everything from her car into the living room. We finish getting food ready while she and her son set up."

"Who is 'she'?"

"She is some cousin or in-law of DeDe Jereske. DeDe's daughter plays with Maria."

"OK." I put a towel around Lucy's head and walked her back to my chair.

"Anyway, the guests come, my mom, my sister-in-laws, my mother-in-law, good friends, neighbors…The party starts, and the Décor lady starts giving her little spiel. The way these parties work, the ladies listen to a little speech about the company and products, and they can start ordering—or that's what's supposed to happen. The lady starts talking, and two sentences into it all, we all start looking at each other because she's really slurring her words. Then she starts repeating herself and gets stuck on the little rhyme, 'A candle with brass is like a home without class…'or something like that."

"She was drunk?"

"Off her home-interior-decorating you-know-what."

"So what did you do?" I began trimming the ends of Lucy's hair.

"I didn't do anything. I couldn't move. I'm like, all these people have come here for a party, and this awkward thing is happening. Theresa gets up and says to the group, 'I think we're ready to start looking through the magazines and placing orders. What do you all think?' Everyone just shakes their heads and starts looking through magazines. Then Theresa takes the lady to a separate room and finds out that woman had just discovered that her husband was having an affair. She found out when she was getting ready to come to my house. Evidently, she drank some vodka while she packed the car."

"She had a little boy with her?"

"Yep, and he didn't look that rattled by it all. Almost like he helped her out a lot. It was so sad." Lucy thumbed through a magazine as I dried her hair.

"OK, so is now a good time to ask questions?"

"Go right ahead."

"Why did you have the party anyway?"

Lucy thought for a moment. "Guilt."

"All of that for guilt."

"I felt bad for DeDe, who felt bad for her cousin or whatever…Then I felt guilty when I asked my friends since I don't want them to feel like they have to buy something but they do anyway. Women are so weird, Ben."

"Ya think?"

"I can't tell you how many basket parties, candle parties, Tupperware parties I've been invited to. It's all about guilt. When you get the invitation, you feel bad because you don't want to go, but you should. Then you feel bad if you go and don't buy anything, so you do. Then you feel guilty since you buy something you don't need or even want. These parties are what little girls do when they grow up instead of chain letters."

"OK, what's a chain letter?"

"You don't remember chain letters? Didn't you ever get one?

"Nope. Remember, I'm not a woman."

"You'd get a letter that would say, 'Copy this letter ten times and send it off to nine of your friends. Send a letter back to the person who sent this to you and keep their name on your list, include a dollar bill or a stick of gum.' You were supposed to put your name on the top of the list that you send to your group, or something like that. If it worked out, you were supposed to end up with a million dollars."

"Or a million sticks of gum. Did it ever work?"

"Never, not once."

"Did you send them?"

"Always"

"Why?"

"Guilt. And fear. The letter usually said that the chain had not been broken in thirty-seven years or something like that, except by one person. And that person suffered a violent and immediate death by fire after throwing the letter away. I wasn't going to risk that sort of thing…I was seven, by the way."

I grabbed Lucy's coat and helped her put it on. "So where does all of the guilt come from, Lucy?"

No hesitation. "My mother."

"All of it?"

"Pretty much. I think that even the really good and fun moms had their share of dumping guilt on their children. I think it's their job. I remember hanging out at Stinky Morrow's house when we were kids. It was around the holidays since I can remember they had their Christmas tree up. Everyone was finishing up breakfast, and Mrs. Morrow walked in the room and screamed when she noticed Stinky's little sister Julie, maybe three or four at the time, sitting on the kitchen counter about to stick a butter knife into the toaster. Mrs. Morrow grabbed Julie and then looked at all of the older kids sitting at the table and screamed, 'What, you want a dead sister for Christmas?' The kids all just looked at her like they didn't know the answer. And Mrs. Morrow was one of the cool moms."

"So, all your guilt comes from sweet, little Ava?"

"Well, not all of it. The Catholic Church had a big hand in it…but I feel guilt when I blame the Church. Is that funny or what?"

"Not really. OK, so how many Catholics does it take to screw in a light bulb?"

"Easy. Twelve. One to screw it in and eleven to watch and feel guilty."

"OK, so, Guilt Queen, what guilt-infested activity do you have planned for today?"

"None. Right now, I'm running over to Theresa's house with this." Lucy picked up a bag that was sitting next to her purse. She pulled out a small plastic statue.

"Who's that?"

"Saint Joseph. We're burying him in her backyard before Michael gets home. He can't know about it."

"Why do I feel like I should call the police or something. Are you aware that it's pouring outside? Could turn to snow with how cold it is. And you're very pregnant. Now why are you burying a statue? And why can't Michael know about it?"

Lucy put the statue back in her bag."We're burying it so that Theresa can sell her house. It's been on the market for a month, so we knew that we needed to resort to Saint Joseph. Michael thinks it's voodoo." We walked past Toby's station to the door; his cheeks were no longer red. I would need to make a call to A.C .about the change of plans for the Husker game.

"And you don't feel guilty about lying to Michael and burying a voodoo doll in his yard?"

"It's not voodoo. I don't feel one ounce of guilt. When you're trying to sell your house, you bury the statue head down facing the house three feet from it. Saint Joseph will help you sell it. You can get these kits at certain bookstores. Even my Jewish neighbor did it, and her house sold three days later."

"OK."

"Don't tell Michael. Promise?"

"Sure."

I walked a little pregnant woman to her car, holding an umbrella over her head. As Lucy drove away, her own words echoed in my ears.

People may be weird about their hair, but women are just weird.

25

# A.C.: Quick Trim, Heading to Colorado

## Saturday, May 17

# 1993

"And we have probably the best seats at Red Rocks. We're packed and ready to go as soon as Ben trims my head." A.C. walked in flanked by Jenae and Virginia, flirting and gushing as he charmed them with each word.

A.C. and I were headed to Colorado to camp near Morrison, a town in the foothills about fifteen miles west of Denver. We had tickets to see Sting in concert at Red Rocks Amphitheater on Sunday night. We were planning on heading back Monday afternoon, the day Vanity Insanity was closed.

"A.C., you already look hot!" Jenae leaned into him as she and Virginia pulled up chairs near my station.

"What is this? The A.C. Entertainment Hour?" I asked as I grabbed an apron for A.C."I hardly have enough room as it is." The Vanity Insanity staff was growing, but the place was no bigger. Tom Ducey had called me months earlier with the news that Tres Chique had decided not to move, and therefore Vanity Insanity was still pretty much landlocked.

"OK, so what's your favorite song from the new CD?" Virginia, our newest stylist, stood an inch or two taller than A.C. and a good fifty pounds heavier. She wore a black apron over her clothes. The front of it read: *What happens at the hair salon stays at the hair salon*. Virginia's beautiful face and long, chestnut hair distracted us all from her unusual size. "Ben's been playing *Ten Summoner's Tales* all week."

"I think we know every song by heart...and there're actually eleven songs." Jenae rolled her eyes and moved closer to A.C.

"That's easy." A.C. sat in my chair and looked at himself. "If I Ever Lose My Faith in You." Do you guys know the story behind the CD's title? It's actually a play on words. A pun. Sting's name, before he legally changed it, was Gordon Sumner."

"Gordon?" Jenae squawked. "Sting doesn't look like a Gordon!"

"I get it!" Virginia shouted. Her voice filled the room. "Like *The Canterbury Tales*. I'm right, right? Am I right?"

A.C. laughed. "I didn't think anyone would catch it!" As an English major, he gloated about literary allusions that he found, many in Sting's songs. Sting was a former English teacher himself. "I'm impressed, Virginia! The title links Sting to the naughty summoner in Chaucer's tales. Kind of funny, if you think about it."

"I don't remember Chaucer." Jenae tilted her head. "Was Chaucer in American lit? I only finished eleventh grade." She stood up and started playing with her hair in the mirror.

"No, he's British," A.C. explained. "If you'd gone one more year, you would have learned about him."

"All I remember about English was my obnoxious teacher who wore a bad toupee. Oh, and I remember Gatsby. I absolutely loved *The Great Gatsby*. He was so loyal to his dream. He was so in love with Daisy. Something about the green light and his purposeless splendor." I wondered if I had read the same book. I'd thought Daisy was a ditz myself.

"Gatsby was a little random," A.C. added as I started shaving the back of his neck.

"Oh, here comes my three o'clock appointment!" Jenae kissed the top of A.C.'s head. "Have fun at Red Rocks, boys!" She ran to greet an older lady at the door.

"Speaking of random," I muttered.

"Drive safely." Virginia stood up and headed to her station. "Hey, look who's here. Lucy!"

Lucy rushed in and reveled in her introduction by Virginia. "I've got a sitter for two hours. I'm free, I'm free!"

"What can I do for you, Lu?" I knew she didn't have an appointment.

"A.C.!" Lucy gave A.C. a hug from behind the chair. "It's been, like, forever! I just stopped in to grab some conditioner, Ben. Ran out yesterday. This is so weird. I was just praying, and the old neighborhood gang popped into my head. I'm not kidding. I was just thinking of you, A.C. When I dropped off my dry cleaning, I saw a vase with a rose in it, and I just knew it was a sign from God."

"A sign of what?" A.C. asked.

"A sign that I would run into you!"

"Roses are Lucy's biggest sign from God," I told A.C. I'd heard many rose stories.

"So I see." A.C. smirked.

"Seriously," Lucy went on. "Roses are signs of answered prayers. I was just praying that I'd see some of the old gang and…"

"Voila!" I said. "A.C. shows up! Just like your moving vans."

"Don't make fun. Last year Tom and I were thinking about moving, and so I prayed and prayed if that was the right thing for us, you know, with all we have going on and schools for the girls. That entire week I kept seeing moving vans, Mayflower moving vans everywhere. I mean everywhere. I just knew that was our sign."

"Or maybe," A.C. looked at Lucy in the mirror, "people were moving. Like they do every day. Some schmuck was moving across town, and you saw his van."

"Hey, aren't you two supposed to be in Denver?" Lucy pulled up the same chair that Virginia had just put away and sat down.

"We'll be on the road in a half hour," A.C. told her. "Lucy, you baby machine, I heard that you have three little girls now."

"And they're all perfect little angels, right, Ben?"

"If you're referring to the last time you brought them all in with you… uh, yes, they're perfect little angels." I smiled. Lucy laughed. "Not a devil in the bunch."

"Speaking of devils." Lucy's voice was serious and softer. "The newspaper had an article about that Saint Walter's priest. Sounds like they settled out of court on all counts. I guess I can see now why that Eddie Krackenier was so creepy. The kid had no dad, and the next-best father figure was… awful. That explains all the stuff he did."

After we were older and no longer ran into Eddie, we'd heard most of the "stuff" Eddie did through the grapevine. The "stuff" included stealing from construction sites, dropping out of ninth grade, attempting to rob an ATM, and dealing drugs. The Eddie lore was always cheap conversation filler whenever I ran into people from the old neighborhood.

"Remember when we used to always run away whenever we saw Eddie?" Lucy's eyes had that glaze she got as she talked about the years on Maple Crest Circle. "When we used to always" was one of her favorite lines to throw out when we got to reminiscing. "Always" was an interesting choice of words in most cases.

"Remember when we used to always build forts in the back of the Morrows' storage closet?"

We did this once, got in trouble, and never did it again.

"Remember when we used to always play Mass and pretend to give Nabisco cookies as the Eucharist?"

I don't remember ever doing that.

"Remember when we used to always sing 'Little Willy Really Won't Go Home' to my brother Will?"

I never did this. Not once.

"I never ran from Eddie," A.C. told Lucy. "I was too tough. I do remember wanting to run from the one lady in charge of our youth group at Pius. Mrs. Plankton, or something like that. She gave me the heebie-jeebies."

"Mrs. Pinkerton," Lucy corrected him. "I liked her!"

"Yeah, well, I remember her taking us caroling. Ben, remember, our moms made us go? Mrs. Plankton thought it would be 'neat' to go sing at an insane asylum."

"It was a home for the mentally and emotionally challenged, A.C.," Lucy corrected him again.

"Right, that's where I want to drive a bunch of naïve fourteen-year-old kids to sing holiday songs. The patients all stared blankly at us as we pounded out a bouncy version of 'We Wish You a Merry Christmas.' That one guy in the back kept screaming, 'Get the F out of here' until they took him somewhere to settle down. I remember not being able to sleep that night 'cause I kept thinking of all those people trapped inside those crazy minds. There had to be a soul down deep in them. If our mothers only knew what the holiday field trip was like."

"OK, on a lighter note," I said, "remember in fifth or sixth grade when Lovey Webber cheated off some kid next to her on a quiz? She mouthed the words 'number six' to him, and he, probably thinking she was cute, whispered, 'visual aids.' Lovey was so mad when she got the answer wrong. The teacher asked Lovey what she meant by 'fish blades.'"

"I remember," A.C. pointed to me as he went on, "when you used to think that the Wicker Witch was watching you." Lucy looked confused as A.C. started singing lines from "Every Breath You Take". He laughed so hard his eyes watered. "Man, those were good times, and we didn't have a clue. Those years on Maple Crest and at Pius were our salad days."

"Salad days?" Lucy looked at A.C.

"The salad days!" A.C. was on a roll with his literary allusions. "Shakespeare's Cleopatra talks about 'My salad days, when I was green in judgment, cold in blood.' Shakespeare was talking about the 'green' youth, when we didn't have a clue. Our salad days were the Maple Crest years when we were oblivious to the problems in life. And when it was OK to laugh at farts."

"You mean it's not OK now?" I asked.

"I get it," Lucy said. "The salad days were when the most important things on my mind were cute boys, getting a really good tan, and making sure my hair looked good. Now it's about keeping my kids healthy, remodeling the kitchen, and making sure my hair looks good."

I took A.C.'s apron off as he stood up and checked himself out in the mirror. "We sure ain't livin' in the salad days no more. Good to see you, Lu. Ben, what can I do to help you shut down so we can hit the road? And remember, no jokes about gas."

"Wait, A.C., you can't leave yet," Lucy said as she stood up and grabbed the bag of conditioner I handed her. "Not until you tell me about your girlfriend and you becoming Jewish. My neighbor's Jewish. Maybe you know her."

A.C. looked at me, and I shook my head as I pulled out the bank bag. I wasn't going to be the one to tell Lucy about the latest stop on A.C.'s religious adventures.

"Sounds like you're a few links behind in the news chain." A.C. looked uncomfortable as he started organizing my station. "Leah and I broke up a few months ago. And as for the Jewish thing, I did dabble there for a while…"

A.C. had practiced the Jewish religion for a few years. His enthusiasm to take in every aspect of the religion only grew when he met a beautiful Jewish woman named Leah, who fed him information on the Jewish faith and encouraged him as he questioned and explored. Their first date was to a Jewish wedding of her best friend. A. C. told me that when the bride and groom broke a glass at the end of their ceremony, he was moved to tears. "Brokenness in midst of great joy. Does that gesture not just capture the human condition? " A.C. had lectured me at the time. "Shattered glass? The celebration of love? Are you following!"

Leah stood by A.C. in his quest for peace. I always liked Leah. I liked to call her Patient Leah since she endured his inquisition for years, supporting him in his insatiable quest for religion and faith.

"OK, fill me in." Lucy sat back down. I reorganized my station as A.C. sat down in the pink chair. Most of the staff had left Vanity Insanity, and Virginia and Jenae were finishing their clients' hair.

"Well, where do I begin? I did practice Judaism for a while. Here's how it works. In the Jewish religion, a child traces his Jewish roots back through his mother. My mother was Catholic, so Leah told me all about the consequence of Emancipation to make Jewish identity a private promise rather than legal status, leaving it a complex combination of destiny and choice."

Lucy squinted her eyes. She really was trying to understand.

"OK, basically the kid of a non-Jewish mother and a Jewish father has to convert, like anyone else."

"So you converted?"

"I did. And I practiced…For a while."

A.C.'s passion and hunger for knowledge and peace were greater than his passion for Leah. Question after question, challenge after challenge, slowly gave way to doubt and arguments, and, in time, Patient Leah became Not-So-Patient-Leah—though I couldn't blame her—as A.C. shared his pending and growing uncertainty in the first principle of Rambam's Principles of Faith: God exists.

In early 1993, A.C. hit a gigantic personal and moral wall as he ventured into the blurry and alarming field of atheism. My own theory is that Arthur Charles Perelman had one too many thoughts in his head, and something just exploded. The guy is one of the most brilliant people I know, but sometimes I think that he thinks too much. I knew that he was experiencing a crisis of sorts when he was barely fazed by Leah's announcement that she was leaving the relationship.

"So you're not dating Leah, and you're not Jewish," Lucy summed up.

"Pretty much."

"Are you still a lawyer?" Lucy laughed.

In 1993, A.C. had walked away from the legal system and God. Not much else was left. "Lucy, I liked law school, but it turns out, I don't like being a lawyer. The laws are black and white, and the world is gray and complicated."

"Like you."

"Like me. Every time I tried to promote justice, I found myself in position that supported the opposite. I'm taking a break from it all right now, Lu."

Jenae and Virginia walked past the serious conversation. Jenae squeezed A.C.'s shoulder as she passed. "Y'all be good in Denver. Don't do anything I wouldn't do!"

"Leaves them nothing to do," Virginia shouted as they opened the door to leave. The bell rang.

"What does that mean? Taking a break?" Lucy moved closer to A.C. and looked directly into his eyes.

"It means that I have some pretty big questions. That's all."

"You still believe in God. Right?" Lucy sounded and looked like a little girl who wanted the tooth fairy to be real.

"Religion makes sense, Lucy. Really it does. People want to have this enormous religion security blanket of a super father figure, keeping them safe. I get it. It works for most people."

Lucy was speechless. If A.C. had instead said that he was signing up to work for the devil, at least she could respond with anger, a slap on the cheek, or clear disapproval. If A.C. was saying what he was saying, then Lucy could not react at all.

A.C. looked down as he spoke. "Religion has its purpose. Really, it does. I guess I'm just sorting out what sometimes seems like, more or less, a mechanical acceptance of a lot of old folklore from people suggesting that people should believe this or that of God. Our world envisions what it thinks God wants humanity to do, and then people sit back waiting sadly for God to do it. And some think of God as a puppeteer, making us do what we do."

Lucy sat down. I went into the back room to turn off the music. As Whitney Houston was singing "I Will Always Love You" from the salon's speakers, I slowly turned down the volume and then turned off the system.

A.C. stood up and unzipped his backpack and pulled out his keys. "I get frustrated when I see some people feeling a sense of entitlement for their faith and their time worshiping. They feel that they should earn some kind of merit badge for following the rules." A.C. cleared his throat and looked down. "I had a professor once who said that religion is the safest place for someone to hide from God…I get that."

Lucy stared at A.C. as I started my unplugging routine.

"Lucy, I've got no problem if it makes a person feel better through his day thinking that there's something beyond this existence; I've got no problem with that. It just doesn't work for me anymore."

Lucy looked down at her folded hands. "You don't believe in God?"

A.C. sat quietly, the kid caught cheating on his spelling quiz. I started shutting off lights and checking outlets. "Way to go, A.C. Way to ruin our salad-days moment."

"How can you not believe in God?" Lucy looked at A.C. and shook her head. "Do you believe in the devil? What do you believe in, A.C.?"

"I believe in you, Lu! Come on! Don't be so serious. This doesn't make me a bad person."

"I…I just, I mean, I just don't get it. How can you face each day if you really don't think that there's a higher goodness? Something bigger than we are? Something more than where we are right now?"

I knew that this whole A.C. crisis would not sit well with Lucy. Sweet and strong little Lucy. Her whole life had been a devotion to God and his goodness, which inspired and encouraged her every movement. I knew Lucy would struggle more with this news more than I had when A.C. had first dropped this bomb on me. I think I still felt that he would try on the atheist hat for while and then move on to learn more somewhere else, like he always had.

Lucy hadn't expected this news from A.C. After all, A.C. fit in a "Good" box. Her entire life, Lucy had clearly and definitively placed people in boxes and labeled them appropriately. I wouldn't say that she was judgmental as much as orderly. If she had to figure this world out, she needed clarification. Just pull out a marker and label the box. Ellen Richter—"Self-Righteous." Mikey Beard—"Weird." Eddie Krackenier—"Creepy," now crossed out and relabeled "Victim."

In the "Atheist" box, all was dark and bad and wrong. I'm sure Lucy thought that if you didn't believe in God, then you would probably just become a serial killer or a pimp. Even atheists had options. But you would still be put in the "Bad" box. If Lucy had to open her mind up to the fact that people were more complex than one label, she would most certainly struggle with the muddy fact that people and their lives, and their thoughts and their beliefs, are very, very complicated.

The silence between A.C. and Lucy was both painful and powerful.

I looked at my two good friends and realized that I was looking at two extremes on a continuum of faith—exact opposites. Blind and pure faith. True and pure curiosity. I envied them both for their absolute fervor, their valiant declaration.

A.C. moved toward Lucy and put his arm around her. "I still believe in goodness. There are lots of good things in our world. I'm just hoping to go out and find more of them."

I stood at the door with the key. "Hey, I've got a concert in Colorado to get to."

Lucy stood up and hugged A.C. She didn't have to say it. I knew she was planning on praying for him.

A.C. knew that, too.

26

# Octavia: Wash and Set, Board Meeting

## Friday, January 14

# 1994

Octavia sat in my chair, looked up at me, and smiled a strange smile.

I said, "Wow, I don't think I've ever seen you this quiet."

Octavia put her tiny, vein-laced hand in her big purse and pulled out a cell phone. "I'm connected."

"You've got to be kidding me."

"Truman thinks he can keep tabs on me now. I'll still do whatever I want when I want."

"Like anyone could ever stop that." I started combing out her hair.

Octavia placed the phone to her ear and pretended to answer it. "Saint Peter? Uh, yes, I will give him that message."

"A direct line to heaven?"

"Saint Peter wanted me to ask you: Would there be enough evidence if you were arrested for being a Christian?"

"I thought Ralph Waldo Emerson asked that."

"I thought you were a business major. I'm not even sure who said it."

"Touché, Octavia. OK, so let's focus on your hair. What do you see us doing today?"

"Well, I look in this mirror and see a young, beautiful woman."

I smiled at the mirror Octavia. "I see that same young beautiful woman."

"Do you know that optical-illusion picture, where, depending on how your brain processes, you can either see a haggard, old lady or a beautiful, young lady?"

"I think I've seen it."

"I look in this mirror every day, and my mind chooses to see the young lady. Not the old lady."

"What old lady?"

"Ben." Patti, my newest employee, tapped me on the elbow. "Excuse me, Octavia. Ben, do you know if anyone picked up supplies yesterday? Jenae is in the middle of a color and can't find a dye."

"Toby picked several boxes up yesterday." Virginia answered Patti's question. "They should be in the back room next to the coffee pot. Sorry, Ben, I couldn't find anywhere else to set them down."

I walked Octavia over to the sink to wash her hair.

"You have chemicals in your coffee? Good thing I've already had mine today." Octavia held her phone and frowned at me as I pulled the apron over her.

"Hey! We're absolutely packed in here, Octavia. We've got boxes on boxes. We added a new lady."

"Virginia? The bigger gal?"

"After her, we added another stylist, Patti. We're elbow to elbow here, lady!"

The good news: Vanity Insanity had a waiting list three pages long. Our crazy salon had been gaining a reputation as the different place: "You know, the place with the pink-and-yellow walls." On three separate occasions, I'd tried to paint them something less repulsive and was met with fierce opposition from both staff and clients. Not many places in town had that oh-so-eclectic feel to them, and I'm not just talking about the décor. The Old Market community had finally embraced Vanity Insanity; the owners of boutiques and restaurants in the Old Market were both clients and advertisements for the salon with the crazy staff. The bad news: we were jam-packed.

"Well, if you're that crowded, why don't you do something about it? Maybe it's time to grow up!" Octavia pulled out her phone from under apron.

"Excuse me."

Octavia pointed to the ceiling. "Grow up! The floor above you has been vacant for as long as you've been here."

"Never thought about that. It would be kind of a challenge to put in a staircase…"

"Challenge? Nobody said it would be easy to go upstream. If it was, everyone would."

"I didn't think anyone used the upper floors on this wing." I checked to see if Toby was near this conversation.

"Well, if you don't know for sure, find out and quit whining." Octavia checked her phone as Jenae came up to my station with a broom.

"Check out my new purchase! I'm putting it in our back room." Jenae's long, feathered earrings moved back and forth as she showed the broom to Octavia and me. "The little man who sold it to me was blind. I kid you not. He makes these brooms and sells them. Isn't that the cutest?"

"Must have been the Reverend," Octavia said as she held out her hands to hold the broom. She ran her little hands along the wood of the handle. "He's still doing his work." She shook her head and smiled.

"Yeah, he did say his name was Reverend something-or-another. He was so sweet; I just had to buy a broom from him." Jenae took the broom and ran back to the back room. "Gotta go, my Miss Uptight's almost here."

Octavia looked down at her phone again.

"You waiting for an important call?" I asked. "Got a hot date or something?"

"I'm supposed to hear from Lee about a change in the board meeting for the zoo. I need to let one of my girls know so I can get a ride down there."

"Lee? As in Dr. Lee Simmons, director of the zoo? "Lee Simmons had been pivotal in the growth and changes to the Omaha Henry Doorly Zoo. Under his guidance, the zoo accomplished unprecedented expansion and national attention. I'm pretty sure that everybody in Omaha has been to the zoo at least once. The only person I knew who had never been to the zoo was Jenae. While people from all over the country flocked to our zoo, she refused. I'd quit asking her why since Jenae always said the same thing: "Going to the zoo is a lot like TV dinners and sex on the beach. They sound like a good idea, but once you get there…not so much for me."

"With all the attention the Lied Jungle is getting, the board needs to talk about the next feature," Octavia informed me. The Lied Jungle, the world's largest indoor rainforest, had opened in April of 1992. "We're thinking about a new aquarium, but you didn't hear that from me."

"I was never here."

"Right. The zoo meetings are pretty interesting. I'm sitting on a few boards for banks and schools that put me to sleep. Truman tells everyone yes before I can tell them no."

Octavia's reputation as that ornery, old, rich lady who really knew what she was talking about had trickled through Omaha through the years, and many Omaha businesses had asked her to voice her opinion on their boards. People got a kick out of the colorful lady with colorful opinions and sometimes language. The commissioners of the College World Series had asked her to throw out the first pitch at Rosenblatt Stadium the summer before. While most people watching the nationally televised game might not have known who she was, the viewers in Omaha knew exactly who the diminutive pitcher was.

"Right now, I'm sitting on the board for First Data Corporation. Michael Beard asked me right after his company merged with First Data. Do you know who he is? Nice guy."

"Think so." I didn't think Octavia needed to know of Weird, Weird Mikey Beard's history. Since she hadn't mentioned him spitting fake loogies on board members at meetings, I figured the Weird, Weird Mikey Beard was staying on his meds.

"At the last meeting, Michael Beard seats me next to this really old man," Octavia began.

"So."

"Ben, we're talking really, really old. Did Beard think I was stupid enough not to realize what was going on? 'Let's put the really old people together. Maybe they have some old people things to talk about.'"

"Maybe he was trying to set you up."

"Not my type, honey. Nice guy but seemed like a recovering asshole. After talking to him for while, I could see right through him. Trying to be a nice guy later in life…too late."

Toward the end of the appointment, Kelly and her sister stopped by to see Octavia. Kelly had finally made enough money to have her sister, Chin, move from Viet Nam a month earlier. Fiercely protective of Chin, who'd chosen the Americanized name Katie, Kelly was working on helping her sister gain American citizenship and helping Katie to learn English, but Katie had a long way to go since "hi" and "have nice day" pretty much covered the span of her English vocabulary.

"Oh, wow, Octavia, you have phone now?" Kelly pointed to Octavia's new gadget.

"I do. And I'm getting pretty good at using it. Now see, this little button here can give me any message I missed." Kelly and Katie moved in and looked closely at Octavia's new toy. "And this one, I don't know what that's for. Oh, if I push the number one and hold it, it automatically dials Truman's number for me. I have a different number for each of the girls who drive me around so I don't have to dial the whole thing."

"Wow, that so neat," Kelly said with genuine interest.

Octavia handed the phone to her to look at. "Now the darndest thing happened to me the other day, ladies. This little phone rings, and I answer it like I always do—'Hello, sweetie' is what I say since I know everyone who calls me. Anyway, the woman on the other line is sobbing. I mean, she is crying like a baby. Finally she settles down to tell me that she found my number in her husband's wallet, and she asked me if I was having an affair with him. More sobbing. More drama. She called me a home wrecker. On and on. I finally said, 'Look, you probably fat-fingered the numbers.' Then she said I was a liar. By this time I'm laughing. 'Honey, I'm a wrinkled old woman, but if your husband was seeing me, he wouldn't be able to keep up with me anyway'—and then I hung up."

Kelly and Katie's laughter moved in unison as their bodies shook. I'm pretty sure Katie hadn't understood a word Octavia had just said.

"Kelly, do you still have that little boyfriend you told me about last time I was here?"

Kelly translated Octavia's question in Vietnamese to Katie, and the two sisters laughed. "No way. He was lazy man."

"Kelly, listen to me, now, you have no time for a bum. You wait for the right guy who deserves you."

"I tell last guy, 'No money, no honey,' and then kick him out." Kelly and Katie laughed again.

Octavia's phone rang, and Kelly and Katie ran to the nail tables. I waited while Octavia spoke.

"Hello…yes, that would work…I will see you then."

"Simmons?" I asked.

"Warren."

"As in?"

"Buffett. We're playing bridge tomorrow. He's actually pretty good."

"You play bridge with Warren Buffet?" Her little buddy Buffett had become a billionaire in 1990.

"Only when he's in town. He's kind of a busy guy."

"You are connected, you poor wretch."

Octavia stood up, and I pulled her coat around her and helped her put her arms inside. "You know, Ben. Change is a sign of the Holy Spirit." She put her phone in her coat pocket as I held out the crook of my arm for her. "Katie and Kelly changing their names is symbolic. They're starting a new life here."

"OK. So what's your point?"

Octavia pointed to the ceiling. "Change. Make some calls. Grow up."

I escorted her to the door and waited with her until one of her girls came to pick her up. I heard Octavia giggle as she walked out, "No money, no honey. I like that. I might have to use that one."

As I walked back inside Vanity Insanity, I wondered where she might fit that line in. Maybe in a bridge game.

Not likely.

# 27

# Theresa: Style for Date with Husband

## Friday, November 11

# 1994

"You have got to be kidding me!"

Jenae was in a really bad mood.

The summer of 1994, Jenae decided that she had secretly always wanted to be a blond, so voila: she was Barbie. She had the figure of a Barbie, which few others could claim; she colored her hair, which had been growing out, a Malibu blond. Jenae's long and straight newly golden locks against her tan skin transformed her into what I'm sure every G.I. Joe that I owned growing up would have crawled across the sandbox to get a better angle on. What made the final look a bit comical was the tattoo of a rose on her ankle and the nose ring on the left side of her nose.

She slammed a brush on her station and looked around the salon.

If you had asked her, Jenae would have listed several things that were bothering her that day. First off, the weather was always a factor in Jenae's moods.

The oppressively high temperatures, the humidity, and the clouds hanging dark and low that day weighed heavy on Jenae. Secondly, she was struggling with that fact that anyone would accuse her favorite actor of all time, O. J. Simpson, of murder. She had no clue that he had ever played football. Finally, and probably most relevant, was the fact that Caroline, our staff's token bulimic member, was throwing up in the bathroom again. In about ten minutes, our chairs would be filled with the first clients of the day. For the moment, we all stopped and looked at Jenae, who looked like a very angry Barbie.

"Am I the only one who can hear that? Hello? Am I crazy?" No one dared answer either question as we all looked at Jenae and then to the bathroom door across from the back room. "That's it! I can't take it anymore." She stomped to the door and pounded on it with her fist. "We know what you're doing in there, Caroline. Come out here right this minute."

The door slowly opened, and we all glanced at the pale face of Caroline. She leaned against the door and pushed the hair from her face. "I'm pregnant."

The staff, including Jenae, remained silent as we took in Caroline's announcement. Ten-plus years with a group in tight quarters translated that bad days had a way of sneaking up on us. Nerves and the day-to-day problems of the staff meant that things would blow up and blow over. Vanity Insanity had celebrated its ten-year anniversary in the Old Market, which was an amazing feat in and of itself in the nomadic and fickle field of beautification. Staff turnover was just an accepted part of the salon process. Stylists and nail people got restless and often left one salon for another. My staff had remained loyal, and while for the most part I could say that was a good thing, I did have my days when I went home exhausted from the drama and energy. We'd celebrated the decade milestone with a wine-and-cheese open house for clients and business neighbors to say, "Yep, we're still kicking and screaming' and, in Jenae's case, slamming brushes.

Jenae was now living with Dirk, a Market Rat and owner of Strange Love, a novelty store I had never been to and most likely would never go to. Dirk and Jenae's tumultuous relationship offered light entertainment for those who had to hear of the big fights and rekindled love affairs. Most of the Vanity Insanity staff had been able to make it to help move Kelly and her sister Katie into a bigger apartment. Toby was still Toby. He was still obsessively methodical and within the last year had been recognized by the national Chicago Midwest Traveling Style Team, which enlisted him to travel once a month with their entourage. Virginia and Patti took on his clients when he was gone. Hope, who was putting in more hours, was responsible for the organized shelves of products. And as for Caroline, who had continued to binge and purge through the years, we were currently not exactly sure what was going on in her world.

Jenae broke the silence. "That's good news…right?"

"It is," Caroline whispered.

I have never pretended to understand the wiring of the brain of a person with an eating disorder. When I'm hungry, I eat. When I'm not, I don't think about food. Pretty simple. I don't think that working in a job that focused on physical appearance could help any issues with self-image, and my years with Caroline had educated me on the real suffering that took place in her every waking hour. From what I could guess, she suffered a lifelong hatred of her body and struggled to gain a healthy relationship with that which she must have in order to live: food. Alongside her, our Virginia struggled with her own relationship with food. The comfort she found in food created some angst and health issues in a different way.

I didn't have long to conjecture about the father of Caroline's baby—we knew of no one that she was dating—since the bell above the door interrupted our unplanned staff meeting. Theresa walked in and stopped as the staff, frozen statues around the room, moved their eyes in unison from Caroline to her.

"I'm too early? I can leave and come back." She backed up toward the door.

"No, you're exactly on time." I patted the pink chair and breathed a sigh of relief.

Freeze time ended as everyone glanced at the clock and hurried to get ready for the day's first clients.

"Save me from this nuthouse, the land of misfit toys," I whispered as I grabbed several combs and a pair of scissors. "Remind me again why I'm here."

Theresa laughed. "You belong here, Ben."

Virginia turned on the sound system to bring an end to the silence. Sheryl Crow's voice filled the room with her ambition to have fun in "All I Wanna Do."

I combed one corner of her bangs out. "Can we talk about what's going on here?"

"Guilty." Theresa covered her mouth as she laughed. "That part was bugging me the other day, so I got out my scissors and chopped…"

"Really? Do you see me going out to schools and doing speech therapy on the orphans? Do you?"

"No." Theresa smiled at me in the mirror. "Orphans…" She covered her mouth and laughed.

"I don't do your job, so don't do mine. Are we good?"

"As gold. OK, so fill me in on the whole A.C. thing."

"You mean the Sudan disaster?"

Earlier that year, A.C. had come across information on the civil war in Sudan and its severe endemic of dracunculiasis that was reported by the Guinea Worm Eradication Program there. The country needed help with allotment of food assistance, and A.C. wanted to be a part of the solution.

"And how he's feeling. Why did he go in to Sudan?" Theresa asked.

A.C. had joined the Omaha volunteers, who were trained by UNICEF's Operation Lifeline Sudan, by flying to the country to deliver cloth filters to villages with endemic disease as part of the accelerated intervention. Maybe he'd run into Faith. Once A.C. came down with malaria, Lucy commented, "Hey, there's a country with a lot of sick people. Why don't we go there?"

I combed out Theresa's long hair and replied, "You know, most of my life, people have asked me why A.C. does the things he does. What the hell motivates him? All I can say is A.C. is A.C. I personally think that A.C. went to Africa to find God. He just doesn't know that."

"And a girl, at least that's what I heard."

"You mean Robin? She's actually from Omaha. She was on the team. She's a nurse. She got sick, too. A lot sicker than A.C., since he got to come back when he was better, still weak, though. Robin's still there."

"I heard he wants to go back and get her. Sounds serious."

"I guess. Until then, he's been hanging out with an old law-school buddy, John Hubbard, who served on the counsel for Willie Otey."

"Is he the one they executed in September?"

"That's the one. Nebraska hasn't executed anyone since 1959 when they killed Charles Starkweather after his killing spree across the state."

"So why was A.C. so interested?"

"A.C. drove by the house with his dad back when they found the girl dead. I guess it always stuck with him. When he connected with his friend, he found the whole story leading up to Otey's death fascinating."

"What could be fascinating about it?"

"Well, according to Eric, Willie had been a model inmate who was even allowed to walk the grounds unescorted. Said he wrote a few books, poetry or something. I guess there were lots of legal mistakes that led up to the execution. He just wanted life in prison."

"Wow."

"So tell me something crazy about your day today," I suggested.

"Well, I started my day handing out pills, you know vitamins and dog worm pills."

"Wow. That is one very wacky story."

"Wait, I haven't even told you the story."

"Captivated. You had me at worm pills."

"Anyway my little Morgan, who's two now, and the boys were running around the house getting the dog, Hawkeye, all hyper. Running from room to room, chasing each other." According to Lucy, it was a good thing that Theresa's "boys"—six-year-old twins Joe and William and four-year-old Jack—were so cute because they were a bunch of wild monkeys. "So anyway, I hear this loud crash from the other room, so I hurry up and take my vitamin and run into my bedroom."

I motioned Theresa to the sink and started shampooing her hair.

"Hello, Theresa." Hope arrived with a big box that she set on my station.

"Hope, how are you?" Theresa sat down by the sink.

"I am great. I bring boxes to help Ben get organized."

"Ben's pretty lucky."

I nodded my head, and Hope continued, "Theresa, did you hear that Peony Park is going to be closed?"

I hadn't even heard that. I knew that the old amusement park's popularity had been fading.

"Are you sad?" Hope asked Theresa.

"I am sad, Hope. We had so much fun there when we were kids. I like your shirt." Theresa pointed at the Charlie Brown shirt that Hope was wearing.

"Oh, thank you. I'm washing my number-eighteen shirt today."

"Your number-eighteen shirt?" Theresa looked at me.

"Jenae and Hope are the two biggest Brook Berringer fans. Number eighteen for the Huskers." I started shampooing Theresa's hair.

"Yeah, we think he's soooo cute." Hope's blue eyes sparkled as she tried to sound and look like Jenae when she spoke.

"He is kind of cute," Theresa agreed.

"He is kind of a great quarterback," I retorted. The fall of 1994 had been a breakout season for Berringer. He started in seven games that year since the Husker starting quarterback, Tommie Frazier, was struggling with blood clots. Jenae bought number-eighteen Husker jerseys for Hope and herself, which they wore on games days.

Nineteen ninety-four was the beginning of a new era for the Huskers. They had been improving throughout the years, and in the fall, Husker fans were feeling a national championship on the horizon. The team was incredible. Mac always had to remind me that in our unstoppable offensive pipeline that year was a "kid" from Mac's hometown, Fremont, Zach Wiegert. Mac spoke of the kid, six feet five and over three hundred pounds, with such pride that you would have thought he'd taught Wiegert how to pancake block.

"Charlie Brown played football, too, Hope." Theresa was looking at the image of Charlie Brown getting ready to kick a football that Lucy was holding. Above the picture were the words *Never, ever give up*. "Charlie Brown is awesome!"

"I know. I think so, too. Do you think Charlie Brown is Catholic?" Hope asked sincerely. " Lovey says no." Hope asked both Theresa and me.

"I guess I never really thought about it," said Theresa as she furrowed her eyebrows.

"Lovey says Charlie Brown is a good man. You know, 'you're a good man, Charlie Brown,' and he wears a uniform like Catholics, that same shirt every day, but she said he's probably Methodist."

"Lovey's just teasing you, Hope," I said as I rinsed Theresa's hair.

"Do you think Charlie Brown's Catholic, Hope?" Theresa asked as I sat her up and dried her hair.

"I'm not sure. I told Lovey that I knew Charlie Brown was a cartoon, but I just wondered."

Leave it to Hope to ask the most challenging question of the day. Do you think that Charlie Brown is Catholic? I guessed that all depended on how I felt about Catholics and how I felt about Charlie Brown. Was being a Catholic a good thing or a bad thing? What did I think about Catholics, being a Comatose Catholic myself, who avoided answering questions like this? What did I think of the little melon head in the funny papers who was always left behind, given rocks instead of candy for Halloween, and messed with by Lucy, who moved the ball when he went to kick it. Was he a pushover or just a nice guy who had a few bad days every week? Was Charlie Brown ever an altar boy? Did he know any bad priests? Did his dad stick around for the Kool-Aid stands?

"Hope, can you help me bring in the boxes from the back alley?" Patti called from the door to the alley. I guessed we all would just have to sit with the Charlie Brown question for a while.

Theresa and I walked to the pink chair at my station, and after she sat down, I began trimming the ends of her hair. "OK, so don't leave me hanging," I said. "What crashed in the other room?"

"Well, I have to set this up, OK?"

"I might never know what crashed."

"OK, last Sunday, about five days before."

"Five days before you were handing out pills?"

"Yes, last week Jack had been at Sunday school while we were at Mass. The teachers in his class talk about the same readings from the Mass that day on a younger level. One of the readings was about God taking a rib from Adam and making Eve. Believe me, he talked about it the rest of the day. The reading kind of bothered Jack."

"Bothered me, too."

"OK, so fast-forward to the day of the crash."

"The mystery crash." I picked up my hair dryer and plugged in a curling iron.

"So I took my pill and ran into my bedroom and found Jack lying on the ground. He's holding his ribs and moaning and rocking back and forth. And you know what he says when I poked my head in the room?"

"Help?"

"No, he says…" Theresa was having a hard time talking through her laughter, "He says, 'I think I'm having a wife.'" She covered her mouth and wiped the tears from her eyes. She kept laughing as I dried her hair.

"So what did Jack crash into?"

"My vanity. I have this little vanity table with a stool that Michael gave me years ago. Joe or William had thrown a baseball at Jack. We're not sure which twin did it. Anyway, Jack dodged the ball but crashed into the vanity. The ball hit the mirror, and the rest is history."

"The mirror cracked?"

"Shattered!"

"So have you fixed the mirror?"

"Heck no. It's on the bottom of the honey-do list, a Z priority. Works for now! I have one little area of the mirror that isn't completely shattered that I use to do my hair. If I stand back, I see all of these tiny images of me in the broken glass."

"Not such a bad thing."

"Ben, I almost forgot to tell you the best part of the story."

"The story that never seems to end?"

Theresa laughed as tears came down her cheek. "I took the dog's worm pill this morning. That's the crazy part. I ate a dog pill for worms. Don't you think that's crazy?"

Saint Pius X student body in the late sixties.
*Photo courtesy of Father Mike Eckley, Saint Pius X*

Saint Pius X First Communion picture.
*Photo courtesy of Father Mike Eckley, Saint Pius X*

Saint Pius X parking lot as busses pick up children.
*Photo courtesy of Father Mike Eckley, Saint Pius X*

Saint Pius the X in 2013.
*Photo courtesy of Father Mike Eckley, Saint Pius X*

The tornado of 1975 as seen from the Ak-Sar-Ben racetrack.
© *Photographer Bob Dunham*

The original headquarters for the Union Pacific Railroad in Omaha.
© *Union Pacific Railroad Museum*

Warren Buffett.
*Photo with permission from Warren Buffett*

Indian Hills Theater.

Brookhill Country Club.
*Photo courtesy of Brookhill Country Club*

Marian High School in the early eighties.
*Photo courtesy Susan Toohey, Marian High School*

M's Pub in the Old Market in downtown Omaha.
*Photo courtesy of M's Pub*

Inside of M's Pub.
*Photo courtesy of M's Pub*

Sacred Heart Church.
*Photo courtesy of Father Tom Fangman, Sacred Heart*

Coach Tom Osborne.
*Photo courtesy of NU Media Relations*

Memorial Stadium in Lincoln, Nebraska.
*Photo courtesy of NU Media Relations*

"Coming and Going" illustration.
*Photo with permission of the Norman Rockwell family and Curtis Licensing.*

# PART III

## The Day the Music Died

## 1995 to 1997

*The three men I admire most, the Father, Son, and Holy Ghost, they took the last train for the coast, the day the music died.*

**Don McLean, "American Pie"**

# 28

## Octavia: Wash and Set

### Friday, December 15

# 1995

A petite, older woman by the name of Elsie sat on the church pew near the window of Vanity Insanity staring at Jenae's long-sleeved T-shirt as though she were witnessing a horrific car accent. Elsie, one of Octavia's girls, visibly shaken, could not look away.

What Elsie was so mesmerized by that December morning was an incredibly tight-fitting pink T-shirt that Jenae had stretched over her astonishing curves. It read: Dirty Blond. I suppose I should have felt more professional guilt in allowing Jenae to wear the possibly offensive shirt to work, but Jenae and I had come a long way to get to the present message on the shirt over her eye-catching chest.

A few months earlier, I'd made Jenae wear one of my Husker sweatshirts over the T-shirt she'd worn during River City Roundup. She had come into the salon in a short jean skirt, red cowboy boots, a cowboy hat, and a T-shirt that hoped to convince the world of her plight: *Save a Horse, Ride a Cowboy*. Elsie should be relieved that I'd spared her that terror.

Elsie now accompanied Octavia to every appointment. Truman said that she was a good friend of Octavia's from the church who, along with Truman, had recognized a change in the matriarch. Octavia was more agitated and absentminded, and so Elsie was her guardian to most of the appointments now. Octavia either ignored Elsie or else was not aware that she did not leave Vanity Insanity when I did her hair. I walked Octavia slowly to my station as she took in all of the obnoxious Christmas decorations covering nearly every inch of the salon.

Since Jenae's first bizarre and atypical Christmas adornment, the tradition of decorating the salon took on a life of its own. Staff and regular customers asked Jenae what day they should mark on their calendar to come help turn Vanity Insanity into the cheeriest and tackiest holiday venue like no other. The decorating kickoff took place the Saturday after Thanksgiving immediately following the last appointment of the day. Those who wanted to attend the party were to bring drinks and a holiday decoration they were planning on throwing out to the evolving tradition. Bad taste was the key. Jenae ordered everyone around until the last glitter-elf statue was perfectly placed, all of the fake snow laid out, and the last glass of wine drunk.

"What is that?" Octavia stopped in front of the plastic Elvis Presley, as tall as she was, wearing a Santa outfit. Santa Elvis had been with Vanity Insanity for six Christmases. He wore dark glasses and held a sack of toys in one hand and a microphone in the other. The slant of one raised lip gave the appearance of someone who was just about to throw up.

"That's the new receptionist. I don't think he's going to work out." I walked Octavia to my chair and helped her sit down.

She looked at me with an expression of pure perplexity. She sat down and tilted her head. She mumbled, "Just as well. He ain't nothin' but a hound dog anyway."

Glimpses of Octavia made me smile. Less and less of those moments had been occurring over the last six months. The woman who had taken over most of Octavia's waking moments was grumpy and confused. The woman in Octavia's clothes, holding Octavia's phone, was agitated by the bright lights and the noise in the salon. And while this woman showed up every Friday for Octavia's appointment, this imposter never talked about the growth of Omaha or cussed out the big-city lugs that were slowing things down.

"These walls are ugly," Octavia mumbled as I put the apron on her.

"I won't argue with you on that one."

"How long have you been here? I remember another place."

"Eleven years, Octavia of the Old Market, of which you are part owner, lady."

"Yes, yes..." Octavia shook her head and looked down at the phone in her trembling hand.

Octavia's name remained on lists of boards around the city, banks, the Henry Doorly Zoo, and schools, but she no longer attended meetings. Elsie took Octavia to daily Mass and "hung out" with her when Truman was unavailable.

"Do you still play with that one black kid? D.C. or something like that?"

I couldn't hold in my laugh. "Octavia, I can't believe you remember A.C. Yep, we still *play* together every once in a while."

In 1994, A.C. had made several attempts to get back to Sudan to see Robin but was denied by his doctor each time since he was still vulnerable to all of the serious diseases in Africa at the time. It would be a month before Robin could come back to the States.

"The atheist, right?" Octavia was on a roll. "You know, I've never met an atheist I didn't like. Some of them are the strongest believers—they just don't know it. They're just thinking. That's all."

After I shampooed her hair and walked her back to my chair, she said, "And don't get me started on the priests that you read about in the paper."

"OK."

"Those priests are not the Church. They are bad people in the Church. They aren't the Catholic Church." Her voice was louder with each word.

"I'll make a note of it." I combed her hair as she relaxed again. She remained quiet for a few minutes.

"I saw in the paper that...What's the name of the place? A racetrack?"

"Ak-Sar-Ben Racetrack?"

"Yes, yes. Ak-Sar-Ben. They shut the place down. Just like that."

"Yeah, I guess attendance to the races had been declining for years. I hear they're going to start putting in some commercial and residential developments instead."

"We were just there last week," Octavia told me. "David and I took the boys. They like to look at the horses after the races. Always make a big day of it."

I knew that Octavia hadn't been to the races in years. I hesitated and then asked, "Win any races?"

"Oh, I'm not much of a gambler." She stopped talking for a while. She seemed agitated, so I let her rest. But suddenly she panicked and asked, "Where's my purse? I need my purse!"

"Right here on my station, Octavia."

"Where's my phone?"

"In your hand."

She looked down and started to chuckle. "I'll be damned. Now what was I talking about?"

"What you're getting me for Christmas." I smiled.

"What I'm getting…Do you know where I put my purse?"

I helped Octavia up and gave her purse, which was sitting on my station, to her. We walked together to get her coat, and Elsie came over to help me put the coat over the fragile body between us. Octavia hooked her hand in the crook of my arm, and I escorted her past all of the staff, who looked up at us but said nothing. Octavia stopped at the Elvis Santa again and looked at him. "Pretty cluttered in here," she muttered. "You really need to clean up. How long have you been here?"

"Eleven years. Twelve in a few months."

"Well, you have a really nice place here."

Elsie and I flanked the old body invaded by an imposter all the way to the car and helped her into the car and into her seat belt.

I missed Octavia.

29

## Michele Mangiamelli: Highlight and Trim

### Tuesday, January 9

# 1996

"Do you have time to do a shave along with the usual trim for Chewbacca this afternoon?" Toby covered the mouthpiece of the phone.

"Sure," I mumbled, hoping that Subby's wife Michele Mangiamelli hadn't heard him over the running water.

"Chewbacca?" Michele asked as I pulled the towel up from her collar to dry her hair.

"Yep. He's a big guy with a lot of hair who kind of looks like…"

"Really?" Michele was one of my favorite clients. Subby's wife was a classy, beautiful woman who could talk sports. After she sat down in my chair, I started to comb her long, auburn hair out.

"Just let me explain. Jenae isn't very good with names, especially those who aren't her clients, so she makes up nicknames," I said as Michele looked at me in the mirror. "Sometimes inappropriate ones. She uses the nicknames so much that we sometimes can't remember the real names. Just one great big, inappropriate family."

The faces of Mrs. Happy, Chunk, Monkey Man, Festus, and Cruella are all clear to me even to this day, but I couldn't give you their real names to save my life. Each nickname made sense and clicked instantly but was never used in the presence of the client. We had class, you know.

"You're not going to report me, are you?"

Michele smiled. "No, I just want to know what my nickname is."

"Sorry, we save nicknames only for the unusual and bizarre, not the beautiful. We remember your name, Mrs. Mangiamelli."

"Whatever," Michele smiled. "Let's talk about this suntan you have going on."

"I do look good," I said as I looked at myself in the mirror and raised one eyebrow.

"I mean, let's talk about where you got it! Tell me. Was it awesome?" Michele was referring to the national-championship game. Sun Devil Stadium, Tempe, Arizona.

"Incredible." A.C. and I had flown down for the game and spent a few days there after watching the Huskers win their second national championship in a row. We hadn't seen this kind of football in our state since the early seventies. "And everyone was betting against us. It was awesome."

The Husker buzz in Omaha was remarkable. The 1995 team in Osborne's twenty-third season was arguably his best and in time would be known as one of the best teams in college football history. Husker fans couldn't have been more proud of a team that followed the 1994 off-season, nicknamed "Unfinished Business," with a national championship only to repeat the success in the 1995 championship led by Tommie Frazier and Brooke Berringer. The year was so great that most fans overlooked the sideline drama of several players who were in trouble with the law; strange incidents of violence and accusations of attempted murder had been challenging for our Husker leader. Coach Tom Osborne told his fans, "It was a terrible year, and it was a great year."

"Subby and I were so jealous. I think I've got him convinced to book our tickets to the championship next year." Michele was the main reason I'd broke down and bought a big colored TV for the salon. She said that she would schedule her appointment during game times if I did. "Oh, Subby wanted me to give you an update on Will."

Will Mangiamelli had fallen off the face of the earth in the last year, and his family members wavered daily between worrying that he was dead in a ditch somewhere and furious that he had taken so many bad roads in life because of his addictions. During a haircut a while back, Anthony Mangiamelli had told me that he'd bought a T-shirt for Will, which he found appropriate and in which Mrs. Mangiamelli found no humor: *I'm not an Alcoholic, Alcoholics go to Meetings.* He never gave it to Will. A.C. and I, after numerous failed attempts to connect with Will, finally stopped calling the friend who struggled like the stupid bird that kept flying into the window, again and again. Our old CCD teacher had told us long ago—in a moment when I was paying attention—that we were like a clean, white shirt when we were born. Sin was that first stain on the shirt. For many, Will included, it was easier to just keep messing up the shirt since it was dirty already.

Mac said it best when he said that free will is the thin line between us and the devil—when we cross that line, the devil has control of us. Something like that. I found myself angry at Will, the guy whom I had always been a little jealous of for most of my childhood, who seemed to have it all, who had crossed the line somewhere through the years.

"Will showed up on Louis and Ava's front porch a week ago," Michele said, "sober." I was shocked. "Neither asked any questions. He's been staying with them since."

"How's everyone taking it?" I asked, knowing that the brothers and Lucy had grown tired of Will's inconsistent and irresponsible behavior that worried their parents so much.

"Well, Stephano didn't even stop by when Ava and Louis killed the fatted calf for the prodigal son. Those are Stephano's words, not mine. Subby and I did go over there for dinner. Will looks pretty thin."

"Bummer."

Changing the subject, Michele looked around the room and then whispered, "Does anyone know yet?" She was referring to the decision I'd finally made to look into the space above Vanity Insanity to make room for the growing business. I had asked Subby Mangiameilli to walk through the space with the realtor to see if I should pursue it. We both agreed the price was steep, and Subby knew a contractor who said prices should be going down within the year. I looked over at Toby and shook my head no to Michele.

"Ask me again in a year. What about you? I heard that you two were house hunting."

Michele perked up as I trimmed her ends. "Great! We finally decided that we want something in the Holy Cross area. We put a bid in on a house Saturday."

I stopped and stepped back in shock. "Did I just hear you say 'Holy Cross area'?"

Michele was a non-Catholic from Chicago who had come to Omaha in 1990 to work at Mutual of Omaha. She'd met Subby through mutual friends, and the two knew instantly they'd be together a long time. Michele had confided in me when she and Subby had started courting each other that she found Omaha to be a little crazy. "If one more person asks me what school I went to, I'm gonna scream!"

"Why? You went to a great school in Minnesota."

"People in Omaha don't want to know that. Most people mean college when they ask an adult where they went to school. But not in Omaha. They want to know if you went to Saint Philip Neri or Saint Wenceslaus or Saint This-or-That. They want to place you in the city, and if you're not from Omaha, they're not quite sure where to place you."

"We're not that bad. We're just playing the Omaha game when we do that. People just want to know what puddle you came from so they can ask you who you know."

Evidently, Michele had jumped into the messy puddles of Omaha. She became Catholic when she married Subby, and from the sounds of it, she was dividing the city by parish puddles. If you can't beat them, join them.

"We looked in the Holy Cross area," Michele said again as she smiled. "Troy will be in kindergarten, and I guess we need to find the area that will categorize him for life. He'll be a Holy Cross kid. I'm OK with that."

"You put a bid in?"

"Actually, the house kind of looks like yours." I had bought a little home in the Assumption area the year before.

The sound of a baby crying came from the back room. Kelly and Jenae made a beeline for the back, elbowing each other to get to Caroline's baby first. In 1995, within the yellow-and-pink walls, we'd added one more to the staff, though he was still in diapers. Caroline's baby boy, Connor, had been born in the middle of July during a record-breaking week of temperatures over one hundred. Caroline couldn't afford day care. We all guessed that the father was out of the picture physically and financially, so the staff agreed to share the tasks of taking care of Connor. We set up a playpen in the small back room and juggled feedings and diaper changes with shampoos and manicures. My initial reluctance waned as clients enjoyed having a baby around. Caroline's "issues" seemed under control, and she looked healthier than ever. Kelly offered her wise two cents' worth: "That baby save her life, you know."

As I finished Michele's hair, we continued the updates.

"A.C.'s girlfriend is back from Sudan and still recovering from the malaria episodes," I told her.

"Robin. Right? I heard you all like her."

"She's too good for him, so he'll probably dump her. Kidding!"

"Fingers crossed. Did you hear that Tom Ducey is considering running for city council?"

"He only knows half the city. He's got my vote."

As Michele stood up, she turned to me. "So who's this Fiona person that Lucy told me about?"

One of my clients had introduced me to Fiona a few months earlier. "She's a sharp Irish woman who runs an Irish shop on the other side of the Old Market. We enjoy each other's company."

"Yikes, that sounds like a relationship with your sister." Michele was savvy in the ways of sports and relationships.

"No, she's really a great gal."

"A great gal? I haven't met your new girlfriend, and I already know why."

"OK, so she's not 'the one,' but we both have something to do on a Friday night," I said as we walked to the UP desk.

Michele cleared her throat after she paid me. "I'm guessing you haven't heard the news." I put her check in the drawer and looked up. I thought we'd covered it all. "About Theresa." She looked down.

Theresa hadn't been in for a while. "I hear she's pregnant. Does this make number four or five?"

"There's something else. Lucy wasn't sure if you knew yet." Michele looked down. I hadn't seen Lucy since before Christmas. "Theresa had some tests done. It looks like she has breast cancer."

I heard Connor giggling in the back room. "But she's pregnant."

"And she refuses to start treatment until the baby is born...while the cancer is growing. Lucy wanted me to tell you since she can't get in here for a while."

I didn't know what to say.

"Ben." Jenae dropped a note on the desk in front of me. "Chatty Kathy needs to change her four o'clock appointment to four thirty. She needs you to call her back."

Michele touched my arm. "I thought you'd want to know."

# 30

## C. Henning, Jenae's client

### Tuesday, April 30

# 1996

"I'm not going. I'm a big fat elephant, so I won't need to come in for my hair appointment."

Lucy was pregnant again.

"You're not going where?" I had been sitting at the UP desk going through mail when Lucy called.

"To this big political event for Tom. He's going to announce that he's running for city council."

"Are you not coming in for your appointment because you're an elephant, you're sick, or you're in a grumpy mood?" I asked as Jenae walked in from the alley in the infamous sweatpants, an oversized sweatshirt, and a Creighton Blue Jay baseball hat over uncombed hair. Kelly and I had our sneaking suspicions that Jenae was off her meds again based on the past two days.

"All three," Lucy responded, pulling my attention back to the telephone.

"Not to sound judgmental, but isn't the wife supposed to stand by her husband when he makes big announcements like this?"

"Not if she's an elephant."

I put the mail in the drawer and pulled out the schedule for the day as Lucy changed topics: "Did you hear about Johnny Madlin's killer?" A call from Lucy was never quick. "They electrocuted him." Nebraska had barely wiped the dust off the electric chair from Willie Otey's execution and apparently felt the need to use it again. "And Theresa has another chemotherapy treatment today. What an awful day."

Theresa's baby, Mary Elizabeth, who was due in May, had been born by C-section in mid-March. The delicate balance between waiting for the baby to be "ready" to be born and rushing to have the baby born so that Theresa could start treatment weighed heavily on her friends and family. While waiting, the cancer in Theresa had thrived with the hormones that helped her baby grow. The very proud godmother of Mary Elizabeth was Lucy. No sooner had the water from the baptismal font dried on Mary Beth's newly baptized head than Theresa was taken in to start an aggressive chemotherapy.

"OK, well, I guess I can't force you to get your hair done," I said.

"It's against the law."

"Hope you feel better soon."

Jenae was sitting in her chair in her station staring at herself in the mirror.

I hurried over to her station, stood behind her chair, and looked at her in the mirror. "So I heard that your number eighteen is about to be drafted, Toots. Ya gonna miss him?" Announcements of the draft were coming up, and the state of Nebraska wondered where Brooke Berringer might end up.

Jenae didn't answer, and then Toby and Virginia walked in from the alley with several coffee orders. They both looked at Jenae and then at me.

"I forgot to tell you something, Jenae," I added.

Jenae looked at me in the mirror; her eyes without makeup made her look very young. Kelly and Katie walked in. Kelly ran up to the chair and stood next to me, looking worried as her eyes met Jenae's in the mirror.

"I threw everyone's name in a hat and pulled out your name. Jenae Tolliver!" I said loudly. Jenae blinked. "Don't you want to know what you won?" Kelly put her hand on Jenae's shoulder. "The day off, Toots." Jenae started crying into her hands and then got up and hugged me. We had about fifteen minutes before the first appointments.

"I got your bag." Kelly was holding Jenae's purse. "You want me to drive you home?" Kelly had just gotten her license. Jenae nodded.

"You want to let us know what's going on," I asked Jenae as she pulled her head from my shoulder. She shook her head no.

Almost in a whisper, I said, "Jenae, you need to go home. I know you're trying to see if you don't need your medicine sometimes, but you do. I want you back here tomorrow in stilettos and sequins or whatever."

Jenae pulled a Kleenex out of the pocket of her sweatpants and blew her nose. She nodded her head up and down as she hugged me again. "Sorry."

"No problem. Stilettos, remember."

Kelly walked Jenae to her car as I looked over the schedule with Toby and Virginia. Double booking was never fun, but no one complained, as we juggled appointments all day. By lunch, I was hoping that Jenae's one o'clock appointment I was covering would be late so I could eat a sandwich in the back room. The bell over the door rang as an incredibly gorgeous woman walked into Vanity Insanity. I looked up at the petite blond in a gray, perfectly fitting professional blouse and skirt. She glanced at Jenae's station and frowned.

I looked at the schedule. "Henning?" I asked.

"Yes, I'm looking for Jenae. I have an appointment with her."

"Jenae went home sick, but I'm picking up some of her appointments. I'm Ben."

Henning looked me over and then looked at the clock on the wall. "Sure. I guess that will work. Where do you want me?"

I was glad that A.C. wasn't here because he would have seen that as an opportunity. All the possible answers to that question. I directed C. Henning to my chair and pulled out an apron. "What are we doing today?"

"Just a wash and style." She smiled. "I'm going to an event tonight, and I'd like something fun and different. What do you think?"

Again with the interesting questions.

"I'm meeting an old friend tonight. I ran into him at the Holy Name Fish Fry. You ever been to one of those?"

I combed out the long locks before directing C. Henning to the sink to wash her hair. "Oh, yeah. Holy Name is the granddaddy of all fish fries. The beer, the fish, the way you smell when you leave. It's all good."

"Anyway, I ran into this friend, whom I haven't seen in years and we just clicked. Just like that. We clicked."

I stopped combing.

"Anyway, he and I kind of have a history… If you know what I mean."

"History?"

"We go way back to grade school. I haven't seen him in years. Then there he was, handing out flyers for his campaign at the fish fry."

The word "campaign" hit me like a bad mythical creature in a poorly lit movie.

"He's having some big party to kick off his campaign. He doesn't know I'm coming. I thought I'd surprise him."

"Are we cutting off your ends, uh, Carol?"

"Charlotte. My name is Charlotte." Of course it is.

So the mythical creature did exit, and she was sitting in my chair. Charlotte the Harlot even had a real last name. I checked out her boob job as I started drying her hair. I felt a bit of that old guilt as I tried not to make C. Henning look too good.

While Charlotte Henning was paying for her services, Katie answered the phone. She was getting better at speaking English, so she was excited to grab the phone whenever it rang. Katie handed me the phone as I watched my one o'clock leave the salon.

"A.C. on the phone. He sound serious."

"What's up?" I answered the phone, wondering if he had news about Robin.

"Brook Berringer died. It's on all the local channels. Plane crash."

I couldn't reply.

A.C. continued, "Not a great day in Nebraska. Sorry to have to be the one to give you the news."

"I'm good." I hung up and turned to Toby, who had been watching me on the phone with concern.

"Everything OK?" Toby asked quietly.

"Some pretty bad news." I turned on our flat screen and turned to ESPN. A man reported, "Brook Berringer, former Nebraska Cornhusker, died in a private plane crash in a field in Raymond, Nebraska. A friend and brother to Berringer's fiancée also died. Berringer was expected to be drafted in the NFL this coming week."

I walked over and sat on the pew near the front door and watched ESPN. Toby came over and sat next to me. "I hope Jenae gets herself together before she hears."

"I'll go over and check on her later. I'll let her know," I said as I walked over to the desk and picked up the phone. I'd been double booked all day. I could juggle one more appointment. I dialed.

"I changed my mind, Lu," I told the grumpy pregnant woman on the other end of the line.

"Changed your mind about what?"

"Your appointment. Get your little elephant butt in here. I'm going to make you beautiful. You have to go tonight, Lucy. Your husband is running for city council. You're going to stand next to him."

"But…"

"No buts except your elephant butt in my chair."

Lucy arrived forty minutes later, still a little cranky.

Her hair looked great that night.

31

# Theresa: Guido the Wig

## Friday, November 1

# 1996

C*ra-zy, cra-zy, cra-zy.*

On the drive back to Vanity Insanity from the Beauty Supply Warehouse, the rain attacked my windshield like an army of uninvited flying ants. A ripped wiper on the driver side was not doing its job as the wipers moved back and forth, making a creepy sound that pounded in my head.

*Cra-zy, cra-zy, cra-zy.*

I parked on the street side of the salon since after seven o'clock most of my staff had gone home. Toby was probably the only one still cleaning up now. I could see the back of Theresa's head in the Vanity Insanity window as I got closer to the door. She was sitting on the pew across from the UP desk. Her hair, as long as it had even been to my recollection, flowed down her back.

"Are you ready for this?" I asked as I walked into the salon. I smiled as I pointed to the box I held in my hand.

"Is that my new friend?" she asked. Theresa and I had gone to the Beauty Supply Warehouse a few weeks earlier to see the selection of wigs. As soon as she'd found out she had cancer, she'd decided to shave her head, donate her hair to Locks for Love, and avoid having her hair come out gradually. She would wear hats around the house and save the wig for outings in public places. Together we found a color similar to her caramel hair, so Theresa ordered a shoulder-length wig, and we waited. I'd called her as soon as the warehouse let me know her wig was in.

"Yep, I say we call your little friend in this box Guido. Just a thought."

Theresa smiled and tilted her head. "Guido? I like it."

"Word on the street, you been lookin' for Guido," I said in scrappy Mafia accent. Toby came out of the back room with a box of supplies.

"Hi, Toby!" Theresa said as she started walking to my chair.

"Hey, Theresa." Toby was always awkward when Theresa came in. I think he suffered from Beautiful Girl Syndrome. I knew that Toby liked Theresa, but his face would turn red and he came off rude whenever she was around. Theresa was always kind to him, though. For the past several months, Toby had been asking me for updates on Theresa's health.

"Ben, I'm in Chicago until Tuesday. Remember," Toby said as he wiped his station down, preparing to leave town for a conference on hairstyles.

"Yep. Come back with some new crazy ideas. I won't let anyone touch your station when you're gone." I smiled. Toby cleared his throat and forced a smile back.

Theresa sat down in my *safe* chair and smiled at me in the mirror. She pulled a ponytail holder out of her purse and handed it to me.

"I guess I won't be needing one of those for a while."

As I combed out Theresa's long hair, clumps began to fall into my hand. I knew I would get through this appointment, but I felt my hands start to shake.

"Bye." Toby carried his box of supplies to the door and set it on the pew.

"Have fun in Chicago, Toby," Theresa said.

"'Have fun stormin' the castle!'" I yelled to Toby.

Theresa's laugh echoed against the walls, "I know this one. Sounds like *Princess Bride*, right? Billy Crystal is dressed up as a really ugly, old guy and he yells it to…Westley. Right?"

From my peripheral vision I saw Toby touch the upper casings of the door, rub the door handle, and dart out of Vanity Insanity. "You are good."

"Dancing Queen" by Abba was playing on the sound system. Toby must have switched to an oldies station when everyone left.

*Friday night and the lights are low*
*Looking out for a place to go…*

Theresa watched me put her hair in a high ponytail. Her smile fell into a solemn expression. I rarely ever saw the beauty before me without a smile. Did Theresa really have cancer? Did the person in front of me really have something in her blood or her system or whatever that was trying to kill her? She didn't look sick to me. Maybe there had been a mix-up in the lab. Maybe this was all just a terrible mistake we'd be talking about ten years from now. "Wow, wasn't that crazy? We thought Theresa had cancer." My hands started shaking again as I picked up the scissors.

"Oh! I almost forgot!" I yelled as I put the scissors on my station. I ran to the back room and came back with a bottle of wine and two wine glasses. Theresa's smile came back. I would do anything to keep that smile on her face.

"Now I'm not trying to be romantic or anything here," I said as I poured the wine. "I wouldn't want Michael mad at me for hitting on you. I just thought that since it's after hours, we could enjoy this appointment." What great irony. Theresa knew we both needed a glass of wine.

"Awesome, Ben. Great idea."

*You are the dancing queen, young and sweet, only seventeen*
*Dancing queen, feel the beat from the tambourine*
*You can dance, you can jive, having the time of your life*
*See that girl, watch that scene, diggin' the dancing queen.*

We both took a big sip.

"Remember how Lovey would murder this song?" I set down my glass, picked up the scissors, and took a deep breath.

"Oh my gosh. In her little two-piece, she would act so cool walking around Brookhill singing at the top of her lungs: 'See that girl, watch her scream, kicking the dancing queen.'" Theresa sang loudly as she mimicked Lovey. We both laughed more loudly than we would have on a normal day. Today was not a normal day.

"But wait, there's more," I added. "Then she would sing: 'Better want a watussie, Everything is fine, you're in the mood to dance.'"

"'Want a watussie'? What's a watussie?" Theresa covered her nose as tears came out of her eyes while she laughed.

"Exactly." I held her ponytail in one hand and the scissors in the other one.

"What are the real words anyway?" Theresa asked, laughing more.

"I don't even know. If I listen to the music, I still hear watussie." I looked down at her as I said this. I could see several large tears spill against her cheek. Theresa was trying to laugh, but the tears came stronger. She covered her face.

"You don't have to do this, you know," I whispered.

Do what? Get her hair cut? Shave her head? Have cancer?

Theresa took a deep breath as she wiped the tears from her face. She grabbed her glass of wine from the station and held it up toward the box that held her wig. "To Guido! My new little friend."

I cut slowly through the thick hair just below her ponytail holder. I placed her long ponytail on Toby's counter. I would need to clean up his station later. I took the electric razor and began shaving Theresa's remaining hair from her head in long rows. The pieces of hair fell in clumps to the floor like an army of dying ants. Theresa smiled in the mirror. Even without any hair on her head, she was beautiful.

I opened the box and set it on her lap. I picked up my wine glass and held it above the box.

"To Guido." I set down my wine glass, pulled out the wig, and placed it on her head. Theresa smiled at me in the mirror. I smiled at her in the mirror.

"You know, it looks pretty real, don't you think?" I said.

"Not bad," Theresa sniffled. "Just for a short time, so it's going to be great."

Theresa kept her new wig on as we finished our wine. The rain lasted into the night, hitting the roof tops of the homes in Omaha, like an army of uninvited cancer cells attacking a beautiful woman.

# 32

## Octavia: Trim, Wash and Set

### Friday, November 15

# 1996

"What a hoot! I haven't guessed the number of jelly beans in a jar since fifth-grade math!"

"Don't even talk about the jar," Virginia mumbled to Lucy as she walked by, her eyes big and threatening.

"OK." Lucy looked at me, confused, and followed me to the back room.

"We had a little contest," I said under my breath, "that didn't work out so well…Actually, it divided the crew. Long story."

"Oh, tell me. Please."

I looked out at the staff and then shut the door to the back room. "The Head JAM saleswoman gave me a huge bag of products and a stipend that was to go toward a contest with clients. For someone to win the bag of products."

"Sounds like a harmless little gimmick. Kind of fun."

"No, not 'kind of fun.' So Virginia had the idea to buy a 'humongous' jar to fill with jelly beans. She bought the jar, the biggest I've ever seen. Jenae went out and bought a carload of jellybeans to fill the jar."

"Still sounds fun to me."

"OK, so Virginia hands out bags to each staff member with the instruction to count the jelly beans. Jenae, Caroline, and Patti felt that an estimated number found on the label of each bag would do. Toby and Kelly felt that the exact number was the whole point of the contest. More than anything Jenae did not want to count the jelly beans. Toby did not think he could trust the others, so he counted all 7,943 beans with a 'humongous' deal of jelly bean resentment."

"Did you have the contest?"

"The jelly bean jar has been sitting on the UP desk since last week when Monkey Man won. He told me that he needed a giant jar of jelly beans and a bag of hair spray like he needed a hole in his head—or monkey head. So he didn't take it. It's been very quiet around here."

"So the jar sits."

"The jar is the center of tension around here. I vow never to have a contest again." I held my hand up in a scout's honor pledge. "Now what brings you in here today?"

"Not the festive energy, that's for sure. I probably won't help change the mood here. I needed to let you know that Theresa finished her stem-cell procedure last week."

"I know you've told me, but what is a stem cell…?"

"It's barbaric, that's what it is. The doctors basically took Theresa to death's door."

"OK, but why?"

"It's a pretty aggressive procedure that's usually saved for high-risk patients. I didn't hear that from Theresa, though. A friend of mine who's a nurse told me. She said that the patient receives a high dose of chemotherapy with a bone-marrow or stem-cell transplant. I think since they didn't get a good start on attacking the cancer in the beginning, they're resorting to this."

"Will it help?"

"I hope. She's been so sick and weak. At the worst of it, in the hospital, Michael said that Theresa started mumbling about all of the little babies crawling around the room."

"Babies?"

"Yeah, she saw them on the bed and crawling on the floor. She told Michael that one was sitting on his lap."

"What?"

"The doctors told Michael she was hallucinating, but between you and me, I think she had little angel babies protecting her."

"Wow."

"The rosary group's still meeting, so we're just turning up the prayers. Your jelly bean contest and the story behind it actually cheered me up."

"Any time my wacka-doodle staff can be of help."

As Lucy walked out the back alley to her car, the bell rang above the front door. Elsie walked Octavia in the front door. Octavia stopped at the big jar of jelly beans on the desk and stared.

"Would you look at that, Octavia?" Elsie spoke in a beautiful, thick Irish accent, "Look at all of those jelly beans. Aren't they beautiful!"

Several staff members looked at the jar and frowned. I helped Elsie take Octavia's coat off as Octavia continued to stare at the jar.

"How you doing, Elsie?" I asked.

"We're not having a very good day today. Perhaps we could make this a quick one."

"Sure."

The past few appointments had been the same. Octavia no longer needed her warming-up time. No more verbal banter. No more stories. She sat in her appointments holding her cell phone with both hands. She might comment on the music being too loud, but mostly she sat quiet. Elsie and I guided Octavia to my chair.

"How about those jelly beans, Octavia. Kind of crazy, huh?"

"Crazy," Octavia muttered as she looked at her phone, her hands shaking. She sat down and looked at me in the mirror with a question on her face. "Amazing?"

"That's me," I said. "Pretty amazing." I combed out her hair.

"Such a resemblance."

"Who are you talking about, lady?"

"Your father. You look just like your father."

Did Octavia even know my father? "My father?"

"Now, does he still farm outside of town?"

"Of what town?"

Octavia paused. "Oh, I thought you were… you look like Donald."

"Donald?"

"A boy who lived by me in Fremont. We used to show sheep at the fair…" Octavia looked at the phone in her hand. "Such a resemblance." Relief came over me like the buzz off a stiff drink. Just what was going on in the beautiful head in front of me? Octavia was quiet for most of the rest of the appointment. The group No Doubt filled the room with their song "Don't Speak."

As I finished Octavia's hair, she mumbled, "I caught one of those TV shows late last night."

"TV shows?" I'd never heard Octavia talk about television before.

"Where they interview someone and talk about their life."

"Like a documentary?"

"Yes, yes, a documentary. With that Diane Sawyer lady. She's doing something funny with her hair now." Was I talking to the real Octavia here?

"*Twenty/Twenty* or *Forty-Eight Hours*?"

"Something like that. A documentary. Late. Very late. And I'll be damned if they weren't doing a whole segment on Elbert True… E.B. True."

"E.B. True?"

"My old man," Octavia spoke in a gruff voice. No, I wasn't talking with my old friend Octavia.

"Your dad?"

"He talked about the farm and the bankruptcy."

"They actually interviewed him?" What was I saying? Octavia's father would have been dead for years now. "Maybe the man just looked like your dad."

"You think I wouldn't remember what my old man looked like?" Octavia shouted. Jenae and her client looked over at the old woman in my chair.

"Sorry."

"Sounded like he'd been drinking, that ole son of a bitch. That's when I knew it was him for sure." Octavia stopped. Elsie saw that I was finishing up.

"Then Diane Sawyer asked about his twelve children."

I put my combs and brushes away. I was intrigued.

"He answered. Right there on national television. He said that he didn't care much for kids. Kind of a pain in the ass. That was what he used to always say about us. I tried to change the channel, and then the old man looked right at the camera and said, 'Octavia, she was the homely one, downright ugly.'" Octavia's lip began to tremble. "That's what he said." She held her phone and began to rock back and forth. Tears filled her eyes.

Elsie walked up as I placed my hands on each of Octavia's shoulders. I consoled her, "Those shows are all a big setup, Octavia. All for ratings. Not real. Anyone who knows you knows that you're beautiful."

Octavia looked at me in the mirror and beamed liked a child being praised by a teacher. Elsie took her hand. "Octavia, dear, we need to be getting along now. We need to get lunch ready."

"We need to go," Octavia mumbled as Elsie and I helped with her coat. "It'll be dark soon."

I walked the girls to the car on the sunny Friday morning in November, relieved that I did not look like my old man.

# 33

## Lucy: Protein Pack, Trim, Cafeteria Duty

### Wednesday, February 19

# 1997

"What's wrong with you anyway?"

"Nothing. Not a thing, Lu," I lied.

I had a lot on my mind since I had received a call from the friend of Toby's client Cruella. Dale Sinnot had called to propose a business offer in which everyone stood to benefit, including Cruella, who had lots of upset friends sitting on the Vanity Insanity waiting list to get their hair done. Sinnot wanted to embark on a business journey as a partner in a huge renovation to Vanity Insanity with a major addition to the salon that could accommodate more room, more clients, and more services. I had been careful to conduct most of my interactions with Sinnot outside of the salon, all the while teetering between excitement at the potential growth of my business and consideration of leaving the industry all together. I hadn't voiced that feeling to anyone yet.

"Well, you're really starting to bug me with this serious and quiet thing you have going on. You haven't even asked me about my girls." Lucy and Tom had added one more girl to the sorority, as Tom called it. Delaney Rose was the fourth and final Ducey, according to Lucy. Tom and Lucy with their four beautiful girls around them had appeared in a picture on the front page of the *Omaha World-Herald* the day after Tom won his election for city council. When Lucy told me that Charlotte the Harlot had showed up at the kickoff party last year, I acted surprised and asked, "How did her hair look?"

"Did I ever tell you that Tom's opponent in the election was Joe Weller?"

"I think I know that, Lucy. His name was on the ballot. The one I didn't vote for."

"Joe Weller, Ben. Do you not remember Joe Weller?"

I shook my head.

"Horror Hall Joe Weller. The jerk who broke up with me when I wouldn't kiss him in the Horror Hall."

"The guy who dumped you in sixth grade?"

"The guy who lied to Sister Annunciata when asked if he had ever been in the Horror Hall following junior-high games."

"What a loser. Serves him right. We could have a devil running our fine city. What a relief."

"Joe Weller's not a devil."

"You said so yourself."

"No, I said he was the jerk who broke up with me. Joe Weller isn't evil. But I do think evil exists in some people."

"You're telling me. I think one of Virginia's clients looks like he's related to the devil." I laughed as I trimmed Lucy's ends.

"Ben, I'm serious. I think that the devil is powerful to weak people, taking advantage of weaknesses, like greed, vanity. He keeps us busy. Don't you ever wonder if at one moment in your life, you might have been standing right next to evil? Maybe in the line to order food at Burger King?"

I was still having a hard time keeping a straight face.

"Let's say Johnny Madlin's murderer was standing right behind me when I ordered a McRib sandwich as a kid," Lucy continued.

I made a face. "You couldn't get a McRib at Burger King. I remember McRibs. Nasty."

"What if the devil himself sat under your nose in your chair?" she asked me.

"Then I'd probably use a stiff gel to give him a real wicked look." This time I made Lucy laugh. Kelly stopped by my chair with a note from Sinnot.

"Speak of the devil," I mumbled as I took off Lucy's apron.

"Oh, I almost forgot to tell you that I bought a Sting CD, *Mercury Falling*." Lucy grabbed my arm. "I'm hooked now. I swear, Sting's voice is like a warm, long kiss on the back of my neck...It sends shivers—the good kind—up my spine. Can I be in your Sting club now?"

"I'll run it by the board."

"You mean A.C.?"

"Yep. And me. I'm the president."

"How is A.C.?"

"Well, I haven't heard any wedding announcements yet."

"OK, so does Robin know that he's a you-know-what?"

"No, but I think she's got A.C. figured out. Just a hunch. Also, my mom got married to her little friend."

"Wow. Good for her. Good news everywhere. Marty and her husband are starting the adoption process. And Theresa got her good news."

"Yep." Theresa had told her rosary group that she was cancer free a week earlier. I still couldn't believe the news.

"And the Huskers?" Lucy asked.

"Let's not go there."

"But you love your Huskers!"

"Lucy, have you not been paying attention?"

It might sound shallow, but the shift in my personal storm that year started when the Big Eight Conference merged with four Southwest Conference Teams to form the Big Twelve Conference at the beginning of the season. After back-to-back national titles, "my Huskers" had suffered two disappointments last season. The first was the 19–0 catastrophe at Arizona. Fans who had been loving the ride we'd been on as an unbeatable force felt the jolt back in August when the Huskers flew to the desert in Arizona, only to get their "butts handed to them," as Jenae had so eloquently commented. The vibes worsened when we lost to Texas in the inaugural Big Twelve Championship game in December, both games confirming an end to the winning streak and the possibility of three back-to-back national titles.

Nebraska does not like being compared to Iowa or confused with Oklahoma, but we really hate being beat by Texas. We were the Charlie Brown kicking the ball, and Texas was our Lucy, pulling the ball out from under us.

"So what wicked soul gets to be the first to see your hair done so well?" I asked.

"That would be the fine young children of Saint Pius X and the ladies who volunteer in the cafeteria. I have cafeteria duty today."

"Cafeteria duty. Sounds like something you step in out in the backyard."

"It's not bad. Actually, this older lady I work with told me that cafeteria duty is a lot like sex for tired moms."

"I'm pretty sure that this is something I don't want to know."

Lucy grinned in the mirror. "They're both events that you should probably do but have so much else to do and you're exhausted. But once you get there, you end up having a good time."

34

# Octavia: Wash and Set

## Friday, May 9

# 1997

"Damn, not what I needed to hear today," Tom Ducey mumbled as he, A.C., and I walked across the street to M's Pub. My two legal buddies, as a favor to me, had looked over the merger agreement that Sinnot was proposing for the renovation of Vanity Insanity. We were going to talk about some of the curve balls that Sinnot had tucked into the contract proposal.

Tom ended his phone call with a buddy, who had given him bad news about the former Nebraska Football coach. "Bob Devaney died," he said to A.C. and me as he held the door open to the restaurant. "Damn."

"The Devaney days," A.C. said, "were some awesome times. Kind of like the early seventies were Husker Nation Part One and we're living Part Two right now." A.C. was referring to our two national championships and the "Three Pete" T-shirts that all the Husker Hopefuls were wearing as we crossed our finger for a third national championship.

"Three," Tom said to the owner, who took us to a table near the window.

The owner paused after she set down the menus at our table, "Hey, Ben, how's our dear friend doing?"

"Not the best. Her son brings her to get her hair done, but that's pretty much it, " I said.

"We miss her around here. We really miss Octavia."

"I'll tell her that." We both knew that Octavia wouldn't know who I was talking about.

"Sounds good," the owner said quietly. "I'll send your waitress over to your table."

"OK, so not to be a buzz killer, Ben," Tom started and looked at A.C.

"But we think this Sinnot guy is trying to screw you," A.C. finished.

"OK, now what?"

"The plans look good," Tom said, "but Sinnot stands to gain more of a profit than we both think he deserves. I mean, he's done nothing but show up with money to add to yours."

"Yeah, and from the looks of this contract, he's hoping to gain the most from all of the work you've put into Vanity Insanity for over a decade. He's kind of like a gold digger." A.C. looked over the menu. "We don't think you should walk away, but Tom and I want to tweak a few things before anything is signed."

We talked a little more about the contract before lunch came, but Tom and A.C. agreed to make the changes on the contract that I would show to Sinnot the next week.

"Almost forgot to tell you both," Tom said as we were finishing lunch. "Lucy wanted me to tell you that Theresa's cancer is back, and…it was probably never really gone."

A.C. looked at me and then shut his eyes and sighed. Because he hadn't seen Theresa much since her cancer diagnosis, he was still having a hard time getting his head around the reality.

"Before the next rounds of aggressive chemo, she took a two-week break, and she and Michael went on a trip." Tom pushed his plate aside. Why had I not heard about this? "They flew over to Lourdes, France, to make what Lucy called some kind of a healing pilgrimage."

"Lourdes?" A.C. asked. "I read about that place. Isn't that where some woman saw visions of Mary? Miracles happen there or something like that."

"Sounds right. Anyway, Theresa was too weak to walk to the Masses and nightly candlelight processions and the grotto, so Michael moved her through the town in a wheelbarrow."

"Wow." I hadn't known that she had gotten to the point of being so weak.

"The best part of the trip, according to my wife, is that she met Richard Madlin, Johnny Madlin's father."

"Seriously?" A.C. rubbed his eyes and shook his head.

"Yeah, so this Mr. Madlin told Theresa that he went on the trip to pray that Mary would take away his anger, which had been causing damage in his life since his son was killed. The man has no cancer or illness, but he makes the pilgrimage so that he can forgive the dude who murdered his son, so that he could move on with his life."

"What about Johnny Madlin's mom?" A.C. asked.

"She didn't go on the trip since she could never forgive the man who killed her son, whose last earthly task was to deliver the evening paper. So the father asks Theresa to pray for his wife. You ever hear of anything like that?"

I paid for lunch as a thank-you to my legal team, and we all walked out to the brick street between the restaurant and Vanity Insanity. Tom lit a cigarette as he walked to his car. A.C. told me he'd call me later, and I walked back to work.

When I walked into the salon, Octavia and Truman were sitting on the front pew near the window waiting for me. Truman, whom I hadn't seen in a long time, looked old and tired. He smiled as he helped Octavia up.

"She's been waiting all morning for her appointment. She thinks every day is Friday." Octavia's hands shook as she held fiercely to her phone, shuffling to my chair. The staff respected the situation as they had for the past year and did not bother Octavia as she walked through the room. The years of chatting with the sassy yet kind old lady, which even Toby used to do, were gone, as Octavia had become increasingly agitated with all of the activity.

I tied the apron around her, and she looked at me in the mirror with furrowed brows. "What am I doing here?"

Truman stood by the chair and patted her arm. "Mother, Ben's doing your hair today, remember?"

Octavia looked up at Truman and then looked at me in the mirror.

"Octavia, you're here so that I can help you to look beautiful," I explained. "Remember, I'm the one who helps you to be even more beautiful."

Truman walked over to the pew and picked up a newspaper. Octavia said nothing and sat with a look of distrust on her face. About halfway through the appointment, a moment of lucidity came over her. "That Truman is too busy for his own britches. He can't even take the time to visit his mother anymore." I looked over at Truman, who looked up from his paper, shook his head, and smiled. He'd probably been accused of this before.

"Be nice if he could take time…and he's gotten kind of chubby lately. Maybe you haven't seen him…"

This time I laughed as I made eye contact with Truman who threw up his hand in the air, shrugging. Octavia was quiet as I dried and styled her hair. I began to take off her apron, and Octavia grabbed my arm with a tight grip.

"Did my husband pay you yet? He has the money to pay you."

Truman walked over to help her get up from the chair.

"He must be parking the car, but he can pay you," Octavia insisted.

"Mother, I'll pay Ben. I'm here," Truman calmly whispered.

"Where's David? Where did David go?" Octavia demanded.

Truman tried to calm her. "He's not here, Mother, not today."

"Where is he?" Octavia panicked. "Where is David? I need to know right now!" The staff and their clients looked over at her.

Truman shook his head as he looked at me. "So sorry, Ben."

"Where is David?" the tiny woman screamed. "Where is David?"

"Mother, Mother, calm down…Mother, Dad died. Remember? It was a really nice funeral. So many people came. I'm here to pay Ben. I'm here."

Octavia began to cry. "David died? Well, this is just awful…This is terrible…We need to call someone…" She put her hands to her face and sobbed as though David had just now died; her shock and grief were both very real. Jenae and Kelly looked at Octavia. Jenae looked down as she pulled open the appointment book. Toby avoided eye contact as he organized and reorganized his station.

Truman turned to me. "Ben, this is obviously not good. Would it be too much to ask you to stop by Octavia's house to do her hair? We have a full-time nurse around the clock. We can pay…"

"Just let me know what you need," I told Truman.

Octavia began to rock back and forth, holding her phone with both hands now. "Hail Mary full of grace, the Lord is with thee…" Truman took one arm as I took the other, and together we got Octavia to the car. She continued praying the rosary as we put her in the car. Suddenly, she stopped, grabbed my arm, and looked directly into my eyes. From all of the years of looking at each other in the mirror, I can't remember ever looking eye-to-eye at Octavia Hruska. She placed her tiny hand on my cheek and smiled a very warm, endearing smile. "Teddy, you're a very good boy. You are such a good, good boy."

The name of Octavia's dead son stung the air, and Truman put her seat belt over her, buckled it, and shut the door. His eyes watered as he shook my hand. "Thanks, Ben. So sorry about the scene. Octavia thinks the world of you…"

I walked back into Vanity Insanity and looked at Toby, who was standing at the desk, pretending to look through the appointment book. Everyone in the salon looked ill at ease. I took a deep breath.

"Toby, could you help Virginia and Jenae cover my afternoon appointments?" I could hear my voice shake. I caught my breath. "I'll be back to close." No one said a word as I grabbed my keys and left. I drove without knowing where I was going. Not knowing where I needed to go.

I drove north of the Old Market and into neighborhoods, just driving around. I drove in circles around the same block several times until I realized that I was driving past Sacred Heart, a beautiful church in the Kountze

Place neighborhood. I parked my car in the church parking lot and sat for a while. I took a deep breath and got out of the car and stood for a while looking at the old, beautiful church. Then I walked inside. It was dark and quiet in the afternoon hours.

The smell of the church was clean and pure. Years and years of Masses and incense and oil and celebrations. I was smelling the odor of sanctity, a smell that I missed. I walked about halfway up the aisle and sat on the right side of the church in a pew by myself. I noticed people coming and going from the a little room on the side of the church. I guessed that this room must have been what Lucy's "open face" or face-to-face Confession looked like. No dark closet to kneel in and feel overwhelmed by my sins and the sins and secrets of those who sat in my chair. Just a room in which I would have to face my sins. Face-to-face with another human.

My heart was pounding.

I slowly walked toward the side room and looked in. A man about my age with a warm smile motioned me into the room. In casual attire, the priest, still in his collar, welcomed me to a chair near his. He put down a book as I walked in. I sat down in the chair next to him and took a deep breath. I knew that I had memorized a little program of sorts as a kid when we went to Confession during CCD. Not one word came to mind.

"I haven't done this in a really long time." I laughed nervously.

"That's fine."

"I mean, really, I have no idea what to say."

The kind, hazel eyes of the priest reminded me of Mac. He smiled and said very quietly, "You don't have to say anything at all."

I felt the tears flooding from my eyes as I cried while the man before me took my hands. Father Saving Grace whispered the most needed absolution to me as I continued to cry.

I said nothing as I shook his hand and walked out of the tiny room.

# 35

## The Stink Bomb

## May–September

# 1997

The summer of 1997 sizzled like the wick of a cheap stink bomb. No loud explosion. Nothing too sensational. Still the slow and repulsive sizzling of problems was the unpleasant reality between May and September.

Working with Dale Sinnot—or Slick, as Jenae referred to my new business partner—on the renovation plans for Vanity Insanity, I learned more about myself than I ever cared to know. All of Jenae's disparaging remarks through the years regarding my control issues began to make sense as I found myself more than uncomfortable sharing control of Vanity Insanity with a man I liked less and less each time I met with him. When Sinnot and I met at M's Pub in June to move forward with the project, he showed me the blueprints of the upstairs addition to Vanity Insanity. The blueprints also included the bay next to us. I had gone to the altar twice with the owners of Tres Chique, and both times the runaway brides had changed their minds right before contracts were signed.

"How can you include the bay next to us?" I asked Sinnot. Tres Chique would not budge; this much I knew.

"Because I'm hoping to strike a deal with them soon. Real soon. Word on the street is they're shutting down in August, giving us plenty of time to order equipment for the massage rooms."

Sinnot didn't run in the Old Market circles. Where would he hear any "word on the street"?

"Massage rooms? I guess that's probably a decision I'd like to have been a part of." Whoever cut Sinnot's hair did a really bad job. This middle-aged man was clearly fighting the age factor, as he kept a mass of hair covering his receding hairline. The mop moved up and down as he talked. He reminded me of my ninth-grade math teacher. I didn't like my ninth-grade math teacher.

Once the renovation was over, Sinnot would be a partner in the financial books only. He knew nothing about the business. He knew nothing about the people I worked with or the clients who had been coming to see my staff for the past fourteen years. He had just come to me with his money to make money.

"See, I knew you were busy, Benny, and I thought I'd be helping out by taking care of the details. Everything is coming together beautifully. This place is going to be big. I mean, really big." Sinnot cut his steak, took a big bite, and then pointed to the blueprints with his fork as he chewed.

I picked them up and looked over the plans. "I thought you said you were going to have several architects bid on the project. I see only one plan here."

"Again, taken care of." Winking at me, Sinnot took his napkin and patted his smug little lips. "My brother's an architect, and I've already saved us money here. Though money isn't a problem." Another wink. From the beginning, Sinnot had played the "money is no object" card enough that I was beginning to wonder. "The decorator's coming by this afternoon to take some measurements."

"Decorator?"

"Her name is Dolly, and I guarantee you will love her, Benny."

I swallowed some water and took a deep breath. I detested this man's insinuation that he could take over my business, even if he was loaded.

I knew he and I would need to talk before any contracts were signed. I could see that we both had a very different vision of the growth of Vanity Insanity.

When the check came to the table, Sinnot let me take care of it. I paid for the meal and felt my lunch sloshing around in my stomach as I walked across the street to the salon. I looked up at the sign and realized that I was starting to have the same feeling about my affiliation with Sinnot as I had about my connection with Fiona. I didn't see a future with her, either. I was good at walking away from things, but I had never been good at the breaking-up part.

When I walked in to the salon, a short woman popped up from the pew and began performing for me like a Shetland show pony. "We've got some changes to make here, Ben. It is Ben, right?" The short woman with—surprise—a bad hairdo held out a clipboard as she grabbed a pen from the overteased, overcolored helmet on her head. "The colors are all wrong, as you probably know, and this monstrosity here..." Dolly pointed to the UP desk. "...will be the first to go." I saw the back of Toby's head as he stormed out to the back alley, slamming the door. "I'm just going to take a little dipsy-doodle upstairs to take a little looksy at the pallet I have to work with." Dolly handed me a card as she pulled a tape measure out of her purse. "Here is my contact information. Call me with any questions you might have."

Dolly doodled to the ladder next to the bathroom, which was the only access we had to the upper bay until the stairs were installed. I looked down at the pink business card, which read:

*Dolly's Decorating*
*At a loss for your décor?*
*Dolly's knocking at your door*
*Dolly Sinnot*

Really? Sinnot had sent his wife—straight from the fifties—with her bouffant hair and her dated clichés to decorate my life? Jenae's spin on the couple was comical. She called them Jim and Tammy Fay of Annoying.

"I don't like her," Kelly said to me as she handed me a bill. "The construction man needs money before they start work next week. That dipsy-doodle lady really bug me."

By July, the workers had made a mess of the upstairs, which they dragged into the salon as the staircase was built. Jenae made several "Please Forgive our Mess" signs that she placed all over the salon. The silver lining that month was that we realized that we had the most loyal clients in the city, as not one left us during that time—while the waiting list to get a haircut at Vanity Insanity grew.

Near the end of July, Robin had organized a surprise birthday party for A.C., and I looked forward to the break from the mess. I'd arrived a little late to Toad's, a bar on the other side of the Old Market. A.C. had already been surprised, and he yelled to me as I walked in, "Better late than never! Get over here." He had an arm around Robin and looked happier than he had in a long time. "Where's Fiona?"

"We called it quits last week. It's all good." I hadn't had to initiate the breakup with Fiona since she beat me to it. I couldn't blame her. I'd been a lousy boyfriend.

"Ben, you missed the big surprise!" Lucy hugged me and handed me a beer. "Look, Marty's in town." Lucy pointed to Marty and her husband. "They're house hunting!" Lucy raised her eyebrows and tilted her head.

"House hunting?" I raised my eyebrows and tilted my head.

"That's right. Our uppity big-city friend finally realized that Omaha is the world's best-kept secret. They just adopted a little boy and will probably move in sometime this fall."

I wondered if Theresa's health had any impact on the decision. "Good for Marty." I looked around the whole bar, taking in all of the people who'd showed up for A.C.

"She's not here," Lucy said above the noise of the bar.

"Who?"

"You know who." Lucy waved to Tom, who had also gotten here late.

Lucy and I had known each other so long that we could kind of read each other's mind. I'd never once told Lucy about my feelings for Faith, but she knew. What was wrong with me? Maybe I was that creepy guy who only liked what he couldn't have and would then die a lonely, pathetic, creepy guy.

"And yet you always look for her," Lucy continued.

"Do not." Maybe Faith still thought about the kiss by the fire truck.

"Do, too." Lucy looked directly into my eyes.

"Not." I looked away from her and saw Theresa and Michael a few tables over. Theresa had stopped treatment for the time being and was growing her hair out, which was coming in darker and curlier. She stood with one crutch on her left side. I looked at Lucy. Lucy looked at Theresa, looked at me, looked down, shook her head, and walked over to Tom.

Each episode of cancer treatment, Theresa had talked about her cancer like it was an annoying summer cold that had hung on too long. Lucy told me it was anything but. A week earlier Lucy, Marty, and Theresa had gone to dinner for a girls' night out while Marty was in town. They had met in midtown Omaha and talked for a few hours. When the three drove away in separate cars, Lucy noticed that Theresa turned the opposite way to go to her house. Lucy was concerned that Theresa may have been overtired and decided to follow her to make sure Theresa made it home safely. Theresa drove to the Methodist Hospital parking lot and went in. Lucy followed her and found her. When Lucy asked Theresa what was wrong, Theresa replied, "Oh, I was feeling a little tired, so I went to get some blood."

The crutch was there to help Theresa as she hobbled around with it. No one was supposed to acknowledge it. Marty suspected that the cancer had moved to her bones. Why would they have stopped treatment?

"Ben!" Theresa called out. I moved toward her so that she didn't have to walk.

"Look at the hair growing back, Theresa. You're going to have to start coming back to my chair."

"Short and sassy. I've never had hair like this."

"Ben, I heard that you're adding on to Vanity Insanity." Michael kept a hand against Theresa's back while we talked, as if protecting her from alien forces.

"Something like that. It just looks like a mess right now. I'm going to have a party when the place is all cleaned up."

Theresa said, "We'll have a big party together. I can't wait until this whole thing is over." The "thing" would be the "cancer" word we weren't allowed to say. "Michael and I are going to have a big party, too, and invite everyone we know. Right?" Michael nodded with a smile on his mouth but not in his eyes.

A.C., who looked like he was high on life, ran over and hugged me. "This..." he pointed to me as he spoke loudly and very near Theresa and Michael's face. "This is the best friend a guy could ever have. This is my best man!"

**

By September of 1997, the renovation project from hell ran into speed bumps at every turn. Workers tore apart walls upstairs and didn't show up for weeks after that. Sinnot, who was in my face and annoying earlier in the summer, was harder and harder to get a hold of. By September, I was ready to pull out of the deal since I could see the toll it was taking on my staff. We were uncomfortable to say the least. Toby, who did admit that we needed to expand, was still overwhelmed by the lack of structure for such a long period of time. Jenae, who was staying on meds and strong as ever, spoke to me one day on behalf of the staff. Virginia stood behind her, a rock to support her words.

"We hate this project."

"OK, Toots. So tell me how you really feel about it all," I said in the sarcastic tone that I used most days during that time. Virginia tried to hide a smile.

"Ben, I mean it. We won't ever complain about how crowded we are ever again. Ever." Jenae was going through what we all called her "country girl" phase. She wore pink cowboy boots with her miniskirt and a shirt tied like Marianne on *Gilligan's Island.* While grieving the passing of Brook Berringer, Jenae had discovered Sawyer Brown, a country group who recorded "The Nebraska Song" in tribute to her favorite Husker. The lead singer for the group had been a pallbearer at Berringer's funeral. Jenae, now an avid fan, was in the front row when the band played at the Nebraska State Fair in August. "Toby's having a real hard time with this whole..."

"We'll all be uncomfortable for a while," I interrupted. "Not a big deal."

"It is a big deal."

"It'll be over soon. I don't have a lot of control here, Toots. I didn't plan for the renovation to get to this point. I planned everything differently in my mind."

Virginia leaned in with one hand on Jenae's shoulder and one on mine. "Hey, if you want to make God laugh, show Him your plans."

Neither of us laughed.

"I know you will make it better, Ben." Jenae galloped off to her station. Virginia shrugged and walked to the door to meet her client.

At that moment, I decided I would call Dale Sinnot and make a date for a breakup meeting so that I could gain control of this project. The minute I began feeling peace about the decision, I felt a sharp pain in my mouth that had been a dull pain I had ignored for the past month or so. I opened the desk drawer and took a handful of aspirin. Kelly shook her head and scolded me.

"You take too much aspirin. You need to fix your pain. Not ignore it."

"I'm planning on making an appointment soon. I promise," I lied. I had no time to make an appointment, let alone go to one, for my tooth.

"Almost forgot to tell you." Caroline came up to me and tapped me on the arm. "Mrs. Happy called and canceled."

"What?" I couldn't tell if I was annoyed at Caroline for telling me three minutes before an appointment that someone had canceled or mad that Mrs. Happy always canceled and expected immediately rescheduled appointments.

"She said that she could come in tomorrow morning."

Tomorrow wouldn't work. I was booked. Mrs. Happy, whom I constantly shuffled appointments around for, was going to be Mrs. Not-So-Happy, and I found myself OK with that. I decided to wash the front window as a time filler since the dirty windows had been bothering me the entire morning. I grabbed some Windex and paper towels and walked outside. A young man in a tailored suit with a smile bigger than the pain in my tooth walked up to me.

"Do you know if they take walk-ins there?" The man tilted his head toward Vanity Insanity.

"If they have openings. What do you need?" Today was this man's lucky day. Walk-in availability had been very rare over the past year.

"Something new. I'll wait as long as needed for an appointment." He was having an awesome day. Maybe his good fortune would wear off on me.

"I could cut your hair. I just had a cancellation."

"You work here? Kind of a different place, huh?"

We walked into Vanity Insanity together, and I pointed to my chair. "Yep, kind of different."

"I heard the owner is wiping out his whole block and putting in some mega day spa. The Old Market vendors aren't too happy about it."

"So what are we doing here?" I used my barber voice. "The same thing, only shorter?"

"Nope. Do something different. Anything. New salon, new look, new life. I've never felt better."

"Sounds like you're celebrating. What's the big occasion?"

"I just decided this afternoon that I'm leaving my wife, and you're the first person I've told. I've never felt so alive."

The words were suspended in the air with the scissors in my hand. I hadn't asked for this man to share his personal life with me. What I wanted to tell Mr. Young-and-So-Alive was to take a number, buddy. I already know half of Omaha's secrets. I wanted no more details of his wicked plans—like maybe he was leaving a daughter or a son who was not yet born. I didn't want to know about the ugly pieces of his life. What was it with this place that made this chair a diuretic to people's souls? I wasn't a psychologist, a bartender, or a priest. I was just here to do your hair. I wanted to yell at this man to get the hell out of my safe chair. And yes, I would say "hell." Over the years, I'd endured the stories of unhappy employees, unsatisfied spouses, tortured children, unappreciated relatives, and more. I was getting tired of being privy, oh so privy. What was in the shampoo that made people feel the need to bare their souls? Just what was in the shampoo?

Mr. Young-and-So-Alive smiled at me in the mirror. I motioned him toward the sink and washed his soon-to-be-divorced hair. I brought him back for a trim and decided to give him the same hairstyle; I would not be party to his happy breakup.

As I cut, I glanced in the mirror to see Toby cutting a young boy's hair. The boy appeared to be six or seven and looked miserable as his mother stood near and watched every snip of scissor. A gigantic tear rolled down his freckled cheeks.

Jenae tapped me on the shoulder, her eyes red and swollen. She handed me the phone. "Truman's on the line. I'm so sorry, Ben."

# 36

## Octavia: Great Plains Mortuary
## The Last Appointment

### Thursday, October 2

# 1997

During the drive to Great Plains Mortuary, I said something that resembled a prayer.

I'm not sure if I was addressing God or Octavia, but I asked for enough strength to make it through her final hair appointment. As long as I was asking, I added that a little bit of peace in my world would be nice.

After my phone call from Truman, I called Sinnot to reschedule our "breakup" dinner until after Octavia's funeral and left a voice mail. I needed to focus on Truman's request; he told me that Octavia had passed away during her afternoon nap, and then added, "It would be really great if you could do her hair for the funeral, Ben. If you're not comfortable with that, I would understand."

"Just let me know when and give me the directions to the mortuary." I knew that I wanted no one else to do her hair.

Back in my college days, I'd made some good extra money moonlighting at a mortuary doing hair of the deceased. The money was amazing since there's not a long line forming to do the hair of dead people, who—by the way—are naked with a thin sheet over their bodies. A.C. commented that the whole thing certainly put a new spin on the phrase "dull and lifeless hair." After which I added, "Yeah, people are just dying to get their hair done by me." The money was good, but after a few weeks into the job—did I mention the dead bodies were naked—I quit. I guess I wasn't cut out for the funeral home scene. Somehow, doing Octavia's hair felt different than when I'd worked on strangers.

Truman told me that the Rosary would be that evening and that the funeral would be the following day at Saint Cecilia's Cathedral with the burial following at a cemetery in Fremont. I was surprised at how calm I had been upon the news of her death. I felt something of a relief since the Octavia I had known had died a few years ago, and the alien that had inhabited her body since then had suffered tremendously. Now the suffering had ended.

With a box full of supplies I'd brought from Vanity Insanity on the passenger's seat of my car, I drove to meet Truman at the mortuary on a Thursday in early October. I parked, grabbed my box, and walked toward the front door to the mortuary. Truman was sitting on a bench outside the door and stood to shake my hand. He had always been a good son to Octavia, but this gesture to make sure that she looked good for her funeral showed how much this man really knew and loved his mother.

"Thanks again," he said.

"You bet."

I followed him to the embalming room where I was to work on Octavia's hair. Truman then introduced me to the man standing by her body.

"Ben, this is Digger Gehring. Digger, Ben's the one I told you would be coming by to do Mom's hair." Digger shook my hand as Truman turned to me. "Digger and I grew up together in Fremont."

"My brother couldn't say my nickname, Tigger, when I was a kid, and so it stuck for life. Kind of a funny name for a mortician, huh?" Digger offered this information as I looked at a picture of a clown on the wall of the room. I found myself resisting a strong urge to laugh out loud at the surreal, dark comedy unfolding before me. Digger, a heavyset man with big, brown eyes, directed me to the table upon which lay Octavia's body, covered with a blue sheet. I took a deep breath.

"I'll see you at the Rosary," Truman said, patting my shoulder as he walked by.

Octavia's head was propped up at an angle with what looked like a wooden pillow. I remembered from my short-lived career at the mortuary that the bodies were staged as they would be in the coffin since when rigor mortis set in, they were harder to position. Hanging next to the table was a navy-blue suit that I'd seen Octavia in about a half a dozen times in her life, mostly in the newspaper or when she had board meetings to go to following an appointment.

"I'll be getting some work done in here, so just let me know if you need anything, Ben." Digger opened the door of a closet in the room and began taking out several boxes.

"Thanks."

I walked over to the table and set down my box of supplies. I pushed a lock of hair from Octavia's forehead. I knew this head of hair very well. I knew the light streak of gray on the left side of her part. I knew the cowlick on the back end of her part that I always hid by strategically pulling the thicker hair to the left and then back-combing the area. I knew that her thinning hair at the front hairline had bothered her. I knew Octavia's natural silver-gray hair well.

I pulled out two combs that I usually used on her each appointment and a can of hairspray. I worked on one side of her head and then moved to the other. Adjusting my position several times, I sprayed over areas that I knew had a tendency to stray. I stepped back to look at the beautiful old woman in front of me. I was really going to miss her.

"Knew her well?" Digger asked after he shut the closet door and moved the boxes against the wall.

"Most of my life." I looked at Octavia. I would never do her hair again.

"It's never easy."

"Yeah." I looked up at the picture of the clown. "You keep that picture in here to lighten the mood?"

Digger grinned. "That's me. My other job. Digger the Clown. The job gives balance to my life. Keeps me sane, you know."

I laughed, maybe a little too loudly. "Got any openings?"

"I'll let you know. You know, I'm not supposed to leave you alone here, but I need to get this box down to the front desk and grab a file. If you want to take a moment alone, this would be the time."

Digger the Clown/Mortician left, and I walked back to the end of the table on which Octavia's body lay. I considered sneaking a cell phone into her folded hands and then laughed out loud again. This tiny old woman had been a powerful presence in my chair, in my life. Octavia had given me so much through the years as she scolded but never judged. She knew me. This woman knew me. I moved one last hair to the side of her temple.

"At least it's clean. It's been an honor, Octavia."

37

# Octavia's Funeral: No Morning Appointments

## Friday, October 3

# 1997

The next morning I closed Vanity Insanity. Jenae, Toby, and the others had all wanted to attend the funeral, so I had Virginia contact clients to reschedule morning appointments while Jenae posted a sign on the door of the salon:

*Vanity Insanity will be closed this morning so that staff and other clients can attend the funeral for our client and friend, Octavia Hruska.*
*She will be dearly missed.*

Before we left, I read in the *Omaha World-Herald* a Midlands-section feature story on Octavia that included a picture of her standing with a young baseball player at the College World Series. She was holding the ball that she was about to throw out at the opening game. Her head was tilted in toward the player, who had his arm around her. The twinkle in her eye with her subtle grin brought the only tear to my eye that day. The story was well written and was an extended version of the obituary that appeared in the listing with all of the other people who died that week in Omaha.

> **Hruska, Octavia Edith (True)**—Age 92, born in Fremont, Nebraska on December 25, 1905. Died September 30, 1997, in Omaha. Preceded in death by her husband, David Hruska, and son Leonard Theodore "Teddy" Hruska. Survived by son Truman Hruska, daughter-in-law Deb, and granddaughter Sara. Octavia was a generous contributor to the Omaha and Fremont communities. She loved classical music, flowers, political debates, and progress. A service will be held at Saint Cecilia's Cathedral on Friday, October 3, at 10 a.m. Memorials to Omaha Alzheimer's Association. Rosary Thursday evening 6 to 9 p.m.

Octavia's funeral at Saint Cecilia's Cathedral was on one of the most beautiful fall mornings that I can remember. The colors on all of the trees were popping against a true-blue sky without a single cloud. I walked into the packed cathedral and saw Mac waving to me halfway down the aisle. He had saved a spot for me next to my mom and sisters. Mac stood up and let me in the pew next to my mom, who leaned into me and whispered, "Warren Buffett is three pews ahead of us." Octavia would be pleased.

People were standing against the walls near the confessionals since there was no room to sit. I saw the owners of M's Pub sitting a few pews behind me. The priest and what looked like staff from the mortuary moved the casket to the front of the church as the organ blared from the balcony of the enormous, beautiful cathedral. Mac elbowed me and pointed to the program for the funeral. Under a list entitled "Honorary Pallbearers" was my name among several names of people I remember Octavia mentioning. "The old gal liked you, Ben."

The last song of the funeral was "Let There Be Peace on Earth." I think I remember sometime through the years Octavia saying that this was a favorite of hers. I would have thought "Amazing Grace" would be more appropriate since it mentions me—the poor wretch—each time the refrain is sung, but Truman honored all of Octavia's wishes voiced before her mind went, before the imposter took over. The organized woman had planned her perfect funeral.

I could hear Hope's voice singing over the others. Her voice was louder than most as she held the notes a little longer than the congregation. I looked across the aisle and saw Hope with her mother. She was wearing a doily on her head that looked like a tablecloth thrown carelessly over a dinner table. I smiled. Why was I feeling so happy at a funeral?

Following the church luncheon, Toby and Jenae went back to Vanity Insanity with the rest of the staff. I drove to Fremont with Mac and Hope. Hope, who insisted that we needed to be there when they buried Miss Octavia, wore white gloves and a doily on her head. Mac drove his big car, Babe, behind Mom and my sisters on the drive to Fremont.

I had thought about skipping the burial. The thought of putting Octavia in the ground forever floored me, but Lucy's good old inappropriate guilt—or maybe appropriate in this case—seeped into my heart in the days leading up to the burial, and I knew that if I didn't go, I would somehow disappoint Octavia. I know that sounds strange since she was dead, but I guess that's what they call respect for the dead. Octavia would probably forgive me, but she'd be mad as hell.

Standing under the tent over her gravesite, we all huddled together behind the seated family members. The priest said a few indiscernible words at the gravesite as he placed a red rose on the casket. Hope leaned into me as we buried Octavia Hruska on a gorgeous fall afternoon.

Prior to the decline of the mind of one of the most incredible women I have ever known, Octavia had instructed Truman how she wanted her tombstone to read:

Octavia Edith Hruska<br>
December 25, 1905–September 30, 1997<br>
"I was right!"

38

# Tom Ducey Drops Off Meal

## Tuesday, October 28

# 1997

Untimely and ruthless.

The ice storm that attacked eastern Nebraska in late October slyly glazed the landscape with a heavy, confused snow that wanted to melt and then quickly froze, clenching the trees and electrical lines with a sinister death grip. No one could have predicted the damage or disruption that followed: the ice storm of 1997.

Untimely and ruthless.

Because most of the trees still held a good number of leaves on their branches in late October, the weight of the heavy, frozen snow on many trees smothered them to death. Many trees fell from the burden and dragged some electrical wires with them; some of those wires were still live. One-third of Omaha, in pockets gathered throughout the city, was without electricity for up to two weeks in some cases. Many families moved in with friends and families or into hotels during the cold temperatures. Others became creative, like my sister, who took several connected extension cords across the street to her neighbor, who had not lost power, and remained in her home with a space heater and a TV.

Vanity Insanity didn't lose its electricity, but the cure of the tempestuous time drizzled into my days as I dealt with picking up the debris from the broken plans for the renovation that had crumbled when Sinnot called me shortly after Octavia's funeral to break up. He informed me that he'd come across a better and more promising deal and that, since he hadn't signed any final contracts, he no longer wanted to work with me. That chapped my hide since Sinnot had stolen my thunder. I wanted to scream to him in the phone, "You can't break up with me. I wanted to break up with you first." When all was said and done, I was left with a mess. I needed to decide if I could afford to move forward with this project alone, or if I even wanted to.

Jenae and Virginia were putting on their coats after a full day in the salon. Virginia grabbed a suitcase that she'd been bringing in all week since she was staying with Jenae while waiting for electricity to come back on. "We're doing a potluck tomorrow, Ben. What do you want to bring. Paper plates and napkins again?"

"Put me down. I'm always good for plates and napkins." My tooth was starting to hurt again.

"And plastic forks?"

"Got it."

The bell above the door rang as the girls left. Tom Ducey came in with a box that he placed on the UP desk. "This stuff does have a unique smell. I'm just saying." Tom frowned at the meal I was going to take to Theresa's house.

In August, Michael and Theresa had returned from an appointment while Lucy watched their kids. Lucy watched from the window as Michael and Theresa walked from the car, Theresa limping more than ever. Both wore large sunglasses covering red, swollen eyes. The doctors had told Michael and Theresa that the cancer had spread to Theresa's liver and that the plan should be to keep her as comfortable as possible in the coming months. The positive couple could no longer call the cancer an annoying little cold. Just how do you move forward from a "there's nothing else we can do for you" speech from a team of doctors who specialized in cancer?

Giving up was never an option. A friend told Theresa and Michael about a book by a woman who had also been given the same speech from her doctors when she had breast cancer. The book claimed a special diet could save lives. A strict diet of macrobiotic food as a therapy for cancer patients with recorded historical success was their answer to the bothersome malignant cells that had invaded Theresa's body. A sister of Michael's coworker made her meals in which processed or refined foods were forbidden, and beans, fish, seeds, and nuts attempted to achieve a balance in the system by applying the oriental principle of yin and yang to the food. The process of making the food was as important as the food itself, and Lucy told me that she gagged every time she delivered a meal to Theresa's home because of the smell of the food.

"I sure as hell hope this stuff does the trick for her. She's not doing too well, Ben." The last time Theresa had left her house was on Morgan's first day of kindergarten. She walked her little girl into school, walked back to the car to go home, and had remained in bed since that day.

"Thanks for getting me on the meal delivery list," I said to Tom. The list had been organized by Lucy and other members of the rosary group. A meal could be an opportunity to see Theresa if she was having a good day, of which she had been having less and less.

Tom grimaced. "Brace yourself, buddy. Just saying."

"OK."

"You'll probably see Michael and Theresa's mother. We call them the gatekeepers. Protecting Theresa. Man, I wouldn't want to be in their shoes. Michael took a sabbatical from work to be home with Theresa and the kids. Oh. One last thing, Ben. Not that you're anything like Lucy." Tom cleared his throat. "But keep your tears at the door. It's all hope and smiles while you're there. Lucy comes home after seeing Theresa with a big headache from holding back the tears. All smiles." He held out jazz hands.

I followed Lucy's written directions and drove to Michael and Theresa's house in West Omaha. As Tom had warned, the smell of the food did take over the car and nauseate me a little. Or maybe my nerves were making me sick. I parked in front of the house, which looked like a picture out of *Family Circle* magazine. To the side of the white, two-story home were tricycles, plastic bats, and balls strewn across a driveway covered with chalk drawings. A tree swing hung from the front oak tree with a doll lying next to it, and a few feet from the tree was a statue of Mary, a green Frisbee leaning against her. Not one sign that a very young mother was very sick inside this mirage of a perfect world.

I walked up to the front door with a broken screen. I shifted the box to one hand and knocked on the door. Michael opened the door with a gigantic smile on his face. *Smiles everyone. Keep your tears at the door.*

"Ben, how the heck are you? Come on in." Behind Michael stood Theresa's mother, Mary O'Brien, who looked so much like her sister, Sheila, Stinky Morrow's mother, that I had to take another look.

"You know Mary, don't you, Ben? Since our little Mary Elizabeth was born, we like to call Theresa's mother Big Mary."

Mary O'Brien laughed and came toward me with a gentle hug. "Please don't call me Big Mary, Ben. Wow, Ben Keller from Maple Crest. You haven't changed a bit." Not something a thirty-six-year-old man likes to hear, but that was all right.

I followed them inside and set the meal in the box on the counter. Toys and kids were everywhere, and I heard *The Lion King* playing on the TV in the other room. An awkward silence transpired as I stood and looked at Michael and Mary, an awkward moment when three people who have a connection with each other meet but the connection was not in the room. I sensed this was my clue to leave. I guess I wouldn't get a chance to see Theresa. I smiled and mumbled a good-bye as I started walking toward the door.

"I think Theresa's awake, if you want to say hi. I know she'd love to see you." Michael picked up a little girl, who held her arms up to him.

"Sure." I hesitated. I turned toward the direction Michael was walking and looked down into the big eyes of a barefooted wild monkey wearing an Aladdin shirt and holding a ping-pong paddle.

"Who are you?" The boy asked.

Michael laughed and put down the little girl on the couch in front of the TV playing *The Ling King.* A meerkat and a warthog were singing "Hakuna Matada" and proclaiming to the room not to worry, for the rest of your life. Strange advice for the moment.

"Jack, this is Ben, a good friend of Mom's. He stopped by with dinner."

"Oh," Jack said as he ran out of the room. I knew why Theresa's mom and Michael so ferociously protected the situation. I felt bad for coming.

"She's upstairs." Michael motioned for me to follow.

With each step toward the next level of this home, I felt like I could cry. I swallowed, took a deep breath, and stepped to the second level. I followed Michael to a room with a closed door. He opened the door and stepped aside. Theresa was sleeping with a rosary in her hand, her body thinner than I had ever seen it. Her hair looked dark and curly against the pillow. Around her neck were several chains, anchored down by medallions of saints, many hopeful pieces of metal dangling against her heart.

Michael touched Theresa's arm. "Hey, hon. You'll never believe who's here. Ben Keller. He brought dinner."

Theresa's eyes popped open, and she smiled immediately. She took a moment to take in what Michael had just said, then tried to adjust herself to sit up as Michael helped her. "Ben, you brought me my macro McMeal? That's too funny. Doesn't it smell nasty?"

"Well, actually, I ate half a container at a red light. Sorry about that."

Theresa laughed, tears gleaming in her eyes. Michael stood in the doorway, removed but present as we talked. Theresa sat up. "I know you're lying. Are your renovations done yet? I bet your Vanity Insanity looks amazing."

"Oh, we're taking a little break." I tried to think of something funny to say, the tears in my throat were starting to burn. My toothache was my saving grace as I concentrated on the pain to avoid tears from coming to my eyes.

"Hey, did Jenae ever get her naval pierced?" Theresa asked me.

Jenae had her naval pierced last spring. "Yeah, she's looking for other parts to pierce." A child cried from a room nearby. I could hear muffled sounds of Theresa's mother comforting voice muffled through the wall.

Michael cleared his throat. "Ben, Subby Mangiamelli stopped by yesterday to replace the mirror on the vanity. Looks good as new, right, hon?"

"It looks awesome." Theresa sounded drained as she smiled and looked toward the vanity. "Good as new." I remembered the vanity when it had been in Lucy's trunk years ago. "Hey, Ben, we have to figure out what my new hairstyle will be when this mop grows out." Theresa's words were starting to slur as she spoke.

"I'll check my schedule. 'I might be too busy counting me holy cards, Danny.'"

Theresa closed her eyes.

Michael came toward the bed. "Did you catch that, hon. *Caddyshack*, right, Ben?"

"Sounds like *Caddyshack*. Easy…" Theresa looked up at me. "So good to see you, Ben."

"Yep, see you later, Theresa."

"See you later." She moved her head toward the window and closed her eyes.

I moved much more quickly down the stairs, stepping on a squeak toy at the bottom. I needed to get out of the house.

"Hey, thanks," I said to Michael and Mary as I moved to the front door.

"Anytime," Michael lied. "You're the one who's helping us out. Thanks for dropping off dinner."

"Anytime," I lied.

By the time I got to the car, I turned on the engine, and Sting's voice played from my CD player. The song "Let Your Soul Be Your Pilot" took over the car. Sting, my constant sage, who had laced the years of my life with background music, found me in my pain. I drove the car to the next block and pulled over. My head hurt. My tooth hurt. I took a deep breath.

*When the doctors failed to heal you*
*When no medicine chest can make you well*
*When no counsel leads to comfort*
*When there are no more lies they can tell*

*No more useless information*
*And the compass spins*
*The compass spins between heaven and hell*
*Let your soul be your pilot*
*Let your soul guide you*
*He'll guide you well*

**

Theresa received the last rites three times in the next week and a half. She died in her sleep on November 2, a day after All Saints Day.

The storm of 1997.

Untimely and ruthless.

# 39

# Theresa's Funeral: No Morning Appointments

## Wednesday, November 5

# 1997

This time Jenae's note posted on the door to Vanity Insanity looked as though an angry child had scribbled it:

*We are closed this morning to attend the funeral for*
*our dear friend Theresa.*
*We are so sad due to our loss.*

"Can we at least try to sit together?" Virginia put some lipstick on as she shut a drawer in her station with her hip.

"We look for each other," Kelly said, "try to save places. If not, we meet at the lunch."

We all met at Vanity Insanity that morning and agreed to get back for a few late appointments after the lunch. Caroline was able to find a sitter for Connor, and Toby and Patti had called all morning appointments to reschedule. Jenae was tying her head into a tight bun at the mirror at her station. She wore a navy dress with a string of pearls.

"I've never been to this church. Can I catch a ride?" she said to anyone who could hear.

The staff walked out the back side of the salon, and I followed and locked the door. I put the keys in my pocket and felt the rosary I had put in there following the Rosary visitation the evening before, a rosary that had been given to me by a lovely lady years ago. I looked over to my parking spot and saw A.C. with no coat, wearing dark sunglasses, leaning against my car. "Mind if we go together?"

"Hop in." The pain in the entire left side of my mouth had been so bad the last several days that I'd lost count of how many Tylenol I had taken. The less said, the less pain, so I hadn't said much since Theresa died. A.C. got in the passenger's side of the car, put his seat belt on, and turned on the radio.

The Spice Girls were screaming about what they really, really wanted.

A.C. turned the station.

A high-pitched woman's voice called out to her Ken that she was his Barbie girl in her world.

A.C. turned off the radio. A.C. turned on the radio.

Barbie Girl.

Spice Girls.

A.C. turned off the radio. "Dumb songs," he mumbled.

I drove several blocks out of the Old Market before it occurred to me that Toby and Jenae were driving together to the church. Years and years of their childish tension had so subtly and quietly waned that I couldn't remember the last time those two had bickered or exchanged insults.

Theresa's funeral at Saint Pius X was on one of the dreariest fall mornings that I can remember. The cloudy sky hovered over a cold morning as we drove onto the blacktop parking lot, which was already packed forty minutes before the funeral was to start. Storm-whipped, distressed trees sagged as they wrapped the landscape of the big box church that I hadn't seen in ages. A big tree lay on the side of the parking lot, its roots pulled out of the ground from the weight of the ice during the storm. The tree was now dead. Dead too young, way too young. My mouth throbbed.

I looked at the school and church and paused. Saint Pius X looked beautiful. I had heard about a few renovations through the years, but I had not been back here since A.C. and I moved the free pews to Vanity Insanity over a decade ago. In the midst of sadness and broken trees, I stood in awe of the changes made to the building in which I attended CCD classes and the church where I served Mass with a kid whose name I couldn't recall. Saint Pius look different; it looked beautiful.

A.C. nudged me. "Let's do this."

Clumps of people stood quiet and serious, debating whether they should enter the church for the funeral or run to their cars and leave. Shocked expressions covered faces that would not look at each other. Had Theresa really died? Clumps of zombies slowly moved toward the door with A.C. and me.

Just inside the doorway in the hallway that wrapped around the church were two easels with large poster boards, each covered with a collage of pictures of Theresa throughout her life. Several grieving zombies stood in front staring at the pictures. Who were these people? A.C. and I moved toward one poster and looked at the biggest picture in the center of the collage. The eight-by-ten photo showed a beautiful little girl missing a front tooth with long, caramel-colored hair, shining with the glow of several months swimming at a pool. A picture of Theresa and Michael at her wedding was to the left of the center picture. A picture of Theresa without her wig holding Mary Elizabeth was to the right. I could see that the collage was not in any order, as though somebody had thrown the pictures of her life against the board, knowing that the different and mixed pieces would make sense to those who knew her. A black-and-white picture of three little girls in uniforms caught my eye. Marty, Lucy, and Theresa had their arms around each other, standing in front of a school gym. They couldn't have been more than ten.

In the lower right corner of the poster board was a blurry photo of a large group of people in the front of the Mangiamelli house on Maple Crest Circle. I bent down and took a closer look at the poorly taken photo of the prom of 1981. Satch, the tree, towered over the group. Everyone in the picture squinted as the wind blew hair and dresses. I found myself in the photo standing next to Theresa in her cream dress. My face was a blur since I had moved quickly, turning to look toward the house of the Wicker Witch just as the photo was snapped. There I was, thrown on the board, fortunate to have been a little, blurry piece of the life of such an awesome woman.

"What a beauty." A.C. shook his head and took a breath.

More zombies stood behind us, so we moved to the side to let them see Theresa through the years, Theresa when she'd lived. As I moved, I bumped into a body leaning against the wall. Will Mangiamelli barely noticed.

"Will." My voiced sounded odd.

Will looked at me with red, panicked eyes. "Ben? A.C.?" He didn't look too good.

A.C. walked around to the other side of Will and nudged him. "Come on, let's go sit down." A.C. and I anchored Will between us as we walked to a pew near the back of the church and sat. I hadn't seen anyone from Vanity Insanity yet. A.C. leaned in front of Will and looked at me. I looked at him with burrowed brows and shook my head. He moved his head toward the end of the pew. Corky Payne was sitting with his head down. Why was he here? His long, gray hair and beard stuck out in all directions. He wore an old brown suit that looked like it had been crumpled in the back corner of a closet and pulled out for today. His posture showed the pain he had been carrying, his lifelong suffering upon the death of a boy born on my birthday. I didn't want to add to that pain. I positioned myself through the funeral so that he might not see me. A.C. moved to shield me from Corky Payne's vision.

I looked around for any sign of the staff. The church was filling up, and I knew the chances of sitting together were slim. A few rows ahead of me were three rows filled with students from the school. Lucy had told me that Theresa's oldest son was in the second or third grade at Saint Pius. Jack's classmates sat with teachers on the ends of the pews, glancing down the rows for any sign of misbehavior. The uniforms were different from the ones I remembered students wearing when I was young. No longer pee yellow or poop brown; the blue and red jumpers on the girls weren't hideous.

The funeral Mass moved like a bad dream. The voice of the priest was monotone and quiet, and I found myself looking around at the people who had known Theresa and had come to say good-bye. My eyes moved from the people to the casket near the altar. People, the casket. People, the casket, closed and cold. I spotted Jenae and Toby across the aisle and a few rows back. Toby kept looking at the back door. Jenae was crying. What I can't recall to this day is if any music was played at Theresa's funeral. I don't remember the music.

Several rows ahead of me stood a very tall man with a beer belly and really short hair. He had to be at least six feet five. He bent his head over during most of the service, visibly sobbing. The altar was covered with a flock of smocked priests. The priests I recognized looked old and tired. Not-as-Big-as-He-Used-to-Be Father Laverty, Used-to-Be-Young Father Gusweiler, Even-Older-Fart Father Dailey and Still-Cool Father Whelan, who always remembered my name, who always smoked so coolly, who never touched me inappropriately. Father Whelan had an oxygen tank at this side. A.C. leaned over to Will and me. "If a bomb went off, every priest in Omaha would be gone."

The casket, cold and closed, was covered with red roses. Roses everywhere. If roses were answers to prayer, I wondered what prayer had been answered. An end to her suffering? An end to the army of cancer cells invading her body? Had the prayers of those who wanted her here for her children been heard? I heard the sniffling of adults crying all around me.

I spotted Caroline, Kelly, and Katie standing by the confessionals at the back of the church. I never did see Virginia and Patti. Across the aisle and three rows toward the altar was the Webber family. Hope with a doily on her head. Lovey and a man I assumed to be her brother, Robert. Next to Mrs. Webber was what looked like the back of Faith's head. Long, black hair shone in the lights of the newly remodeled interior of the church. Was it really Faith?

Mac and my mother were sitting in front of the Webbers. I saw Subby and Michele Mangiamelli sitting in a pew with Lucy and Tom, Anthony,

Stephano and his wife. Ava and Louis. I looked up to the altar and saw that one of the altar servers was a young girl. When had they started allowing girls to be altar servers?

In the front row, I could see Michael and his children. Mrs. O'Brien was holding the baby next to him. They were listening to the sermon, which was given by a younger priest I didn't recognize. I had never met Theresa's father, but a man sitting next to Mrs. O'Brien took out his handkerchief and blew his nose. Mr. and Mrs. O'Brien were burying their daughter today, something no parent should ever have to do. Grief and questions hung above them in the pew. *Why take her so young? Why not us?* I'm sure those same questions hung above Octavia as she buried her Teddy. Hadn't Corky Payne asked those same questions every day of his life since Tommy died? Jane McManus, who was murdered near Ak-Sar-Ben twenty years ago, had parents who must have asked the same questions. The parent of Johnny Madlin, the father who forgave the murderer and the mother who didn't, still asked those questions today. *Why my child? Why not me?*

Sitting directly behind Theresa's parents was Mrs. O'Brien's sister, Mrs. Morrow, the sister she resembled, my former neighbor. Mr. Morrow stood next to her. He looked different. He looked much older than the Mr. Morrow I remembered standing behind Stinky as he blew out his candles on his birthday cake. The perfect father. He looked older than the man sitting in a car down by the creek with the Morrows' baby-sitter. Had Mr. Morrow ever confessed that sin to his wife as she still sat with him all these years later, both of them carrying that cross together? Or had he held that sin secret from her and carried both the sin and guilt as two large crosses alone to this day? Mr. Morrow looked different in the pew next to his wife, burying his niece. He looked older and not as perfect.

The pain in my mouth and the grief in my heart took a back seat to an anger that had been lurking in my heart for years, though I hadn't felt angry until this moment. I looked at Mr. Morrow, who had changed a naïve teen that day by the creek. I guess I had allowed that change. The perfect father was not perfect. His sin had changed that, whether I was the only person who knew that along with him or not. Mr. Morrow had failed like so many other fathers. Like Eddie Krackenier's father, who had failed and abandoned him, and like the "Father" Eddie had turned to after that. Had Willie Otey's father failed him? Had Otey not had a man in his life to keep him from running from good and doing bad? Like the man who used to be married to my mother? The failure of fathers flooded my heart, and I felt an anger I never knew I had. I was angry.

Will interrupted my anger with loud, uncontrollable sobbing. He was losing it as the funeral ended. A.C. and I both grabbed him as he started to crumble to the pew. I wasn't sure he would make it to the cemetery. Following the funeral Mass, we walked out of the church holding on to Will as we took him to my car. We drove silently to the cemetery, each of us staring off into our own private grief.

Hope found me at the cemetery that cold, gray, and windy afternoon. She came to stand with me. She adjusted the doily on her head and then patted my back as we watched the priest speak over the coffin. Hope patted my back. "Ben, you are my angel." She patted and said, "I think Miss Octavia and Grandma will be waiting for Theresa in heaven. Grandma will have a big, sloppy kiss for her." I took a minute to realize that the "Grandma" Hope was talking about was the dog we'd lost years ago, the dog that had lined our youth and our driveways with her presence. "Ben, I know a secret." Hope stopped patting and looked at me. "Faith got a job yesterday. In Omaha." She then held my hand during the service at the cemetery.

A.C. blocked me from Corky's view as we stood close enough to the plot so that we could see the family gathered around the casket, suspended above the grave. We were far enough away that we couldn't hear the young priest say a few words through the wind. Theresa's plot, which had no headstone yet, was positioned on the far corner of the cemetery tucked on the corner of two very busy streets. Nothing about her death seemed right. Nothing. Hope nestled into me for warmth.

We needed the luncheon. We all needed to gather together after the awful funeral and the less enjoyable burial. Flavors of funerals. I had actually enjoyed Octavia's funeral, which seemed like a celebratory closure to a long, beautiful life. Theresa's funeral had left a bad taste in my mouth.

The flavor of the funeral made me angry and frustrated. We needed the luncheon.

I saw Lucy across the cafeteria, sitting at a table alone. A.C. and I waved and walked through the outdated room with acoustic tiles and low ceilings. Lucy waved back, her eyes red and puffy. A.C. and I sat down across from her. Lucy shook her head.

"She was supposed to be the poster child for hope. Theresa was so hopeful. And then she died. She really died. Not once did she talk about dying."

"Probably better than the alternative, to mope and groan and have the same outcome," A.C. said.

"Did you see the article on her in the obituary paper?"

Neither A.C. nor I had.

"*Woman Dies So Her Child Could Live.*"

"As if one line could sum up her life," A.C. sounded as though he were talking to himself. Theresa had been sick for so long that I had forgotten that she'd delayed chemo for her baby. "Mother Theresa, Princess Diana and...Beautiful Theresa. Nineteen ninety-seven, not a good year. We lost some incredible women."

"What am I going to do without her?" Lucy cried.

I got up, walked around the table, and sat next to Lucy. I put my arm around her. Lucy sniffled as she continued, "She and I used to play this one game. Long time ago. When we were in junior high. We would take her cousin's yearbook, and we would each look over a two-page spread of pathetic class photos; and when we were ready, we would count to three, and on three we would point to the person who took the worst picture and then laugh our heads off. Every once in a while we would land on the same photo, but mostly we would just laugh at how funny people are. Looking at a photographer in their favorite clothes. In what they thought was cute hair. Really bad smiles or closed eyes. We just laughed."

Lucy took a deep breath. We waited for her to continue. "A good friend will tell you that you have something hanging out of your nose or tell you that you have a long hair growing out of your chin." A.C. looked at me with raised eyebrows. Lucy went on. "But a really, really good friend will pluck the hair out. She was that friend. Who's gonna do that for me now?"

A.C. put his hand across the table, and Lucy put hers out to him. A.C. said, "I'm here for you, Lu. Do you want me to pop that zit on your nose?" We all laughed out loud, and it felt good.

"I have to admit it, too," A.C. said softly. "Theresa's death hit me like a bullet."

"'It was a bullet that jumped up and bit you?'" I threw out a line to break up the tension.

A.C. and Lucy stared at me as if I had made an inappropriate noise.

I continued, "'Oh, yes sir. Bit me right in the buttocks.'"

Nobody caught it.

"'Never did see any money from that million dollar wound.'"

A.C. shook his head. Lucy frowned.

*"Forrest Gump.* Hello? *Sounds like* a line from… Anyone?"

Theresa was really gone.

Lucy started crying again. "Why did God give Theresa cancer?"

"God didn't give Theresa cancer!" A.C. proclaimed and then sat back.

Lucy stared at him. Strange words from an atheist.

A.C. continued, "People are born. People die. Some have car accidents. Some live to one hundred. Some die of cancer. God doesn't decide to give cancer."

Lucy stopped crying.

A.C. added, "Why do you think they call it faith? It's not supposed to be easy. Cancer is…like a thorn on your roses, Lucy."

Lucy smiled.

"Lucy," I asked, "who was the really tall guy with the short hair?"

"The one who was having a hard time keeping it together?" she asked.

I nodded.

"Ted Ellerby."

"What in the heck is a Ted Ellerby?" A.C. asked.

"Chewey. Remember Chewey? He was the guy Theresa dated for while."

"Chewey from prom Chewey?" I asked. I'd never met the guy. I was glad to hear he had a real name.

"Yeah, he was kind of a jerk. I guess he turned out all right. Married a really nice girl."

"A recovering asshole?" I asked, borrowing Octavia's line.

Lucy laughed. "Speaking of, I'm sure I saw Mikey Beard at the funeral."

No "Weird, Weird," still Mikey. I looked around the cafeteria, which was filling up. Friends and family of Theresa Marie Gerard O'Brien Davis.

"Well, here's her party. She always talked about having a party when this was all over…" Lucy's eyes welled up as Tom walked over and handed her an iced tea.

"Hey!" Tom was never comfortable with sadness. "You know what Woody Allen says about death?" Lucy looked horrified at her husband. "He said, 'I'm not afraid to die. I just don't want to be there when it happens.'"

A.C. shook his head and smiled. Lucy hit Tom in the arm. "That's about the only good thing about this, Tom. I'm not afraid to die now. Theresa will be there."

"That's only if you make it to heaven, baby doll."

Hope walked up to the table with plates of food. Behind her followed the priest who had spoken at the cemetery. Lucy got up, put her arm on the priest's shoulder, and introduced him. "Did you all get a chance to meet Father Steve?"

I looked at Father Steve, who looked familiar.

"Stinky?" A.C. said. "Father Stinky?"

I'd heard that Stinky was thinking about the seminary years ago.

A.C. spoke as he shook Stinky's hand. "Man, you were great today. I don't know how you made it through."

Marty and her husband, holding their adopted son, Sean, came up to the table. We found room for everyone to sit at the table.

*Margaret, are you grieving?*

The line of a poem I remember from my one year of English at UNO suddenly popped into my head. "Margaret, are you grieving?" I couldn't remember much more, but I remember the overly excited professor explaining the poem to our class. The poem was about a little girl named Margaret, who was crying as the leaves fell from the tree in the fall, sad that their beauty is dying. The voice of the poem was speaking to the little girl and telling her that she wasn't crying for the leaves. She was crying for herself.

*Margaret, are you grieving?*

We sat in the cafeteria, the gang from the old neighborhood, telling stories of our youth while feeling sorry for ourselves. What would we do without Theresa? In my heart, I knew that she was at peace now. She was laughing. She was goodness. But as for us, we were in pain. We were suffering our loss.

I felt two hands on my shoulder from someone behind me. I turned around to see Lovey Webber. I stood up and turned to her.

"Hey, Ben!" Lovey shoved her hand out in front of me. "Did you hear I was engaged?" To Triple-Flip Jimmy, I was guessing.

"Congrats…uh, what are your colors?"

Lovey leaned into me as she laughed. "Ben, you were always so funny. Did you know that I had the biggest crush on you when we were growing up?"

"Are we grown-up now?"

"See?" Lovey grabbed my arm and laughed. "That's what I mean. I used to practice writing 'Lovey Keller' on the back of my notebook, over and over again. I had such a crush. Big." She walked away, wiggling her body as she walked, as only Lovey could.

"Lovey? And you?" A.C. shook his head. "No way, man."

All those years of watching her cute little body swerve and flirt, I'd had no idea. I felt two hands on my shoulders again and turned to see if Lovey had heard us. Faith Webber stood behind me in a gray suit. Her dark hair framed her beautiful face.

"Hey, Ben. Long time no see." Faith's blue eyes smiled at mine.

"Faith," I said.

"Sorry to interrupt for a second, Faith." Stinky had a gift in his hand. "Ben, I was wondering if you could do me a favor. Could you drop this gift off at my parents' house?"

"Sure, no problem."

"Mom and Dad just left. I missed them, and I had their anniversary gift in the back seat of my car. My brother's going to run me to the airport to catch a flight right now, so I won't be able to get it to them. Just put in under that back deck. I'll let them know. I really appreciate it, Ben." Stinky shook my hand.

I hadn't been back to the neighborhood in years. My mom had moved from our old house years ago. "Will do," I said.

"Can you believe they've been married for forty years?"

"Wow, hard to believe." My mouth was starting to throb with pain again.

A.C. came up as Stinky left. "Jenae's waving to you." Jenae motioned to me to come over to their table with the staff from Vanity Insanity. I looked back to see Faith, but she was no longer there.

I walked through a long aisle of several tables to get to Jenae. My eyes panned the room looking for Faith. I felt a hand on my arm. Corky Payne was beside me.

"Ben?"

I looked into his deep, sad eyes.

"Ben Keller?

"Yes, sir."

"How old are you now, boy?"

"Thirty-six, sir. I'm thirty-six."

Corky dropped his hand and walked away.

*Margaret, are you grieving?*

*I went down to the sacred store where I'd heard the music years before,*
*but the man there said the music wouldn't play.*
**—Don MacLean, "American Pie"**

## 40

## Monkey Man: Trim Sideburns

## Thursday, November 6

# 1997

*There was an old woman who swallowed a fly*
*I don't know why she swallowed a fly*
*Perhaps she'll die.*

Jenae had been singing the obnoxious song all morning, ignoring perturbed glances from Toby. Caroline shook her head as she worked on her client's nails. I was in the middle of trimming Monkey Man's sideburns when Kelly came up to my side.

"Did you call the tooth doctor?"

"I did." I'd broken down the day before about my extreme pain. The pleasant voice on the other end of the call said that the soonest they could get me in was Monday morning. I asked her if there was anything I could take for the pain in the meantime. The pleasant voice took my name and number and said that she would ask the doctor and get back to me. I knew that four more days of this pain would be unbearable.

"You talk to the contractor about the mess upstairs?"

"Not yet."

Kelly sighed. "OK…Tom Ducey gave me this envelope to give to you. He came by when you ran to the bank."

"Thanks. Just put it on the desk, Kelly." If the information in the envelope had anything to do with Sinnot or the legal breakup, I didn't want to open it. I would avoid it as long as I could.

"And one more thing. This is for you." Kelly handed me a small piece of paper with a name and number on it. "Rose or Rosie called. She said it was an emergency." Kelly slowly and clearly pronounced "emergency." "Long distance."

*There was an old woman who swallowed a fly.*

Jenae was wearing a red sweater, red pants, red boots. Must have been a red day.

*I don't know why she swallowed a fly.*
*Perhaps she'll die.*

Jenae looked up at me with an apologetic grin, after she straightened the magazines in the rack against the wall. "Sorry, I can't get it out of my head. Do you remember that little song?"

"I forgot it…until today."

"Sorry, hon. Can't help it."

I knew nobody named Rose or Rosie. Client, family, or friend. It had to be business. Product sales.

"Emergency, Ben. She sounded pretty upset." Kelly raised her eyebrows, picked up the phone, and brought it to me, then walked back to her manicure client. With Kelly's eyes on me, I dialed the 208 area code number. From what part of the country did this number come? A woman's deep scratchy voice picked up on the other end.

"Yeah."

"Yes, I'm returning a call for Rose or Rosie."

"Who's this?"

"Ben Keller. My name is Ben Keller. I received a call from this number." I had a million things to do today.

"About time. I've been calling insurance companies all morning." The voice was lined with years of nicotine. "Finally, one says that you were his customer, but he couldn't give out personal information. He said you owned the Vanity Insanity. What's a Vanity Insanity? Mental institution?"

"I'm sorry. Is this Rose?"

"Yeah, I'm Rose, and we've got a problem."

"Does this have to do with my insurance company?

"No, that's just how I found your name and number. I just figured that his wife had remarried, and I knew he had one son, and I knew your last name wouldn't change. I tried to find his sister, but she must be married 'cause she ain't in the book under Keller. The operator gave me the number of a Vanity Insanity. That a clinic or something?" Rose coughed for a really long time and then said, "Right off, I called the insurance companies to see if he had any insurance."

"I'm sorry. If this isn't about my insurance company, then I don't think I can really help you. Who is *he*?"

"Your old man. I need some money to bury him. He din't have no money, but I hoped that he might have some in Omaha. I need to bury the man. It's only right."

I couldn't reply.

"I couldn't find his sister's name since she must have gotten married. Like I said, she must be under a different name. He said that his son's name was Ben. Aren't you Ben Keller?"

My dad had a sister?

Rose coughed again. "This is the number the operator gave me."

My brain was on overload. First, my dad really did exist. He really did go off and live another life. He had a sister? And this piece about him dying? My mom had severed all ties to the family of the man who had fathered me, so in time I'd lived with the absence by believing that he really didn't exist. It had worked so far. At least up to this moment. Now some lady named Rose wanted money to bury the man that I'd pretended never existed. How did you bury an imaginary man? I finally spoke.

"Where are you, Rose?"

"Idaho. Sandpoint, Idaho."

"How can I help you, Rose?" My tooth hurt. My head hurt.

"I just need money to bury the man. S'only right. Man, do you know how much a casket is? The man at God's Grace Mortuary wanted over a thousand dollars just to put his body in a casket and bury him. Where would I get that kind of money? I just want him to have a proper burial. That's all."

"Do you have phone number of the mortuary?"

"God's Grace Mortuary?"

"Yes, God's Grace."

"Just a sec." Rose left, and I heard her coughing louder than ever. I glanced up to see Kelly watching me. I could hear Jenae singing in the back room. Rose came back to the phone. "Here it is." She read the number to me. "You have to dial the area code. Did you know that?"

"Yes."

"You know someone who can help?"

"I'll find someone."

"Trust me. I'd do if I could. I just don't have the money." Rose coughed. "It's only right. Christ, the man needs a proper burial. He lived a hard life. He lived a very hard life. It's only right. Howard was a good man." She dropped his name like an ice cube into a cold drink. As though he were real.

"I'll take care of it," I said numbly. "Do you need anything else?"

"That'll do. It's good of you, ya know."

I didn't want to hear any more. He was a good man? He was also a man who'd walked away without another single word to his family. I didn't want Rose to say another word. I didn't want Rose to tell me anything this man had done or said about me. I wanted to hang up. Kelly, the little mother hen, was still watching me.

"Have a good day, Rose," I said loudly and then hung up.

Kelly came up to me after she finished her client's manicure. "You make that call?"

I nodded.

"Everything all right?"

"Wrong number, Kel. Wrong number."

Jenae came out from the back room.

*There was an old woman who swallowed a fly.*
*I don't know why she swallowed a fly.*
*Perhaps she'll die.*

"Wrong numbers don't take that long," Kelly mumbled as she shook her head and walked away.

# 41

## Last-Minute Appointment: 9:30

## Saturday, November 8

# 1997

I made three phone calls Saturday morning.

I'd driven to Vanity Insanity earlier than usual after a long night of little sleep, a lot of pain in my mouth, and an overload of new information in my head. I'd sat at the chair by the UP desk and made my calls before the staff came in. The first call was to my dentist's office. The nice voice on the other end said that the doctor had called in a prescription to the downtown pharmacy for pain medication that should "get me through" till Monday's scheduled double root canal. I thanked her and hung up.

The second phone call was to God's Grace Mortuary in Sandpoint, Idaho. I had decided—not long after hanging up with Rose—that I would not let Mom or my sisters know anything about the phone call. Maybe in time I could get back to my normal life of pretending that no father of mine had ever existed. I would allow this roller coaster of emotions only for a time. The nice voice on the other end told me the cost of a simple casket and "proper" burial as I pulled out my credit card: $3,344. The nice lady gave me her sincerest condolences, and I thanked her. I remembered my good friend Digger the Clown. I wondered what the mortician at God's Grace Mortuary in Sandpoint, Idaho, did for grins. What did he do to keep his sanity? Mime? Skateboard? *Oh, the insanity.*

My third call was to First National Bank. I transferred money from my savings, which was starting to decline, what with business interactions gone bad and burials of estranged fathers and all. The nice voice from the bank was glad to shuffle my money around. By the end of that phone call, Toby, Jenae and Virginia were walking in and setting up for the day. Jenae turned on the sound system to an oldies radio station. Sting's voice poured out into the salon as he sang about a little black spot on the sun.

"Oh my gawd! I have not heard this song in, like, forever." Jenae turned up the Police classic song: "King of Pain."

"Hey, Ben, this is you." Virginia came out from the back room with a bottle of chemicals. "King of pain. Get it? Your tooth. 'King of pain,'" she sang loudly along with Sting.

The bell rang as Caroline and her son, Connor, opened the front door. Connor ran into the salon in red cowboy boots, shouting, "Donuts! We got donuts!" Caroline had let Connor's blond curls grow until a client asked what her little girl's name was. His new short hair made him look older and boyish.

"Ben, want a donut?" Connor asked. He grabbed my hand and walked me over to the box on the UP desk. "We got skrinkles on 'em."

I really had no appetite with the throbbing in my mouth, but I took one. "Thanks, buddy."

"Is the TV broken?" Toby asked, annoyed.

"No, why?"

"The Missouri game is on tonight, and as much as I like hearing old Police songs, I'm sure that ESPN is already talking about the game."

Back in August, when I had first seen the Husker schedule, I'd had my eye on the Missouri game. As the fall had quietly twisted into a sad season, I lost my focus with the Huskers, who were well on their way to a third national championship. Toby and I were going to meet A.C. and a group of friends at the Upstream Brewery in the Old Market that night.

"That's right. We'd better start talking about it!" Jenae mocked.

Jenae's hair was darker and shorter, and I wasn't sure where she was getting her inspiration these days. She had taken a two-inch area of hair on one side of her head and colored it a pink-copper color. I didn't ask why since I knew she'd probably tell me.

"Let me guess what those cute little ESPN sports guys are going to say, hmmm? How about, 'Man those Huskers look good. If they play better and are stronger and execute and penetrate'—whatever that means—'they'll probably win the game.'"

Toby ignored her and looked at me.

I sighed. "Virginia, turn off the radio. Turn the TV on, Toby."

Toby went to turn on the TV and then stopped. "I forgot to tell you that you have a nine thirty haircut. I couldn't fit him in, and I saw that you had an opening..."

I looked at the clock. It was 9:28. At this point, all I really needed was relief from the pain in my mouth. I wasn't sure if I could make it through the shift. "Caroline, when's your first manicure?"

"Ten. Why?"

"Could you and Connor run up to Richard's Pharmacy and pick up my prescription? My first appointment should be walking in any minute."

"Yay! A walk, Mom. Go for a walk!" Connor jumped down from the pew he was standing on. He'd been looking out the window at the dark clouds rolling into Omaha.

As Caroline opened the door, the wind blew in and almost knocked Connor over.

"Whoa! That was fun!" Connor laughed.

The weatherman had been hinting at a big front, possibly bringing severe weather. The bell rang repeatedly as Caroline and Connor left, and a small man entered Vanity Insanity, wearing worn jeans and a work shirt: my nine thirty appointment. I looked at his hair first. He didn't even really need a haircut, so this could be a quick one. I was already thinking that I might throw a few other appointments at staff. I didn't want to handle too many today.

"Have a seat." I looked over my last-minute appointment. His hair was thinning and turning gray at the temples. His face looked much older than his hair suggested. Miles and miles of small wrinkles lined his weather-worn complexion—probably from working construction at a big project downtown, a few blocks from the Old Market.

"What do you need today?" I hoped this one wasn't a talker. I didn't feel like talking.

"Just a trim." The man's quiet and polite voice didn't match his rugged looks. He did look a little familiar to me. Maybe he looked like some actor. I couldn't place it.

I looked at the clock as I placed the apron over the man in my chair. Hopefully, Caroline wouldn't run into any problems at the pharmacy. As I buttoned the back of the apron, I looked down at the back of the man's neck. He had a large birthmark just below the bottom of his hair.

"It doesn't have to be too short," the man mumbled.

The misshapen birthmark brought me right back to Maple Crest in a flash. I was cutting the hair of the Chief. Eddie Krackenier, the bully from Saint Walter's, was sitting in my mom's pink chair. I started cutting his hair as I got my head around the fact that I was touching a man who had scared Lucy to death and entertained the old neighborhood with his reputation. He seemed old. He seemed small. He seemed beaten. I was no longer the boy who played by the creek. He was no longer a bully. We were both older and a million miles away from the years on Maple Crest.

As I finished wiping off the extra hair from Eddie's neck, Hope opened the door, the bell ringing like a school bell. She looked rattled. "It's really bad out there."

Eddie cleared his throat as he asked, "How much do I owe you?"

"Are you working on the renovation of the old Union Station?" I pointed to the Wehner Construction logo on his shirt. The Union Pacific railroad station was getting an art deco facelift.

Eddie looked down at this shirt and mumbled, "Yeah."

"We've been giving you guys free haircuts this week." I hoped the staff didn't hear me.

"Oh, uh, thanks," Eddie said as he threw down two bucks for a tip. "Thanks," he said again as he awkwardly opened the door and left Vanity Insanity. He bumped into Connor as he ran into the salon. Caroline mumbled an apology, and Eddie mumbled, "No problem."

"Here, Ben!" Connor handed me the bag from the pharmacist. "Guess what we saw!"

"The Cookie Monster?" I asked.

"No, silly. We saw a funny man." Connor closed his eyes, pretending to hold a cane, and walked around the room.

Caroline smiled at her son. "A blind man was selling brooms."

"I remember that man from when I was a kid," Virginia said as she picked up the schedule from the UP desk. "He must be two hundred years old."

"Ben," Caroline said as she lowered her voice, "the pharmacist said this is some pretty strong stuff. You must have some toothache."

I set the sack of medicine on the manila envelope from Tom Ducey that I hadn't touched since he'd dropped it off on Thursday. As the day inched by, I eyed the sack, looking forward to heading home and checking out of this pain shooting across my jaw. By three o'clock, the sky outside Vanity Insanity's windows looked as dark as night, and the howl of the wind sounded spooky to Connor. At three thirty, I gave in, opened the sack, and looked at the bottle. I sat down, read the warnings and directions, and decided that since I had just finished my last appointment, I would take two pills. The pain was now sharp, severe, and no longer bearable.

"What time do you think you'll get to the Upstream?" Toby asked me.

"Toby, I'm gonna have to pass on the Upstream. I wouldn't be much company anyway. I'm heading home. Tell A.C. that I'm watching the game at home with my sack of codeine." I pointed to the pharmacy sack on the desk and smiled.

Toby smiled awkwardly and then said, "Will do." He swept around the chair with Jenae's broom and then set it near her station. "I hope you feel better, Ben."

Jenae came out of the back room singing, "'There is no place like Nebraska, good old Nebraska U.'"

I felt a little murky as the medicine kicked in. In the fogginess, I thought about a mortuary in a small town in Idaho. I was burying my dad. The pain was starting to lift.

"'Where the girls are the fairest, the boys are the squarest…do, do, do, do…'"

"Could you sweep up the back room while I start unplugging everything?" I asked. The light of the salon changed the streak on Jenae's hair from copper to pink, pink to copper, as she flitted around the salon.

"I have one more lady at four thirty," Jenae replied. "A cut and style with…what's her name?"

Toby walked out of the Vanity Insanity, and the bell rang. "If you change your mind, we'll be upstairs by the pool tables near the bar."

I walked over to the UP desk and started collecting what I would need to take home. Suddenly I stopped. Toby hadn't touched the upper casings of the door. I looked at Jenae, who was digging through her purse. Maybe I'd just imagined that Toby had just walked out of the door without his normal routine. A calm wave slowly started to take over me. My codeine was working. I needed to get home before I got too loopy.

Had Toby really not touched the upper casings of the door? Had I really paid for the funeral of a man who lived in Idaho, a man I'd never met? The lights of the salon changed the color of Jenae's copper streak as she moved around her station. I needed to get home.

"After my color and style with Glenda the Good Witch: game time."

"You're killing me, Jenae. Why so late on a Saturday? "

"I thought we were watching the game here. Don't we usually?"

"That's for day games, Jenae. Look around, Toots. Everyone's gone, and I really need to get out of here." I could hear the downpour of rain outside the front window, a cold rain. A degree or more lower and the rain would be snow.

"I can't cancel. Besides I don't think I could get a hold of—what's her name?" Jenae ran to the UP desk and looked at the appointment book. "Susie James. Don't you think she looks like Glenda the…"

"Jenae, I'm dying here."

"I won't take too long. Oh, I almost forgot to tell you that Faith called this morning, sorry. I guess she's back in town. Wow, can you hear that rain? This weather is so cool. It kind of feels like when the apostles were all huddled in that one room after Jesus died. I think it must have been storming. That's what I think. Don't you think?"

I had never heard Jenae talk about religion. I shook my head and looked out. Faith had called?

"Remember?" Jenae asked as if we'd been there. "When Jesus shows up in that upper room and tells them to calm down and stuff. Remember?"

A buzzing sound started to fill my head, and I knew that I needed to get home soon. I couldn't wait to take another one of those little pain stoppers. Peace, be with me.

"I think there was fire, something about fire when Jesus told them to…"

"Jenae." I pulled out a key ring from my pocket. "Please, please, check every outlet twice. Make sure every hot iron has cooled. All lights off except that back one."

"Whoa. Wait, let me catch my breath." Jenae put her hand to heart. "Is the control freak really going to trust someone other than himself with the *key*?"

I took the key off my key ring and handed it to Jenae.

"I'm just not sure if I can handle the power of the key," she mocked.

"Every outlet twice, Toots. I mean it."

"Feel better, Ben."

I grabbed the bag of checks and cash from the day, the manila envelope, and the bag of pain meds that were becoming my new best friend. I was going to float home and watch the Huskers. Just my painkillers, the Huskers, and me. I ran out to my car, the cold rain pelting my face as I smiled. I was going home to get away from funerals, songs about old ladies who had swallowed flies, a salon that still had equipment in the upper bay from a renovation stopped in midstream, fallen and weaker neighborhood bullies, and caskets in Idaho. I was running away.

I drove to my house and sat in the driveway for a moment. The pain in my mouth was softer, distant. I took the money but left the Morrow gift and manila envelope on the passenger seat. I locked the car door, walked up to my front porch, unlocked my door, threw my jacket on the floor, took another pill, and plopped on the couch. On my pain-free island, I watched the first quarter of the game against Missouri, which was being played in Columbia, Missouri. The Huskers were ahead fourteen to seven in the first quarter when I fell into a very deep sleep.

My dreams were sketchy and pointless until I floated into the most vivid, wonderful dream I can remember.

*Tom Osborne knocked on my door and walked into my living room. This was the Tom Osborne from the seventies era. He was much younger, his hair redder, and he was wearing a jacket that I remember him wearing during the championship time when I was eight years old. I felt awkward that I was too tired to get up and greet him. He looked at me.*

*"Don't get up, Ben. We've come here to ask you something."*

*I didn't know who the "we" was, but I sat up and listened. I didn't want him to know about my tooth.*

*"We need you, Ben. We really need you right now."*

*I couldn't believe that Coach Osborne was standing in my living room. And he needed me.*

*"I'm putting together a new staff of coaches, and we think that you'd be a great addition to the Husker coaching staff."*

*"Me? Really?" I tried to get up, but I couldn't move.*

*"My new assistants are with me. We want to add you to our team, but you can't tell anyone. You have to promise not to tell anyone."*

*The silhouettes of two more bodies were in the door. The smaller one came into the room. Octavia was wearing her blue suit and holding her cell phone. Her hair looked good. "I told him all about you, you poor wretch."*

*The other body entered my living room. Theresa was in her cream-colored prom dress with long and full, caramel hair. She was laughing. "Ben, is this a hoot or what! I'm coaching football." It was really Theresa. As clear as day. Without cancer. I wanted to get up and hug Octavia and Theresa. I wanted to tell them how much I missed them, but I knew that this was an important meeting, a serious meeting with Coach Tom Osborne, so I smiled at them both.*

*"Will you help us, Ben?" Tom Osborne asked me in a gentle voice.*

*"We need you, Ben. We'll have so much fun," Theresa said as she came a little closer. Octavia's phone rang. She answered as she started to walk toward the door.*

*"It's for you, Ben. It's Faith. I forgot to tell you she called. She's in town."*

*Octavia held the phone out toward me, but it kept ringing. How could it be ringing if Faith was on the phone?*

*"We need you, Ben," Coach Osborne said.*

*Ringing.*

*I tried to move toward Octavia to get the phone, but I couldn't get up. I was being pulled back down when I tried to get up.*

*Ringing and ringing.*

*Ringing and more ringing.*

# 42

## Phone Call

### 1:45 a.m. Sunday morning, November 9

# 1997

Ringing and more ringing.

I struggled to wake up. I needed to find the phone that was ringing and ringing.

"If you order now, we want to send you the entire line of my product."

The television was still on from when I'd been watching the game. I focused and saw Victoria Principal imploring me to buy her amazing skin products. "Just look how they work for me." The ringing was everywhere. I heard the phone ringing in the kitchen and my cell phone ringing from the pocket from my jacket on the floor. Slowly, I pulled myself out of my dream residue and realized that I hadn't just seen Theresa and Octavia. Tom Osborne didn't really need me. Somebody in the real world was trying to get a hold of me. I pulled my cell phone out of my jacket pocket and answered it.

"Hey."

"Ben, where the hell have you been?" A.C.'s voice sounded tinny on the other end.

"Sorry about missing the game. My tooth was killing me." I looked at my watch. It was 1:45 a.m.

"Ben, you need you to get down here now..." A.C.'s voice was breaking up.

"Not tonight, A.C. I'm wiped out." The last thing I needed was to party with A.C. till dawn. I was guessing Nebraska had won.

"Ben, Vanity Insanity is burning. It's on fire. Get down here."

I wasn't completely awake until the cold night air hit me as I ran to my car. The medicine was wearing off, and the throbbing in my mouth had never been worse. What kind of fire? I couldn't call A.C. back since I had forgotten my cell phone and jacket in my rush to get to the Old Market. I would have to get the details when I got to the salon.

Two blocks from the Old Market, I saw flames shooting into the sky and heard several sirens blaring. I turned the corner to the street where Vanity Insanity was and saw three fire trucks and a crowd of people across from the salon. I picked out A.C. in the crowd and what looked like Mac and my mom and her husband huddled together, looking at the flaming building. Flames were flashing and spitting out of the salon onto the adjacent bays. The Vanity Insanity sign was bent and melting; the only letters that were discernible were ANITY.

A.C. ran toward me with his hands in his pockets. "Where were you? I've been calling everywhere trying to find you."

"I'm here now."

"We left Upstream around one and saw the flames from your place. Then we called nine-one-one. The operator said someone else had just called. I think the owner of Trini's had just called in. We were starting to get worried, dude. That you might be..."

I looked at the snow gathering on A.C.'s hair. The Upstream. I'd never thought about it, but now I figured out the name of the restaurant was probably an allusion to the Indian name of Omaha, which meant "those who go upstream against the current." Maybe the owners had paid attention during the fourth grade history of Nebraska unit.

"Ben!" My mom screamed and ran toward me. She hugged me and through her tears mumbled, "We were just about to drive to your house. I was afraid you were in the..." She covered her mouth and looked at me. "Where have you been?"

"Home sleeping."

"But we've all been calling! Did you not hear your phone? A.C., Mac, and I have all been calling!"

"I'd taken some codeine for the pain in my mouth. Two root canals Monday." I looked past the firemen who were knocking out the front windows of my building. I thought of Jenae.

Mac walked up as I was talking to Mom. "Must have just been in a pretty deep sleep, Ben. We're just glad you're OK."

"Your dad had bad teeth, too," Mom muttered as she ran to a car. My sister, Tracy, was driving up. "Tracy, we found him. He just got here."

Wait.

Had my mom just said something about my dad? Really? Years and years of not talking about "you know who" and then, bam, she just threw a casual comment in the fire like the man still lived with us. As though he were real. *Your dad had bad teeth? You've got to be kidding me.* I could not believe that my mom had so matter-of-factly dropped his name into the smoky night air when she had never once mentioned the man in the past thirty years. Strange timing.

Mac walked up to me and put his hand on my shoulder. "Once this mess is all cleaned up, I can help you get back on your feet, Ben. You'll bounce back. You always do."

"Mac, do I have an aunt somewhere?"

Mac tilted his head. My business of almost fourteen years was blazing in front of us, and I'd asked him about an estranged aunt.

"Do I? On my dad's side of the family?"

"Yes."

"Does she live in Omaha?"

"Your father's family suffered a great deal, Ben." Mac looked at the fire. Snow started to fall on his head and gather on his stray hairs. Mac needed a haircut.

"What's her name?"

"People didn't talk about mental illness back then like they do now, Ben. It was hidden in shame. Not treated. Your dad suffered. Eleanor had her own battles, too."

"Eleanor? Is she still alive?" The last fire truck finally turned off its sirens. Two policemen walked past us to talk to the fireman coming from the blazing building.

"Yep. Never leaves her house. Afraid of people or the public or something like that."

"Did she ever marry?"

Mac burrowed his eyebrows, brushed some snow from his face, and looked at me. "Where's this coming from, Ben?"

"Please just tell me her name, Mac. My whole life, we've pretended that this family didn't exist. I know nothing of the man you call my father. Of his family. Of his problems. I know nothing."

"Eleanor Wicker."

"Eleanor Wicker?"

"Eleanor married. The man left after a year or two. She's got problems."

A.C. came up to Mac and me and grabbed my arm. I stared into the fire and thought of a little green house that I'd driven past about a billion times in my life.

A.C. shook me. "Y'OK?"

"Just fine," I mumbled. I was pretty sure that the old black radio was melting somewhere in the glow of the flames inside the salon. I thought of Jenae closing Vanity Insanity about nine hours earlier. I looked up at the ashes flying above the salon, and I thought of my shoebox and all of the lives on my index cards. I looked up at the ashes and thought of my clients. I thought of Octavia. She had placed that little scapular under my chair when I was at Maple Crest to collect my prayers and protect me from eternal fire. The little piece of material had fallen off somewhere in the move to the Old Market thirteen years ago.

Damn, should have asked for another one.

# 43

## Gentle Dental Office

## Monday Morning, November 10

# 1997

The happy little lady at the front desk of Gentle Dental asked me to take a seat and fill out several forms.

My trip to the dentist's office on the Monday following the fire was a much-welcomed reprieve from the hurricane of phone calls and concerns I'd been dealing with since early Sunday morning. My last phone call was to Toby to ask him to contact staff for help to call clients. Most people had already read about the fire since it had made the front page of the *Omaha World-Herald*: "Old Market Salon Destroyed in Fire." The article ended with "Vanity Insanity salon owner could not be contacted for comment."

I had never looked more forward to two root canals in my entire life. My goal was to escape. I didn't want to talk to one more friend or family member consoling me, asking about my plan to rebuild. Maybe my plan was to walk away. I hadn't voiced that to anyone, though. As I sat down in

Gentle Dental, I tabled any thoughts about the fire or Vanity Insanity. I didn't want to carry all this "stuff" anymore. I wanted to be carried.

After I'd filled out my paperwork, I picked up the sports page of the *Omaha World-Herald* that had been lying on the seat next to me. I was still pouting about the play that everyone was talking about—at least, those who weren't talking about funerals, fires, or aunts formerly known as witches. The Miracle in Missouri. Somewhere between when I'd fallen asleep on my couch on Saturday night and when Vanity Insanity was consumed by flames, the Nebraska Cornhuskers had beaten the Missouri Tigers in a game that included a play that has since been called many things: the Great Escape, Immaculate Reception II, and the Miracle in Missouri. Had the play not happened, the Huskers would not have challenged the number-two Tennessee Volunteers in the FedEx Orange Bowl. That play sealed an ideal season for the Nebraska football team.

The article described in detail how Husker quarterback Scott Frost, with only seven seconds remaining in the game and the Huskers down by seven points to Missouri, hit wingback Shevin Wiggins at the goal line. When Wiggins lost control of the ball, the ball deflected off of his foot and into the air. I watched the replay of a diving Matt Davison catching the ball before it could hit the ground five times on ESPN before I left for the dentist office. The article finished with the statement that the Huskers scored in overtime with Frost running in from the twelve-yard line. The Husker defense secured the win by stopping Missouri in four plays.

Davison had actually caught the ball that bounced off Wiggins's foot. You've got to be kidding me. ESPN had been replaying the play throughout the past two days, so that I could repeatedly feel a pit in my stomach for missing the game. I folded the paper and crossed my arms. I think A.C. knew that I wasn't happy about missing the play, so he hadn't yet brought it up.

When Miss Short-and-Happy called me to the desk, I handed her my paperwork and turned off my cell phone. Part of the escape plan. She led me down the narrow hallway to the small office and into a room where I was to wait for the doctor. She motioned to the chair where I would be undergoing my root canals. I lowered myself in the chair and closed my eyes. I lay back. I allowed myself one final sulk about the game and capped it with the solace that I would probably not have had my dream if I had stayed awake for the game. The residue of the dream still made me smile. Theresa had looked so healthy, and Octavia, who had really been gone for years, was as lively as ever.

As I relaxed, I considered asking the dentist for an extra shot of Novocain, enough to numb my mouth and soul. I opened my eyes and looked at the ceiling of the root-canal room. It was covered with pictures and posters with sayings. Someone—I'm guessing a receptionist with too much time on her hands upon the suggestion of a poor wretch who had sat for hours in this chair—had come up with the idea to entertain the people being drilled who had no other choice but to look up at the ceiling. Clever idea, really. I had never been in the room, so I found myself amused at the scattered sheets taped to the ceiling. The center picture, held with yellowing pieces of scotch tape, was an obvious Norman Rockwell picture.

Mac had a Norman Rockwell calendar from the year 1967 that he kept up because so many people liked looking through the months. The picture on the ceiling of Gentle Dental was one that wasn't in the calendar, one I had never seen, but I knew the picture was a Norman Rockwell. The faces in his pictures seemed familiar to me, like I knew these people. The picture on the ceiling had two scenes, one on top of the other. The top scene was a family car with a canoe on top, heading to what the viewer could only assume was a vacation or an outing. The father was driving, the mother watching the road, and the older woman in the back was more than likely the grandmother. Kids with excited faces and a family dog filled the windows. One little girl was blowing a huge bubble with her gum. The bottom picture was of the same family with the car going the opposite direction, looking as though they were headed home. Mother was asleep. Dad was slouched down. The kids and the dog looked tired. Grandma was the only one who looked pretty much the same.

The door to the office opened as an older man and a young, attractive woman walked in. The old man looked serious and busy, so I decided not to ask about the Novocain. The woman with long, dark hair and incredible eyes carried a tray of utensils and smiled at me.

"Ben, I'm Gerilyn, and this is Dr. Hamilton. Just let me know if you need anything during the procedure. If you're unable to talk, you can just tap my arm, OK?" Gerilyn had a beautiful smile. "Do you have someone coming to pick you up today? You might be a little woozy when we get done."

Dr. Hamilton cleared his throat. I gave Gerilyn a lying nod. I hadn't asked anyone for a ride. Part of the escape plan. Once Gerilyn propped my mouth open with some sort of contraption lined with a rubber remnant that smelled funny, Dr. Hamilton came forward with a large needle that I welcomed wholeheartedly. The slight poke on the side of my mouth was nothing compared to the weeks of pain that I was ready to be done with. Dr. Hamilton and Gerilyn, the lovely assistant, began their hour-and-forty-minute session—the first of several—on my mouth. My mouth numbed and my entire body relaxed. My eyes took in other fun sayings covering the ceiling as two people focused on my mouth.

*If it's tourist season, why can't we shoot them?*

*Funny thing about trouble, it always starts out being fun.*

I considered a few of my own sayings:

- People who own salons should learn to embrace chaos.
- Neighborhood witches should receive special tax breaks.

Gerilyn sucked the extra saliva from my mouth. "Are you doing OK?"

Her eyes were a beautiful light brown with dark edges. I blinked. I was really enjoying my lovely state of loopiness. Gerilyn looked like she might be a good kisser.

*A mediocre person is always at his best.*

*A truly wise man never plays leapfrog with a unicorn.*

- Children should not pay the price for the failures of their fathers.
- Just because something is in your blood, doesn't necessarily make it good. Case in point: cancer, cutting hair, bad teeth.

I looked up again. On the other side of the Norman Rockwell print were other interesting questions.

*Why is the word "abbreviation" so long?*

*Why do they sterilize needles for lethal injections?*

- Was Walkin' Willie, who had walked horses and the green mile, walking in His Grace?
- Was Charlie Brown Catholic?

*Can you be a closet claustrophobic?*

*Do cemetery workers prefer the graveyard shift?*

- Why did Theresa have to die so young?

*If the cops arrest a mime, do they tell him he has the right to remain silent?*

- Should a victim of a root canal ever consider asking out the cute hygienist?

*What's another word for "thesaurus"?*

- Do emotionally and mentally unstable people ever find peace in this life?

*If at first you don't succeed, skydiving is not for you.*

I looked up at the face of the man above me, his eyebrows furrowed, his forehead filled with many ridges. He looked to be about sixty-five or seventy, about the age of the man who had been married to my mother. About the age of my father. The dentist focused on my mouth as though it were an object under a microscope. His dark-brown eyes held many years of serious focusing. I wondered if this man had any children. I wondered if he had a son. If he had failed his son.

*When companies ship Styrofoam, what do they pack it in?*

*If we knew the value of suffering, we would ask for it.*

The value of suffering? That wasn't funny. We would ask for it? I looked at the Norman Rockwell print on the ceiling and found the little blond girl, who in each picture, top and bottom, was blowing a bubble from a big wad of gum. I looked at the dog, whose face looked forward in the top picture, ears blowing in the wind with great eagerness, but appeared tired and panting in the bottom print. The father had the same serious look on his face, top and bottom, the same serious focus. I wondered if the Norman Rockwell's "vacation father" had failed his children. Had he made mistakes that disappointed them? I knew he must have.

"We need to move to this side at a different angle." Gerilyn's voice sounded far away. I moved a bit. I looked up at Dr. Hamilton and could see in the deep ridges on his face that, yes, he had most certainly disappointed others in his life. He would have had to at some time. He had made many mistakes in his life. He was human. I wondered if this man's son had ever forgiven him for his failures. Had his son ever seen the humanity in this imperfect man? I suddenly felt sorry for the man drilling my mouth.

*If your mom is mad at you, don't let her brush your hair.*

*If a book about failures doesn't sell, is it a success?*

Failure. Who hadn't failed? Who hadn't disappointed another to some degree? Forgiveness. Now that was an entirely different bird. Most people could fail almost flawlessly, flawlessly fail—but could not forgive. Forgiveness was not something practiced in the Keller home on Maple Crest Circle. I'd had a great role model in forgiveness denial. My mother couldn't forgive the man who'd run out on her in 1963. She couldn't forgive the Catholic Church. She couldn't forgive my sister Tracy for clogging the bathroom with extra hair from her brush the day before Christmas. I'd learned from the best. I struggled to forgive my mom for leaving me in the business I was in because I wanted to help her, and then struggled to forgive myself for never leaving it since I'd had no idea where I was supposed to go. Yes, I was positive that Dr. Hamilton had failed many people. I would not go so far as to put a wager on if he'd ever been forgiven.

Failure and forgiveness flitted and floated on the ceiling above me. Failure and fires. Forgiveness and funerals floated and flitted. I stared at the focused father in Norman Rockwell's picture. The focused and failing father driving his family home from a vacation on which he probably failed them all.

Gerilyn nudged me and whispered, "I'm going to help you up now. Just need you to rinse and spit a few times." Her hands helped move me up in the chair. She smelled like heaven. She was even more attractive now than she'd been when I first saw her two hours earlier. She walked me down the hall.

"Your friend is here to pick you up. He's been waiting for a while." Gerilyn walked me to the lobby and pointed to A.C. What a great friend I had. I must have mentioned my appointment to him, somewhere among the smoldering pain and the smoke blowing off my burning business. What a guy.

A.C. stood up looking serious. Even too serious for a root canal. I tried to speak around the rolled-cotton cigar fitted into my mouth, absorbing extra drool, keeping me from biting my lip. My salutations and thanks sounded like a muffled groan.

"Did you turn off your phone again?" A.C. sounded like a disapproving father I'd never had.

I wanted to introduce him to Gerilyn, my future wife. I needed to let him know that I wasn't upset about the fire. I wanted to talk to him about the Miracle in Missouri. I needed him to lighten up. The mushy words pushed through the cotton.

"Oh, great. This is not good." A.C. gave a half smile to Gerilyn and thanked her as he pulled out his cell phone. Gerilyn walked back to the receptionist desk.

"Whuuuh?" I asked.

"We've got problems, Ben. And you sounding wasted is not going to help matters. Follow me. Do you need to talk to the lady?" He motioned toward Short-and-Happy, who was looking at me. I was somehow able to communicate by sign language that I would call to set up the next appointment when I could speak coherently, when I would no longer be confident enough to ask for Gerilyn's phone number.

"Give me your keys," A.C. said. "I'm about out of gas after driving all over town trying to find you. Good thing Toby knew the name of your dentist."

OK, A.C. was really starting to bug me. I hadn't asked him to pick me up. The peace of my Novocain was wearing off. But because I wasn't verbally or physically in a place to defend myself, I handed him the keys.

"We need to go down to the police station. What's all this junk in here?" he asked as we got into my car.

I picked up the Morrows' gift and the manila envelope and threw them into the back seat. I plopped down in the passenger seat and hoped to go to sleep. Had A.C. said something about the police station?

"The officer who questioned me Saturday couldn't get a hold of you so he called me. Ben, you have some serious things to think about here. When did you and that Sinnot guy break things off?" A.C. started the car and pulled out of the strip-mall parking lot of Gentle Dental.

Sinnot? I hadn't spoken with Sinnot in several weeks. A.C. was quickly trashing my whole escape plan.

"Ben, the officer mentioned that you would have reason to burn your place down if you were looking for a way out of a deal gone bad. Probable cause. What happened with you and Sinnot? You were the last one out of the salon on Saturday, right?"

I shook my head no.

"No? Someone else closed for you on Saturday?" A.C.'s voice was getting louder each time he spoke.

I nodded and attempted the word "Dunnay."

"Jenae? Are you kidding me?" A.C. pulled the car over to the side of the road and parked. "Ben, you let Jenae close? You trusted Jenae with the keys to your business?"

I looked straight ahead.

"Ben, who hands his livelihood over to a woman with tight-fitting clothes and a pink stripe in her hair? Even if she is having one of her really, really happy days. What were you thinking?" A.C. spit as he was screaming.

I pulled the cotton out of my mouth.

"Ben, we need a plan here! The fire department has been working since yesterday to find the source of the fire." A.C. hit the steering wheel. "Are you picking up on the fact that you just might be going to prison for arson? Are you following this at all?"

I nodded yes but didn't look at A.C. He turned on the car and started driving.

In a calmer voice, he asked me, "Is there anything about the Sinnot deal that I should know before we go in there?" I guess my lawyer had taken over. Buddy A.C. had left the building, folks.

I shook my head no.

A.C. looked straight ahead as we drove quietly to the police department. I really didn't have any feelings about the whole thing. I felt pretty peaceful in spite of his attack. Wishing I could go back to the chair at Gentle Dental and hang with my friends Norman Rockwell and Gerilyn, I refused to allow panic to enter into my mind. After all, a pretty good thing had happened today. I'd forgiven my father in the dentist's chair today.

The father who left before I met him. The father who died before I knew him. The father for whom I paid for his burial. I had forgiven my father.

I was feeling pretty peaceful.

# 44

## The Creek

### Monday afternoon, November 10

# 1997

By the time A.C. and I arrived at the Omaha Police Station, the fog of my root-canal intoxication was beginning to lift. My peace was replaced by the unpleasant reality that I might be going to jail for a fire I'd never started.

"Just keep quiet. I'll do the talking," A.C. said under his breath as he opened the door for me. He looked up to a tall man with a mustache who appeared to be waiting for us outside of an office.

"Are you Arthur Perelman?"

"Yes, and this is Ben Keller. He unfortunately just had some major dental work done on his mouth, so…"

"I need to have you both come into my office. I have some news." The man was neither rude nor friendly as he ushered us into his office. He cleared his throat as he shut the door and moved to the seat behind his desk.

"Take a seat." The man looked at me and shook my hand. "Ben, I'm Eric O'Donnell. I've been working your case since the fire early yesterday morning."

My case? I really hadn't signed up for this.

"I just received a phone call from Kurt Taylor, the fire chief at the Omaha Fire Department. He and his team have been looking over the rubble of Vanity Insanity alongside three investigators from the police department and two men from insurance companies."

Companies? I had only one company and a flawless track record. I wished I could speak.

"All groups seemed to agree that the fire started in the upstairs unit in a circuit box near a large pile of lumber."

A.C. sat back and looked like he was going to ask a question when the officer continued. "The pattern of melting and charring suggests that the fire started inside the box rather than outside. Kurt's team found a splattering of the copper wiring that indicates an electrical short followed an inflamed circuit, more than likely set off by the storm that night. I'm thinking an overload in the system caused a short in the system. I'm just guessing at this point, since that entire eastern wing of the Old Market lost electricity around that time."

"So, is Ben good to go here?" A.C. was rubbing his hands back and forth on his slacks.

"Well, uh, yes. But officers from both the fire and police departments still need him to stick around for an hour or two to answer some questions. You're welcome to stay with him. Did you say you were his lawyer?"

"Yes, I am representing Mr. Keller." A.C.'s serious and professional demeanor was comical yet comforting as we moved with the officer to a different area of the police department.

As my lawyer and best friend, A.C. sat with me for the next few hours, translating my words here and there. The officer's questions mostly pointed toward my motivation to burn down my business for the insurance money to be gained from such an endeavor. Was Vanity Insanity losing money? Did I have the financial security to move forward with the renovation project? What exactly was my relationship with Sinnot?

"Were you aware that Sinnot had filed for bankruptcy?" one officer asked me.

*Are you kidding me?* Sinnot had implied the entire time we were in the "wooing" stages of planning that he would carry the project financially to gain greater control of the salon. So much had been going on for me personally in those weeks that I wasn't myself. Usually, I would have asked for his financial information or demanded more control of the project. My anger diminished when I remembered that I had signed no contract. I was done working with Sinnot.

I began talking in the second hour of questioning, and I answered all questions with less and less of a slur in my speech and more and more confidence. I had done nothing wrong. The good news on several accounts was that my business was thriving, and bank accounts could attest to that. My financial contribution to the project and my capability of finishing the project—had I wanted to—helped support my case.

"I think that went well," A.C. said to me as we walked down the hall toward the exit.

"You don't have to use your lawyer voice anymore."

"I'm serious, Ben. I was pretty scared for you. You have no idea how serious this all looked this morning."

Regardless of the outcome, no one could take away the peace that I had found in the dentist chair earlier that morning.

A.C. apologized—sort of—in the parking lot about his abrupt behavior when he'd found me at Gentle Dental. He hadn't wanted to see his best friend go off to jail for a crime that, at that point, he was not sure I hadn't done.

"I'm starving," I announced as A.C. started the car. I wasn't sure if I could chew, but I knew that I needed something, so A.C. went through a McDonald's drive-thru. I ordered two large vanilla shakes, and A.C. got a Big Mac combo. We needed comfort food. Neither of us had any idea where to go, so we sat in the parking lot of McDonald's while he ate and I enjoyed my shakes.

"Who's the present for?" A.C. asked in between bites as he pointed with a french fry to the gift in the back seat of my car.

"Stinky…I mean *Father* Stinky asked me to drop it off at his folks' house. It's a fortieth wedding anniversary gift."

"The Morrows have been married that long?"

"I guess so."

"When do you ever go back to the old neighborhood?"

"Never. But what was I gonna say? 'Sorry, I don't want to help you out'? Last Thursday his parents had left the funeral before he could get it from the car. He was heading out of town right after the funeral, so I…"

"Well then, let's head over."

My business had just burned down, and I didn't know where to go. How about back to my childhood?

We crumbled up our wrappers and threw our trash into the McDonald's parking lot trash bin. I don't know how A.C. was feeling about heading back to the old neighborhood, but I was feeling kind of conflicted about it all. I had been putting the trip off and was relieved that I would not go to Maple Crest alone.

A few blocks from the old subdivision, we drove past Brookhill Country Club and its empty parking lot. The pool was empty, and the tables and umbrellas had all been stored away for the winter. A big oak tree had fallen over the fence by the diving board.

As we drove into the area, my stomach did a double-large-vanilla-shake flip, and I picked up the gift from the car floor. We drove closer to the cul-de-sac, and I mentally prepared myself to see the Wicker house for the first time in a different light. As much as I felt that I could tell A.C. anything, the news of my relation to the Wicker Witch was something I was not yet ready to share.

"Hey, look!" A.C. pointed to a new sign that welcomed visitors to the subdivision. *Maple Hill.* They had changed the name of our neighborhood.

"What's up with that?"

I thought of Octavia. She had told me more than once that change was the sign of the Holy Spirit. That in the old days, Hebrews changed their names following conversion as a symbol of that change. Saul and Paul. Maple Crest and Maple Hill. Had the Holy Spirit been hanging out in our old stomping grounds?

"Check it out, check it out!" A.C. screamed. "Did we really live here? Good Lord, the houses are itty-bitty." We both started to laugh, A.C.'s hearty laughter drowning out my nervous laughter. Had we really grown up on this circle? My childhood seemed so much bigger.

A.C. drove to the Morrow home and parked on the street in front of the small house. Nobody was home. Stinky had said that if that was the case to take the gift around to the back of the house and put it by the basement door, under the deck in case it rained before his parents got home.

"I'm gonna run this down to their back door," I told A.C. "I'll be right back."

"You sure you don't want me to? You've had a crazy day. I'd do that for you."

"Nah, I got it." Stinky had asked me, and I was the guy people felt comfortable asking a favor. The safe guy. I was Ben "You-Can-Count-on-Me" Keller.

I walked around the side of the little, yellow house, wondering how a family with five kids could fit in there. Near the edge of the back covered patio was a rosebush with four or five buds still holding on in November, a week after the ice storm. I put the gift by the door and turned to head back to the front of the house. When I got to the side of the house, I turned around.

I had to see it. I had to see the creek.

I walked to the back edge of the Morrow backyard, right before the pitch became severe and sloped down to the creek. I stood high and looked down low at the sadder, beaten, and broken creek. In my youth, the trees that surrounded the water's edge had seemed mammoth in size. The creek that I remember, so full of life, had cradled my childhood and later seemingly had stolen a young boy from Omaha who was trying to deliver papers. That same creek later pilfered my innocence by exposing me to an infidelity that shattered my hope that a father could be good. Before danger and sad events, the trees seemed to protect us from the world. Now the trees seemed weak and spindly and empty, many of them broken from the impact of the ice storm.

The creek was not evil.

Bad things had happened at the creek, but that didn't make the creek bad. The creek wasn't guilty; it, too, was a victim. A victim like my mother. Like Eddie Krackenier. Like Theresa. Like the man who had once been married to my mother.

Like my father.

We were all victims, just like the creek.

We were all sinners.

My whole life I had feared to find my own dreams. To find myself. If I did, I just might lose myself. And it was to be in that losing of myself, of my business, that I found myself. But in order to lose myself, I had to forgive myself. And it was then that I was carried. By grace, I am certain.

Tom Osborne had written as the last a line of his book *On Solid Ground,* a line that I'd underlined. "It's not just children or college football players who deserve a second chance. I believe we all need to be more forgiving and understanding of each other. What each of us does with a second chance is up to us."

I had forgiven.

I was forgiven.

My cell phone rang as I moved back from the hill. I looked to see who was calling, but I didn't recognize the number. I decided I should probably get this. Fire station?

"Hello?"

"Ben," Jenae sobbed. "Ben, do you hate me? Please don't hate me." I could hear in her voice that she was in her dark place.

"Jenae?"

"Ben, I did everything you said…I unplugged everything. Everything! Don't hate me. Don't leave me!"

"Jenae, Jenae, everything is all right. It's all fine."

"But the fire…your business. What are you going to do? Where am I going to go? I'm so sorry."

"Sorry? For saving my life?"

Jenae was silent. Silent for the time ever since I had met her.

"Jenae, listen to me. And listen carefully. You didn't start the fire."

"What?"

"You didn't start the fire, Jenae. And if you had, I would still need to thank you for helping me move on in my life. I'm not so sure that I was ever cut out for this hair thing. Get it? Cut out?" I laughed fully as I looked down at the creek again. "Thank you, Jenae. Thank you."

Life did exist and flourish beyond the chair. Things would look different without a mirror.

"I don't understand. You're leaving us?" Jenae sobbed.

It hadn't occurred to me until that point the impact my personal decision would have on the staff. After all, Omaha was filled with hair salons.

"You can't leave me, Ben." Jenae was sobbing again. "You can't leave me."

Jenae and I had an interesting relationship. Though I might have been physically attracted to her for seventeen minutes or so at one time in my life, my love for her had evolved—though I hadn't known it—through the years into a fatherly love. She had never talked about her father; apparently he had failed her, too. I would always take care of her. I would always be her rock, her hope that a fatherly God might be possible. Jenae looked to me for strength; she looked to me to keep her stable. I was her Mac.

"Jenae, I'm here for you, Toots. I'm not going anywhere."

"Ben, I need you."

"Jenae, go take your meds and take a nap. I'll never leave you. I promise, everything will be just fine."

"I love you, Ben."

"Love you, too, Toots." I ended the call and walked up the worn path in the lawn alongside the Morrow house. I looked out to my car to see A.C., leaning against the car, holding the envelope with a silly grin on his face.

"The woman really loved you."

How could he have heard my conversation with Jenae? I was behind the house the whole conversation.

"That old lady really loved you, Ben." He began waving the envelope through the air.

"What are you talking about?"

"Octavia Edith True Hruska. She remembered you in her will." He poked the envelope at me. "You been carrying this around just for grins?"

"That's her will?"

"You haven't read this? None of it? At least the part that pertains to one Benjamin Howard Keller?" A.C. handed me the envelope on top of which were several typed sheets. "You don't really need to read through all of the jargon. As your lawyer, I can help you with that, but believe me, she did remember you. Remember her cute, 'little' house in the Saint Cecilia Cathedral area? Yours. How 'bout that little old radio station in the Dundee area? Yours. How 'bout a little financial gift to the tune of $250,000?" This time he sang the word in a high-pitched voice: "*Yours!*"

I was numb.

"So even if you do go to jail—which you won't—but if you do, you'll be sitting pretty when you get out of the slammer. Of course, I'd take care of your money and property while you were in prison. As your lawyer, I would do that for you."

I shook my head slowly. "Wait, what about Truman?"

A.C.'s head went back as he howled in laughter. "Benny, did you not know the lady was loaded? Tom Ducey told me that her son Truman is set for life. You just got a little drop in the bucket. Octavia was sitting on endowment after endowment toward the end of her life. Tom was having a hard time finding where to donate all of that money. According to Tom, she got her will in order when she was still, you know, sharp Octavia… Ben, what's wrong? Maybe you don't hear so well: the old lady loved you!"

"So much…"

"You never knew?"

"…to me…"

"You were good to her." A.C. was more serious. "You were very good to Octavia, Ben."

I sensed that I was being watched, and I turned to the back door of the green Wicker house. I saw a curtain rustle in the kitchen window. A.C. looked over where my eyes had stopped.

"Great idea, Benny! Let's take the Wicker Witch out for drinks. On you, of course. Wonder what ever happened to that lady…" he mumbled as he walked toward the car.

"Throw me the keys, A.C., and don't call me Benny. I'm going to take you out for a big dinner. Even if I can't chew, I can watch you." I handed him the will. "Now read this to me while I drive. I guess this is your lucky day, Arthur Charles."

"My lucky day?"

"Yep, Bucky's flying and buying."

"Awesome. Can we talk about the Miracle in Missouri now?"

As I drove out of the Maple Hill subdivision and glanced over at the Wicker house, I drove away in peace.

## EPILOGUE
# Faith of our Fathers

Baby bookmarks serve a purpose. They truly do.

However, no baby marked the year 1997 for me. With no baby, my mom sometimes stumbles to remember that year. I admit, I stumble, too. I now end up finding my place with the suffering that marked that year. Funerals, failures, fathers, and fires. Many of those who lined my life that year allowed me to find myself, to find my place. And while reminders of death seem sadder than the birth of a baby, I felt a rich relief in the suffering that year, though it made no sense at the time.

Tom Osborne made an announcement two months after the fire of Vanity Insanity that he would be retiring from the head-coaching position at UNL. The announcement came out a month before the Huskers won their third national championship with Osborne as the head coach. His retirement marked the end of an era, for the Huskers and for me personally.

I did end up calling Faith Webber. I helped her move into her new home, and for the most part, the two of us have been inseparable since she has moved back to Omaha. We talk very little about the time she spent away. We mostly talk about our plans. We have lots of plans. Most days Faith can find me at my radio station working on a sports story or lining music up for the DJ. We've also gotten into the little habit of going to daily Mass at Sacred Heart. Cramming, I guess. In the beauty of my "purposeful splendor," I realize that my good looks and others' prayers alone won't get me to heaven, or so I've been told.

I moved into Octavia's beautiful home in the Cathedral area after giving my little house to Caroline and Connor. My neighbor is a friend of A.C.'s who went to Creighton. I met him years ago during a night out with A.C. He's the guy from New York who proclaimed "This city sucks" after only a month into his first semester at Creighton in 1980. He is now raising his family here.

With two new houses, Faith and I have been doing a lot of cleaning. We're going to need a few more brooms. I told Faith I knew of a guy who might have some. I'm keeping my eye out for him walking through my streets. It's been a while since I've seen him, but I haven't really been looking for him until now.

Following the cleanup of the fire, I used the insurance money to rebuild Vanity Insanity. I sold all of the extra bays and added nothing to the original salon. I hired Toby to man the business that I own but no longer work at. I go in every two weeks to get a trim from Jenae and look through the meticulous books that Toby maintains.

Vanity Insanity has been a thorn in my life for many years. Vanity Insanity has been a rose. Each day over the past decade, I have touched and been touched by the many suffering people with so many beautiful crosses, of all different sizes. And all chose to carry those crosses differently. Some stumbled daily. Others held them high. All who came to me, without words, spoke thousands. "Help me look beautiful while I walk with this cross."

Not much to ask, if you think about it.

When I consider all of the heads that I've held in my hands, some good, some bad, mostly good and bad together, as I shampooed, cut, and listened, I know that I held God's grace in my hands every day. A grace for which I had not asked.

A grace that I never deserved.

Reverend Livingston Wills selling brooms
on the streets of Omaha.
*© Photographer Jeff Bundy, Omaha World-Herald*

## *Vanity Insanity* Questions and Topics for Discussion

1. The story begins and ends at the creek. Discuss the creek's presence in the book and how and why Ben's feelings toward it change.

2. While he is surrounded by people with clear and strong feelings about faith and religion, Ben appears to be spiritually numb. He admires the clear—though extreme—stances that Lucy and A.C. take, since they are, at least, feeling something about God. What events and people move Ben away from ignoring his own beliefs?

3. Though he is not about self-importance and vanity, Ben finds himself immersed in an industry that focuses on appearances. What are some of the problems in the novel that come from characters thinking too much about their physical appearance? What are some funny scenarios regarding vanity that Ben witnesses in the novel? How does Ben come to terms with helping people feel better about their looks?

4. Mentally and emotionally suffering people envelop Ben's life throughout his years in his salon. Why is it interesting that he discovers that mental suffering was at the core of many problems in his own life? Do you think that his attitude and treatment of mental disorders impacts his reaction to the news of his father and aunt?

5. Corky Payne is a man whose lifelong suffering paved his life in a negative way. What other characters handle their pain—mental or physical—differently than Corky? Ben, who in the end of the story feels like the king of pain, suffers a toothache in the midst of his personal pain. What does Kelly mean when she tells Ben, upon her urging to get to a dentist, "You can't ignore your pain forever"? How is her message symbolic?

6. Michael gives Theresa a vanity as a Valentine's Day gift. One of her children shatters the mirror, which remains broken until she is dying. What is Michael really attempting to do when he has the mirror fixed?

7. One of the dominant motifs of the novel focuses on forgiveness. How do the lives of Johnny Madlin and Willie Otey address the theme of forgiveness? At what point does Ben forgive his father? What final incident moves him to ultimately do so? When does he forgive himself? Why does Ben's Confession following the news of Octavia's death move him to tears?

8. Ben labels himself as the "not-quite Catholic kid" since he feels disconnected from many of the traditions and common normalcies of being a Catholic. While this is an easy out, and the silly formalities are poked fun at, the true essence of the Catholic faith is elevated for Ben, mostly through Octavia's words and the suffering he experiences. What are some of the times of suffering that impact Ben's faith the most?

9. Octavia's and Theresa's funerals, one right after the other, are two completely different "flavors" of funerals. How are the two different? How are they similar?

10. Lucy, Theresa, and Marty have a strong devotion to Mary to which they hold tightly through good and bad times. For Lucy, roses are signs that prayers have been answered. Why is she so upset by the roses at Theresa's funeral? Why is it interesting when Ben receives a call about his father's death from a woman named Rose? At what other times do roses "show up" for Ben?

11. If Faith, Hope, and Love are also symbolic of the implication of their names in the novel, how do you see their significance in Ben's

life? For example, Ben walks with Hope up the hill from the incident with Mr. Morrow by the creek. Faith is elusive throughout the book. Lovey is misunderstood.

12. Will Mangiamelli is a symbol of free will and the liberty to choose the right or wrong path. Will has been given many perks and opportunities that Ben has not: good looks, athletic ability, a present father. How does Will choose the wrong path?

13. One of the themes of the novel is the necessity of and the difficulty of suffering in order to understand the grace of God. Ben sees this very clearly in the lives of Octavia and Theresa. How do you see this theme in relation to the Wicker Witch? Ben's father? Ben?

14. Ben can identify with Eddie Krackenier, both having been abandoned by fathers. How is Eddie's life different? Who are people in Ben's life who show him the kind of unconditional love of a father similar to the love of God?

15. The reverend who sells brooms represents the silent Holy Spirit in Ben's life. Take note of when he appears in the novel. How does Ben think of him in the epilogue?

16. Right before the fire, while Ben is ready to go home and take his pain medicine, Jenae talks about the upper room when the disciples were hiding after Jesus died. She is referring to the passage in Acts 2 about the first Pentecost. The fire she talks about is the sign of the Holy Spirit. How is her statement foreshadowing? Fire is often a symbol of the Holy Spirit and Confirmation in the Catholic religion. How is the fire of Vanity Insanity symbolic of a change in Ben's faith?

# About the Author

Mary Kay Leatherman grew up in Omaha, Nebraska, where she had a secret love affair with Atticus Finch when she was a teenager, unbeknownst to her parents. While daydreaming about living happily ever after in Alabama with Mr. Finch, Leatherman discovered her love of the written language.

Leatherman majored in English at Creighton University in Omaha and went on to teach English and creative writing to high school students for thirteen years. In 1996, Leatherman was chosen as one of the recipients of the Buffett Award for excellence in teaching. The award was personally presented to her by Warren Buffett.

Leatherman lives in Omaha with her husband and three children and teaches for and manages 3MT ACT Test Prep.

*Vanity Insanity* is her debut novel.

For more information, visit mkleatherman.com.
Look for her new novel, *Cowboys to Camelot,* in 2015.

# Acknowledgements

I have so very many people to thank for help along this journey.

Special thanks to the 'readers' through the course of *Vanity Insanity's* evolution: my mother, Mary Mangus, my sisters Robin Boeck, Patti Grimes and Julie Hahler, my aunt Sister Barbara Markey, my mother-in-law Ande Leatherman, my nephew Michael Boeck, my dear friends Michele and John Trout, Diane O'Malley, Geri Casey, Deb Ward, Sara Smith, Geri Kunkel, Dave Ulferts, Father Tom Fangman, Kirk Redding, Kim Kroger, Mary Pat Raynor, LaDonna Konsel, and Ann Marie Davoren. Thanks also to my "rosary girls" of Omaha: Michele Trout, Sara McKeon, DeDe Salerno, Katie Alitz, Colleen Johnson, Julie Gallegos, Susie Shoemaker, and Lynn Weist. I also want to thank Julie Brown of Cincinnati and Janet Kohll of Omaha for sound advice.

A huge amount of appreciation to Kirk Redding and Scott Barrett, for their shared stories of life behind the chair at their salon Over our Heads.

A special thanks to the LaMar family of Fremont, Nebraska, whose stories of a beloved dog named Grandma became an inspiration for Lucy Mangiamelli's dog.

Great thanks to the people and places of Omaha who allowed me to use their pictures, which only enhanced the story of Ben through the years. Thank you to Marsha Kalkowski and her time with the picture of Marian High School.

Thanks to Tom Osborne, Warren Buffett and Sting, for inspiration, because babies aren't the only bookmarks in this novel.

Special thanks to the team of experts at CreateSpace. Their guidance and wisdom through this process was priceless.

I want to thank Jessa Diebel for her expertise and creativity in promoting and marketing this book through my website.

Great thanks to my dad, Richard Mangus, who became the technical wizard as I gathered pictures for the book.

I especially want to thank my sister Robin, who was an amazing editor, marketing rep, cheerleader, and tear catcher, often all on the same day.

Finally, I thank my husband Mike and children, Connor, Morgan, and Sean, for their incredible patience on the days that I was lost in the story. A special thanks to my husband for his relentless encouragement for a project that was so important to me.

*Therefore, since we have been justified through faith, we have peace with God through our Lord Jesus Christ, through whom we have gained access by faith into this grace in which we now stand. And we rejoice in the hope of the glory of God. Not only so, but we also rejoice in our sufferings, because we know that suffering produces perseverance; perseverance, character; and character, hope. And hope does not disappoint us, because God has poured out his love into our hearts by the Holy Spirit, whom he has given us.*

- Romans 5:1-5

CPSIA information can be obtained at www.ICGtesting.com
Printed in the USA
LVOW04s1135150715

446288LV00014BA/282/P